# NOW
# AND
# AGAIN

## CHARLOTTE
## ROGAN

FLEET
2017

FLEET

First published in the United States in 2016 by Little, Brown and Company
First published in Great Britain in 2016 by Fleet
This paperback edition published in 2017 by Fleet

1 3 4 5 7 9 10 8 6 4 2

Copyright © 2016 by Charlotte Rogan

The moral right of the author has been asserted.

A CIP catalogue record for this book
is available from the British Library.

ISBN 978-0-349-00581-2

Printed and bound in Great Britain by
Clays Ltd, St Ives plc

Papers used by Fleet are from well-managed forests and
other responsible sources.

Fleet
An imprint of
Little, Brown Book Group
Carmelite House
50 Victoria Embankment
London EC4Y 0DZ

An Hachette UK Company
www.hachette.co.uk

www.littlebrown.co.uk

Charlotte Rogan studied architecture at Princeton University and worked for a large construction firm before turning to fiction. She is the author of *The Lifeboat*, which was nominated for the *Guardian* First Book Award and the International IMPAC Dublin Literary Award and which has been translated into twenty-six languages. After many years in Dallas and a year in Johannesburg, she now lives in Westport, Connecticut.

'With wit, humanity, and extraordinary clarity of vision, Rogan has found the uniting thread that weaves together contemporary American life. *Now and Again* is breathtaking in its scope and insight, revealing the interconnectedness of the prison-industrial complex, mass surveillance, environmental devastation, the moral vacuity of televangelists, failures of recent US military adventures, and the brutality of life for those on the margins. This is America from the ground up, full of ordinary people trying to make sense of their lives, driven by that brand of frontier idealism that might yet be our last best hope' Patrick Flanery, author of *Absolution* and *Fallen Land*

'With consummate command of narrative, Charlotte Rogan nimbly brings together whistleblowers and soldiers in a damning – and pageturning – critique of America's military-industrial complex and its massive amount of collateral damage. It's the novel we deserve for the war we didn't' Teddy Wayne, author of *The Love Song of Jonny Valentine* and *Kapitoil*

'*Now and Again* doesn't disappoint. All the ingredients of a tense thriller with a domestic slant that got my heart involved' Sarra Manning, *Red*

'Dazzling layering of different people and different stories and of the leaps their minds make as they learn to open their eyes. The prose is strong, supple and sometimes infused with a magisterial rhythm that reflects the novel's commanding scope. This is a novel of the American dream, and of how that dream is shattered and betrayed' Christina Patterson, *Sunday Times*

C334089993

ALSO BY CHARLOTTE ROGAN

*The Lifeboat*

*For my parents*

# NOW
## AND
# AGAIN

*Do it or don't do it—you will regret both.*
—Søren Kierkegaard

# 1.0 AMMUNITION

*If you were to measure east to west and draw a line down the center of the country, the line would not pass through the town of Red Bud, but it wouldn't miss it by very much. Most things missed Red Bud by a lot more than that.*

—Robert "Buddy" Hutchinson, Mayor

*There wasn't any warning. One day Maggie was gossiping in the lunchroom with the rest of us, and the next she was all righteous and judgmental. It was like she was born again, but not in a good way.*

—True Cunningham

*It started when she realized we were making bombs. She had always known that—of course she knew it. But you can know something and not really know it, if you know what I mean.*

—Misty Mills

*Word got out that something important was missing from Mr. Winslow's office. Whatever it was, I don't think Maggie would have taken it. I mean, she was trying to do something good in the world, and that wouldn't include stealing.*

—True Cunningham

*I could get in a lot of trouble if anyone knew I had misplaced a top-secret report, so I decided to keep it to myself.*

—August Winslow

*The word "depleted" is inserted to make the uranium sound harmless. Believe me, it's not.*

—Professor Stanley Wilkes, Oklahoma State University

# 1.1 MAGGIE

Maggie Rayburn had just come from eating birthday cake in the employees' lunchroom when a document sitting in plain sight on her boss's desk caught her eye. It was one o'clock, and a shaft of late-winter sun was stabbing through the plate-glass window behind the desk, blinding her enough so that at first she wasn't sure exactly what was signified by the thick red border on the document's cover or by the stern capital letters or the string of acronyms and slashes. Curiosity—was it a useful trait or a dangerous one? But who isn't curious, she thought as she lifted the cover and peered inside: *Discredit the doctors,* she read. *Flood the system with contradictory reports.*

Footsteps sounded in the corridor, causing a shiver to prickle her neck. She glanced out the window and cocked her head to listen. It was getting brighter out—or no, it wasn't really, but now and then a band of light cut through the pervasive cloud cover and illuminated the stretch of farmland she had been looking at for what seemed like a thousand years. It was gray and frozen now, but in a few more months it would burst with life, aided by the antlike tractors that crawled along the corn rows and the spindly wheeled irrigation contraption and, a few months later, the big green harvesting machines. And in the distance . . .

But she didn't have time to think about the distance, where the corn gave way to wheat and where a phalanx of oil rigs were drilling into the sub-shelf of the Arkoma Basin, and beyond the oil rigs, Oklahoma City, and beyond that . . .

Beyond that, an entire world she had never seen.

The footsteps were coming closer, pausing—surely they belonged to Mr. Winslow, who would have finished up his meeting with the army brass by now—and anyway, there was never time. There were documents to be typed and filed, telephones to be answered, an outfit to be chosen for the special birthday dinner Lyle was planning for her—in secret, he thought, but Lyle was an open book. The more furtive his movements, the easier it was to guess what he was up to. All of the hours in the day were spoken for!

Unless she made time. Unless she announced: "Thursday evening you boys are on your own" and went to get her nails done or meet up with True and Misty for a girls' night out.

But today something was different. Whatever it was caused Maggie's heart to clench with a dangerous possibility, and before she knew what she was doing, the document was in her hands, and then it was tucked up inside the baggy sweater Lyle and Will had given her that morning for her birthday—Lyle, who had no fashion sense! Will, who wanted her to be presentable, but not the kind of mother his friends eyed from under the brims of their baseball caps. Where had the years gone? She might as well slap a used-up mother sign on her forehead if she was going to wear a sweater like that.

But as she stood in a stray shaft of February sunlight, watching the distant oil rigs pump their greasy dollars out of the ground, she wondered if certain seemingly indelible aspects of her life and personality might change. If Lyle might become her

4

accomplice in whatever lay in wait for her as the earth made its lonely way around the sun and Will spun off into ever-farther orbits and she took another step along the Path to Becoming, which was something she had read about in a magazine she had bought herself as a birthday treat just, coincidentally, the day before.

She was thirty-nine. In another year she would be forty—she still had time. Time for what? was the obvious question, but like all the other big questions, it couldn't be easily answered, if it could be answered at all. The author of the magazine article had stressed boldness of action in the process of becoming, so Maggie, who had been struck by the aptness of the advice for her stage in life, heard Mr. Winslow hesitate and reached for the document almost without thinking. Almost without realizing that the acronyms and slashes referred to control systems and compartments, which were divided into sub-control systems and sub-compartments as part of a security clearance system she knew about but didn't completely understand. Almost without looking over her shoulder to make sure she was alone, but in the back of her mind picturing a letter she had received out of the blue several weeks before.

She moved some papers into the blank spot where the document had been before scurrying back to the secretarial bay, and at the end of the day she took it home with her and hid it away in the tall mahogany chest of drawers that had been handed down from her grandmother to her mother and from her mother to her, not daring to look beyond the cover with its red Top Secret banner for another week and a half, but now and then catching her own eye in the mirror that sat atop the old chest and seeing there—if not exactly boldness and youth, then not timidity and middle age either. She had never been timid, but maybe she was a little too predictable. Or a little too content. A little too willing to be what other people wanted her to be.

On the first Saturday in March, Lyle announced that he was going to drive Will to the tryouts for the baseball team just the way he had always driven him, but instead of quietly acquiescing, Will planted his feet on the speckled linoleum and said, "Thanks anyway, Dad, but now that I have my license, I can drive myself."

"I'll tag along," said Lyle. "You know I like to watch."

"Okay, Dad, okay. But after today, I drive myself."

"Unless I need the truck," said Lyle, winning a small battle in the unwinnable war of keeping Will from growing up. "Or maybe you happen to have a little money stashed away and can buy your own set of wheels."

"Don't make me laugh," said Will, sounding just like his father as he said it. The money from his summer job had run out months before, and now that baseball season was starting up, there was no chance of working on the weekends for a little pocket cash.

Maggie listened to the sound of the tires spinning down the gravel driveway and out onto Old Oak Road before sitting down on a scrap of carpet she had hooked in what seemed like a previous lifetime. Her hands trembled as she opened the bottom drawer of the dresser and tried to understand the difference between alpha particles, which persisted in the environment upon detonation, and gamma and neutron radiation, which quickly dissipated but were extremely destructive before that point. The document, which was called *Countering Misconceptions,* made the point in no uncertain terms that the weapons manufactured by the company she worked for had no unintended health effects on the people who made, transported, or deployed them. They were perfectly safe. People who said otherwise were misguided or politically motivated or, in some cases, mentally ill. Here were ten talking points on the subject along with four things to do if a colleague poked his nose where it didn't belong.

That night, Maggie and Lyle lay with their arms around each other and talked about their son. "He's all grown up," said Lyle wistfully.

"Yes," said Maggie. "He certainly is."

"He's a nice young man," said Lyle. After a moment he added, "I think we've done a good job at being parents."

This was not a new conversation, and always before, Maggie had gone to sleep feeling satisfied that she and Lyle had done their best. "He's a fine-looking boy," they would remark in the darkness of their bedroom, and occasionally one or the other of them would say, "He's an old soul. It's almost as if he's been here before."

But now Maggie sweated and tossed and thought about the world Will was entering, how filled it was with hidden dangers. She wondered what it would be like with Will gone off to college or wherever his own path led him—would she be able to escape the gravity of her role as wife and mother, or would she collapse into herself, becoming hard and dense and dying? She thought about the article on becoming, which stressed the need for agency, and about the letter from a person named Dolly, who had decided not to sit idly by, and about how any person could point to a handful of moments that changed everything: The first was when her father had slammed out the door for the last time. The second was the evening she had taken her sister's turn at washing dishes so that she could wash them with Lyle, who up until then had been her brother's friend. The third was the moment the footsteps paused, giving her an opportunity to take the document that now lay pulsing beneath the sweaters in her bottom drawer.

# 1.2 DOLLY

Dolly Jackson worked as a midwife at a women's health clinic, and because of the clinic's location near a large VA hospital, it attracted a lot of veterans and veterans' wives. She loved her job despite the fact that her family had tried to dissuade her from entering the field. "You're doing a doctor's job, but you're getting paid worse than a nurse," they said when Dolly went home for Easter or Christmas.

It was true, but Dolly didn't care. More and more women were joining the armed services, and she liked to think of herself as soldiering bravely on the battlefield of women's rights. She also liked to think she was helping her boyfriend, Danny Joiner, who had enlisted in the army when his college scholarship ran out and whom she hoped someday to marry. Her work allowed some of the women to have their babies at home, where Dolly lit candles and soothed them with soft music. "I'd like to see a man go through this," she'd whisper to the women, and when the babies plunged mewling from their mothers' wombs, their first glimpse of the world was softly lit and rose scented and the first thing they heard were the violins and cymbals of *Appalachian Spring* if they were white babies and the Oklahoma City Gospel Choir if they were black. "It's a beautiful world!" Dolly told the babies. "Me oh my, it's a beautiful world!"

She taught the husbands and boyfriends how to help the women breathe, and then she wrapped the babies up in soft cotton blankets and placed them in their mothers' arms. But lately, Dolly's work had taken a frightening twist. Three babies in the past year had been born with horrendous defects. One had been born without face. The head was the size of a grapefruit; its only feature was an open mouth, and out of the mouth a tumor protruded, purple as a plum and big as an orange. She deserved to go to hell for wishing the baby would die. She wished it would die quickly, before the mother saw it. What else could she wish for?

Over the next few days, she tried excising the thoughts as neatly as the pediatric surgeon had excised the tumor, but ugly images kept penetrating her resolve. She saw ripe fruit everywhere, even in her sleep. She sat bolt upright in bed with the words of the attending obstetrician ringing unbidden in her head: "Why in the world did you let the mother see it?" As if it were somehow her fault for wanting everything to be perfect in a world where nothing was.

I wish that baby would die, she had thought then, and she thought it again whenever the horrendous image of a baby with a head like an orange and a grapefruit stuck together popped onto the screen of her inner vision. It had been the worst moment of her life when, in the soft winking light of the candles, with Copeland's magnificent crescendo evoking the thrust of new life from the earth, she had said to the mother, "We need to call the doctor," and the mother had taken the baby in her arms and screamed and fainted, and only Dolly's quick thinking had prevented the baby from falling to the floor.

The grandmother, who had been waiting in the next room, rushed in when she heard her daughter scream. "What's going on here?" she shouted as the father grabbed at the soft bundle, and Dolly had allowed him to take it from her.

She was glad when the baby's tiny weight was no longer in her grasp. She had hurried out of the room to use the telephone—to call the doctor, of course, but also to evade the family's dawn of derstanding. When she returned, she announced, "The doctor ill be here in twenty minutes." During those long minutes, Dolly didn't know what else to say. She pretended to be busy with her bag of instruments and then with the mother and the blood pressure cuff, but she could tell that the family blamed her for the baby's condition—not because it was her fault, but because there was no one else to blame.

Dolly wished the doctor would hurry. She knew he had a new car with a powerful engine, and she wished he would use it as aggressively that night as he used it to get to his weekend trysts in Norman or Shawnee. She wanted a second set of shoulders for the burden of blame the father and grandmother had handed over the way she had handed over the baby, but she wondered if they would feel the same way about the doctor, who hadn't been complicit in the actual birth—and also, the doctor was a man. Dolly knew people preferred to blame women if there was a choice. For one thing, women were smaller and presented a lesser physical threat, and for another, the women she knew, herself included, were more than eager to blame themselves.

That had been the worst night of her life until the sunstruck October evening less than two months later when a baby had been born covered with a cracked white coating, a coating like a potter's glaze, a powdery white crust crazed by deep black gashes where there should have been skin. Dolly could hold her tongue no longer. "Don't we need to tell someone?" she had asked as carefully as she could. Long ago, she had learned which things would encourage the doctor to speak and which would cause him to say, "So you can see that I'm a busy man, with no time for idle chatter." She kept her voice low, which made it hard to get the tone right. "About the birth defects, I mean. That's two now, just eight weeks apart."

"I know what you're thinking," said the doctor, stroking the stethoscope that hung around his neck and giving the appearance of listening.

In a normal conversation, that's when Dolly would have said something, and the conversation would have proceeded with the usual back-and-forth rhythm. But Dolly didn't have normal conversations with the doctor, and she knew silence didn't mean he was waiting for her to speak. He was merely pausing for effect. He was merely letting the tension build to make adequate space for his next pronouncement. But she liked it when he talked as if she wasn't there. That was when she learned things.

"You're thinking there are multiple factors to take into consideration—genetics, parental health and drug use, environmental toxins, both naturally occurring and man-made. And you can't forget about random mutation and plain old bad luck. Not to mention that these women neglected to get adequate prenatal care."

The doctor thrust the file he was holding at her, indicating the end of the discussion. But then he muttered, almost to himself, "And then there's the concern about munitions safety. I've been sent an eye-opening report."

That was the night Dolly started to look into things. That was when she started to listen extra carefully whenever the doctor was on the phone. But it wasn't until January, when she heard about a baby that had been born with cleft ears and no eyes, that she started writing letters and emails. She wrote to politicians and to captains of industry and to the heads of research institutes, and when she didn't receive any satisfactory replies from those people, she wrote to their secretaries and administrative assistants. She even put a classified notice in the newspaper, but six weeks had passed since then, and she had yet to receive even a single form letter in reply. Now she guessed she never would.

# 1.3 WILL

Will Rayburn slouched in front of the television set and watched the penguins string out single file across the ice. Each step transformed four or five inches of the snowy expanse in front of them into the snowy expanse behind as the sturdy bodies trudged across the ice floe, shuffling footstep after shuffling footstep, a testament to survival through unquestioning singleness of purpose. The scenery was bleak—gorgeous and deadly. The narrator announced that the temperature was eighty degrees below zero, that Antarctic winds rose regularly to one hundred miles per hour, and still the penguins put one stubby leg in front of the other as they made their way back to the ancestral birthplace—home! Will's blue eyes watered to think of it. There was honor in conformity, beauty in unquestioning obedience to instinct, comfort in knowing what the next step was, even if it was genetically programmed and identical to the last million steps, which, he calculated in his head, was how many four-inch increments it was from the edge of the ice to the inland nesting ground.

A commercial for deodorant came on just as his mother entered the room. "Are you crying?" she asked. "What are you crying for?"

"Just something in my eye," said Will without looking up. It certainly wasn't because he, too, struggled with hormonally induced odor or because neither of his parents had thought to clue him in about bodily changes in general or about the difference between antiperspirant and deodorant in particular, both of which it appeared he needed, or because Tula Santos had turned him down that afternoon when he'd finally gotten up the nerve to ask her out.

"Here, let me see."

"No, no, it's gone now," said Will, batting her hand away and sinking farther into the shapeless cushions of the couch.

"Well, you can't sit in front of the television all day. Don't you have homework?"

"Okay, okay," said Will, hoping she would leave the room. He liked to be alone. He liked to think of himself as coming from and going nowhere—untethered, unaffiliated, even unnamed. But he couldn't figure out whether conformity or nonconformity was what he wanted. Of course he wanted to be an individual, of course he wanted to do something no human being had ever before done, but he also wanted to fit in. He wanted to merge with something bigger than himself, to be an integral part of something transformative and grand, though he also wanted to be completely recognizable and unique in case Tula ever looked in his direction and said "Hey" in the breathy way Sammi Green said "Hey" to whichever of the football players she was dating at the time.

"Look, Will. This letter is addressed to you."

His mother was going on about something from the state university she had found among the junk mail and bills, an envelope with his name on it—what did it have to do with him! The show was coming on again, a distant shot of a lone penguin, a tiny black speck against the ice. Just as the narrator, his voice heavy with inevitability, started to explain what happened to stragglers, his mother hit the off button and repeated, "You can't sit here all day." Then she went out of the room, leaving Will behind to ponder what lessons the penguin's plight might hold for his own.

He couldn't sit there all day.

He knew he couldn't, but somehow he was powerless to move. Where there's a will, there's a way, he told himself the way his parents had always told him, as if his name conferred special powers, but all he could do was twitch his wrist in the direction of the remote control, which had fallen to the floor on top of the envelope from the university. Not that he had any doubt about what happened to stragglers and not that the next day wouldn't find him going through the motions at school—not because of some burning desire to better himself, but because he didn't know what else to do. Sitting on the worn corduroy couch, he was suddenly assailed by questions of free will and self-determination that couldn't be easily answered, not by the narrator, who was clearly reading from a script, and not by people who willfully stepped out of line but who were still completely bound by convention—if not the convention of going along with everyone else, then the convention of reacting against them—the way they were all bound—or were they? Suddenly the answers to such questions seemed critical before Will was able even to consider taking the next step.

He sat for a while deciding what he would need to survive in the Antarctic, what he would take with him if he had only a sled dog and a sled to carry his gear, or if he had only snowshoes and a backpack and the clothes on his back—no dog, no sled, and certainly no GPS. He would take a down parka with a fur-lined hood, a box of matches, a compass, a pair of sturdy boots, a sharp knife in a leather sheath. He would take a magnifying glass because he liked magnifying things and because a full-sized microscope probably wouldn't fit. Then, with a huge effort of will, he bent forward and stretched his right hand toward the remote control, clawing until he could just reach the edge of the envelope it had fallen on and slide it toward him, inch by inch, until both the remote and the envelope were cradled in his big outstretched hand.

# 1.4 TULA

As a young girl, Tula Santos had been able to convince herself that her lowly birth was an advantage, that her feet were firmly planted on the hard rock of existence instead of on unstable elevations, but at sixteen, she knew she was deluding herself. She now suspected that she had been invited to join the Order of the Rainbow for Girls more as an experiment or an act of charity than as a statement of equality, and that her mother's employer, who was next in line for the position of Mother Advisor and who had no children of her own, thought of her as a project. "I am fortunate to be in a position to give back," Mrs. August Winslow would proclaim whenever the spotlight shone on her silken shoulders and well-coiffed head. Tula knew that Mrs. Winslow wouldn't have chosen a project who was ugly or blemished, which is why she spent her pocket money on lotions and oils—not out of vanity, as her friend Sammi Green did, but out of self-preservation, as a stay against the sucking circumstances of her birth.

It was her induction as a Rainbow Girl five years before that had first allowed Tula to see being fatherless as an advantage, for the Rainbow organization was meant to celebrate womanly virtues, and who was more womanly, a girl who spent her days in a house ruled by a man or a girl who had been raised solely by women?

Tula had often fantasized about an eighth bow station with white as its color. There were already stations for virtues like love and patriotism. The eighth station would stand for purity, which n Tula's mind was the epitome of the female principle, unmixed with anything hard or protruding or loud. She had harbored this idea ever since the Virgin Mary had come to her in a dream, but she was waiting until the end-of-summer ceremony to bring it up. If all went well, her idea would be adopted for the all-assembly project, which would solidify her position as a leader and set her up for eventual election as a jewel officer. She was confident that her plan for establishing an eighth bow station would far surpass the offerings of the other girls, who came up with ambitious but predictable projects like sending clothing to remote corners of South America or tutoring people with skin even darker than Tula's skin while they cooed over them and called them cute. One of the girls wanted to plant a garden of biblical herbs in a weedy patch of land behind the church, and Sammi Green talked about honoring the famous men of Red Bud with handmade plaques describing their heroic deeds.

"What about the women?" asked Tula.

"Of course I'll honor the famous women too—if there are any," said Sammi.

"Don't forget Sandra Day O'Connor," said Mrs. Winslow when Sammi bragged about how many influential men she knew. "She was the first female Supreme Court Justice, and once upon a time she was a Rainbow Girl too."

"I'm talking about local heroes," said Sammi. "They can be men or women, but they have to be from around here."

Most of the proposals seemed derivative to Tula, while her own, which she kept secret even from Mrs. Winslow and her mother, had never been attempted before—never even thought of!—while still being in keeping with the spirit of the founding charter. Her idea would change the very structure of the order—or not really change it, but build on what was already there, making it better for future generations of Rainbow Girls and freeing them from their subjugation to men.

From the time she was a middle schooler, Tula had seen how Sammi and her friends curried favor with boys—some of them in a very direct and obvious way. Even Sammi, who was athletic and strong and mostly resistant to peer pressure, rolled the waistband of her skirt so that the slightest lifting breeze would have shown the edges of her panties if Sammi had worn the kind of panties Tula wore underneath the pleated skirts that even the updated version of the Rainbow Handbook said were supposed to come within two inches of the knees.

But Tula didn't. Tula, who was modest inside and out, could only marvel as Sammi teased the boys by flexing her abdominal muscles and arching her back. Even when Tula stood alone in front of her full-length mirror, she couldn't twitch in a way that made her skirt swing from side to side the way Sammi's did, so she watched uneasily as the boys and girls paired off and wondered how their behavior fit with their avowed submission to a patriarchal religion. Tula herself had sworn fealty to the same God and Savior, but in her heart she revered the Virgin Mother above all other deities and saints. Who was more pure than Mary, the mother of Jesus? She knew from the stories her own mother told her when they lay together at night, unable to sleep because the full moon, which her mother said was male, was pulling at the female tides within them the way men had always pulled at women, causing the tides to shift the way women had always shifted—even physically fit women like Sammi shifted, women with rock-hard abdominal muscles and intelligence. They all shifted like the tide the minute a handsome man winked in their direction.

After such a night, it was a relief when the sun rose, restoring to earth the female principle of sunlight and, even Tula had to

17

mit, fertility. When Tula had mentioned the gravitational effect of the male moon to her benefactress, Mrs. Winslow had smiled indulgently and said, "You have it backwards, darling. The moon is the female principle. It is we women who affect the tides of men!"

Tula was still trying to figure out which made more sense, but whichever it was, she knew she owed it to the Virgin Mother, who smiled down at her from the niche above her bed, to resist the male principle for as long as she could. So she said no when Will Rayburn asked her out. She said no out of principle, but she also said it because Will Rayburn scared her. Or it wasn't really Will who scared her, it was the feeling of the tides within her shifting whenever Will walked by.

## 1.5 MAGGIE

The cherry trees on Main Street were blooming big and pink when Maggie decided she could no longer continue in her current line of work. "You'll lose your pension," warned her friend Misty Mills, and True Cunningham added, "You don't actually shoot the bullets, do you? Technically, you don't even make them."

"Bullets," said Maggie as the three friends stepped from the cool aluminum shadow cast by the munitions plant onto the crazed asphalt surface of the parking lot. She stopped short of saying that she might have been able to make her peace with bullets, but the company they worked for produced everything from missile components to armor-piercing artillery shells, and the solid core of the shells was made of a toxic substance that had a half-life of four and a half billion years.

"We're not the only ones making bombs," said Misty. "We're making bombs in a world where other people are making bombs. Do you really want to live in a country that doesn't have them?"

"You don't even work on the line—you work in the office," put in True, but nothing anyone said would change her mind.

"Does that mean we won't drive to work together anymore?" asked Lyle, and Maggie replied, "No."

"No, we won't drive together or no, that isn't what it means?" asked Lyle.

"We won't drive together anymore, Lyle. That's the part that breaks my heart."

When Lyle had lost his job at the prison, it was Maggie who persuaded him to apply for a job at the munitions plant, and for the past four years she had packed turkey and cheese sandwiches for Lyle and Will and turkey without cheese for herself, and then squeezed her knees against the truck's gearshift until they dropped Will off at his school before continuing down the New Road, past the turnoff to the Choctaw Casino and along the New Road extension to the plant, but now she wondered how she could have been so glibly confident when she had said to Lyle, "Come work with me! You'll know half the people there, and you won't have to worry that an inmate will take you hostage if you make a mistake or turn your back." Years before, there had been a riot at the prison, and people still talked about it as an ominous and continuing threat.

"What will you do?" asked Lyle, his eyes wide with love and regret as he and Maggie ate their last sad sandwiches in the munitions plant lunchroom, where they were constantly interrupted by people who stopped by their table to ask Maggie questions or offer advice.

"I'll find a different job," said Maggie with her old optimism, but it went without saying that her job perks and benefits would be hard to replace. In fifteen years, she had risen to the position of administrative assistant to Mr. August Winslow, civilian chief of operations, which gave her a far greater status than Lyle and their friends who worked in shipping or production. And if she were to stay on for another ten, she would get lifetime health care and a burnished wooden plaque.

"I guess you know that good jobs are hard to find," said Lyle.

"I do," Maggie replied.

"It seems like you're giving up an awful lot." But once Maggie had made her decision, she wouldn't reconsider.

Lyle wasn't the sort of person to ask "Why?" but that was the first word out of Will's mouth when Maggie could no longer put off telling him about her plans.

Maggie was proud of her big, strapping son, who took in bits of information and then, when no one was expecting it, let them out again, rearranged. Like the time he asked Pastor Price if the identical Farley twins each had only half a soul and the time he asked if it was a sin to starve your children. "It's not only a sin, it's illegal," said the pastor, which prompted Will to ask, "Then why is it also a sin and illegal for people without any money to steal?" The teachers in the lower school still talked about the day Will had surprised them by standing up at quiet time and asking if spilling seed was tantamount to murder. "Tantamount!" said the teacher gaily. "Now there's a big word. Let's all take out our dictionaries and look it up!"

"I've made my decision," said Maggie, gently setting out the chipped rose-pattern dessert plates and a cinnamon raisin cake with drizzle icing. "I can't pretend I don't know what the bombs and bullets are used for. I can't pretend innocent people aren't getting killed."

This led to a discussion of duty and if it was based on a person's own imperfect sense of things or handed down by a greater authority.

"What you're saying is that because a person can't know everything, that person is obligated to do as he or she is told," said Maggie.

But Will and Lyle insisted that wasn't what they were saying.

"It's just that each person is looking through a tiny peephole," said Will, which was a reference to how, in years past, Lyle had taken his young son to look through the circular holes cut in the plywood barricade whenever there was a construction project in town.

"Two heads are better than one," added Lyle.

"Is mine one of those heads?" asked Maggie. "Or is it everybody else but me? Anyway, I haven't suddenly become a fanatic, if that's what you're worried about."

But she didn't tell them about the top-secret document she had taken from Mr. Winslow's desk or about the letter from the Department of Defense she found and copied a few days later or about the book she had subsequently checked out of the library, which was called *The Economics of Nuclear Waste* and which made a connection between the waste disposal problem of nuclear energy facilities and the need of the munitions industry for cheap and lethal raw materials. She didn't tell them how 40 percent of the dart-shaped bullet tips broke off before impact, causing secondary explosions and widespread dispersal of radioactive dust or about the Internet articles documenting the effects of radiation poisoning on unborn babies in Iraq or about the ones questioning whether their own drinking water supply was safe. Will was optimistic and she wanted him to stay that way, so she didn't tell him that she sometimes wondered if the earth was the thing with a soul and if human beings were a boon to the planet or a curse.

"I love you too much to make a product designed to harm somebody else's child," she said as she cleared away the rest of the cake.

"Don't make this about me," said Will, getting up to do his homework. "Tell her, Dad. Tell her this has nothing to do with me."

Maggie didn't say, It's always been about you, Will, ever since the day you were born, but she smiled to recall the day she and Lyle had brought Will home from the hospital in his blue-striped cap and how they had worried when he never cried. "Do you think it's normal?" asked Lyle. Maggie replied that she wouldn't have married Lyle if she'd thought he would father a normal son. "He's going to do something good in this world," she had said. "Maybe even something great." But now it seemed to Maggie that it was unfair to pin the burden of her hopes and dreams on Will. Parents had a duty to lead by example, and that was all she was trying to do.

Two nights later, Maggie unintentionally let it slip to Lyle about the Iraqi babies, and Lyle must have let it slip to Pastor Price, because the pastor cornered her at Sunday coffee and exclaimed, "What's this I hear about quitting your job?"

"I want to set a good example for Will," said Maggie. "Besides, if I had to live my life over again, I wouldn't want to regret my decisions—or worse, to feel ashamed."

Rain was pelting the tall parish hall windows, and a flash of lightning made the bulbs in the sconces flicker as if God was trying to tell them something. Maggie was a believer, but she wasn't the sort of person God spoke to, so she figured He must be communicating with Pastor Price.

"Don't get me wrong," the pastor said after Maggie had

explained everything to him as well as she could. "I'll support you any way I can, but monkeying about with definitions can lead a person seriously astray."

Maggie didn't think she had monkeyed about with anything unless it was Mr. Winslow's files. "I'm not sure I understand," she said, hoping old Mrs. Farnsworth would come forward with one of her questions about adultery and lust, but Mrs. F. was eyeing the donuts and eavesdropping while she patiently awaited her turn.

"Exactly!" said the pastor. "We run the risk of hubris whenever we think we understand."

Even though he said "we," Maggie knew he wasn't talking about himself. Still, she thought it best to admit she understood very little and would be extra careful of hubris in the future, whatever that was.

"We run the risk of heeding false prophets," said the pastor, and Maggie merely nodded her head and said she had to follow her heart.

"Don't get me wrong," Pastor Price said sternly, "but following your heart can be a tricky business, especially for a woman with a heart as big as yours."

The next Sunday, the pastor and his wife Tiffany approached Maggie after services. "Lex Lexington told me one of his administrative assistants up at the prison is leaving," said the pastor. "If you're interested, I can put in a good word for you."

"The prison!" Maggie didn't like to think about the fortress filled with the nameless and forgotten where her father had worked when she was a child.

"If there's one place on earth that needs someone like you, it's that prison," said Tiffany. "Besides, my Mothers of Mercy group is conducting an education outreach for the inmates, and we need a few dedicated people on the inside."

"On the inside!" exclaimed Maggie. "That makes it sound so dangerous."

"It's one thing to avoid doing harm in this big old world," said Tiffany. "But it's quite another to do some good. That's what the education outreach is all about. Believe me, that prison is just crying out for people like you."

"Just so long as your expectations for what you can accomplish are modest," said the pastor. "Don't get me wrong—Tiffany can work miracles when she puts her mind to it. But if you set your expectations low enough, you won't be disappointed."

The pastor had a habit of saying "don't get me wrong" the way Misty Mills said "no offense." The phrase proved so useful to him that Maggie started using it herself. She said it when she went to collect her final paycheck and the payroll clerk said, "I hear you're taking matters into your own hands." She said it when Misty Mills called her high and mighty. And she said it when Mr. Winslow lectured her about patriotism and exploding weapons. "Why, they even talk about shrapnel bombs in 'The Star-Spangled Banner,'" he said. "They're as American as apple pie."

## 1.6 PASTOR PRICE

Even though he vowed that his growing church and weekly radio show wouldn't change the way he looked at other people, Houston Price couldn't deny that he sometimes felt a slight sense of superiority as he watched the solid citizens of Red Bud file into his church every Sunday morning. There was Garner Hicks, pressed and frayed and dying of cancer but hopeful of reprieve, just as they were all dying and hopeful. Behind Garner tiptoed Mrs. Farnsworth, iridescent in her polyester pants suit and squinting about for telltale clues of sexual indiscretion. Her eyes lit on Lily De Luca, who was all dolled up and ready to flirt if the opportunity arose, which, for Lily, it always did. There was the new baby Hollister, born out of wedlock but saved just the week before through the holy baptism of the Redeemer. Edging away from the baby and its mother was Tyler Hicks, who only came to church to snitch from the collection plate, and behind Tyler was Sammi Green, surpassingly sulky and adolescent until things got going and she started to stretch her hands up to heaven and shimmy mightily in a show of what God could do with bodily glory when he chose.

He had outdone himself in that regard when He created the pastor's wife. Tiffany was the daughter of the largest landowner in the county, so marrying her had turned out to be as much an alliance as a love match. The union had led to the donation of the land the new church building was sitting on, the one condition being that Tiffany would participate in the design consultations and take charge of a healthy budget for good works. And if Tiffany had progressive ideas about the relationship between buildings and the earth, she also had progressive ideas about intimate relations, which more than made up for any architectural compromises the building committee had to make.

Before each service, Tiffany arranged a clean surplice on the back of a chair and set out the scented powder that kept the pastor's feet from sweating. "Sealed with a kiss" was always the last thing she said before he walked out into the swoop-ceilinged nave, and thrusting her tongue in his mouth was always the last thing she did. She did it, they both agreed, in order to free his spirit from his body for the task ahead, and it always worked—if he could resist Tiffany, he could resist anything.

"Bless you my child," he always said when she handed him his prayer book and leaned in for the freeing kiss, careful not to stand where people passing by the door to the sacristy could see them.

"Sealed with a kiss," she always said, but sometimes instead of kissing him, she just gazed into his eyes as she put his fingers on her breast, right where the nipple poked through the lacy cloth of the undergarments she wore beneath her choir robe. All of that added spice to the weekday humdrum of his job: the marital spats he had to adjudicate, the patient explication of texts to people who wanted to use the Bible to prove this or disprove that, and the more delicate approach he needed when the town scions he depended on for his livelihood sought his support for their favorite political causes.

It was six minutes to ten on a bright spring morning, but now, instead of Tiffany rushing into the sacristy and apologizing for her tardiness, it was August Winslow who filled the doorway. Winslow, who was not only civilian director of the munitions plant and husband to the Woodford oil fields heiress, but also a senior member of the pastoral council, now came charging in demanding to talk about Maggie Rayburn and how a reporter from the *Sentinel* wanted to write a story about her. "I called the publisher and put a stop to it," bellowed Winslow. "There's no sense giving the woman a megaphone. There's no sense giving all of my other employees ideas."

"I hope you handled the reporter carefully," said the pastor. "That kind of thing can backfire."

"Of course I handled him carefully. It was the publisher's nephew who apparently had the bright idea for the article, but I have no doubt we can count on the Fitches to do what's right for the town."

"I've already had a talk with the Rayburn woman," said the

pastor, who had come to rely on what Tiffany called his pregame routine and who was sweating because things were sliding off track. According to the sunburst-shaped clock on the wall, there were less than five minutes left, and if the pastor was known for anything, it was for exploding through the curtain at exactly ten o'clock on a crescendo from the organ, just when the stage lighting went from an expectant blue to a pulsating blaze of silver magnificence, and once his lighting manager had surprised him with giant sparklers and another time with a crazy purple fog. His entrance was hardly the most important part of the service, but it pleased him when Tiffany said he got a ten for showmanship on top of his ten for execution.

Winslow was saying, "She's a loose cannon. She worries me, to tell the truth."

"She's lost her way, but with a little help and understanding, she'll be back on track before you know it."

Back on track is where the pastor wanted to be. Three minutes to showtime, and his body was still fused to his spirit. His feet weren't the only thing sweating. Even his tongue felt coated and thick.

"Excellent, excellent. But I was hoping you could talk to Fitch."

Winslow showed no signs of leaving, so the pastor said, "Call me tomorrow. We can talk about it then." Panic was gathering in his bowels in spite of the fact that another thing he was known for was what Tiffany called his grace under fire.

She must have been detained. The women of the parish were always coming up to her with ideas for the ladies' outreach, and the men were always coming up to her because even standing next to Tiff was its own reward. With less than sixty seconds left, he'd have to oust all bodily concerns himself. He could do it—Tiffany hadn't always been there to help him. They hadn't even celebrated their three-year anniversary.

Winslow finally said, "Okay, okay," and backed out the door, leaving the pastor with the troublesome notion that his talk with Maggie hadn't seemed to resolve things. He had forty-five seconds to clear his mind. He closed his eyes. He kept a mental box for occasions like this. In his imagination, the box was made of inlaid precious materials like lapis lazuli and ivory and rare endangered woods from the Brazilian rain forest. Now he put his earthly concerns into the box so he could take them out again later. It was a beautiful box, but strong as steel, and once a worry had been locked inside, nothing could let it out again except the pastor himself. He was ready. The crescendo came. The flash of lights.

He didn't remember August Winslow or Maggie Rayburn until that evening over hot compote and potpie. "What does it mean," he asked his wife, "that some of my own parishioners have heard the Truth and rejected it? What does it say about them, but more importantly, what does it say about me?"

"Not everything is about you, baby," said Tiffany, and she was right. Hubris was an occupational hazard, and the pastor vowed to guard against it. But first, he had to reconnect his body to his spirit, and he needed Tiffany for that.

## 1.7 LYLE

It was the information age, but Lyle Rayburn had been left behind by it. He had dropped out of school just before his fifteenth birthday, which had left him with deep insecurities about his ability to know or understand.

"I won't try to convince you," Maggie told him. "I have my reasons, that's all."

Lyle was happy to let silence do the work of words, to stare open-mouthed through the windshield and express his injury by lingering at the Main Street intersection long after the light had changed and the cars behind them had started to honk. It was Will who piped up from where he was pressed against the passenger-side door. "If you really wanted to make a difference, Mom, you'd have to convince other people. That's what they tell us in church. That we have to witness to other people if we want to be saved."

"This isn't about saving myself," said Maggie. "This is about saving other people. This is about doing the right thing."

"But what makes you right and everybody else wrong? What if other people know something you don't?"

"Those are good questions. But if I had to have answers to everything, I'd never even get out of bed."

"Are you sure you won't change your mind?" asked Lyle over the efficient sound of the turn signal and the crunch of gravel under the tires as they made the final turn toward the high school. "We can't afford to buy another car, and we'll need one if you're going off in some completely different direction every day."

"I have the bicycle, and if I get the job at the prison, I can take the bus."

"What if it rains?" Lyle wanted to know. And then he added gravely, "What if it snows?"

"I haven't worked out all the details yet," said Maggie.

"Well, don't you think you should?" The closest Lyle ever came to getting angry was to suggest there was something that was not being done. He liked things to be squared away and he counted on Maggie to square them, even though he usually stopped short of assigning actual blame.

Lyle had known Maggie Sterling since before he had dropped out of school. He had been friends with her older brother and had taken to stopping by in the afternoons, not so much on the brother's account or even on Maggie's, but because of the rambling house where no shouting was allowed. "My mother is allergic to shouting," Maggie's brother told him. "It literally makes her sick."

Lyle, who thought he might be allergic to shouting too, started going there regularly to escape his own household, which was so full of siblings and cousins that Lyle was never missed. He took to showing up at dinnertime and standing at the screen door until the old flop-eared dog awoke from its nap and barked at him before going back to sleep or until one of the four Sterling children noticed him and let him in. He was careful not to let the screen door slam behind him, for when he did, Maggie's mother would scurry from the quiet depths of the house with an alarmed expression on her face and ask in a hoarse whisper what all the commotion was about.

Over the years, Lyle came to associate the comfortable chairs and steaming bowls of spaghetti with Maggie, and one day, instead of going to sit on the corner chair in the TV room after dinner, he had gone into the kitchen to help with the dishes, and Maggie had pushed her sister out of the way and said, "Isn't it your night to clear?" Their hands had bumped under the soapy water, and Maggie had splashed some bubbles into Lyle's hair. "Where would you go if you could go anywhere?" she had asked him.

"Niagara Falls," replied Lyle without hesitation. He had heard about a man going over the falls inside a rubber ball named the Plunge-O-Sphere. It seemed like a crazy thing to do, but also brave, and the idea of doing something like that on purpose filled him with curiosity and dread. "What about you?" he asked Maggie.

30

"The Grand Canyon," said Maggie. "I want to see what's inside the earth—what you'd find if you dug deep down."

"I hear you can ride donkeys all the way to the bottom," said Lyle.

"Donkeys!" cried Maggie, her eyes sparkling as if Lyle had said something shocking or funny or wise—he had never been sure which, but his heart soared to know he could have such an effect on her.

The answers to the travel game had changed over the years, and now it was Will who was apt to choose somewhere dangerous or impossible, while Maggie and Lyle were drawn to major cities and beach resorts. Now and then Lyle would catch Maggie's eye and say, "Where would you go?" not because he wanted an answer, but to remind her about how the game had started and about everything that had happened since. Six months after they first washed dishes together, Lyle dropped to his knees during a commercial break to ask her to marry him, and right in front of her gaping family, she said yes.

When they reached the school, Will clambered out of the car, grabbing his backpack and sack lunch out of the truck bed as he did five days out of seven. Also as usual, Maggie blew him a kiss good-bye and Will ignored her, hoisting the pack to his shoulders and hunching slightly under its weight. Now that Will had been safely delivered and he didn't have to concentrate so hard on the road, Lyle was able to glance across at Maggie, who still could melt his heart with a look.

"Oh, Lyle!" cried Maggie. "It's just that ... " But instead of finishing her thought, she laughed, filling Lyle with the hope that his wife had been playing a practical joke on him or that she saw something he didn't see, and that if Lyle didn't see it now, he soon would—the way Maggie always heard the freight train coming before Lyle did, or said what he was thinking before he could find the words and get them out. "We're on the same wavelength," they liked to say whenever that happened, but sometimes, lately, he wondered if they were.

## 1.8 MAGGIE

I haven't worked out all the details yet," Maggie said again at dinner. Again she burst into laughter, partly because Lyle looked so sad and funny and partly because the crushing weight of indecision had finally lifted from her soul.

But Lyle only turned his face, still sagging with disbelief, toward Will, as if he might find the answer there. He bumped his glass up and down on the varnished tabletop and asked again, "Well, don't you think you should? Before certain actions are taken, I mean? Actions, I mean, that can't be taken back?"

Maggie had seen it many times before: Lyle's anger short-circuiting before it could gain steam and the passive voice pointing a vague finger while absolving everyone present from responsibility, because the minute he started to criticize someone else, he would be reminded of his own shortcomings, which invariably caused him to think, Who am I to say! Sometimes he said it out loud: "Who am I to say!" On those occasions Maggie would stroke his hair and croon, "You have as much right as anyone, honeybun." Humility was one of the things she had always loved about her husband, but now all she felt was irritation. "If your car

32

was headed at a crowded sidewalk, you wouldn't work out all the details before you turned the wheel!" she exclaimed.

But Lyle said thoughtfully that yes, he would. "There'd be no sense turning it toward a more crowded sidewalk, now, would there?"

He laid his heavy hands on the table and examined his fingernails, which were dirty and chipped. Maggie had never before noticed how blocky his hands were, how his fingers were all nearly the same length, as if they had been cut from the same chunk of wood as the table and never properly shaped. "If I was headed toward the sidewalk outside the Multiplex on a Saturday, I'd turn the wheel toward the Merry Maid, but if I was on Main Street during the homecoming parade . . . "

"You wouldn't aim it at a more crowded sidewalk!" said Maggie impatiently. "You'd aim it at a less crowded one!"

"Exactly which sidewalk are we talking about?"

Lyle was like one of the heavy hand trucks they used to move ordnance at the plant—slow moving and hard to turn. Maggie could tell from his expression that he was trying to come up with some way to justify doing nothing, some way to put himself in the passenger seat and so be absolved of having to steer. She tried to catch Will's eye the way Will always caught hers when the subject of the conversation was Will. The boy was poking at his uneaten vegetables when, suddenly, he came out with a justification of his own. "It's the lesser of two evils," he said slowly, looking up from under his pale eyebrows at his dad.

Maggie swelled with pride in her first and only born. How many times had she stuck up for Will to Lyle or the teachers at the school? And now, just when she needed him, Will was sticking up for her. "You see!" she crowed. "Will knows what I'm talking about!"

But Will surprised her again by saying, "I'm not talking about the crowded sidewalk. I'm talking about the munitions plant. I'm talking about guns and even about killing people. That's the thing that's the lesser of two evils. Do you really want us to wait for the terrorists to use their weapons on us?"

"Lesser evils—" began Maggie, but for the first time in many years, the proper words came to Lyle before they came to her.

"I think your mother just wants to do something she can believe in," he said.

But that wasn't quite it either—there was more to it than that.

After the dishes were washed and put away, Maggie took one of the Internet articles out of the dresser drawer where she kept a brown accordion file of what she had begun to think of as her evidence and showed it to Will and Lyle. "I wanted you to see this," she said, spreading the printouts on the table, and to Will she added, "I think you're old enough."

"They haven't proved the birth defects are caused by the depleted uranium, have they?" asked Will, so Maggie showed him a newspaper article about the strange freaks of nature being spawned in their own backyard.

"There are frogs with eight legs!" she whispered, sounding exactly like her own mother, who had taken to whispering after Maggie's father had left, as if that would somehow cancel out the years of arguments and shouting.

Will offered up a scientific theorem about causation and correlation. "Not to mention reverse causation and coincidence. Umbrellas don't make it rain," he said.

Lyle nodded his head and said, "Tell me something I don't know," as if Will had taken the words right out of his mouth. Lyle was always saying "tell me something I don't know" the way Pastor Price said "don't get me wrong" and Misty Mills said "no offense," but for Lyle, the phrase was a way to avoid having to comment on subjects he knew nothing about.

"Oh, Lyle!" cried Maggie in frustration.

"We're only saying that you don't have all the facts," said Will.

"Who in tarnation does?" asked Maggie. "What does anyone base a decision on? Partial knowledge, that's what." She had practiced the line, but now it sounded flat and inadequate. Even Lyle could poke holes in it.

"That's what we have experts for," he said.

Of course other people knew more than Maggie did, but that didn't absolve her. "That doesn't absolve me," she said. "I have a duty to act." She wanted to add something about wisdom, about how it didn't always depend on facts. She wanted to say that the more facts people knew, the more they were blinded by them, but Lyle interrupted her.

"Lay off, Will," said Lyle. "Can't you see your mother's upset?"

This only increased Maggie's aggravation. Her family was allied against her, both coddling her and making a joke of her determination. It was as if Lyle had grabbed on to her sleeve and was pulling her back from an important edge.

Maggie had shown Lyle and Will the newspaper article, but she didn't show them the document she had taken from Mr. Winslow's desk that remained hidden in a separate folder at the very bottom of the evidence pile. She didn't even like to think of it, yellowing there beneath her sweaters and flannel nightshirts, yellowing except for the crimson border and the threatening red letters marching across the top of the page—and tucked just inside the cover, the letter from the Department of Defense.

Tucked inside the folder too was the letter from Dolly Jackson describing her experiences as a midwife at a women's clinic and asking Maggie if she had ever come across evidence that the munitions produced at the plant were making people sick, and if she had, could she copy it and send it on. Maggie hadn't bothered to write back saying she hadn't and she wouldn't—of course she wouldn't take something that wasn't hers! But she had. She had, and now she had to do something with the evidence—evidence that was more like ammunition than she liked to think.

When True came up to her at her going-away party, which was no more than Dr Pepper and a store-bought sheet cake in the lunchroom, and said, "So, you think you're better than us, do you?" Maggie only had to put her hand on True's sharp little shoulder blade and say, "Don't get me wrong," for True to burst into tears and splutter, "I'm going to miss you, Maggie! Of course I'll still have Misty, but you know how bossy Misty is."

"I suppose you're going to work at that chicken farm out by the highway," said Misty, covering up her own dismay with her usual air of superiority.

"Oh, no!" exclaimed Maggie. "I can't take a job that will bring suffering to someone else."

"Someone! Chickens aren't people!" True and Misty laughed 'til they cried over that, and the story spread like wildfire throughout Red Bud and north to Glorietta that Maggie Rayburn was giving up everything to live a moral life.

# 2.0 ORDERS

*It started with the surge, which was officially called The New Way Forward. In order to build up forces, tours were automatically extended by presidential order.*

—PFC Pablo Hernandez

*It's true I didn't relay the information to the men in a timely fashion. For a long time it seemed too soon to tell them, and then, suddenly, it seemed too late.*

—Lieutenant Colonel Gordon Falwell

*I was standing in the back. I'm not saying we always understood what the colonel was talking about, but usually we could at least hear the words.*

—Specialist Win Tishman

*Some of the men went fucking crazy. The captain had to do something about it, and he did.*

—First Sergeant Vince L. Crosby, aka Velcro

## 2.1 GORDON FALWELL

Two weeks before Lieutenant Colonel Gordon Falwell's Forward Support Battalion was scheduled to go home, Falwell was informed that all tours were being extended. The order had come down "effective immediately," but whether he did it out of fear or compassion, the colonel put off telling his troops. He had considered writing a letter on official stationery that they could have in their hands as he made the announcement, but he couldn't get the wording right. He liked to write things. He liked the feel of ink from his West Point pen flowing onto a fresh sheet of paper and he liked the crisp credibility of the final word-processed document. Above all, he liked finding the perfect word for a particular sentiment. But what was the perfect word for "fucked"?

As the day of liberation neared, discipline had deteriorated to the point of insubordination, which reflected badly on all of them, but mostly on Falwell himself. All day long, irritation had been squeezing his eyebrows together and forcing itself into the cavity behind his lungs, and now he was being called to brigade headquarters to get their new orders. Which meant he had to tell his troops ASAP.

One leadership lesson he'd learned was to get his ducks in a row before making a pronouncement, but his ducks depended on other people's ducks, all the way up the chain to the president, who had the upcoming election to consider. Meanwhile, did he continue to send supplies to the northern bases? What did he tell the news crew that had come to interview him about the New Way Forward, which was also being called the Surge? And where did he put the incoming troops if nobody was leaving? He was jumpy. The jumpiness, combined with the guilt he was feeling, made him snap at Miller, his Command Sergeant Major, when Miller came in with yet another stack of reports. Lunchtime came and went. By midafternoon he could put it off no longer. He slammed his fist on the desk and told Miller to muster the troops. An hour later, 300 men and women stampeded into the DFAC, tipping over chairs and telling high-spirited jokes because they still believed they were going home.

"One more trip to Tikrit and we're free," said one of the soldiers.

"Too bad we missed Mardi Gras," said a second soldier, and a third said, "There's always Burning Man."

"Haven't you seen enough of those right here in Iraq?" asked the first.

"Yee-haw," said the third.

"They can celebrate after we win the war," grumbled the colonel as he followed Miller to the front of the room. Washington promised that a surge in troops would be accompanied by a surge in support for the war, not only among Americans, but among Iraqis. But Falwell thought they should have fucking surged back at the beginning instead of committing to that zip-in-zip-out light-footprint strategy, which had been the only way to sell a war without raising taxes and upsetting the folks at home and which someone or other had described as "just enough troops to lose."

Not that political considerations were any of his concern, but now and then he couldn't help thinking, What the fuck?

Whenever the door opened, a gust of wind puffed the cheeks of the tent in and out according to some unseen geophysical rhythm, and still the colonel stood silently next to Miller, waiting while the men scraped into the chairs, some of them whistling and others laughing and punching each other on the arm. The ones who were sitting were banging their fists on the tables, and the latecomers, who had elbowed their way into the gaps between the tables in order to hear, were now pushing at one another and asking what was up before deciding it didn't matter: just two more days and they'd be gone.

Falwell thought how easy it would have been only a year before to bark out the facts and turn on his heel, but an unfamiliar wave of indecision washed over him, leaving him unsure of how to proceed. Sometimes he liked to shout out "Terror and ecstasy!" at strategic places in his inspirational speeches. Even though the troops didn't know the words referred to Nietzsche's view that only by joyously affirming suffering could man transcend meaninglessness, and even though the colonel didn't remember anything about Nietzsche but that, it still felt good to say the words. Now he wanted to say something that would penetrate their thick buzz-cut skulls and detonate their centers of understanding, but he didn't know what that something should be.

Falwell appreciated that the male prefrontal cortex didn't mature until the mid-to late-twenties, which was why young, uneducated men made such good soldiers and why college students, like Falwell had once been, admired Nietzsche's early writings and also why, at forty-seven, he couldn't think of anything pertinent to say that would transcend the wide gulf that separated a man with a developed brain from a room full of men without. Men and women, he corrected himself. He didn't know much about women, and what he thought he knew was always turning out to be wrong. Just ask his ex-wife and his daughters how much he knew about women and they would say jack shit.

His mouth was dry. His lips were cracked. His tongue felt like a hairless animal caught in a trap. Not to mention that lately he'd had a persistent, hacking cough that he should probably see a doctor for. "Fucking desert," he said to Miller, and Miller said, "Yes sir," in that well-oiled, agreeable way he had.

The noise in the DFAC was deafening. Even though some of the sound was absorbed by the soft canvas ceiling and the plywood floor that had been laid over the shifting desert sand, Miller had to shout to be heard. "At ease the noise!" he bellowed.

One by one the stragglers collapsed into the remaining chairs or shuffled forward from the back of the room or stood against the wall with their legs apart, increasingly alert to the long shadow of silence cast over the room by their commander. After a few seconds more, most of them had stopped pounding on the tables, and when Miller barked, "I said, lock it up!" the last of them stopped talking too, until the only thing Falwell could hear was the flapping of the canvas roof and, somewhere, a loose board banging in the wind. Even the tent seemed to be holding its breath and waiting for him to speak. Still, he gazed a fraction of a minute longer at his men, seeing in them his own youth, his own heedlessness, and also his own desperation to believe in something larger than himself.

Finally, Falwell cleared his throat. He confined himself to pointing out that full participation in life involved disappointment and tragedy and that the troops should enthusiastically embrace their lot, first because they were soldiers and second because there wasn't any other choice. He added a few sentences from his Center

42

of Gravity speech, which was loosely based on the theories of the great Prussian general and strategist Carl von Clausewitz. "Where the U.S. Army tends to conceive of the COG as the thing standing in the way of accomplishing a mission," he said, "I see it as an individual's source of moral and physical strength. That's something every one of you is going to need." Then he bluntly announced that the tours were being extended, no exceptions, end of case. "I am headed to Command Headquarters this afternoon to receive new orders. I will brief you again as soon as I return."

Miller was standing stiffly at the colonel's side, glaring at the troops arrayed before them until one by one the men and occasional woman stood at attention. One by one they stood tall and straight and focused on the middle distance, not looking at their colonel—just as he was not looking at them—but at the nothing the army had taught them to look at in order to avoid distraction, in order to be completely attuned to the form of things, in order to be tensed and settled and ready for whatever might be coming next. Content would follow form, the army had promised them, and for the colonel, it had. He believed in the mission completely and in the soaring American spirit backed up by the taloned might of American power. But sometimes he wondered if anyone knew what they were trying to accomplish. Sometimes he asked himself, What the fuck?

Falwell was nearing the half-century mark, and what lay beyond the middle distance when he dared to look that far was no longer what he had seen there as a young man or what the young men before him would see if they refocused their eyes. What lay beyond the middle distance, for him, was not the terror or ecstasy of youth, but resignation and a belief in partial truths. And beyond those things was the face of Sarah as she had been on the day of their wedding and also as she had been on the day of their divorce. He arranged his features to convey fierce devotion to duty. He straightened his already straight shoulders, and then he barked out, "Dis-missed!"

The men in the front started talking quietly, but the men farther back resumed their jokes and laughter.

"But sir," said Miller, "I don't think they heard you."

The wind was blowing again, shrieking, really, and maybe it had never stopped.

"Not now," said the colonel. "It's already past fifteen hundred hours. I've got a chopper to catch. I'll get my gear. Have the driver bring my vehicle out to the yard."

## 2.2 PENN SINCLAIR

Captain Penn Sinclair's outlook had changed since joining the army. For one thing, he no longer heard his father's voice in his head saying, "You're a Sinclair, son, and the Sinclairs have never been Keynesians." He led a logistics unit, tasked with making sure supplies got to the soldiers who needed them, and it was more likely that the voice in his head would say, "You name it, we'll get it for you or die trying." He no longer needed to decide if existence preceded essence or if the universe was a grand illusion perpetrated by an unseen force or if there was a foolproof way to distinguish right from wrong or if numbers were real or constructed. "I no longer wonder if you and I see the same thing when we look at the color red," he had told his girlfriend of four years over the telephone only the day before. "But I could build a school for you in less than six weeks."

"I like you better this way," Louise had replied.

"So do I," said Penn.

"I've changed too," she told him. "The old me would have tried to convince you that red is only good as an accent color. Of course, I still believe a little red goes a long, long way, but now we're meeting somewhere in the middle—conversationally, I mean. What's halfway between macro and micro?"

"Six to eight trucks," said Penn, because at just that moment his NCO, a steady man who was known as Velcro, came over to remind him he was late for a briefing.

"You see?" cried Louise triumphantly. "I was thinking the exact same thing, except about bridesmaids. The optimal number is six, seven including the maid of honor."

"Big enough to cover each other, but small enough to move quickly," said Penn.

"Exactly right," replied Louise.

And it no longer made him angry when his father said, "What do you say you put those government-issue leadership skills to work for me?" He could reply, "I'm not cut out for finance, Dad," without feeling he had to scrape the glue off of his feet or ace his serve to win the set.

Immediately after the meeting in the DFAC, the colonel sought the captain out for a quiet word. "Hold tomorrow morning's convoy for a couple of hours," he said. "Just in case something changes and the supplies are needed somewhere else. I'll let you know by eight hundred thirty hours."

Sinclair followed the colonel toward a vehicle that was waiting for him near a row of containerized housing units. "Where might they be needed?" he asked.

45

"I'm guessing Anbar Province, but I'll know more after my meeting at HQ."

"Al Anbar Province? We're abandoning our projects in Tikrit?"

"We're not abandoning anything yet, Sinclair. Did I say I'd have more information after my meeting at HQ?"

"Yes sir, you did. It's just that we've collected some books and other supplies for that school we're building on the outskirts of Samarra. I thought the men could drop them off on their way north."

Some months before, Sinclair had joined forces with a construction unit that was building a school in its spare time. He saw it as a way not only to make a lasting contribution, but also to foster cohesiveness in his cobbled-together logistics unit, which increasingly seemed to be made up of misfits transferred out of units where they had gotten into trouble or failed to fit in. And the unit had gelled—at least it was gelling. Now Velcro only had to say, "Look sharp!" for whomever he was addressing to jump away from the computer where he was playing solitaire or trying to discover what his girlfriend was doing behind his back and say, "Yes sir! What can I do for you, sir?"

Now and then he or Velcro laughed and said, "Don't forget that we were transferred in from other units too. What does that say about us?"

"Good," said the colonel as he got into the waiting Humvee. "Building infrastructure is an important benchmark. But the strategy is changing, which means the kinetics will have to change as well. This isn't just about winning hearts and minds, Sinclair. This is about searching out the bad apples before the rot spreads. This is about clearing neighborhoods and safeguarding residents from violence and intimidation. We'll have to wait to see if and how your school fits in."

"Finishing what we started is important to the men."

"*No campaign plan survives first contact with the enemy,*" said the colonel. "Do you know who said that?"

"Yes sir." It was Moltke the Elder, but it could have been Penn's father, who never tired of stressing the Darwinian need to adapt.

"What we started is a war," said the colonel. "Not that we started it."

"Yes sir."

"Everything in war is simple, but the simplest thing is difficult," said the colonel. "Clausewitz," said Penn.

"*The little things are the big things.*"

"I don't know who said that, sir, but the school nicely illustrates the point."

"I said it, and you can quote me. I'll let you know about the school."

The colonel squinted at something over Penn's shoulder. Then he signaled the driver and shouted above the noise of the revving engine, "The stop-loss is bound to hit some of the troops pretty hard. Don't let them sit around bemoaning their fate. Don't let them skimp on safety. Tell them they have the rest of today to get it out of their systems, and then you expect them to buckle down. I'll let you know where to send the convoy. And give any troublemakers something to do!"

The wheels of the colonel's Humvee dug in and then spun free, causing it to buck forward while the wind sent a column of dust spiraling across the yard. Sinclair stood watching the vehicle drive off and trying to get the grit out of his mouth and eyes and deciding he'd continue with the convoy briefing just in case they got lucky and were able to finish the school and also trying to ignore his father's voice, which suddenly intruded on his thoughts.

"You make your own luck!" his father liked to say, as if luck and opportunity hadn't both come up sixes for him and his

47

children, all boys, all athletic, all destined to follow the trajectory of Sinclair success—all of them quick to shout out "Buy!" or "Sell!" or "Anti-fragility!" which was an investment strategy that not only withstood a turbulent market but performed better under such conditions, just like the Sinclairs. Of the four brothers, only Penn had no interest in finance or the family business, but he had internalized the lessons about running down the hall and shouting, "Follow me!" What he had learned was that people tended to do it without asking where they were going. It was a useful skill for a leader, although unlike his brothers, he had a tendency to over-think things, the way he was doing now.

*Facta, non verba,* he reminded himself. Deeds, not words.

This led to a thought about how the word "fact" was more closely allied with actions and fabrications than with bits of dis-coverable truth and how words sometimes contained elements of their opposites, which was the kind of insight he loved and the kind his father hated. "Interesting thought," his old man would say. "But who's going to pay you to think it?"

Deeds, not words, Penn reminded himself just as Velcro came up and said, "I'm a little worried about the troops."

## 2.3 DANNY JOINER

Their tours were being extended. That's what the colonel's long-winded meandering had been about. That's what the muffled grumbling in the front rows and the funny silence meant. The

48

news reached Danny Joiner where he was sitting in the shade of a makeshift shower stall taking his weapon apart in order to clean and oil the action for the third time that afternoon. He had been absorbed in this task and only realized something was going on when Pig Eye ran around the corner of the yard shouting, "Can they do it? They can't do it, can they?" As if somebody had a definitive answer as to what the U.S. Army could and couldn't do.

Pig Eye was desperate to get home, and with each passing day, new fantasies about his wife's infidelity blossomed in his brain. "Extending our tours would be illegal, wouldn't it?" he whined. But they were talking about the people who both made the rules and interpreted them.

"What planet you livin' on, man?" asked Specialist Le Roy Jones, and Staff Sergeant Mason Betts, who was their squad leader and who happened to be walking by just then, batted the side of Pig Eye's head with an open palm and said, "Toughen up, man," before he disappeared into the shower stall.

Everybody had some factoid to contribute, some phrase from their enlistment papers, some personal theory of right and wrong honed on the steel of their childhoods, some favorite chapter or verse guaranteed either to make sense of their personal situations or to start an argument if not a war, until Le Roy got everyone's attention by whispering, "Slave labor, that's what it is!"

The whisper passed through the unit like a pressurized stream of combustible gas. Le Roy kept whispering, "Slave labor," over and over again to anyone who came within earshot. He said it to Danny just as Danny was trying to convince himself that the trickling sound of water from the shower stall was rain. What he wouldn't give for a downpour—send in fucking Katrina if that's what it took to break the heat that sucked the spit from his mouth and the sweat from his pores and the glaze from his ever-aching eyeballs.

"Jeezus, Le Roy," he said. "Can't I have some peace?"

"You heard, didn't you?"

"Yeah, I heard."

"Then why are you just sitting there?"

"What am I going to do about it? You tell me that and I just might consider it. Meanwhile, I'm oiling this rifle so if I ever need it, it doesn't jam."

Le Roy ran off to find someone more excitable to talk to. When Betts emerged dripping and the water sound abruptly stopped, Danny tried to sustain the daydream—wet dream, he thought—ha! That brought to mind his girlfriend Dolly, who was waiting for him at home just the way Emmie was waiting for Pig Eye and E'Laine was waiting for Le Roy and someone was waiting for all of them: girlfriends and parents and wives.

Or not waiting. The women back home were always posting pictures of the fun they were having on Facebook, where anyone could see them in their low-cut dresses, raising their glasses and blowing kisses ("This one's for you, honey!"), which made the men crazy because it was hard to tell the difference between passing-the-time-'til-you're-home-baby prowling and a full-bore, cat's-away, see-ya-later-buster hunt, and anyway, what were they going to do about it here?

Danny wiped his fingerprints off the barrel with a ragged chamois cloth, the sweaty skin of his massive forearms shining more brightly than the metal of the gun, and then he ambled around the corner into the yard just in time to see Corporal Joe Kelly climb up on the hood of a Toyota flatbed pickup and bow his head as if in prayer. But something about how Kelly's muscles were twitching told Danny that prayer was the last thing on his mind. Even when Pig Eye climbed up beside him, Kelly faced ahead and slightly down, not turning the way Pig Eye turned to check on who was watching and not smiling or catching anyone's eye before ramming his fist into the bone-dry air just as Captain Sinclair opened the sagging canvas door of his office and stepped out into the yard, followed by Velcro, whereupon both men jumped down, but not before a television crew that was passing through camp on its way to Tikrit caught the incident on tape and afterward went around asking the soldiers what the stop-loss orders meant for them.

Having an audience fired Le Roy up again, and he repeated his incendiary message into the microphone and also to a truckload of new recruits who drove up looking both shocked and optimistic. But by dinnertime, the furor was dying down and the men trooped off to eat, anger already giving way to resignation.

Danny watched the scene unfold from a corner of the yard, trying to remember the last lines of a Shelley poem that might sum up what he was feeling, if a creeping sense of desolation and inadequacy shot through with a deeply percolating anger was even subject to summation. He knew that most anger was born of misunderstanding, and he wanted to understand. More than that, he wanted to fit in. But he had never fit in, not in school, where he had wanted to study literature, and not in the army, which was why he had been transferred to the logistics unit and why, if he had asked Kelly the proper technique and thrust his own fist into the air and called him and Pig Eye "brother" or whatever the proper word was in order to let them know he shared their disappointment, they would have stared at him without a speck of comprehension. He understood that their identity in a funny way depended on his, and his was alien to them, which was just the way they wanted it. Men like Kelly wanted solidarity and separateness at the same time. It would have filled him with sad-ness if it hadn't first filled him with other things, one of which was anger, but another of which was something he couldn't quite put his finger on.

"It's not good enough to be an American anymore," he said to Harraday, who was standing near him.

"What?" asked Harraday. "I'm with them. This stop-loss bullshit really sucks."

Harraday spat and walked off, and Danny would have given anything to have an exclusive hand gesture to wave in Harraday's face, a gesture that defined the knife-edge of identity and proved to Harraday that, whatever Harraday was, Danny wasn't that.

Instead of going to dinner, Danny made his way to the latrine, where he took off his uniform jacket and carefully rolled the sleeves of his T-shirt in overlapping folds, which made his bulging biceps look almost as big as, if a little softer than, Kelly's biceps looked when he rolled his sleeves the same way. Danny glanced behind him to make sure he was alone, listening carefully for the sound of footsteps on the packed earth outside the door. But most of the troops were in the DFAC and all was quiet. He stood at attention in front of the rectangular sheet of metal that served for a mirror and searched his face for signs of what he was thinking and was glad when he couldn't find any. Then he took a deep breath and thrust his fist into the air. The exposed ridge of arm muscle hardened, and for a moment he didn't recognize himself. His gray eyes darkened a shade closer to black, and his brows soared above his nose like the wings of a raptor.

Danny was startled to find that the gesture had both an out-side and an inside. All he had known of it before was what it had looked like when someone else did it and also that it had worried him, the kind of worry that turned to anger before you knew it was really fear. But now, standing in the latrine where the only observer was a tinny mirror image of himself, he felt the adrenaline rush and almost understood what Kelly and Pig Eye had been thinking when they had practiced the gesture on the rest of the battalion. He could almost feel, rising within him, a big Fuck You to the war.

## 2.4 LE ROY JONES

Le Roy had to laugh. All he had to do was say "slave labor" and everyone's panties were in a twist. He had to laugh at the fresh, unbaked faces of the new recruits, who didn't know the first thing about war but were about to find out. And there was Pig Eye, waving a torn envelope and wondering now that the US of A had them in Iraq, was it allowed to keep them there?

"Shit, man, they can do anything they want," said Le Roy. "Isn't proving that the point of the war?"

"But," said Pig Eye, and then he just stood with his mouth open and his eyes bugging out and the letter hanging limp at his side.

"Slave labor," he said to Kelly, and it was a beautiful thing to see that man's muscles tense and his eyes become hard and dense, like if you touched Kelly's trigger, they'd come shooting out of their sockets straight at you. Kelly could be a politician, the way people automatically looked in his direction—if he could control his temper, that is. If he could control his mouth.

Velcro said, "Nobody here cares what color you are, Jones. You have to go back home for that." But Velcro was like an android, strictly by the book. If something wasn't written down in a manual, Velcro didn't know about it. So Le Roy said, "Slave labor" to the new recruits, and he laughed to see their jaws drop open and their eyes go wide. Jeezus, it was funny. What did they think they were getting into? What did they fucking think?

It was funny until a current of something that wasn't quite so funny ionized the air around him. It was what his girlfriend E'Laine would have called paranormal because she believed in electromagnetic fields and how energy was neither created nor destroyed, which meant that when people died, their life force had to go somewhere—and where it went, she insisted, was either into other people or into the atmosphere, so that at any given time a person might be surrounded by a hundred souls or blobs of plasma and electrons or whatever it was that hadn't yet found a new body to inhabit.

So it was natural Le Roy thought of E'Laine when the current made the hairs on his arms stand up, for even though he considered E'Laine's energy conservation theory to be superstitious and probably false, he couldn't deny that the tremor coursing through him was more than an idle premonition. It was as if the mood of the world had changed or the air molecules were bunching up and crowding in on him. He'd felt that way before—in moments of despair, but also in moments of wild but unrealistic hope. Like the time his computer science teacher had asked, "Have you ever thought about college, boy?" The question had caused the atmospheric molecules to shift and part, and Le Roy had seen a path to a different future, a path that lingered in his imagination long after the teacher forgot all about the college talk. He didn't meet anyone so optimistic about his future again until that army recruiter had said, "You interested in computers, son? Damn right we can teach you that."

It was better to laugh it off. It was better to say, "Fuck that shit" and go about his business. It was better to be the one who said the words that got other people all riled up than to be the one who took the words on board and started to hope. Meanwhile, he had E'Laine, who was a whole hell of a lot steadier than Pig Eye's wife, even if Pig Eye's wife was smoking hot. E'Laine would be there for him when he got home. One hundred percent she would be there waiting. Whether it was tomorrow or a year from tomorrow or a year or two years after that, she'd be waiting for him with one of her special recipes sizzling on the stove and a cold beer in the fridge and an eternal flame of love for Le Roy Jones keeping vigil in her heart. Meanwhile, he didn't mind finding his fun where he could get it. Meanwhile, he told Hernandez he'd better get someone to check on Maya and his little boy, and then he whispered, "Slave labor" into Garcia's ear.

"It sure don't seem fair," said Garcia.

"Now we'll see who the real men are," said Harraday, who, along with Kelly, had transferred in from a combat unit and who never smiled except when he was telling stories about his old team and the fun they'd had until he'd gotten into trouble for something he said he preferred not to talk about but hinted at anyway now and then. But now even Harraday's shoulders sagged, and suddenly Le Roy's heart wasn't in it. Still, he passed the news to a few more men and had to laugh at how their eyes went dark and their faces started to smolder. He had to fucking laugh because it all depended on what you meant by "fair." And then he was thinking about E'Laine again and seeing her as she would be when he told her he wasn't coming home, not yet anyway. She would cry. He could see it clear as the dragon tattoo on his arm: the softening of her features, the downturn of her mouth, the leaking of her eyes the way they had leaked the day she drove him to the airport, acting like it was his last day on earth.

And then his heart *was* in it, even though it wasn't funny anymore—*because* it wasn't funny and because he was feeling the rage spiking out of Kelly and the panic from Pig Eye and feeling a slow, sure burn in his own guts as well.

## 2.5 PIG EYE

When the commotion broke out, Pig Eye had been thinking about his wife Emmie. He alternated between thinking she was unfaithful to him and thinking she wasn't—but if she wasn't, why not? She was beautiful, while he was short and funny looking. Even though Emmie had only had drug-dealer boyfriends before meeting Pig Eye three years before, he knew he didn't deserve her. But whenever he said, "Why do you love me when you could have anyone?" she would reply, "You might be small, darlin', but you're all muscle." Or she might say, "Every girl needs a superhero, and baby, you're mine."

Pig Eye ran a car repair shop with his buddy Earl, and when he left, Earl promised he would prioritize diligent bookkeeping and quality control exactly the way Pig Eye always had, but now he wondered if Earl was cheating him moneywise or if he was prioritizing Emmie behind his back. In her most recent letter,

Emmie had written, "Earl is taking care of business." Pig Eye's eyes stuck on that line like it was glue. He had to read it over and over, and still he wondered if she had left out the word "the" on purpose or if it had been a mistake—or if it was just a casual way of writing, kind of like a person would talk. And if it was a mistake, was the letter telling him a bigger truth than Emmie meant to tell?

Kelly's gesture released something that had been trapped in Pig Eye for a long time, something to do not only with skin color but also with the fact that he had round cheeks and small eyes and a drop-dead gorgeous wife. He didn't stop to think before stepping up on the truck beside and slightly behind Kelly—he knew not to stand right next to him, of course he knew that—and putting his arm in the air too. It felt good to glare out over the heads of the men and women who paused as they went about their duties to look at him with surprise and new respect. It felt good to stare straight at Kelly without looking away first. Now he knew what it was like to be tall and powerful, not just because Kelly was tall and powerful and anybody Kelly liked shared in that power, but because he was acknowledging something about himself, freeing some un-free thing that was the reason for his insecurity and stepping beyond his short, awkward exterior to show who he was deep down inside.

It only lasted a couple of seconds, but afterward, people thumped him on the shoulder or made a point of knocking into him in a friendly way, and he knew he had done the right thing in stepping up beside (and a little behind) Joe Kelly. After marrying Emmie and opening the car repair shop, it was the most right thing he had ever done.

## 2.6 PENN SINCLAIR

Sinclair followed Velcro out of the office to where a commotion was brewing in the yard. A few minutes earlier or later and he would have missed the whole thing, but he didn't miss it, and it worried him. It wasn't only that the men looked angry and inscrutable and that anger was catching. It wasn't only that he and the colonel had known for two weeks before springing the news on them that they wouldn't be going home, though of course that added to his sense of complicity and guilt. It worried him because he was losing control—not only of his troops. He too wanted to go home. He too had a girlfriend who loved him and a future to plan.

"Should we put a lid on it?" asked Velcro.

"They're just letting off steam," replied Penn, even though he knew that something little could easily turn into something big and that it was up to him to stop it. The little things are the big things, the colonel had said.

"We'll give them the rest of today," he told Velcro, remembering the colonel's advice. He walked farther out into the yard. "Listen up," he barked. "You have the rest of the evening to let off steam, and then I want your heads back in the game." The mere act of shouting relieved a little of the tension that had built up inside him ever since the stop-loss order was announced. "Convoy briefing at zero seven hundred hours," he added.

"I thought we were waiting," said Velcro.

"We're waiting on the go/no-go, but we're sticking to our

established battle rhythm. The more we stick to routine, the better for the troops."

At the morning briefing, Penn said that the convoy had been postponed and that he'd know more soon.

"So we're going, we just don't know when or where," said Kelly.

"That's about right," said Penn.

"Shee-it," said Le Roy. "That's bad juju right there."

"The key to survival is the ability to adapt," said Penn. Then he pulled Staff Sergeant Betts aside and told him to keep an eye on the pre-checks. "Make sure they don't slack off," he said.

"What are we supposed to do with the stuff for the school?" asked Betts.

"I'm worried about that too," said Penn. "I should know more in a couple of hours, but meanwhile, put it in the last four trucks. Your squad will take those."

Sinclair was proud of his men for wanting to help extend educational opportunities to girls. *"Facio liberos ex liberis libris libraque,"* he had said when the idea had first come to him, and it had become a kind of motto for the men.

"Make free men out of children by means of books and a balance," said Betts now, but he frowned at Velcro when he said it, and Velcro spat in the dirt.

"Building infrastructure is an important benchmark," said Penn before moving off toward the communications center for the intelligence update. He was almost out of earshot when he heard Harraday say, "Try books and a bazooka. Maybe that would work."

The grumbling started up again during the pre-check, and now two of the squads were fighting in the yard. The more restless the men became, the more Penn worried, and the more he worried, the more he thought he couldn't wait for the new orders before he sent the convoy. "Give any troublemakers something to do," the colonel had told him. Taking the supplies north would be doing something.

"If you're holding a wolf by the ears," he said to Velcro, "is it worse to continue to hold it or worse to let it go?"

"You've got to kick that wolf in the balls," said Velcro. "You can't put up with any shit."

Penn had to agree. They needed a mission pronto, so when he hadn't heard anything by zero nine hundred hours, he released the convoy to start heading north. He told the men to monitor the radio in case the new orders came through, and he told Betts to take an extra gun truck so the vehicles destined for the school could make the short detour while the rest of the convoy continued on to Tikrit. Things would calm down once the men had a mission to focus on. They always did.

"Yes sir. I'm on it," said Betts, taking the need for further action out of Sinclair's hands.

"You made the right call, sir," said Velcro. "You're killing two birds with this—giving the men something useful to do and getting the supplies up the road for wherever they're needed."

"Three birds," said Penn, thinking of the school and feeling the familiar sense of accomplishment that always accompanied a tough decision.

And then, suddenly, Penn didn't want to go home. He didn't want to go back to a life where nothing he did would matter in the grand scheme of things and probably wouldn't matter in the not-so-grand scheme either. He liked the high-stakes missions and calling the shots when the shots were not easy to call. Sinclairs did better in turbulent conditions! He thought about his place in the continuum of history and how he was carrying on a legacy bequeathed by the ancient Greeks and Romans, who had determined that war and peace were flip sides of a single coin, and by the philosophers and scientists, who had figured out that in some ways people were not much different from insects, with their workers and soldiers and queens, and that in other ways, people were not much different from gods.

## 2.7 PIG EYE

Things might have settled down if a wispy cloud hadn't obscured the sun just as Le Roy was saying that thing about juju. They might have stayed settled if Pig Eye hadn't shown Hernandez a letter from his wife or if Hernandez hadn't taken it from him and passed it on to Tishman, who passed it to Kelly, each man reading it as if it were his own wife or girlfriend who had penned the description of what she was wearing and how she was going to take the items off one by one once her honey-man was home. Garcia slapped his thigh and said, "Oooeee Momma!" just as Kelly grabbed the letter back for another look. "Wait a sec," said Kelly. "Who's this guy Earl?"

"I told you about Earl. He's my partner in the shop," said Pig Eye. "He's handling things while I'm away."

"I'll say he is," said Kelly.

"What do you mean? What do you mean by that?"

Harraday walked over and cast a shadow on the letter, which was smudged and wet where someone had put his lips to it and tongued it. His eyes were puffy and his breath was as rotten as if he had just rolled out of bed after a night on the town. "He means your friend Earl's porking your wife and now you're stuck here and there's nothing you can do about it," he said.

"What do you mean?" asked Pig Eye again.

"Handling," said Harraday. "Your partner is handling things at home."

"The letter doesn't say 'handling,'" said Pig Eye.

"But you did. You wouldn't have said it if you didn't suspect something was up."

"Don't listen to Harraday, man," said Danny. "He doesn't know what he's talking about."

But Pig Eye didn't have to listen to Harraday to know he didn't trust Earl worth a damn. It was all he could think about when he was checking the fuel. He overfilled one tank and forgot to replace the cap on another. "Jeezus, what's wrong with you?" asked Betts when he hurried past to see if the orders had come through.

"Nothing," said Pig Eye, but he could tell that Betts was down too when he walked past thirty seconds later muttering that he couldn't find his cargo manifest even though he was holding it in his hand.

Pig Eye found a detonator on the ground and slipped it into the pocket of his uniform where he kept what he called his escape kit. Now and then he stroked his thigh to make sure the kit was still there or adjusted the Velcro closure to make sure it was secure. He had made the mistake of telling Hernandez and Le Roy about the kit, and now and then Le Roy would say, "Stick with Pig Eye in case you're captured. He's got a magnifying glass that can burn through rope or zip ties using solar energy."

"You don't use a magnifying glass to escape from zip ties. You'd burn your arm!" said Pig Eye before he realized it was a joke.

Pig Eye didn't mind the teasing until Harraday joined in. "Anybody need a tampon, Pig Eye's your man. He's got emergency supplies."

Pig Eye tried to laugh it off because nobody wanted to get cross-wise with Harraday, but sometimes he imagined revenge scenarios where Harraday's fate was in his hands and he could save him or not. In the scenarios he always ignored Harraday until he was crying and pleading for his life. "Die, motherfucker," a tougher version of himself would say in the fantasy, but then Harraday would beg for forgiveness and the tougher Pig Eye would soften and do whatever needed doing to set him free. Thinking about Harraday gave Pig Eye a pain in his gut, so it wasn't always worth it to picture him crying in the desert. Sometimes it was better not to think of him at all.

"Hey, man, you're riding with me," said Danny. He slapped Pig Eye on the shoulder, and together they walked to where the trucks were waiting.

## 2.8 LE ROY JONES

Le Roy could smell Pig Eye's sweat. He had noticed it earlier, when they were checking the load. Pig Eye's going to be a problem, he thought, and when Joe Kelly walked up with a map of their route, all he had to say was "Pig Eye" for Kelly to frown and nod as if he was thinking the same thing. But because it was more important to make sure the radio was operational and to identify danger spots than to confirm each other's worries about Pig Eye, they didn't say anything out loud.

"Do we have maps of both routes?" Le Roy asked Pig Eye,

who was standing around patting his pockets and fiddling with something he had picked up off the ground.

"What do you mean, both routes?"

"Christ," said Le Roy. "Didn't you hear the captain say we might be redirected? And locate Sergeant Betts while you're at it. Tell him it's SP minus five. And Rinaldi—where's he at?" Rinaldi was one of their gunners. He and Le Roy, who was the radio operator, would be riding in a converted Humvee with their medic Satch and whoever was driving. "Who's driving this Humvee?" he asked, but Pig Eye was already sprinting back to a row of supply shacks in search of the second strip map. "Anyone seen Harraday or Rinaldi?" he asked when Danny and Kelly came by with the cargo manifest.

"They were with Betts and the captain," said Kelly. And then he said, "This can't be right—just two cases of H2O? Don't tell me they're hoarding water again."

"Per truck," said Danny. "I'm sure that means two cases per truck."

"Two per truck isn't enough," said Kelly. "Trucks might run on diesel, but soldiers run on water."

Kelly went off to see about the water just as Pig Eye came back with the map and said, "Betts says we need to get going. It's getting late. It's only going to get hotter, and they're getting a buzz about some kind of movement up north."

They were ten minutes late. Then fifteen. Danny was going over the cargo manifest item by item one last time when Betts came up and said, "Five minutes. Tell the others to be ready in five."

"I'm just checking the list," said Danny, and Le Roy said, "Shit, man, you can check and recheck, but that sucker's already been fired."

"I know," said Danny with a grin. "But I'm checking anyway."

It was an article of faith among the troops that there was no rhyme or reason to who made it and who didn't. The bullet with a soldier's name on it had already been fired if it was going to be fired, and if it wasn't, well, you were good. It was the kind of comforting fatalism that appealed to Le Roy. Whenever E'Laine worried about him, he said, "Don't you worry, baby. If my number's up, it's up, and if it ain't, it ain't."

But they did what they could anyway, so Le Roy made sure both radios were in working order and the tanks were full of fuel while Danny checked and rechecked the straps that secured the equipment and Kelly rustled up the cases of water and filled his CamelBak and an extra canteen because water was important to Kelly, not that it wasn't important to all of them, and Harraday paced back and forth and got himself into what he called "mission mode" and Rinaldi fished out his cross and kissed it and Pig Eye patted his pockets and looked around kind of wildly.

"Pig Eye's going to be a problem," said Le Roy, but he was talking to himself because everyone was busy taking care of last-minute tasks before hoisting themselves up into the trucks just as Summers blasted the horn of the vehicle Le Roy was riding in and Tishman climbed up into the front right seat of the extra gun truck and Finch and the other gunners climbed into their slant-sided turrets and the line of trucks ahead of them ground into gear. Then Betts shouted, "Okay, boys, let's roll," which Le Roy remembered was what that guy on one of the 9/11 planes had said just before it exploded over a field in Pennsylvania.

## 2.9 PIG EYE

Pig Eye spent the boring hours driving or on patrol imagining different escape scenarios where he not only had to get away, but also had to make it back home under his own steam. A major component of the fantasies was imagining what he would need in order to accomplish the task. It gave him something to do to plan elaborate lists of supplies and to keep an eye out for useful items. When he found one, he added it to his kit: a protein bar, a travel alarm clock, an extra pair of paracord laces, a spool of wire, a folding knife, and now the detonator. The pocket wasn't big enough for everything in his collection, so he had to rotate what he kept in it. He stored the items he didn't have room for in a drawstring canvas bag in his locker.

When they were together on patrol, Le Roy or Hernandez would come up with a situation and ask Pig Eye how he would get out of it, or they would quiz each other about escape techniques. "What's the breaking strength of paracord?" Pig Eye might ask. Or Hernandez might want to know, "When is the best time to escape?"

"Right away," Pig Eye would say. "Your first opportunity is always the best one you'll have."

On patrol the previous evening, Hernandez had taught him a time-slowing trick that involved imagining he could throttle down the surrounding action so it played at low speed, giving him more time for whatever he was doing, and Pig Eye had imagined a scenario where barbed wire figured in. So that morning he had switched out the cigarette lighter for a pair of wire cutters he had won off another soldier in a poker game. "Just in case," he had said when Hernandez caught his eye, and Hernandez had said, "Yeah, man, just in case."

The only book Pig Eye had ever read voluntarily was *The Things They Carried,* and the idea that what a man carried with him said something profound about who the man was had stayed with him. He had come to disdain the sentimental and useless treasures most of his comrades pulled from their own pockets to moon over at night. A letter from his mother wasn't going to save his life. A picture of Emmie wasn't going to get him home. Still, among the things in the cargo pocket was just such a picture. He knew it said something about him, and what it said was that he was irrational and soft. It was awareness of his weaknesses that made him extra meticulous in his plans for escape, even though he also knew that escape was impossible, for let's say he could get away from his captors, where would he go in that forbidding and alien land?

One of Pig Eye's most shameful secrets was that his escape fantasies didn't always entail escaping from Iraqi captors, but from his unit. When he had thoughts like those, he felt like a traitor. But even when he closed his eyes and forced himself to imagine he was being held hostage by both Osama bin Laden and Saddam Hussein, he couldn't always get the bad kind of fantasy out of his head.

"What are the two most important things in any escape?" asked Pig Eye, trying to start a conversation with Danny, who was sitting next to him in the front seat, alternately scanning his sector and siting down the barrel of his M4.

"A howitzer," said Danny.

"No. These things are commonplace and they don't take up so much room."

Danny thought for a minute and then said, "Water."

"I'll give you a hint," said Pig Eye. "I don't have either of them in my kit."

"Why the hell not?" asked Danny. "If they're the most important thing."

"Because everyone has them and no one does."

"Okay, riddle man, what are they?"

"Time and opportunity," said Pig Eye. "Opportunity and time."

After that Danny fell silent again and Pig Eye went back to thinking about Emmie and how because of Harraday "taking care of" had morphed in his mind into "handle" and "handle" had morphed into "pork."

# 3.0 PRISON

*It didn't take her long to get a job up at the prison. She told me being around criminals day after day didn't bother her, but I wonder if it did.*

—True Cunningham

*She said her eyes were finally open. She said saving someone else's son was the only way to save her own.*

—Tiffany Price

*I like fairy tales as much as the next gal, but Maggie actually believed she could change things. She wanted to save them all.*

—Valerie Vines

*I think there was another side to her. I'm not saying she didn't love Lyle. I'm just saying that he was her ticket out of that house way back when, and maybe she was looking for another ticket now.*

—Lily De Luca

## 3.1 MAGGIE

Hurry, Maggie said to herself as she rushed down the prison steps in the evenings, and then she said it again as she took the bus to the shopping plaza to buy something for dinner, after which she waited impatiently in the parking lot for Lyle or he waited impatiently for her. Mornings, it was the same thing in reverse. She would arrive at the prison breathless, her head spinning with competing admonitions: Move a little faster! Haste makes waste! Nobody cares if you're late or not! She shivered to think that defeat was lurking and might be inevitable. But late for what? And why defeat?

The prison was set on a rise, dwarfing the people who flocked every day from the employee parking lot up the long flight of granite steps and through a gauntlet of metal detectors and guards charged with keeping the prisoners in and contraband out. Every time Maggie stepped through the gate into the chilly welcome center, she winced as if she were guilty of something, as if the metal detector could see the image of the top-secret document that was squirreled away in her brain or as if the escaped one-eyed men with hooks for arms her father had invented to scare his children into obedience were watching her from wherever they were hiding. It was easy to imagine her father waiting in the shadows too, to shout at her for something she had done or not done—a shoe unlaced, a toy left carelessly on the stair instead of put away in a closet, for crying or not crying when he smacked her, or the only jam to be found in the cupboard was strawberry when didn't he always like peach—or to chase the four of them into their rooms, bolting the doors from the outside as if order in the house, as in the world, depended upon incarceration.

And where was her mother while all of this was going on? By the age of thirty-nine, Mary Sterling had taken to the shadows too, her body shrunken inside her paisley dress. She sent the children for the shopping and rarely ventured out. Maggie had looked helplessly on as her mother was buffeted before the winds of her father's rages. That will never happen to me, she promised herself, and it hadn't. Lyle always asked her what she thought before voicing his own opinion, and even though her father was long gone by the time Lyle had come along, Lyle seemed to understand that paternal absence was a kind of presence, so he tiptoed around it and helped with the dishes and remembered not to slam the door.

Every morning, Maggie took off her bracelets and put her purse on a conveyor belt so it could be x-rayed and searched. Every morning, she smiled at the guards and wondered if they too shouted at their wives. The head of the morning detail was a narrow man with furrowed skin and furtive eyes whose name was Louis, but in the evenings, the burly Hugo was in charge. Hugo exuded an air of tense restraint, as if he was holding his manliness in check or training for some test of stamina and determination. He seemed to find the intimacy implied in searching Maggie's purse or running a scanner over her body amusing, and their thirty-second interactions began to feel like aggressive physical encounters. Hugo would say, "We have to stop meeting like this," in a way that could be interpreted as a joke or as something more serious disguised as a joke. Or he would scrutinize Maggie's face or dress with a savage gleam in his eyes until she blushed and fumbled for just the right lighthearted comment that would acknowledge his superiority in terms of size and strength, while also reminding him that she had a family and that she wasn't available now and never would be.

But something about her interactions with Hugo suited Maggie. The layers to their little conversations fit with a growing sense that she was leading a double life, and she wondered if Hugo also thought of himself as two people: as the determined warrior he was at work and as the virile masher she imagined him to be when he went out on the weekends with his friends. Occasionally she allowed herself to respond to him in a way that hinted at the dual roles both of them were playing. "I see you're wearing your Schwarzenegger smile today," she might say, or "Prison guard by day, lady-killer by night." And then Hugo would smirk at her and reply, "I haven't killed anybody yet."

This wasn't the kind of banter Maggie was used to, and she was shocked at her own boldness. But something about it meshed with an inner readiness, as if she had spent the last sixteen years not only mothering and keeping house, but also training for a clandestine project she didn't yet understand.

"She's too old for you," Louis would say to Hugo if he was working a double shift, and Hugo's face would become a cartoon of regret. Or Hugo would say, "Good morning, Momma," and Maggie would reply, "So now they're giving badges and guns to children—what is the world coming to?"

But most of the time Hugo and the other guards only leered silently as they pawed through her things, and then Maggie would give her best imitation of a sultry smile and call them heartbreakers before gathering up her belongings and hurrying along the corridor to another set of locked gates and a walkway that led past the prison yard to the office block where she worked and thinking only about practicalities and the logistics of her day.

## 3.2 DOLLY

Dolly could smell whiskey on the doctor's breath when he flicked his fingernail at the lab results for an underweight baby and thrust the folder back at her, saying, "Don't you damn women know enough not to drink?"

Dolly knew he didn't mean her. She knew she was only a convenient ear when the doctor complained about inadequate insurance reimbursements or working conditions at the big city hospital where he spent most of his time or when he told her about a vacation he was planning or about a task force he had been asked to chair. He had been divorced twice from the same woman. He had a daughter in San Francisco and a son in New York. Over the years Dolly had learned many things this way, while the doctor would have been astonished to find out that she came from a family of seven children, all born at home, that her boyfriend was a soldier in Iraq, that many of her clients paid her late or not at all, and that there was an entire consciousness ticking behind her eyes.

But the doctor also worked many cases for free, which was what convinced Dolly that underneath the gruff exterior a heart of gold was beating, trapped there like a caged bird and just waiting for something to free it. Each time she caught his eye over a swollen belly or a wriggling newborn, she thought she saw a window slide open, and sometimes she swore she could see right through the window to where the bird was flapping its wings against the bars and singing. But then he would cow a pair of anxiously waiting newlyweds into silence by barking, "While you've been sitting here reading magazines, I've been saving lives!" and she would go back to thinking he didn't have a heart at all.

Dolly liked the feeling of lives in her hands too, but for her, it wasn't the power she liked, but the mystery of new life springing from the very atoms of the earth, animated by love and the merest puff of grace. She could imagine vast potentials in the tiny curls of the fingers with their even tinier nails. "You can be anything you want to be," she would whisper to the babies. Even though she knew that half of them would succumb to drugs, abuse, or lives of crime, she had to believe that each little life she brought into the world would be one of the lucky ones, that each word she whispered into its ear would make a difference, that each happy thought would help it beat the odds.

Mostly she only listened as the doctor talked, breathing out "Mm-hmm" or "Oh, my!" when a response seemed called for. Or she just hummed a song inside her head if the doctor waved his hand for silence. So she wasn't quite sure what to think when he sought her out one afternoon and said, "What would you say if I told you they had altered a scientific report? What would you say if I told you the data had been fudged?"

The doctor's eyes were wide and searching, but what Dolly saw in them now was more a mine shaft than a window.

"What report?" she asked him. "Does it have to do with the damaged babies?"

Before the doctor could answer, the second-to-last patient of the day came into the waiting room, drenched from a pelting rain and calling out behind her, "Okay, Frankie. Come back for me in half an hour."

The woman had suffered a miscarriage and seemed both teary and relieved. After assuring the doctor she was fine, she started sobbing. "It's just that Frankie came back from the war without his feet. Some days it's all I can do to take care of him. What would I do with a baby? And Frankie has trouble sleeping, so then I have trouble sleeping too. Can you give him something to help with that?"

"This is a women's clinic," said the doctor, but then he relented and took out his prescription pad.

"These pills are for you," he said. "It's against the law to share them."

"Oh," said the woman.

"However, I doubt anyone would find out if you did."

"And he stopped going to physical therapy. He says there isn't any point."

"I can't solve everything," said the doctor, tearing the leaf off the pad and giving it to the woman. "He needs to see his own physician.

"I can't solve everything," he said again when Dolly put her hand on his arm and said, "You're a good man." Of course the doctor had hopes and dreams! Of course he had a beating heart!

"Tell me, then. What would a good man do if he knew what I know? Would he make that knowledge public even if it ended his career, or would he close his eyes and continue to help his patients the best he can?"

Dolly was certain the doctor was talking about the report on munitions safety he had mentioned several weeks before. She took a deep breath and asked, "Was it the report on birth defects and munitions safety that was altered?"

The doctor looked startled, as if he hadn't meant to speak his thoughts aloud. "Oh, that," he said. "Whatever caused the birth defects, it wasn't the munitions. The revised report was absolutely clear on that."

"The revised report," said Dolly carefully. "What did the original say?"

But the window was closed now, closed and shuttered. And then the doctor was glancing at his watch and asking about the last patient—wherever had she gotten to? Did she think he had all night? While they waited for her to arrive, he talked pompously about the heroic things he had done, the influential people he knew, the exotic places he had traveled to, the new car he was going to buy. "So I really don't have time to wait," he said.

"Doctor," whispered Dolly. "Do you have copies of both reports?"

"Do I have copies?" asked the doctor absently. His eyes had lost focus, and Dolly couldn't tell if he had been drinking again or if he was merely lost in thought.

"Yes, of the two reports."

The storm was turning the orange clay of the parking lot into an orange pond. The owner of the building had dumped a load of pea gravel in a corner of the lot, but no one had ever come to spread it, so it sat like a miniature mountain near the rusting trash receptacle. Dolly liked to imagine the improvements she would make if she were the owner of the facility: curtains at the windows instead of broken mini blinds, pots of geraniums at the entrance, a fresh coat of paint on the flaking stucco, and in the waiting room, a basket of magazines and comfortable upholstery rather than metal folding chairs like the one the second-to-last patient was sitting on while she waited for someone to pick her up.

"Do you have a ride?" asked Dolly.

"Yes," said the woman. "We got the truck fitted out with hand controls. Frankie's still getting used to them, so he says I'm not to worry if he's a little late."

"I guess she's not coming," Dolly said when fifteen minutes had passed and the last patient had failed to arrive.

The doctor put on his coat. "Who would have thought?" he muttered. "Who in tarnation would have thought?"

"What's done in the dark always comes to the light," said Dolly.

"Unless it doesn't," said the doctor.

"What about if we give it a teensy push?"

"No, no. I can't afford to ruffle feathers," said the doctor. "That would be disastrous."

"But I can," said Dolly. "What if I were the one . . ."

But the doctor was pulling a rain hat over his ears and she couldn't tell if he was listening or not.

After he left, Dolly made her way through the rooms locking cabinets and making sure the bathroom was presentable. She had just finished, all except the lights, when a rusty pickup pulled into the parking lot and honked, the beams of its headlamps illuminating the heavy raindrops and the gravel pile. The woman who had had the miscarriage jumped up and ran out the door, slamming it behind her and holding a paper grocery sack over her head to protect her from the rain. Just when she reached the passenger-side door, the truck lurched forward, causing her to fall to her knees in a puddle.

Dolly opened the door and called out, "Are you all right?"

"It's not Frankie's fault!" the woman called back as she scrambled to her feet. "It's the hand controls! They can be a little bit tricky at first!" The gears ground and caught. Then the truck shuddered backward until it was clear of the puddle, and she opened the door and climbed inside.

# 3.3 WILL

The A students sat up front, their faces smug with knowledge. After school, they streamed out the doors to the waiting minivans, the waxed and buffed high-riders, the sleek four-doors and rusted rattletraps, taking their secrets with them while Will was left with the mystery: "Were the ghosts in *The Turn of the Screw* real or not? Explain."

He had a 50 percent chance of getting the first part of the question right, but how could he explain what he did not know? And how did it make sense to ask if something in a made-up story was real, especially when that something couldn't be real in reality. At first he thought it was a trick question, and after hesitating, he had written "No," comforted that the letters, scratched out in soft pencil, were easily erased—something he quickly did. "Yes," he then wrote. But "yes" was an answer he couldn't explain, while "no" had years of experience to back it up, not to mention Sunday school instruction if he chose to get into that, a tactic that went over well with most of his teachers, but somehow not with Mr. Quick. Besides, the Y looked shaky, about to topple over on its stick, so he erased "Yes" and replaced it with the more solidly grounded "No," which he made as bold and as black as graphite and his wavering conviction could make it.

"I'll show you what a nice guy I am and give you ten more minutes," Mr. Quick announced to Will and the three other students who had only slouched more deeply in their chairs and clutched their pens and pencils more tightly when the dismissal bell sounded.

The classroom window looked out onto the courtyard, where a line of cars snaked and waited for the students to emerge. In the distance, a stand of budding apple trees stretched their branches to the sun, and beyond the apple trees, the gentle slope to the ball field where Will's team gathered every afternoon. If he stayed to finish the quiz, he would be late for practice and jeopardize his starting position, but if he didn't stay, he'd get a failing grade.

Will scribbled the word "corruption," which he knew was a euphemism for sex only because Mr. Quick had pointed it out to the class. He wrote quickly, finishing with a statement about how it was fear that was destructive, not corruption or ghosts. Then he hurried to the locker room and changed into his practice uniform before sprinting down the hill to the ball field.

"Hustle up," called the coach, and after that, Will could breathe a little easier.

Because he'd been late, Will had to run extra laps, so it was after six when he walked up the hill to the courtyard. Most afternoons he could catch a ride with a teammate, but at that late hour the turnaround was deserted, leaving him to walk the two miles home. We should have cell phones, Will thought, but he knew it was hard enough to make ends meet without wasting money on things they didn't need.

It wasn't until he was passing the Car Mart that he wished he'd put down "Yes" for the first part of the answer. Even if ghosts didn't exist, the idea of them did, and besides, the word "ghosts" could refer to inner demons as well as outer ones. There were a lot of unexplained things in the world, so maybe the story was about how things were what you thought they were and what they *really* were didn't come into it much.

Was it *really* wrong to think about sex multiple times a day? Was it *really* wrong to imagine Tula with no clothes on even though he liked her just as much when she was wrapped up from head to toe in tights and sweaters? Was it wrong to steal food if you were starving? Some people were forced into lives of crime by the way the world was—the way it *really* was. And then he decided that this whole line of inquiry was his mother talking—she had gotten inside his head somehow and was controlling it the way she had wanted to control Will and Lyle until she decided to go out and control the world.

When Mr. Quick passed back the quizzes the next day, he said that the most interesting answers came from the people who had answered "Both."

"But that wasn't an option!" Will blurted out. He started to raise his hand, but Mr. Quick was in speech mode, beaming down at the high-achieving front row, who were looking primly at their papers and trying not to gloat. Will could feel the pride radiating off of them, and when Mr. Quick said, "thinking outside the box," Will could feel the bars of the box closing in on him, penning him in with the hicks and the stoners and the mainstreamed autistic girl who sat every day in the back of the classroom gently banging her head against the wall.

"The ghosts were both real and not real," said Mr. Quick. "The genius of the story lies in its ambiguity and its open interpretation. Literature is meant to engage the reader, not present some unassailable truth." And so on until Will thought his head was going to explode.

"It's only a grade," said Mr. Quick when Will shuffled up to him after class and burst out, "But both wasn't one of the options!"

Mr. Quick was different from the other teachers. He talked about critical thinking, and there wasn't always a particular answer he was looking for, which was why Will thought going to English class was kind of like standing on tiptoe in a rocky boat.

"Did you learn anything?" asked Mr. Quick. "Was your mind expanded?"

"I guess so," said Will, for he had thought about the questions all the way home.

"Isn't learning the point?" Mr. Quick chuckled in a friendly manner, as if learning was not only the point, but also a lot of fun.

"I guess it is," said Will. One of the things he was learning was that the choice wasn't always between right and wrong. Another was that the all-important grading rubric was the thing that separated the college-bound from those whose only options were the munitions plant or the chicken farm or a life of petty crime.

## 3.4 MAGGIE

Maggie told herself that working at the prison was better than working at the munitions plant, but by the second week, her illusions were in shreds. When she walked past the exercise yard, the prisoners whispered things at her—sexual things or half-formed words she imagined to be sexual in nature, words mixed with kissing sibilations and falsetto imitations and doglike yelps. Even if the words weren't explicit, she knew the thoughts lurking unsaid beneath the shiny skin of the shaved skulls were.

Maggie didn't like the inappropriate yammerings to go unanswered, but how could a woman answer a man without inviting more unwanted attention? And how could any person respond across the great divide that separated the free from the imprisoned, the explicit from the unexpressed? Any sentence she devised or uttered would have whole power structures encased in the grammar, which hinted at dense philosophies she knew nothing about, not to mention the entire history of race relations, for it only took one glance at the exercise yard to see that a disproportionate number of the inmates were dark.

Maggie held her head high and walked as if she didn't notice the hulking presences, but was it right to pretend they didn't exist? She tried not to swing her hips but also not to walk too tightly, which would have been an admission that they had already succeeded in drying up some of her essence.

"Don't let it get to you," said Lex Lexington, who was the director of corrections and whom everyone called DC.

His first assistant, a voluptuous woman named Valerie Vines, added, "You have to have a pretty thick skin around here."

"It doesn't bother me," insisted Maggie, but whenever she passed the yard in the succeeding weeks, she felt as if she were walking past a long row of x-ray consciousnesses that beamed out through the chain-link fence and lit her up for all to see—not only her private parts, but the things she believed in—and not only for all to see, but for Maggie herself to be made aware of—of fears and prejudices and attitudes she didn't know she had.

One day, one of the men pressed his face against the links and whispered, "Miss, Miss. I'm innocent."

Maggie kept her eyes high, as if she were thinking elevated thoughts. Above the dull expanse of metal fencing, rolls of concertina wire gleamed in the sharp light, and high in the sky, a plane was writing a puffy contrail across the sky. But something in the man's voice caught at her attention, and instead of hurrying past, she stopped and turned to face him. The prisoner was small, with a lean frame and girlish muscles. Maggie looked at the creased skin at the corners of his eyes, the flecks of dandruff in his short hair, and the speck of gold in his iris and instantly believed him.

While she pondered what to say, another man came up and leered at her. "I'm innocent too, Momma."

And then another came, and then another, until a crowd of men jostled for position at the fence, all of them innocent, all of them clawing at one another or at the wire mesh, all of them shoving at the small man and shouting out about fabricated evidence and false prosecutions. Maggie tried to imagine what their lives were like, but she couldn't do it. She could only stare at them, her eyes wide and her mouth open, while the concertina wire coiled above them, singing in the rising wind and glittering with the hot, high notes of the sun.

Luckily for Maggie, footsteps were approaching along the walkway that led to the office block. Cheerful voices rose in good-natured argument, breaking the spell and causing the prisoners to stop talking and to back away from the fence. A moment later, the grizzled Louis and the virile Hugo came around the corner and slapped their batons against the chain links, scattering the men like frightened pigeons and replacing the horror of the clawing clot of humanity with the horror of how easily they were cowed by uniformed authority. Maggie found herself suddenly and unexpectedly allied with the prisoners against the guards and glad to be exactly where she was to witness—well, to witness what, she couldn't say. Tiffany was right that the inmates were needy, and now it seemed to Maggie that an unseen force had been guiding her and had purposely dropped her down just outside the chain-link fence so that she could finally do a little good.

Maggie tried to do nice things for the men she came across in the course of her duties. Some of them were longtime inmates who had earned positions of trust, and she would see them working in the gardens or re-shelving books in the prison library. In addition to joining the education initiative, one day a week she gave up her lunch hour to visit men whose families had stopped coming to see them. She would sit on a folding chair and listen to them describe a fishing hole under a cypress tree, a cabin in the woods, a favorite recipe for smoking deer. One day she baked a cake for a prisoner's seventy-fifth birthday and held his hand as he talked longingly of a flaxen-haired wife and children who must by now be half a century old.

Valerie called her aside to say, "You can't befriend the prisoners. You think you're being kind, but you're not. Listening is bad enough, but if you act like you believe them, they'll start hounding you with all kinds of sob stories. It's best if you can think of them as not quite human. Really, it's the only way for any of us to survive, and by us, I mean all of us—them included."

The education initiative consisted of a group of volunteers who worked in the prison school, where Maggie was assigned to help the prisoners on good behavior learn basic computation skills.

"They won't forget me, will they?" asked an earnest young man who chugged his finger dutifully under the columns of figures and word problems Maggie wrote out for him to solve. The class was half over when she realized it was the young man from the exercise yard. His name was Tomás, and he had served three years of his thirty-year sentence for killing a gas station attendant with a knife.

"Of course not, Tomás. Who could forget you!"

"My family, that's who. They live in Arizona, but I was transferred here."

"I assume there was a good reason for that," said Maggie.

"What is it? What's the reason?"

"I don't know anything about it," said Maggie. "But people usually have a reason for doing things. Just like there's a reason you're in prison in the first place."

"But I didn't do anything," said Tomás. "You believe that, don't you?"

"I honestly don't think about it. Besides, it doesn't matter what I believe."

"Why not? Why doesn't it matter?"

"Because I don't know the facts of the case and because I'm not in a position of authority."

"If it doesn't matter to you that I'm innocent, why would it matter to anyone? Why wouldn't it be okay to lock up anybody for any reason, just because you wanted to?"

"But I don't want to," said Maggie. "Why would you think I'd want a thing like that?"

"Because ... " Tomás peered at Maggie as if she was supposed to guess, but she had no idea what he was thinking.

"I would never want that," she said. "Now, here's one I'll bet you can't solve." She wrote out a problem involving complex fractions.

"Yes, you can write in the book!" she cried when Tomás's pencil hovered indecisively. "You see? It has your name on it—right there! Every time you come, this very same book will be yours!"

Maggie hurried across the room to erase the whiteboard, to file the attendance form, to turn on one bank of overhead lights and turn off another. One of the other inmates called out, "Over here, Miss. I have a question too!"

The men scraped their pencils against the paper. A man with a scarred face blew his nose against his arm and then wiped it on the seat of his pants. Maggie straightened the stack of notebooks belonging to the Tuesday class before glancing back to where Tomás was sitting, toiling away over his workbook, writing as neatly as he could. "Good job!" she exclaimed when she circled back to check his answers. "Four out of five correct!"

She was glad when the class was over, but the idea of innocence stayed with her. The next day she asked Valerie, "Does it ever occur to you that some of the inmates are innocent?"

"It occurs to everyone, darling. I was wondering when you were going to ask."

"What do you do about it?"

"I said it occurs to everyone. I didn't say they *were* innocent. In most cases, they're guilty of more than what came out at their trials."

"But most of them didn't have trials," said Maggie, who had started to research the criminal justice system and been shocked by what she had found. "Did you know—" she started to say, but Valerie cut her off.

"I know, I know. And if you kiss them, they turn into princes."

"Maybe someone should kiss them then."

"They're guilty," said Valerie. "Hand on heart. I wouldn't lie."

"But isn't believing you without question the same thing as believing the inmates without question? Or believing ... well, believing anything without looking into it for yourself?"

"That's a little too close to the deep end for me," said Valerie. "My motto is to keep it simple. Besides, the police don't go around arresting people willy-nilly. Someone would have to be awful unlucky to end up here if he was innocent."

"Yes," said Maggie. "Someone would."

Maggie thought of luck as a giant primordial atom that had fractured the day God made the world, unleashing particles of good and bad luck into the atmosphere where they could rain down at random, and now it occurred to her that she was sitting at a desk on the outside of the bars rather than wasting away inside of them not because she was inherently more virtuous than other people, but because she was luckier.

"Do you know why they arrested me?" asked Tomás when Maggie saw him in class the next Wednesday.

"Why no, I don't," replied Maggie.

"Because I ran from the police."

"What were you running for?"

"To get away from them."

"But why? If you hadn't done anything, why didn't you just say so?"

"Because . . . " Again Tomás peered at Maggie as if she could read his mind.

"And why did you plead guilty if you were innocent?"

"I had to plead guilty. If I didn't, I might have gotten life."


## 3.5 LYLE


It was Lyle's belief that bombs prevented bloodshed, and now that Will was backing him up, he felt more sure of it than ever. "I know that sounds like a contradiction," he said to a co-worker named Jimmy Sweets, "but if you think about it . . . " His voice trailed off, not because the explanation was hard to find, but because it was obvious. If anyone would know what he was talking about, it was Jimmy, who had been a fighter pilot in Vietnam.

"We pretty much proved that in nineteen forty-five," said Jimmy. He rolled up his sleeve to reveal a long scar. "Christmas in Hanoi," he said.

When some metal filings flew off a carelessly operated lathe and embedded themselves in Lyle's left biceps, he thought of it as a war wound. "I have shrapnel in my arm," he would say after a beer or two at the Merry Maid, which is where some of the men hung out in the evenings and where Lyle had started to go with Jimmy whenever Maggie worked late or when he wanted to get away from the creeping suspicion that he and Maggie were growing apart and that the new arrangement had left him without a necessary piece of equipment, like a leg.

Jimmy and Lyle thought alike about a lot of things. "What would happen if they turned around to reload their guns, and presto! the ammo was gone," said Jimmy. "Just frigging gone. That's what we do. We replenish the ammo pile."

A Merry Maid regular named Lily De Luca pushed her prom queen hair back over her shoulder to expose the fullness of her pink sweater and said, "Heck, people can convince themselves of all kinds of things."

Lily worked as a bookkeeper at McKnight's Chicken Farm, and despite the tight pink sweater and her breathy renditions of "Desperado," she thought of herself as one of the guys.

"We're not convincing ourselves, Lily," said Jimmy.

"Become convinced, then," said Lily. "People can become convinced."

"We didn't *become* convinced. You make it sound as if we sit around waiting for opinions to fly in and out of our heads. We always thought this way, didn't we Lyle?"

"Yeah," said Lily. "You were born knowing—a real know-it-all."

"We looked at the facts and assessed them. Or is that a concept that's too advanced for people who work with chickens all day?"

"Notice that it's the hens that are useful," said Lily. "Do you know what happens to the cocks?"

"I know what happens to one of them," said Jimmy, but Lily ignored him.

"At egg farms, anyway, the roosters are suffocated or ground up live because they're not useful. Not a use for them in the world."

The two went on in that fashion for a while, but Lyle was happy just to sit and soak up the atmosphere: the polished bar, the crazed mirror in which he could see his new aviator glasses pushed up on top of his head, the television screen showing a mild-mannered weapons inspector getting drowned out by the talk show host, the smell of old beer, Lily's gravelly voice, and the row of regulars with drooping, bloodshot eyes. It was a new world for Lyle, who had gone straight from camping out at the Sterlings' dinner table to being married to Maggie. He had never been in the thick of it before, and suddenly, here he was, going mano a mano with people in a bar. Maybe he wasn't missing a leg after all, or maybe it was growing back.

"Just after our fifth anniversary, my ex *decided*," said Lily. "Does 'decided' work for you, Lieutenant Sweets?"

"Okay, okay," said the bartender, butting in. "This isn't the grammar society. What did he decide?"

"That it was a good thing to have an affair. It took the edge off, is what he thought—or at least that's what he allowed himself to think. People don't like to think they're doing a bad thing—Bertie was no different from anyone else in that regard, and I guess we aren't either."

"Dang, Lily," said Jimmy. "You didn't hear a thing I said."

"I heard you all right," said Lily. "I guess people think what they think and come up with the reasons why after the fact."

"That's not what we do, is it Lyle? We're *critical* thinkers. Rational man—notice how they don't say woman, Lily? Notice how they don't say chickens? We're warriors in pursuit of truth."

"We're almost like troops ourselves," said Lyle, flexing his muscle against the bandage just so he could feel the pain of the place where the filings went in. He was surprised to find his ideas were so fully developed and easy to express. Then he realized it wasn't the ideas that were new, but the words, and definitely the attitude. He probably wouldn't have said anything if Maggie had been there to finish his sentences for him—to drown him out, if he was to be honest about what she did. It was almost as if he was finally arguing with her, as if his words had developed in reaction to the words she would have said, words he could picture flying out of her mouth, slippery and persuasive, but which he didn't agree with at all. He glared at Lily and said, "Did you ever consider that he had an affair because you were smothering him, Lily? And Jimmy's right, we didn't have to convince ourselves."

"Gosh, Lyle, it's just my opinion, that's all. Can't a girl have an opinion around here?"

Lyle felt kind of proud that Lily was fidgeting in her seat and looking at him as if he was a bully or something, as if he was some kind of untrained alpha dog.

When Lily left to go home, Lyle went after her, settling the aviator glasses on the bridge of his nose even though night had fallen and the dark lenses made it harder to see. He had nothing in mind but to prolong the sense of competence and belonging that had enveloped him in the bar and possibly to apologize for treating her roughly, but as he walked into the fragrant springtime air and followed Lily into a side street, the feeling turned into something new and disquieting. She walked with her head down and didn't turn around even though Lyle's shoes made clacking sounds on the pavement. Doesn't she know I'm here? he wondered. A dog barked at their passing, but still she didn't seem to notice him. She must be hard of hearing—or she was purposely ignoring him, leaving the decision to follow her entirely in his hands. Something is beginning, thought Lyle. It was like watching the first part of a movie as he settled into his seat, taking off his jacket or unwrapping his candy bar and listening half-interested/half-annoyed to the whispered conversations coming from the people around him who were still settling in too, until suddenly he was swept up in the on-screen action and hurtling with the hero toward the point of resolution or disaster.

Lily turned left on Maple and left again on Pine, where a row of two-story dwellings had been turned into apartments. Only when she was standing on the porch of a downstairs unit did she turn and say, "You might as well come in," in a low, come-hither voice. Lyle had stopped behind a row of crape myrtle trees, still trying to decide if he was going to declare himself or walk away. Just as he was about to step forward, a tall shape detached itself from a rocker and followed Lily into the house.

Now Lyle was just as eager to remain hidden as he had been to be seen a moment earlier. He kept to the shadows as he went back up Pine to Maple, walking on the grassy verge to muffle his footsteps. To be honest, he was relieved that it wasn't up to him after all, and he drove home newly aware of a great web of networked futures and how he could live just one of them and how that one would only be revealed slowly and how he could quickly get tangled up in an alien future merely by stepping out from behind a crape myrtle tree at exactly the wrong time.

# 3.6 MAGGIE

The file room was accessed through a maze of stairs and corridors that tunneled through the hill on which the prison was set. Its only natural light came from two windows that were set too high up to see out of except by wheeling one of the access ladders to the window and climbing up the steep steps. Every time she entered the room, Maggie felt an urge to climb up and look out, but the ladders were never in the right position and some of them were missing rungs or wheels, so she never did.

On hot days, she liked to linger in the cool, dark room that smelled of concrete and dust. A central dehumidifying system worked day and night to keep the room dry, and when she closed her eyes she could turn the white-noise sound of it into the roar of a rushing river just by imagining it. Sometimes she paged at random through the files, and with the men reduced to paper abstractions, she could feel sorry for them in a way that was hard to do when she was confronted with the hissing reality of the convicts in the yard: *fostered since the age of seven; history of mental illness; abused by alcoholic father; resorted to crime after dropping out of school; after being orphaned; after losing job.*

The file room held the essence of the men, but not the body odor or bad teeth. Not the hopes and dreams. Some of the despair was there, though, and some of the heartbreak, so when she located Tomás's file in a dark recess of the room, she experienced a blast of tenderness. It was only when she opened it and saw the fuzzy mug shot and fingerprints that she remembered his fawning and guile.

It was silly to think anyone knew what she was doing, but as she read, she couldn't help sensing eyes on her—on her neck, on her back side, peering up under her skirt from beneath the ladder she had climbed to access the file or down from the dingy egg crate fixtures, as if someone had put hidden cameras in the room or opened a folder containing intimate facts about her—facts and vital statistics, but also photographs and things she didn't want anyone to know.

But the feeling of being watched didn't stop her from poring over Tomás's record with the idea that she might find something that would tell her whether he was guilty or not, which in turn might tell her what her attitude toward him should be. Only when she came upon a list of the things that had been in his pockets when he was arrested (a book of matches, a dollar coin, a picture of his girl) did she think, I don't want to know anything about Tomás. I know quite enough already! Just as she was closing the folder to return it to its slot, a sheet of paper fell to the floor. It must have been tucked up between the pages, not affixed by the two-prong binding but stuck in casually, almost as an afterthought.

The page was dated two years after Tomás had been convicted, and a penciled note was scrawled across the upper right-hand corner: *Witness recants.* The rest of the page contained only a short paragraph purporting to be the words of John Gill, who now claimed that he had testified against Tomás in order to reduce his own sentence, that he had no knowledge of the crime Tomás was supposed to have committed, and that he had never met Tomás or even heard of him until he was being interrogated by detectives who offered to go easy on him if he could provide information that would help them get a conviction in the murder of the gas station attendant. Gill did his best to help them, but then he had found Jesus, and Jesus would want him to tell the truth.

The file also contained the notes from the arrest. Tomás had been apprehended miles away from the scene of the crime. When the police approached, he had started to run. Two officers had chased him down and arrested him. At the time, the only thing they had charged him with was resisting an arrest that, as far as Maggie could make out, shouldn't have happened in the first place.

Maggie glanced up at the two high windows as if they would shed light on the mystery. Then she took the file upstairs, and when Valerie went to lunch, she copied it. But she didn't know how to get it out of the prison past Hugo and the army of guards who were entitled to pat her down or feel her up, which, according to the other female employees, often amounted to the same thing. For two days, she kept the papers in her desk, but they weren't safe there either. The duties of the secretaries were apt to change unexpectedly, and on any given day, one or the other of them might sit at someone else's desk. Nothing in the prison was private. It made her miss the days at the munitions plant, where she had her own locker and where one of the desk drawers came with a tiny key. While she pondered how to remove her new evidence from the prison, she made a file for a fake prisoner, whom she named Max Gray, filled it with the copies she had made, and slipped it into the "G" section in the basement room. Hide in plain sight, she told herself.

Maggie left Tomás's name out of it when she said to Valerie, "I learned about a prisoner who is only here because he ran from the police. Does that seem right to you or not?"

"Why was he running?" asked Valerie in her weary here-we-go-again tone.

"He had every reason to run!" cried Maggie. "Look what happened to him!"

"Good lord," said Valerie. "It makes no sense to say he was running from a thing that hadn't even happened yet!"

"But he knew it would happen."

"Now he's not only innocent, but he's some kind of a genius. Good lord, Maggie. I'm beginning to see what Misty was talking about."

Soon after Maggie started working at the prison, Valerie had said, "You have quite a reputation. Misty Mills told me all about you." At the time, Maggie had made a self-deprecating gesture and said, "Whatever it was, I hope it was good." But now competing thoughts about what Misty might have said about her wrestled in her brain. Too much time had passed for her to bring it up again and ask Valerie for specifics. Besides, Maggie didn't want to let on that there was anything to tell, which could prompt Valerie to talk to Misty and Misty to put two and two together if Winslow had let on that he was missing a document.

Instead, she approached Misty at church the next Sunday. "What did you tell Valerie about me?" she asked.

"I told her to keep an eye on you."

Again, there were multiple interpretations. Was it a friendly gesture, or was something a little more sinister being implied?

True was standing nearby and must have sensed her hesitation, for she came over with her plate of donuts and linked her arm through Maggie's. "Everybody knows you have a good heart," she said.

"No doubt I do," said Maggie. "But what does having a good heart really mean? Having a good heart is meaningless if you don't do good things."

"You're kind, for one thing, and you don't do anything bad, do you?"

"Thank you, True, but everyone does bad things. I always

thought the key was for the good to outweigh the bad, but now I wonder if that's even possible. And just try putting those people with good hearts in a difficult situation and see what they do then. What if it's the circumstances and not the people that are bad?"

"I don't see how circumstances can be bad," said True. "That's like blaming a road for having potholes."

"But people could fix the potholes," said Maggie. "Instead of worrying so much about whether people are good or bad, maybe we should pay more attention to changing their circumstances."

"I thought you were against changing circumstances," said Misty. "Don't go to war against a dictator. Don't try to free an oppressed people. Don't make an omelet because you might break a few eggs."

"Maggie doesn't believe in eggs," said True with a giggle. "Not if it means upsetting the chickens."

"I'm just saying that there are plenty of people to free right here—people who have done less wrong in their lives than I have," said Maggie a little recklessly, given the documents hidden in her drawer.

"Just so you know, this is what I warned Valerie about," said Misty. "This is a perfect example right here."

## 3.7 LYLE

Lyle started taking an interest in what other people had to say on various subjects, and without Maggie with him night and day, it was as if he had an open socket that was now free for other connections. Sometimes Jimmy sat in Maggie's old chair in the lunchroom, and for the first time since high school, Lyle was reminded of the term "best friend." He made ball-and-chain jokes with Jimmy, and just talking about how a wife tied you down made Lyle feel kind of liberated.

In early March, Lyle towed Jimmy's car to the shop when it broke down. A few weeks later, Jimmy used his chain saw to clear a branch that had fallen on the shed during a winter ice storm, after which Jimmy asked Lyle and Will to go fishing with him up at the lake the next day.

"They can't," said Maggie. "Will is taking the SAT next weekend, so he needs to study."

"What am I going to learn in a week?" asked Will.

"That's like saying it's no use saving a penny," said Maggie. "Every little bit helps."

"Your mother's right," said Jimmy. "Love does much, but money does more."

"My point was about education, not about money or love," said Maggie.

"Anyway," said Will. "I know all of the test-taking techniques. Mr. Quick has been drilling them into us for weeks."

"Say, I've got an idea," said Jimmy. "Will can bring his book in the car. I'll quiz him on the way up."

The next morning Jimmy tooted the horn when it was still dark. While Will settled into the back seat, Lyle stowed a cooler full of sandwiches and drinks in the trunk, along with the SAT review book. As they drove into the rising light, Jimmy switched on the radio looking for the top-of-the-hour news and weather. "They do the weather last," he said.

*Just over half of the thirty thousand additional troops being sent as part of the so-called surge have arrived in Iraq, yet political pressure at home calls for quick results and a firm pullout date,* said the radio announcer.

"Firm pullout," said Jimmy. "That's the problem right there." Then he called back to Will. "'Oxymoron.' There's an SAT word for you."

*Poor construction has resulted in generators that don't work, overflowing sewage systems, and unreliable distribution of food and fuel,* said the radio announcer.

"We're supposed to build their country for them?" asked Lyle.

"If you break it, you own it," said Jimmy. "I guess that's the thinking there."

After the weather, Jimmy turned the radio off and said, "Okay, Will, now for the quiz like I promised your mom."

"I might have put the review book in the trunk," said Lyle. "If you pull over, I can get it out." Outside the car window, the landscape heaved and buckled. Scrubby pine trees clung to the rocks and a stand of post oaks pushed out their soft new leaves.

"It's not that kind of quiz," said Jimmy.

"What kind of quiz is it?" asked Will.

"Multiple choice," said Jimmy. "Here's the first question. If you're interested in a girl, do you (a) tell her how much you like her; (b) wait for her to make the first move; (c) invite her on a romantic date; or (d) ask out someone else?"

"Let's see," said Will. "I'm guessing A might scare her off, and I can eliminate D, so I'm guessing the answer is C."

"B worked for me," said Lyle, and Jimmy and Will laughed.

"Even if that's what you did with Mom," said Will, "it wouldn't work with most girls. Most girls like to be pursued."

"Correctamente," said Jimmy. "And what if the girl doesn't think she's interested in you? In that case, you have to change her mind. So B is out, and telling her how much you like her not only scares her off, but it makes you look weak. Women like strong men. They like men who have options, not some sad sack who's mooning after them like a sick dog. I suppose you could ask her out on a romantic date, but that isn't as good as D."

"No way," said Will.

"You've got to establish yourself as a player. Then the women will come to you."

"Jeezus, Jimmy. That's not how it was with Maggie and me."

"You have to keep them guessing. It crossed my mind that all that weirdness up at the plant is just because Maggie needs a little excitement in her life."

"What weirdness?" asked Lyle. "All she did is quit her job."

"But why did she quit it? That's the buried question. People are curious if all that do-gooding talk was just a smoke screen for something else."

"Who's saying that?" asked Lyle. Then he added, "And what would it be a smoke screen for?"

"Forget I mentioned it. It's just rumors, anyway. The point is that a romantic date is good too. The strategy has to fit the man. No percentage in acting like a player if you can't pull it off."

Lyle had never been a player, but now he wondered if he had let Maggie down in some way, if he should have worked harder to keep their romance alive. And then he wondered if she had let him down too, if they were missing a crucial part of life because of something she had done or failed to do. Nah, he told himself. It was Jimmy who was missing something. "There's more to life than dating," he told Jimmy. "You'd figure that out if you had a wife and kids."

"I won't try to tell you your business," said Jimmy. "But Will here has a chance to learn from a master."

"A divorced master." Lyle laughed before turning in his seat to look at Will. "Consider the source, son. Always consider the source when people are giving you advice."

"Love and war," said Jimmy. "Or, rather, love *is* war. Specifically, it's maneuver warfare. You have to feint and circle, and then you overwhelm. Women like a show of force—nothing over the line, that's not what I'm advocating. I'm just saying, who likes a pussy? Frankly, about the only thing more fun than seduction is war."

"And fishing," said Lyle.

"That goes without saying," said Jimmy.

Lyle hadn't been fishing in a long time, and now he remembered what it was like to feel at one with the world around him instead of looking on from the bleachers while other people made the plays. As a young man, he'd had a vague notion that when he was called upon to provide for a wife and family, he'd do it by casting his line out into the world and reeling whatever he caught back in. That wasn't the way things turned out to be, though, and he'd been silly to think it. Still, he liked the way his hands knew what to do without his brain having to tell them. He liked knotting on the shiny lure and flinging it toward a far-off shore and then feeling it tug against the water and trying to spot it beneath the murky surface of the lake as he jigged it in. He settled into a soothing rhythm: the buzz of the line stripping off the reel as he flung it forward, the musical plunk when the lure hit the water, the ratcheting purr of the reel, the smooth arc of his arm and flick of his wrist for the back cast, the cool spray of drops against his skin as the lure whizzed above his head, and finally, the shooting line and agreeable plink as it hit the surface of the lake. He liked watching the water smooth over it and imagining a whole mysterious world roiling beneath the surface, filled with creatures that would live and die without knowing a thing about Lyle's world, just the way he wouldn't know a thing about theirs.

## 3.8 MAGGIE

By April, Maggie had changed her mind about the prison, not only because the idea of helping the prisoners filled an important requirement for her new life, but also because of the adrenaline rush she experienced when she found out shocking things—that Tomás might be innocent, that profit-driven private prisons relied on a steady stream of bodies for their cells, that "growth" was an industry buzzword, that she suspected her boss was cheating on his wife.

"Do you think DC is having an affair?" she said to Valerie one day when the director was out of the office.

"What makes you say that?" asked Valerie.

"He's been so cheerful recently, and he's lost a bit of weight."

"Good lord!" said Valerie. "You seem to be just as eager to convict the innocent as you are to let the guilty go free. That seems to be a thing with you."

Maggie had hoped she and Valerie could be friends the way she had been friends with True and Misty, but whenever she made overtures in that direction, Valerie would find an excuse to remind her who was the first assistant to the director and who was the second. "Let's not forget who you work for," she said.

"I work for the director."

"On paper, perhaps, but he hired you to help me."

Valerie sold makeup out of her car, and as a gesture of friendship, Maggie bought a pot of eye shadow even though she worried that the makeup had been tested on defenseless rabbits. While

Valerie was dabbing pastes and powders from her sample kit onto Maggie's face and showing her the results in a handheld mirror, she chattered about the great loves of her life and running off with her current husband to Las Vegas while she was still married to someone else.

"Oh, Johnny and I are all respectable and settled now," she said. "But we sure had some fun first. Now, tell me about all of the terrible things you've done."

Maggie couldn't think of any that would interest Valerie. She had once been spanked for losing her house key, and another time she had burned a pan of lasagna and blamed it on her sister. By far the worst thing she had ever done was to strap baby Will into his car seat and forget all about him for an entire hour one autumn afternoon. The idea that if it had been a hot summer day he would have cooked still kept her up at night, but she knew this wasn't the kind of thing Valerie was after. She had never had an illicit rendezvous in a forest or unbuttoned her blouse behind the bleachers or engaged in heavy petting in the back row of a movie theater or been groped by a stranger in a bar or on a bus. She had never had a doomed first love. Now she knew she never would, and the thought filled her with sorrow for the dark swaths of experience she would never know.

But when she skimmed the prisoners' files for indications of suppressed evidence or incompetent legal representation, it was as if she had circled around and was approaching the forest from the other side. Whenever she found something particularly egregious, she copied the document and slipped it into Max Gray's file, and then her nerves would tingle and her lungs would feel as if they might collapse for all the pressure put on them by her heart. What if she was discovered? What if Valerie or DC himself walked in and caught her in the act? On those days, she would breeze through

103

her duties as if she had taken one of the little violet pills Valerie claimed to have taken in her youth.

It seemed as if her energy and confidence was catching, for even Tomás straightened his shoulders and started to speak up in class. He didn't seem to notice when Maggie forgot to bring him something special, just a bag of candies for the entire group. Instead of whining and looking hurt, he only inquired if she and her family were well.

"Very well, thank you," Maggie replied, pushing away from the table rather than leaning forward as she usually did.

One day, it was Tomás who leaned forward into the vacant space and asked, "Do you have a dog?" And then he asked, "Why not?"

"No good reason," said Maggie. "We had a big ol' cat once, but it ran off."

"If you had a dog, what would you name it?"

Maggie told him she neither had a dog nor wanted one, so any name she came up with on the spur of the moment wouldn't mean anything.

"Don't you like dogs, then?"

"I like dogs as well as I like all God's creatures."

"So you like me," said Tomás.

"Of course I do!" Maggie exclaimed, but she was beginning to wonder if she did.

"If I could change into a dog and go home with you, I would. I'd do it this second. I wouldn't even think twice."

"No you wouldn't," said Maggie cautiously. She was already aware that she had begun to think of Tomás as not quite human, but this was her first inkling that he thought of himself that way. "To be perfectly honest, I don't really like dogs," she said.

"Go ahead, tell me to sit," said Tomás. "Go ahead and tell me to stay."

He was like a dog with a bone, and he wouldn't let it drop. "I'd do it. I'd do it for you," he said a few minutes later, but she didn't want him to do it. It was the last thing in the world she wanted. "Just give me any command you want," he said, loudly enough for the whole class to hear.

"You're not a dog, Tommy!" The instant the diminutive left her lips, she wished she could take it back. A look of triumph spread over Tomás's features, and he rocked in his chair, leering stupidly at her. All Maggie could do was repeat, "You're not a dog, and you shouldn't say you are."

"But I can be loyal. I can be loyal and true."

She told him sharply to act like an adult.

"Okay, so then I won't be loyal if that's what you want."

"It's not about what I want!" cried Maggie in exasperation. It wasn't Tomás, she knew, but the prison. Still, it was hard to be kind to him after that.

"Well, it's certainly not about what *I* want. I want to go back to my girlfriend. I want to live in a little cabin in the mountains. A little cabin with pine floors and a fireplace and maybe a river outside the door. What I want is to be free."

"Do you Tomás? Do you really?" Maggie was leaning forward now, and Tomás was leaning back. "Then why did you wind up in prison? Why were you wandering around on the streets that day? Why weren't you in school or at a job?"

"A job," said Tomás. "Do you really think jobs are so easy to find?"

"And why did you get kicked out of your foster home?"

Tomás had the hangdog expression again, his eyeballs settled in their sockets, his chin tucked, his brow slightly furrowed, and a quivering half-smile tugging at his lips as if he was trying not to cry. But then a light flickered and caught behind his eyes and he said, "How did you know that? How did you know about the foster home?"

Maggie couldn't have known unless she had read his file or asked some questions about him; either way, it was evidence that she had shown more than the usual interest in him. She ignored the question—what was there to say? Instead of answering, she strode to the front of the room, snatched up the bag of candy, and then marched up and down the rows of desks, passing it to everyone, Tomás last. By the end of the hour, she had recaptured enough of her earlier high spirits to smile and say, "If you really wanted to be free, Tomás, you'd start taking responsibility for yourself. You'd buckle down and use these sessions to pass the high school equivalency test."

"But how did you know?" asked Tomás again, sucking his yellow teeth as if they were lumps of sticky caramel.

"I only wanted—" But then Maggie stopped herself. Why admit to anything? Why awaken in Tomás something he couldn't have? She wondered if she was turning callous, like Valerie and the other volunteers, all of whom wore friendly masks and unwavering robotic smiles. What was she supposed to say to someone who couldn't be free for over two decades even if he got time off for good behavior?

But she was starting with the conclusion. If Tomás was telling the truth about his innocence, it would lead to a different conclusion altogether. "Why did you run from the police, Tomás? Why in God's name did you run?"

But Tomás was celebrating his little victory over her by smiling and drawing hearts in the margin of his book.

# 4.0 BLOOD

*We were almost to Samarra when the call came to turn the convoy west. The captain told us to deliver the supplies to the school and then catch up with the others. We figured the detour would take us ninety minutes, tops.*

—Staff Sergeant Mason Betts

*I remember thinking, You're shittin' me—the school? But Betts said we were doing it, and he was in charge.*

—Specialist Win Tishman

*The best way to promote peace is to educate the women. I'm probably quoting someone, but I can't tell you whom.*

—Captain Penn Sinclair

*Counterinsurgency meant building infrastructure and relationships. Some people believed in it more than others. The captain, he was one of the believers.*

—Corporal Joe Kelly

*Just after we turned the convoy, we got reports that the road-clearing crews had been pulled from the main supply route north of Samarra. I remember saying to the captain, "It's a good thing our guys aren't going there."*

—First Sergeant Vince L. Crosby, aka Velcro

## 4.1 DANNY JOINER

Danny raised his binoculars to his eyes and peered up the road, searching for the rest of the convoy. "We should have caught up with it by now," he said.

"You're sure this is the right road?" asked Pig Eye.

Danny pulled out the strip map and said it had to be, because of the canal that was visible down a slope to their right. But just in case, he radioed up to Betts, who was in the second vehicle.

"Affirmative," said Betts. "This is it."

As Pig Eye drove, Danny fingered his weapon and scanned the roadside from eleven to three o'clock and back again, looking for shadows or movement, but all he saw was an endless expanse of brown-upon-brown that faded to blue at the horizon but was greener down by the canal. Now and then they passed a burned-out vehicle or a ramshackle farm or a farmer and, once, a kid on a bicycle who stopped and waved at them as they passed and then a group of kids who didn't wave, and through it all, the dusty and colorless road.

He wondered vaguely what Dolly was doing now. It was very early at home, so she was probably still in bed wearing the animal-print nightgown or the one with the hearts on it. He wondered if she had rubbed lotion onto the calluses on her feet and if it was the almond-scented lotion or the stuff that smelled like milk. He wondered if she had replaced the torn coverlet or gotten new curtains for the windows the way she kept talking about.

Then something wasn't right—a shift in the color spectrum, an eddy in the shimmering air. He scanned the road for the hundredth time: left to right, then right to left, then a glance at the driver's side. There! Movement behind the low wall of an animal enclosure. A glint of metal by the side of the road. The lead vehicle slowing down. It was probably nothing, but a prickle of alarm jumped across the synapse separating him from Pig Eye.

"What is it? What is it?" asked Pig Eye, twisting toward him from the driver's seat. Danny saw a wrinkle of worry cross his brow just as the lead vehicle exploded and the next one swerved into a ditch. Pig Eye slammed on the brakes, causing the top-heavy cargo truck to wobble and roll and catapulting Danny forward while Pig Eye fell away and down, as if he had pulled a rip cord or performed a trick and disappeared. Before he lost consciousness, Danny heard a daisy chain of detonations. He tasted cordite and heard the beginning of a shout just as he remembered the last lines of the Shelley poem: *The lone and level sands stretch far away.*

## 4.2 PIG EYE

Pig Eye was thinking about the day he had first met Emmie. He hadn't been called Pig Eye then; he had been called Nerf. And she hadn't been called Emmie. She had been called E.Z.

It was back before he had joined the army, back before the two big guys came looking for him and before the altercation in the bar when one of the guys insulted Emmie and grabbed her by the hair. Back before Earl had said, "I'll take care of things here if you need to get out of town for a while." And it was before, just when they were getting the repair shop on its feet, the landlord raised their rent. He cited improvements in the property even though Pig Eye and Earl had been the ones to improve it. They had converted a corner of the shop to a convenience store, and the neighbors were grateful because the nearest grocery store was two miles away, right smack next to a second grocery and a Walgreens and a Stop-N-Go and a bank, but too far away for them to easily get to. The landlord cited the new laundry and the Dollar Mart, despite the fact that without the convenience store, the laundry and the Dollar Mart would never have opened. Instead, the crack dealers would have moved in and property values would have gone down, not up. Now there was talk of a bus stop and a school.

Pig Eye had arrived one morning to open the shop and found Emmie passed out in a corner of the second bay, blood on her clothing and a pool of vomit crusting over on the concrete slab. With a high forehead and tangled hair and knobby knees that stuck out from underneath her satin dress and, he found out later, slanted eyes with a hint of green in them, she was the most beautiful thing he had ever seen.

"What kind of a name is E.Z.?" Pig Eye asked her after she had been there a week and had started to smile.

"I'm from New Orleans," she said. "The Big Easy is too long for a name, doncha think?"

"But you're not big," said Pig Eye, not putting two and two together about her name because that was when he was noticing the slanted eyes and the dimples in her cheeks and the hole in her earlobe where something had ripped clean through.

"And you're not a Nerf," she replied, so even though Pig Eye kind of was a Nerf back before he had joined the army and muscled up, it seemed to him like the nicest thing anyone had ever said to him.

"I'm going to call her Emmie," he told Earl when she had been there a month and Earl had started asking when she was going to leave. "She's going to stay for a while, and I'm going to take care of her."

"She's not a pet," said Earl. "Are you going to teach her to fetch the coffee in the morning? Are you going to teach her to roll over on command?"

That was the first time Pig Eye laid Earl flat, and Earl let the subject drop until the day a couple of big guys who seemed to know Emmie showed up.

"She's going to cause trouble," Earl said, and Pig Eye laid him flat again.

"They don't call her E.Z. for nothing," Earl said when Pig Eye announced that he and Emmie were getting married and if Earl didn't like it, he could be the one to find other accommodations.

And she had caused trouble, but she hadn't meant to. Trouble followed Emmie, and after she moved with them into the apartment over the shop, trouble seemed to follow Pig Eye too. It followed him in the form of the two big guys and the raised rent and the expensive things Emmie needed and Pig Eye wanted her to have. Even so, the vision he had of Emmie was one of near perfection. He thought of her as flawless and still, like the exact center of the universe, like the shining point around which the stars and the planets and even the truck he was riding in were spinning—spinning and veering out of control.

# 4.3 PIG EYE

Pig Eye thought he was having one of his escape fantasies. He was face down in the dust, pinned by a force he couldn't name. Situational awareness was a prerequisite to forming any plan of action, but he couldn't turn his head far enough to see more than a patch of what looked like earth from a distance but was, up close, a mix of powdery dust and desiccated vegetable matter and glittering crystals mixed with stones of various sizes and also unidentifiable bits of garbage and ash and, for all he knew, bleached and pulverized bones from the years of strife and fighting that had taken place in that desert since the dawn of civilization. Gradually he realized he was stuck underneath the truck, and all that kept him from being crushed was a shallow depression in the earth.

As a precaution, he took an inventory of his body parts as if he were doing a vehicle pre-check or filling out a spreadsheet of parts for Earl to order. He could wiggle his fingers and toes—check. He could move his legs—check. And although his right arm was lodged beneath him and starting to go numb, his left hand and arm were free—check. When he raised the arm as far as it could go, he could feel a flange of hot steel, but whether it was hot from the explosion or hot from the sun, he couldn't make out. He pushed against it and it moved slightly, but his arm was weak in that position, so he scrabbled in the dirt until his right arm was free too. This opened up another inch between his shoulders and the metal above him, which he now suspected was the heavy armored door of the truck. He thought of his escape kit and recognized the folly of believing that a few miniature tools would help him against all of the machines of war. A spool of wire, for Chris-sakes. A powerberry protein bar. A tiny slingshot and a miniature frigging clock. Even if he could have reached the cargo pocket, the things it contained were useless for raising the reinforced slab of metal that was holding him down. Still, he despaired that he couldn't reach the pocket. He despaired until he remembered what the colonel had said about his center of gravity, which wasn't the pocket after all. The most useful part of his escape kit was his body, and the most useful part of his body was his wits.

He inched his fingers into an indentation in the edge of steel, and instead of pushing, he pulled at it with all his might. And miracle of miracles, it shifted slightly. He pulled again, and it shifted more—he gasped to feel the pressure on his legs and would have cried out if his mouth hadn't been pushed into the dirt and if he hadn't now been able to engage both of his shoulders with the metal, so that when he heaved up against it, the pressure eased slightly, allowing him to maneuver in a way that gave him even better leverage. Then he adjusted the left side of his body, and again he could shift his legs a fraction of an inch. By working within the narrow range of available motion and space, he positioned his hands more solidly underneath him. With a mighty heave, he pushed upward and then from side to side. The metal rocked and shifted until finally he was free to shimmy backward into a deeper part of the ditch.

He sank exhausted into the dirt, depleted and disoriented and slightly afraid, but then he remembered something else that was tucked into the bottom of his kit, and the fear was replaced with jubilation. He rolled onto his side and carefully extracted a tiny foil-wrapped package containing two pills Joe Kelly had given to him after the black power salute. "For when you want to really escape," Kelly had said. And then Kelly had winked at him and slipped him the pills.

Pig Eye unwrapped the package and studied its contents—one bullet-shaped capsule and one baby blue disk. He tried to decide which one to take. Then he put both of them onto the sandpaper of his tongue and wished he had a drink of water before pulling himself up just high enough to peer into the front of the destroyed truck, where Danny was slumped against his seat belt. "Hey, man, you okay?" Pig Eye whispered. He could tell Danny was breathing, but his eyes remained shut, so Pig Eye slid his knife from its sheath and cut the strap of the binoculars that were still hanging around Danny's neck. As he was searching for his weapon, which had been stowed behind his seat, a spray of bullets pinged metal, and he dropped down behind the heavy shield of the truck door that had almost killed him. Using the wire cutters and spool of wire from his kit, he looped some lengths of wire around his arms and legs and neck and then tucked bunches of weeds and grasses into the loops before raising his head out of the weedy ditch that bordered the east side of the road in order to assess the situation.

## 4.4 DANNY JOINER

Danny forced himself to open his eyes. He remembered going over the equipment list. He remembered Kelly going on about the water and Tishman about the time, everybody focused on the one or two details they could actually control—or not focused, just shuffling through the motions, their thoughts on how they weren't going home after all or on the endless stretch of weeks that lay ahead. But something else tapped at the door of his consciousness. Something he should be noticing but couldn't quite grasp. He could see that the front of the truck was tilting strangely, and he understood from a stray flap of canvas that the top had ripped loose despite the double-and triple-checked fastenings—triplechecked because that's the way Danny did things.

Gravity pulled his body against the seat belt, and his legs were angled toward the steering wheel as if the truck had been re-configured. He could taste the dust and smell the acrid odor of explosives, which is when he realized that the top-heavy cargo truck had rolled and that the thing he should be noticing was the silence, the complete absence of sound except for a muffled ringing in his ears. And he understood that Pig Eye wasn't slumped on the seat beside him and that his helmet had come off and that he had hit his head and that his weapon was wedged between the gearshift and his knee.

IEDs were deadly, but they weren't precise. Shouldn't the men from the other trucks be scrambling around and shouting? Shouldn't they be calling out for survivors and coming to find out how he was? His instinct was to assess the situation without moving—the condition of his body, the position of the enemy, the status of the other men—but he couldn't get his thoughts together because of the ringing and the thick, mashed ache in his head. He remembered climbing into the truck beside Pig Eye, who wasn't slumped beside him, who wasn't anywhere that he could see. He remembered reaching over to beep the horn of the truck as the convoy rolled out that morning. He remembered checking the straps on the canvas that covered the cargo, and he remembered helping Kelly stow the extra cases of water even though Tishman kept chasing at his heels like a terrier and saying, "Hurry up. We should have left when it was dark."

He remembered Kelly asking for the updated strip maps, and

even though checking the vehicles had been Tishman's job, Danny had double-checked everything himself. Then Harraday and Rinaldi and Finch had climbed into their turrets—most of the vehicles had crew-served guns, but not the long cargo truck—and Danny had climbed in beside Pig Eye and tooted the horn just as they pulled into line behind Hernandez and Harraday and Betts and in front of Tishman and Kelly and Finch, who were bringing up the rear. He remembered tooting the horn, but he didn't remember anything after that.

It was too quiet. Could he have gone deaf? He wanted to test his hearing by saying something, but he thought he should wait until he knew exactly what was what. Meanwhile, the silence pressed in on him, but little by little, his vision cleared. He remembered checking the cargo straps and reaching over to beep the horn. But where was Pig Eye? Not on the seat next to him. And where were the men in the two vehicles in front of him and the one that had been behind? As he struggled to free himself from his seat belt, a volley of gunfire broke through the silence and he hoped it was Rinaldi or Finch or Harraday, giving the bastards hell.

## 4.5 PIG EYE

Pig Eye crab-walked backward, trying to see around the carcass of the truck. Because it was too risky to raise his head very high, his eyes had to burn through a jumble of brush and spiky grass in order to assess the status of the convoy: the blackened husk of the lead vehicle, the second Humvee swerved into the ditch, his own rolled truck, and the rear vehicle, which had been hit but not destroyed. It made sense now. There had been a series of explosions, explosions that must have come from IEDs wired in a daisy chain. It was an increasingly common tactic. A purposely ill-concealed decoy bomb would stop a convoy, putting the line of vehicles in position for a buried chain of smaller bombs that were then detonated by trigger men—men who were probably still hunkered down somewhere not too far away, ready to take potshots at anything that moved. From the sound of sporadic gunfire, Pig Eye guessed the hide position was a low wall that formed part of an animal enclosure about one hundred meters off the road.

Just as Pig Eye was wondering what had happened to the other men, Finch stood up in his turret, his face bloody and his helmet skewed. C'mon Finch, get down, he thought. Then a spray of bullets and Finch was reeling drunkenly in a slow collapse. After that the guns were mostly silent and everything was mostly still, but Pig Eye knew the Iraqis were out there waiting, invisible behind the wall.

Where the hell were the other men? The same marine who had taught him about using vegetation for camouflage and moving through the landscape undetected had said, "If you don't fight back, you die." But they were mechanics and drivers and communications specialists. Still, they couldn't retreat, so why the hell wasn't anybody firing?

Pig Eye tried to recall what his truck was carrying. The tables and chairs and sheets of galvanized metal had been unloaded at the school, along with a toilet and sink and the books they had collected. If only he had studied the cargo list as carefully as Danny had studied it. There had to be something he could use to lay a trap for the insurgents the way the insurgents had laid a trap for them. But if he stood up to look for it, the men with the guns would see him. He was bellying back toward the bed of the truck when he saw it—a hand grenade nestled in a patch of brown weeds like a prehistoric bird's egg in a nest.

## 4.6 JOE KELLY

Waking up was like coming up from the bottom of the creek in Wimberley, up from the deep pool where the creek bent around a grove of cypress trees, like coming up through the muck and the slime and over a slick of limestone rock, up through the fronds of light that penetrated from the surface like bendable knives, up through the heavy quiet, measured not in decibels, but in pounds per square inch or atmospheres. It was like breaking through the tensive surface to the air above, and once the broken water had healed itself, it was like seeing the trees soaring up toward the clouds and also down through the glassy water and not knowing which set of trees was real.

Kelly could hear his mother calling to him: "Joe, honey, you still asleep?" Her musical voice echoed off of what he presumed to be bathroom tile. He tried to swim up and out so he could answer her that he had been awake for a long time, but it was hard to call out from down at the bottom of wherever he'd been—where he still was. He could measure it in atmospheres, but not in seconds, not in inches or miles or feet.

He must have gone back to bed, which is why she thought he was sleeping when he wasn't. He couldn't be sleeping because he heard her talking to his father, who everyone called Joe Senior even though he kept saying, "Call me Dad, son. A boy should call his father Dad."

"Okay, Dad, okay." He was awake. It was the month they had moved to New York, the week he had started his new school. "Whatchu you lookin' at?" asked a police officer who had been staring at him from the opposite corner as Kelly crossed the street. "Whatchu lookin' at?" he asked again as Kelly mounted the curb and headed toward the brown brick school building with plywood still nailed over the window where a rock had been tossed through.

"Keep your head down," Joe Senior was always telling him. "Don't act like you know everythin'. When I was your age, I thought I knew everythin', and nothin' good ever came of it, so however you act, don't act like that." His hair was grizzled and his face was gaunt, and it was hard to believe he had ever been young.

"Okay, okay," said Kelly.

"I walked around like I was king of the world, but I wasn't king. I wasn't nothin', and then I went to prison, and I was less than nothin'. So keep your head down. That's the way to stay out of trouble."

But that day in the Bronx, Kelly's head was up. He was looking around at the other stragglers, who were loaded down with satchels full of books or not loaded down and kind of slinking in the shadows as if they too were deciding whether to go to school or bolt. He was looking at the blinking traffic signal and at the passing cars, at the way the morning sun painted the bricks the color of dried blood and at the cop who was kind of snarling at him and rocking back on his heels with his thumbs stuck in his belt.

"Smile," Kelly's mom had told him. "That's the way to make new friends."

"You hard of hearing?" asked the cop.

Kelly gave the cop a neutral smile. He didn't want new friends. He wanted his old ones, but they were back in Wimberley, probably still lolling around in bed because of the time difference.

"Answer me when I ask you a question, boy!"

"I'm lookin' at you 'cuz you're lookin' at me." Even though it was true, Kelly suspected it was the wrong thing to say.

Kelly's head was up when he looked at the officer, and it was up when he climbed onto the Toyota and rammed his fist into the air the way Tommie Smith and John Carlos had done at the Summer Olympics in Mexico City the same year the Reverend King was assassinated in Memphis and Bobby Kennedy was shot in Los Angeles and anti-war activists seized five buildings at Columbia University to prove the people were ready to take their country back, all of which Kelly knew because it was also the year his father was born, and his father liked to talk about those things as if his lowly birth to an unwed teenager was part of some grand and inspiring civil rights trend.

In Mexico City, the two track champions had stood shoeless and determined on the podium, fists thrust into the air and heads bowed prayerfully while "The Star-Spangled Banner" played and while the Australian silver medalist stood beside them in silent support for which he was later ostracized at home. But first, Carlos and Smith were evicted from Olympic Village and suspended from the U.S. team. "But they stood up for themselves," Joe Senior said every time he talked about them. "They stood up for themselves and eventually their medals were returned." There was a lesson in it, that's the thing he wanted his children to remember. "What's the lesson?" Kelly wanted to know. "Justice prevailed," his father always replied. "Don't you forget that justice prevailed."

Kelly heard his mother calling him to come for breakfast and then it was his father, reminding him to vote. "I lost that right when I went to prison, so you have to vote for the both of us," he was saying. "Every Election Day, you make sure to get up early and exercise your constitutional right."

For some reason, one of their new neighbors started a rumor that Joe Senior had killed a man back in Texas, which is why he'd come to New York. "It explains a lot of things," the neighbor would say, and the other neighbors would nod sagely to each other. "That would certainly explain it," they said.

Kelly preferred to believe his father had been locked up for killing a man than for bungling a robbery, but either way, Joe Senior hadn't been home much, and then, suddenly, he was. He was home and they were moving across the country for a fresh start and a job. Another story went around that Kelly was the one to throw the rock through the school window. What would you expect from a boy whose father was a killer? They were only rumors, but once a story took hold, it didn't matter if it was true. So Kelly started to say, "I'll set my old man on you," whenever anyone gave him trouble, and whether it was that or the fact that he grew four inches over the course of that first year in New York, no one gave him trouble anymore. He didn't need his old man to handle things. He could handle them himself.

It was handling things that led to his first night in jail. It was a minor scuffle over a girl that did it, but Joe Senior sat up late, wringing his hands. "They'll take away your vote if you're not careful," he said. "You ain't a real American if they take away your vote."

The night in jail had scared Kelly. He had looked out through the bars at the dog-faced deputy and realized something about the world and also about his place in it. But then he had gone back to being angry, and after a couple more years of barely scraping by at school, he had given up and joined the army.

And then his mother called out again, "Joe, honey, I've saved two big ol' pancakes just for you. That's surely worth waking up for."

Kelly thought about telling his parents that sleeping was something he hardly ever did these days, but then it seemed not to matter anymore, so he sank back down to the quiet place, the place where the frogs were buried in the silt and the tadpoles slid on their bellies across the stones, smooth as coins, turning inexorably into frogs, their slippery skin evolved through eons of living in water, which surged relentlessly over them, oblivious to all of the life that depended on it in its search for the lowest point.

## 4.7 PIG EYE

Just as Pig Eye was worrying he was out there alone, Hernandez started gunning the motor of the second Humvee, rocking it out of the ditch and repositioning it up the road, farther away from the insurgents' hide position. Harraday got his .50-cal. going, and Betts joined in with his M4, holding the triggermen down and forcing them to fire mostly blind, which meant Pig Eye could move more freely. Now you're talking, he thought. Now they had a fighting chance! He held his breath, fondling the grenade and thinking that if Harraday could keep the Iraqis occupied, he might be able to get close enough to lob it over the wall of the animal enclosure, which would fix the triggermen once and for all.

The plan he settled on was to move twenty or thirty yards back along the ditch before cutting away from the road and making a run to the east side of the enclosure, out of the line of fire. He stuffed some more brush into the loops of wire, hoping to blend in with the landscape and counting on the others to keep the Iraqis busy. Then he bellied along the ditch, cradling the grenade in his hands and every now and then raising his head slightly to check on Tishman, who had gotten Finch back inside the vehicle and was now wrestling with the .50-cal., which seemed to be jammed or broken.

How close should he get before he tossed the grenade? What if his aim was bad and he missed? What if his aim was good, and one of the hostiles caught the grenade and threw it back at him? As he pushed himself nose-first through the dust, Pig Eye thought about all the hours he had spent working through various scenarios, none of them remotely like the one in which he found himself. Danny had been right about the howitzer—that's the thing he needed now—that or aerial support.

Thirty seconds more, and he'd leave the road. Once he pulled the pin and threw, the grenade's handle would fly off, releasing a spring that would throw the striker against the percussion cap, igniting the fuse. The fuse would take about four seconds to burn—more or less depending on variables in the design of the device that Pig Eye had no way of assessing. Then the detonator would ignite, setting off the main explosive charge. He imagined the blast wave and the fragments of casing ripping through anything they encountered and, if he was lucky, slicing the hell out of whoever was hiding behind the wall.

Everything was set. The only thing left to do was to run and aim and toss—or it would have been the only thing if one of the triggermen hadn't peered over the wall and pointed his weapon down the road at a distant puff of dust that signaled a vehicle approaching from the direction they had come. Through the binoculars, Pig Eye made out a small pickup truck, a Toyota HiLux, he guessed. It seemed to be riding low, which meant there were probably people in it, but he couldn't see any people, only the driver, so there was no way of telling how many others might be hunkered down in the back of the truck and if whoever it was were insurgents or civilians. So far, Harraday and Betts had the triggermen mostly pinned, but a truck full of reinforcements would drastically lower their odds. He calculated the Toyota was three or four klicks away. If it was traveling at forty miles per hour, he would have between three and four minutes to do something that raised their chances of escape. If it was moving more slowly, he would have longer. He refocused the binoculars, which was when he noticed that, in addition to riding very low to the ground, the approaching truck was old and had black temporary plates—all signs that it was filled not with passengers but with explosives.

## 4.8 PIG EYE

Kelly's pills worked even better than Hernandez's time-slowing trick. They brought everything into sharp focus so that Pig Eye had a chance to appreciate the shimmer of the pebbles under his hands and the rustle of dry grass and the scratch of the spiny seed heads against his skin as his mind squeezed off a round of calculations: thirty miles per hour, he decided, but gaining speed, which meant that in approximately two minutes the pickup would reach the Humvee that contained Tishman and Kelly and Finch. It was a bomb and it was going to blow the Humvee to kingdom come, killing the men it contained and lowering the odds for the rest of them.

"Never change the plan at the last minute unless you have to," the marine had told him, but what if he had to? He had to neutralize the truck.

Once he understood the situation, his indecision and doubts vanished. Unless it was the pills that chased them, for suddenly he wasn't worried anymore. Suddenly he felt like Superman, drenched in a downpour of rightness and karma and luck. Above him, the sun was a hot lid on the day. The earth embraced him from below as if he were not quite separate from it, as if he were poised somewhere between what he had been and what he would become. Then he pulled the pin on the grenade, holding the handle tightly in place and tensing his muscles for a run.

He couldn't slow time down, but he could speed it up. He could speed it up by running toward the truck, which floated soundlessly toward him on its cloud of dust like a low-flying desert-colored bird. He couldn't stop the bomb, but he could detonate it prematurely, before it reached the Humvee. And he could improve his accuracy by tossing from close range into the truck bed, where he figured the explosives were packed. In his imagination, the vehicle would sail by, continuing on for another three or four seconds while the fuse burned and while he kept running another three or four seconds past it, putting him outside the primary blast zone if he was lucky and exploding the truck before it reached his buddies.

It was the best he could do, given the situation and the fact that he didn't have any more time to come up with a better plan. Time and opportunity were the two most important elements in any escape kit—he had them, he just didn't have enough.

## 4.9 DANNY JOINER

Danny spent a moment trying to find his binoculars, which would have been useful in assessing the situation, but they weren't around his neck and they hadn't fallen to the floor. He slid out of the truck and took cover behind it before shouldering his rifle and firing frantically at the wall before settling down and aiming, which helped to pin down whoever was there even if he didn't hit them.

The seconds ticked by. Whenever one of the Iraqis showed himself, Harraday would pop off a round, or Danny would, but then Harraday's big gun went silent—jammed or out of ammo—so now Harraday was crouching in the gun turret and blasting away with his M4, which is when Danny noticed a vehicle that looked like a pickup truck approaching from the east. Danny figured the truck would have to leave the road at some point to get around the debris, but it didn't leave the road. And it didn't slow down. It was then that he noticed how the truck was riding very low to the ground and how it was heading straight toward Tishman and Kelly's Humvee. "Incoming!" yelled Danny, but his head was pounding and he couldn't even hear himself.

The best thing he could do was to stop the truck before it

reached the Humvee and detonated, which was what was going to happen if he didn't do something quickly. He rammed another round into the chamber and steadied his arm. He remembered to breathe. He remembered that his left eye was dominant. He remembered to flip the safety. Now that he had a plan, his hands were weirdly steady. His head was clear as glass. He could have been a sniper, he was so cool and controlled. As he squeezed the trigger, elation flooded through him because he knew even before the windshield shattered that it was a money shot and that his buddies in the Humvee were safe because of him. The driver pitched forward. The pickup swerved and abruptly stopped. And then the feeling changed into whatever was the opposite of elation as his laser focus opened out again and he saw that something had detached from the roadside and taken human form. The figure had time to run a few steps farther up the road before the truck exploded and with it, Pig Eye and everything predictable about the world.

## 4.10 PENN SINCLAIR

Penn Sinclair woke with a start to the enormity of what he had done. He lay sweating on his cot for over an hour before rising and dressing carefully in the dark. By the time the pink desert light filtered in at the plastic window, he had written a two-page statement outlining what had happened between the announcement that the tours were being extended and the encounter with the IED.

The men had been insubordinate. He had worried about losing control and overreacted. He had justified his actions by telling himself that the school was a priority, as was getting the supplies up the road for when the orders came through. But the truth was, he hadn't asked enough questions or adequately assessed the intelligence or understood the implications of the surge for road-clearing crews or the general confusion that accompanied the implementation of any new strategy. He re-read the statement and thought again about how facts weren't much different from fabrications. But it was the best he could do.

At 06:30 he knocked at the door of the colonel's quarters. Falwell was blessed with a permanent interrogatory look that made people answer questions before he could ask them. When he opened the door, Penn wished him good morning and handed the two sheets of paper across. Falwell's expression turned from Who's bothering me so early? to What the fuck is this?

"It's my statement, sir."

Statement? asked the look.

"Confession, rather. To attach to the after action report."

Falwell opened his mouth for the first time and said, "I was just about to have coffee. Why don't you come in and join me, Captain."

Penn didn't want coffee. He didn't want to sit down next to a picture of Falwell's teenaged daughters or notice that in the picture, the daughters were lounging on a beach holding some kind of fruity drink while two dark-skinned people with trays hovered behind them and smiled for the camera. But he found himself sitting with a coffee cup balanced on his knees and blurting out the story of how he had sent the convoy before receiving the orders and how, once he had received them, he had allowed a unit to continue north to deliver a load of supplies to the school. "My actions were almost certainly the reason the convoy was attacked."

"Almost certainly," said Falwell.

"Certainly, sir."

"How many things in life are almost certain, Captain? Death and taxes, crabs—that's about it."

"Likely, then."

"I see," said Falwell. "Was it yesterday? Or was it the day before? Or maybe it was Wednesday of last week or the week before that."

"Yesterday," said Penn, his eyes straying to the daughters, who wore oversized sunglasses and strapless dresses and the confident smiles of girls who knew how to get what they wanted. "It was the day after the troops found out they weren't going home."

"My point is that it could have been any day. It's too dangerous to send supply convoys every day of the goddamned week. But, of course, it's also too dangerous not to send them because that would hang the guys on the front lines out to fucking dry."

The colonel swallowed a slug of coffee and said, *"The line between disorder and order lies in logistics."*

It was Sinclair's turn to give Falwell a questioning look.

"Sun Tzu," said the colonel.

"But I sent them before the orders came through."

"I heard the men were causing trouble," said Falwell. "And the supplies got to where they were needed way ahead of schedule. It's conceivable that the entire convoy would have been ambushed if it had started later. You might have saved something even worse from happening. Did you ever think that those first trucks only got through because of you?"

"Five of my men were killed and others were injured. What could be worse than that?"

Penn blinked and lowered his eyes. When he raised them again, the colonel was blinking too and the questioning look was gone.

"No person on earth is sorrier about that than me. No one. Not a single fucking person cares more about his troops than I do. But it sounds like they were out of line and you tried to control them. You just couldn't control the Iraqis. If you could, you'd be sitting here instead of me."

The rising sun cast the room in a warm and almost otherworldly glow so that with a little effort, Penn might have convinced himself that he would walk outside to find a row of beach umbrellas and smiling waiters peddling the illusion that the world was a beautiful place and that those who weren't yet happy would be after another mai tai or a hot stone massage or a leisurely swim in the blue-black infinity-edge pool.

"So, what?" asked the colonel. "You want to be punished, is that it? Well, that won't solve a goddamned thing."

"I made two bad decisions in a row. First to send the convoy before receiving the orders, and then to split the platoon."

"And why were those bad decisions?"

"Because they led to unnecessary deaths."

"The end justifies the means, then? An action is good if it leads to a state of affairs that is better than the one you started with? Setting aside the well-worn tropes about torturing or killing some people in order to save others—we've all heard those arguments a thousand times—how does focusing on the consequences provide guidance about what a person should do? Here you are, assessing your options, and you decide that sending the convoy will accomplish more than not sending it. But in the end it doesn't, so now you determine that your action was bad. The problem with this theory is that you can only see what you ought to have done after the fact."

"In any case, I want to take responsibility for it. And I want to keep from doing any more harm."

"There's an easy answer, then," said the colonel. "Go ahead and shoot yourself now. Or join a monastery."

Penn tried to take a sip of his coffee, but the cup was shaking in his hand, so he put it back down and checked out the daughters again, calmed somewhat by their innocence or whatever it was that allowed them to look so alert and oblivious at the same time. One of them was prettier than the other, but he could tell that the second one had bigger—well, the word that came to him was "balls." She reminded him of Louise, except that Louise would have managed to convey that behind the perky smile was an important itinerary, and only by rigidly sticking to it had she carved out that moment of relaxation and fun. Still, they had the same assured look, a look he recognized because he used to have it himself. He owed Louise a letter or an email, but he didn't know what he would say to her or what he would want her to say in reply.

"Call me a pragmatist," said the colonel, "but I don't believe there's a single, unified answer to any of the questions we might ask ourselves about how a person decides what to do. Should I be concerned with the consequences? Of course I should. Mostly I don't lie, but when the Nazis come knocking, I don't tell them where Anne Frank is hiding. I take my best shot given the available time and information—that's the thing I'm paid to do. Anything more than that is above my pay grade, and certainly above yours."

"But if I'd waited a little longer, thought a little harder ..."

"There are the thinkers and there are the doers, Sinclair. The thinkers sit around in their libraries talking in circles about what is morally required or permitted—you can't judge a person without considering his actions, and you can't judge actions without considering consequences. But consequences can't be predicted with any accuracy, so you talk about intentions—and where does all that mumbo jumbo leave us? It leaves us exactly where we are.

Someone has to be out here on the front lines doing something about all the shit in the world, and that's us. We're the doers, Sinclair. We don't have the luxury of waiting until we've got the theory all worked out. While those guys are trying to come up with answers—and don't forget, they've been trying for thousands of years—life is happening all around us."

"And death," said Penn.

"Which is a really lousy part of life," said the colonel.

"It's not really part of life," Penn started to say, but he wasn't sure of his ground, so he stopped.

The colonel got up and poured himself another cup of coffee. He looked at Penn and then past him at the scratched plastic window and the yard where groups of soldiers had started to move about, their faces glowing in the morning light as if lit from within. *"To avoid criticism, say nothing, do nothing, be nothing,"* he said.

"Aristotle?" asked Penn.

"Elbert Hubbard, whoever the hell that is."

The colonel rose and moved toward the door. The morning light hit the crevices of his face, but when he turned, his features were erased by shadows. "I'm going to be perfectly honest with you, Sinclair. I don't much like confessions."

"Sorry sir."

"Do you know why I don't like them?"

"No sir."

"They create problems is why. And I think you'll agree we've got problems enough."

"Yes sir," said Penn, gesturing toward the pages Falwell was holding but hadn't read. "Anyway, it's all in there."

"Which computer did you write this on?"

"My personal computer, sir."

"Are there other copies?"

133

"No sir."

"Good." Falwell walked to where a waste receptacle was nestled in a corner of the room. He put the pages in the receptacle and lit a match, and they both watched as the paper burned. "You didn't email this to anybody, did you? You didn't save it on a disk?"

"No sir."

"See that you don't. You go delete that file and then you empty the trash bin on the computer and then you never mention this to anybody again. And when the incident report is written up, make sure it's routed through me."

"Yes sir," said Penn. Then he added, "I think I cared too much about the school. And I cared too much about how I looked to the other officers. I let those things overshadow my duty to my men. That's the thing I can't forget."

"You sent some troops on a mission that might or might not have been poorly timed, which had the side benefit of letting some hotheads cool off. The orders changed and you adapted the best you could according to the information you had at the time. Hindsight is twenty-twenty, Sinclair. But I'm glad you told me about this. I'll write a press release. We'll inform the next of kin."

Penn said, "Yes sir." He moved the untouched coffee from his knees to a table.

"You're like me, Sinclair. The army needs us, but we need the army too."

As Penn left the hut, the weight that had been pressing down on him since the afternoon before left his shoulders, but it settled somewhere deep inside his rib cage. When he got back to his quarters, he deleted his confession, but only after emailing it to his civilian account and only after enclosing a printed copy in an envelope and addressing it to himself care of his mother, who would recognize the handwriting and wonder vaguely why he was writing to himself. Then she would carefully sort the envelope from the bills and invitations, and the next time she went upstairs, she would put it in the top drawer of the antique chest that stood in the hallway underneath the Sinclair family crest with the rooster on it and the words they repeated at holiday gatherings but otherwise forgot: Commit Thy Work to God. She would recognize his handwriting, but she wouldn't open the envelope the way Louise would open it if he sent the letter to her.

## 4.11 GORDON FALWELL

I should have been a priest," said Falwell before the door closed. "I should have been a fucking priest."

He'd been told to cancel all logistics missions until after the meeting at HQ, which he had done. But now he had five casualties to explain in an incident where supplies were being skimmed off for an unauthorized school and who knew if that was just the tip of the iceberg as far as the supplies went, not to mention that certain road patrols had been temporarily pulled, which is a detail he had known but hadn't passed on in a timely fashion because he'd thought canceling the missions was enough. If he had, though, Sinclair would have made a different decision when it came to disciplining his men, and this rat fuck could have been avoided. It was ultimately his fault. Something like this could stall his career. Now he'd have to change the date on the incident report. Or fudge the time line. Hell, he'd figure it out. At HQ he'd talked to combat commanders, and all of them had reported that insubordination among the troops was on the rise, as were visits to mental health personnel, as were IED attacks, as were demands on soldiers to do things for the Iraqis that the Iraqis should be doing for themselves, as was the belief in counterinsurgency of exactly the school-building kind, and as was the inability to tell who was the enemy or where he was hiding. The war was 360 degrees with surround sound, so how were he and his officers supposed to make good decisions when either way they were fucked.

"Lessons learned" had been the catchphrase of the meeting, and now Falwell had to submit yet another after action report that would be scoured for useful observations, information, and lessons—OIL. The report would trigger still other reports and analyses that would be sent up the command chain, where new policies would be crafted and handed back down with the hope that past mistakes could be avoided. Ha!

He winced at the AARs already littering his desk—the one where the lesson learned was about keeping engines from overheating in this blast furnace of a country and the one where it was about destigmatizing mental health care and the ones about combatting complacency and up-armoring cargo trucks and conserving water and building trust and preventing rape and recognizing likely ambush points. And now the one about how the light footprint strategy had been a—well, people had started to use the word "fiasco." Just thinking about the piles of paper and analyses one more incident would spawn was enough to make him weep.

And yet, the optimism he had brought back with him from HQ hadn't completely dissipated. There was something about tragedy that strengthened resolve and annealed the soul, and there was something about the surge that spelled "Fresh Start." A new strategy always conjured up in his mind a pristine set of pages, ones with that fresh-ink smell and the lines not yet filled with fuckups and confusion. He called his CSM and said, "Everyone in the DFAC in thirty." Then he spent a few minutes pondering the HQ briefing and deciding what to pass on to the troops. He'd keep it short. *In war, only the simple succeeds,* he told himself, quoting Field Marshal Paul von Hindenburg. He liked the words "simple" and "focused" and "decisive."

By the time he was walking across the yard, optimism was tugging his center of gravity by its string. The men were sitting quietly this time, waiting and wary, but they snapped to attention when he entered the room. As he spoke, he amped up his speech a little, and instead of "attempt," he said "high-octane effort," and instead of "senseless deaths," he said "magnificent contribution." And then he talked about balancing kinetics with human intelligence and diplomacy. As he spoke, he saw that there were valuable lessons to be learned after all and that he was articulating them forcefully. Fuck the papers and reports. It was he, along with the men and women arrayed before him, who would make the difference in this war.

"There is nothing you cannot do," he said, and he saw his belief reflected in the faces in front of him. The troops who had been sitting back leaned forward, and the ones who had been leaning forward squinted and tensed their jaws.

"If you fall," he said, "you will pick yourself up and do your job. And if the enemy pushes you down, you will pick yourself up and you will push back harder, and then you will do your job. But if he pushes you down and steps on you . . . "

Now the colonel was feeling the old sort of ecstasy, the kind that could only be forged of forces that were nameless and primal. He thought of quoting General Patton, who had said, *We will twist his balls and kick the living shit out of him,* decided not to, and then the words burst past his lips and had on his own mind the effect he hoped they would have on his troops. And for an instant, in spite of everything that had happened before that moment and everything that was to come, he felt pretty goddamned ready for the surge.

# 5.0 EVIDENCE

*A cougar, isn't that what you call it? I think she was looking for a little action on the side.*

—Hugo Martinez, Prison Security

*It was Will who was the love of her life, and he didn't need her anymore. I think that hurt her feelings more than she let on.*

—Lily De Luca

*I have to admit that I underestimated Will. He was one of those kids who blossomed almost overnight.*

—Timothy Quick, Language Arts Teacher

*Months after I started making inquiries, I got a call from a professor at OSU. But that was right around the time Danny was coming home, so for a while I put it out of my mind.*

—Dolly Jackson

*There was a small notice in the classified section seeking people with information about environmental toxins. So I called.*

—Professor Stanley Wilkes, Oklahoma State University

*That notice scared the pants off Winslow, so he and the mayor and I went on down to the Sentinel offices, right there behind the Main Street Diner. The publisher, whose name is also Martin Fitch, assured us his nephew was under control.*

—Pastor Houston Price

# 5.1 WILL

Soon after taking the SAT, Will had fractured his wrist sliding home. He had gone for x-rays and a cast, which is what he was thinking about as he filled out a questionnaire aimed at getting the juniors to consider college and the future. For many of them, that meant following their parents into local jobs, with the more adventurous signing on to an oil rig or enlisting for the war if it wasn't over by graduation, which was still a year away. Will was picturing the curvy nurse in the tight white uniform who had pressed up against him as she set his arm and remembering how the word "x-ray" sounded like "sex-ray" when the nurse mentioned retakes to the technician. The long, thin bones of Will's arm stood out in sharp relief, edged by shadowy soft tissue, and nestled into the radius just above his wrist was the BB that had been there since the day he'd gone rabbit hunting with Tyler Hicks and Tyler had gotten angry about something and banged his air gun against the ground, causing it to catch on a root and go off as it fell.

"Is that an old war wound?" asked the nurse in a gravelly voice.

"Yeah," said Will. "I guess it is."

"Tough guy, huh?" said the nurse, and the way she said it still set Will's heart racing whenever he thought about it.

Will's test scores surprised everyone. Because he was quiet in class and so was a relative unknown, the doctor idea caught hold among the teachers, who were eager to have a story of unexpected success to put in their end-of-year report. Even Will was not immune to the fiction, and the day the report came out, he sat for a while in an echoing stairwell as students flowed past him like a river around a sturdy rock. He started to see paths and possibilities. He started to wonder if he actually was becoming the person profiled in the report, if a shifting idea of who a person was could change things about the person himself. Just that morning, the principal had stopped him in the hallway and put a hand on his shoulder. All he had said was, "Well done, Will," but the words carried a freight train of meaning, as if Will and the principal had many such conversations behind them and many more ahead. He felt like Bon Jovi for a moment, or Spider-Man, or Barry Bonds. He wasn't arrogant, just newly aware that packed within his body and brain was something unusual, something most people only recognized in others and wished they had.

But then Tyler Hicks thumped into him and said, "Jeezus, Rayburn. What's up with that report?"

"Anybody can fool some of the people some of the time," said the boy who was with Tyler. "Even Rayburn."

"I guess they can," said Will amiably. But then he muttered to Tyler's retreating back, "Why the hell not!" He could do anything if he put his mind to it. He took a sharpened pencil out of his backpack and pressed the point against the skin of his arm until it went in a little way. He had a high pain threshold, and now that he had proved he was smart, he wanted to prove the nurse had been right when she had called him tough. Tough enough to kick Tyler's ass if he wanted to, but smart enough to leave it alone.

That's what he was doing when Tula Santos appeared in the stairwell and said, "Hello."

"Why hello, Tula," he said, without hesitating and without putting his hands in his pockets the way he would have done only the day before.

To his surprise, Tula paused with her hand on the railing even though they were blocking the way for the other students. When one of them muttered, "Move over. Can't you see you're in the way?" Will glared at him in a way that made Tula laugh.

"I've got to get going anyway," she said. "I don't want to be late for class."

"Can you meet me later?" asked Will. "I could use a little advice."

"I guess so," said Tula. "Is tomorrow okay?"

Will sat for a little while longer contemplating how one thing led to another in the chain reaction of cause and effect. When he finally got up to change into his practice uniform and make his way down the hill to the ball field, he could feel his aura moving with him, perfectly in sync with the movements of his muscles. The cast on his arm was due to come off in another week, but now it seemed like an enhancement rather than a deficit. It felt sturdy, like the arm of a cyborg, and the scrawled signatures of his friends seemed confirmation of his new status despite the fact that most of them had been written before any mention of doctoring or college had been made: WAY TO GO, GENIUS AND SEE YOU AT STATE.

"When's that cast coming off, Rayburn?" asked the coach. "We need you back at third."

"Next week," said Will. "I'll only miss one more game." He had missed four games already, and he was worried about losing his position to a skinny freshman.

The next day Tula was waiting for him after practice in a grove of apple trees that had been an orchard way back before the school was built. Will settled himself beside her and pulled the most recent letter from the state university out of his pocket. It was crumpled, but the words hadn't changed even though he'd practically worn them out by running his index finger over the lines of text, something he did again as he read the letter aloud. All the while his aura stretched and flexed, and occasionally it intersected with Tula's aura, which retreated slightly in deference to their comparative forces, but advanced too, in response to the magnetism that had an attractive as well as a repelling force. The letter talked about his accomplishments and test scores and indicated that the college gave generous scholarships to promising student-athletes like Will.

"Why, Will! That's wonderful news!" exclaimed Tula. Her eyes shone, and when she looked at Will, he saw himself reflected in her expression of surprise.

Will rested the dirty cast on his knee and said that college was only the first step, that after that came medical school. The notion that the idea had been planted there by the headmaster's report landed briefly in his consciousness before taking off again.

Tula didn't blink as she asked him what kind of doctor he was going to be.

"An orthopedic surgeon," replied Will.

"I volunteer at a health-care clinic!" exclaimed Tula. "I've already gotten all seven Rainbow merit bars, so I'm working on getting my service jewel. You could come along with me some time if you want."

This was an unexpected invitation, and Will readily accepted. It wasn't a date, exactly, but it was the next best thing.

# 5.2 MAGGIE

One morning, apropos of nothing, Valerie stopped what she was doing and said, "Of course people make mistakes. We're only human, after all."

Since there was no one else in the room, Maggie assumed Valerie was talking to her. "Excuse me?" she said, but Valerie just snapped her gum and made little huffing sounds as if what she was doing was physically exhausting.

Maggie spent the rest of the morning pondering Valerie's strange outburst. Had she been talking about the justice system or about something else? Did she know more than she was letting on about prisoners who had been wrongly convicted? If so, why was she so glib in denying it whenever Maggie brought the subject up? And what had made her mention it on a quiet day when the director was out of the office?

When Valerie went on her break, Maggie sat in her co-worker's chair and flipped through the neat stacks of papers on her desk, but she found nothing out of the ordinary. Then she prodded Valerie's computer to life, but she didn't have the password and wasn't able to get past the log-in screen. By the time Valerie returned, Maggie's curiosity had gotten the better of her. "What mistakes?" she asked. "A few minutes ago you said something about mistakes."

"Oh," said Valerie. "DC's in a twitter because he can't find a top-secret report some muckety-muck sent him. I'm sure I don't know where it is, but you know DC. It's always someone else's fault."

Ever since taking the document from the munitions plant, the word "top-secret" had held a special meaning for Maggie, and she hoped she didn't look as eager and unsettled as she felt. Now she wondered if she was being accused of something. She had copied Tomás's file, but she hadn't really taken it, and as far as she knew, it wasn't secret. "What's so top-secret?" she asked as casually as she could.

"Lord if I know," said Valerie. "I just push the papers, I don't read the damn things."

Maggie had begun to notice how importantly Valerie presided over the office and how quick she was to pass the boring or unpleasant tasks on to Maggie. "You don't mind if I delegate, do you?" Valerie would call to DC through the glass partition of his office, and mostly he would wave his hand dismissively. "Just so the job gets done, I don't care who does it," he would tell her, although now and then he would shake his head and say, "I want you to handle this personally. Give it that special Vines touch." Then Valerie would laugh knowingly and pass something more menial on to Maggie. It wasn't as if Valerie was shirking, for even though she left every day at exactly five o'clock, she worked hard and often arrived half an hour early. Lately, though, she seemed to be going out of her way to make it clear to everyone what the pecking order was.

A few days after telling Maggie about the missing report, Valerie wore a blouse that was so sheer in the back that the black hooks on her bra were entirely visible and anyone standing behind her could read the writing on the label that said *36 D*. The front panel of the blouse was made from a respectable navy fabric and from that angle, Valerie looked proper and businesslike, but from behind, she looked like a slut. The blouse bothered Maggie out of all proportion to what it was, for it seemed to say something not only about how Valerie had hidden sides to her, but also about how everyone did.

All morning, Maggie kept sending irritated glances in her coworker's direction, but mostly Valerie ignored her, answering the phone and making neat stacks of documents for DC to review or for Maggie to cart down to the file room. It was almost as if someone had snuck up behind her and altered her blouse without her knowledge. At one point, the lanyard that held her ID badge looped over one of her breasts in a way that would have embarrassed Maggie, but Valerie did nothing to fix it. She only stretched her arms above her head when DC walked by, further emphasizing her anatomy before getting up and walking to the hallway alcove where the copy machine was kept. The director had his head down, but if he had looked up just then, he would have been treated to a view of the see-through part of the blouse and the thick elastic of the bra. Maggie could stand it no longer, and when DC went off to an afternoon meeting, she cried, "Valerie! Your blouse is completely inappropriate!"

"And what are you, the clothing police?" Valerie smiled and coughed out a hoarse little laugh.

Maggie immediately regretted her outburst. In an attempt to cover up her disapproval, she said, "It looks great on you, don't get me wrong. I just wouldn't have worn it to the office."

"You wouldn't have worn it at all," said Valerie. "Frankly, you don't have the body for it—but no offense." She didn't sound at all like Misty when she said it. Misty would have added, If you've got it, flaunt it. Or she would have said, Hell yeah, it's inappropriate. I'm trying to shake things up a bit. It's high time we had a little fun around here.

But Valerie wasn't Misty. For the first time since quitting her job at the munitions plant, Maggie thought about her old life and wondered if she had made a mistake. Of course people make mistakes, she thought, and when she realized those were the very words Valerie had used that morning, she wondered if someone was using Valerie to send her a message the way Pastor Price said Jesus sometimes did.

Just before she left for the day, Maggie tried to patch things up with Valerie. "I'll walk out with you," she said. "Will has a game this evening, so I can't stay late."

The two women gathered up their things, but just as they were going out the door, Valerie said she had forgotten something. "You go on. I'd forget my head if it wasn't screwed on."

"Okay, see you tomorrow," said Maggie, but a niggling suspicion made her loiter in a dark elbow of the hallway to see what Valerie would do. Instead of retrieving some forgotten item, Valerie took a piece of paper from her purse and tucked it into DC's locked bank of files before closing everything up again, hiding the key in her desk drawer, and breezing down the corridor in a whirl of efficiency and Shalimar perfume. Maggie followed quietly behind. It was only when she got to the parking lot that she discovered the reason for the charade. Valerie didn't head toward her own parking space at all, but walked the entire length of the asphalt lot and got into a car that was waiting at the far end. Even though the car was too far away for Maggie to identify, she knew it belonged to DC. She should have known it all along.

Everybody has secrets, she thought. She found the idea both comforting and disturbing. It made her own transgressions less unusual, but it also suggested that if the law took an interest in a person—Tomás, for instance, but also Valerie or DC or even Maggie herself—it could probably find evidence that that person had done something wrong.

Valerie's attitude toward Maggie changed after the blouse incident. She still snapped her gum and made jokes, but she no longer went out of her way to include Maggie in the gossip sessions she presided over during breaks. She no longer showed Maggie a new eye shadow color and said, "This would be perfect for you." Being ostracized emphasized to Maggie that she wasn't and couldn't be on the side of things where Valerie and the others were, where gossiping and comparing notes on clothing and men provided satisfaction and where morality was elastic, if it came into things at all. She pretended not to notice when Valerie stood sternly under the fluorescent strip lights and watched Maggie walk past as if Maggie were the one with the see-through blouse, but it always made her feel self-conscious, just as she knew Valerie knew it would.

## 5.3 MAGGIE

Maggie sat at her desk and tried to appear busy, intermittently craning her neck to get a glimpse of a visiting group of representatives from the ACLU. When they filed into the conference room to get the badges she and Valerie had prepared, she asked, "Should we find out if there's anything else they need?"

"We don't want to make them too comfortable," said Valerie, who seemed to view the visit as an unwelcome intrusion. "You don't see DC this nervous very often."

"Why is he nervous?" asked Maggie.

"It's the ACLU! They only come sniffing around if they think there's something to find."

"Like innocent prisoners?" asked Maggie.

"Like overcrowding. Like lack of medical and dental care. Like exposure to hazardous substances."

"What hazardous substances?"

"Lord if I know. I doubt there are any, but it's the kind of thing they look for. I guess we should set out more cookies for them after all. Along with some of those yummy tarts."

Maggie was grateful when a woman with disordered clothing and a large brooch pinned awkwardly to her breast stuck her head through the door and asked where the restroom was, giving Maggie an excuse to walk past the conference room, where the director was holding forth on the subject of "humane rehabilitation" and "market solutions to the overcrowding problem."

"The visitor's lounge is in another wing of the building, but you're welcome to use the employees'," she said. "I'll warn you, though, it gets a bit stuffy in there."

"Thank you, thank you," said the woman, hoisting a large bag onto her shoulder and rubbing a fat pink cheek with a sweaty hand.

Maggie hurried before her down the corridor and said she didn't mind waiting outside to lead her back again, but the woman took longer than expected, and by the time they returned to the conference room, the rest of the group had already gone off on their tour.

"Come with me," said Maggie. "I'm sure we can catch up."

The woman nodded and cast her eyes fearfully behind her. "This is a maximum security facility, is it?" she asked as they waited for a guard to open a locked gate for them.

Maggie told her it was.

"I thought so. The ACLU is on a tear about solitary confinement, so they're visiting prisons where they suspect it's in use. My specialty is federal. Nonviolent. Although solitary confinement is used there too—oh, I don't like to think about it. Imagine being shut away by yourself for years. Decades, in some cases. It's really too, too much to bear."

"I don't think they do that here," said Maggie, not because she knew anything about it, but because the woman seemed as if she was about to cry. On an impulse, Maggie grabbed her arm, which caused the woman to fall against her, almost knocking her over.

"Don't be so sure," she said, recovering her balance. "It's a shockingly common practice."

"I'd have heard about it," said Maggie.

"Don't be so sure about that either. They count on people closing their eyes to things."

The woman glanced up the hall and then down it as if she were checking for eavesdroppers before she took a tiny copy of the Constitution out of her pocket and said, "Take a look at this." She pointed to a chunk of text and said, "See? Right there. It's perfectly legal for people who have been convicted of a crime to be enslaved."

"That can't be right," said Maggie.

"As I said, they count on people closing their eyes to things."

Maggie doubted it was true that slavery was legal. If it was, wouldn't there have been an outcry on *Geraldo* and *Oprah,* and wouldn't people be marching in the street singing "Let My People Go"? She found the woman's air of superiority irritating, but as soon as she thought the word "smug," the woman's face collapsed in doughy misery and tears welled in the corners of her eyes.

"What do you do for the ACLU?" asked Maggie in an attempt to change the subject.

"I'm not part of the ACLU—not really. A colleague invited me, so I came along. Oh, I give them a little money now and then, but I'm a prisoner advocate for a different group, a group called PATH, which stands for Patrick Henry. You studied him in school, I imagine: *Give me liberty or give me death!* Why doesn't anyone believe that anymore? In any case, that's what we're committed to. Our mission is to free the wrongly incarcerated case by case, although sometimes I think we're going about it the wrong way. And now I might have crossed the line, and I'm trying to figure out how to uncross it. It's all terribly upsetting."

"What line?" Maggie pictured the yellow lines that striped the floor of the prison, marking the various places where the prisoners had to stand for services or inspections.

"The moral line," said the woman coyly, as if she knew exactly which word would staple Maggie's wandering attention to her face.

"I don't understand. What did you do?" Maggie tried not to sound too eager, but a fragile hope expanded in her chest that there were other people like her out there, people who cared about something other than sex and makeup and what to cook for dinner, people who were used to righting wrongs and could tell her how it was done. People she could turn to for help with Tomás. "Freeing people is something I'm interested in too," she whispered, just in case the prison was riddled with listening devices. Even though Maggie was watching carefully to gauge the woman's reaction, she wasn't prepared for the joy that spread across her face.

"Then you know." The woman was beaming quietly now, and Maggie could see that she had once been beautiful. "Then you know what it's like."

"I'm not sure," said Maggie. "At first I couldn't understand why the people here weren't rushing about trying to fix all the things that are wrong, and then I thought, How can I expect other people to do something I'm not willing to do myself?"

"Be the change," said the woman.

"I'm not very experienced, so maybe you could give me some advice."

"I ... Well ... First, I should probably fill you in on exactly what my group does."

A metallic sound rang from somewhere ahead of them. They had reached an anteroom past which Maggie had no access, so she turned to the woman and said they would have to wait for the guard to call ahead.

"It's just as well, just as well," she said. "I couldn't bear to see anyone in solitary confinement."

"I don't think they do that here," Maggie said again, and again the woman responded, "Don't be too sure." This time, though, there was nothing smug about the expression on her face, which was filled instead with hope and yearning. She reached out and grasped Maggie's sleeves, pulling her a little closer as if she too was worried that the walls had ears. "My George was in solitary confinement for four years," she said. "It's why I took him on."

While they waited for the guard, the woman told Maggie that the members of her group adopted specific nonviolent prisoners and tried to help them. "We publicize their cases and bring injustices to light. We find attorneys who will donate their services, and then we run various errands in order to keep the cases from falling through the cracks."

"How noble!" said Maggie. It was the kind of thing she was hoping to do, and she could see she had gotten off track by merely befriending Tomás and teaching him math.

"Noble? More like exhausting! But you start off filled with idealism, anyway. Then, at some point, you become aware of the line. Oh, you pretend not to see it. You act all prim and dance around it like a schoolgirl, stepping very carefully whenever it's in sight. But after a while, you want to be close to it."

The woman opened the swimming pools of her eyes wide, as though she were noticing something unexpected or trying not to cry.

"And eventually you just step over it. But you don't cross it in a blaze of righteous glory, which is how you thought it would be. You cross it, really, on a dare. Or you cross it because you want a bigger and bigger dose of whatever it was that made you step up to it in the first place. You cross it because you are now an addict. Because, frankly, it is exhilarating and because it's a lot more fun than housework or your day job."

The moment ended, and the woman's eyes snapped shut. When she opened them again, the hope had vanished, and everything about her sagged with defeat.

"I don't understand," said Maggie.

"Of course you don't. How could you?"

"But what did you do when you crossed the line?"

The woman's face softened, and her lips quivered into a smile. "I fell in love with George," she said. "But now I'm about worn out, which is why I came here today. The ACLU people—they're very structured and focused. And disciplined! They all respect the line. That's what I came for—to get advice on that." The woman's mouth settled into a tight barrier between her running nose and quivering chin, and she seemed to be waiting, as Maggie was, to hear what words would come out of it next. "No, that's not entirely true," she said. "I came to pass George on to someone else."

She held up a quilted bag with the name George appliquéd onto the side in contrasting fabric. "Of course the work can be very rewarding if you get your prisoner out of jail, which is why it's so frustrating to be representing George. There seems to be a vendetta against him. If you read the file, you'd see for yourself.

Not to mention that George is very . . . well, dashing. It's been an honor to advocate for him, but nothing I did made one bit of difference. So I came here to find a replacement, and then I'm going home—if I still have a home to go to."

At first Maggie felt cheated—why couldn't Tomás be dashing? Why couldn't she be passionate and strong? But then a rush of excitement and possibility surged through her. If befriending Tomás was murky and ambiguous, representing George would be a completely good and noble thing. There was a vendetta against him! He was handsome and nonviolent! He had been kept in solitary confinement for four long years! "I'll represent George," she blurted out.

Relief flooded the woman's eyes. "I want to assure you that the advocacy program is completely rewarding," she said.

While they were talking, they had circled back toward the director's office. When they reached the conference room, the woman thrust the quilted bag into Maggie's hands and said, "The appellate attorney's name and contact information is in the first folder. He's part of a network of attorneys who take these cases on."

Maggie asked if he might represent Tomás too.

"That depends on where Tomás's case was adjudicated. Anyway, you'll find a lot of information here—telephone numbers and email addresses and official documentation, as well as copious handwritten notes—everything indexed and color-coded."

When they reached the conference room, the woman snatched up her jacket and hurried back along the corridor and down the stairs, not even bothering to call the elevator. Maggie was left with the quilted bag sitting in her lap like a bloated and limbless child and the sinking feeling that even if she took on George's case, she couldn't abandon Tomás. And then, from the heaviness of the burden emerged a sense of sureness and direction. If she really wanted to help Tomás, she would stop buying him little presents. She would stop trying to make prison tolerable. Instead, she would start trying to free him.

When Valerie and DC left for the day, Maggie picked up the telephone and dialed the number for George's lawyer. "Send me the fellow's paperwork," said the lawyer. "I can't promise anything, but I'd be happy to take a look."

Maggie said she would, but first she had to get the file out of the prison, which, given the tight security, might prove problematic. If she couldn't handle Hugo, she told herself, she didn't deserve to be George's advocate. She didn't deserve to be anyone's. Besides, the blouse incident had given her an idea, and one soft summer evening, she was able to smuggle the file out of the prison by unbuttoning an extra button on her blouse. She laughed at the way Hugo, with his handsome face and muscle-bound physique, had fallen so easily into her trap.

# 5.4 TULA

The health-care clinic where Tula worked was twenty miles away. To get there, she either had to borrow her mother's car or ride the bus, which took a lot longer. Because Will had baseball practice every afternoon, it wasn't until school was out for the summer that she was able to arrange a day that was convenient for both of them. Tula was so preoccupied with the logistics of the trip that it was only when they were in the car that she thought about what the clinic was set up to do. How was she going to explain to Will that most of the clinic's patients came in for gynecological services and prenatal care?

The car rattled whenever it reached cruising speed, making it noisy and hard to talk. After a few attempts at conversation, Tula pushed the button to turn on the radio, but the sound was mostly static, with only a few bars of music coming through. Will opened the window and let his hand lift off like the wing of an airplane. When a pebble flew up from the wheels of the truck they were following and made a tiny star pattern in the corner of the windshield glass, Will said, "Now they're attacking," as if Tula would know what he meant by it. And she did know. At least she almost did, for it seemed as if the car was traveling right along the frontier that divided the land of safety from the land of peril.

"They," she said.

"You know, aliens, or terrorists. What would you do if they did attack us?"

"We couldn't outrun them in this old rattletrap, so I guess we'd have to fight them off."

"Never fear," said Will. He pulled a scouting knife from the pocket of his jacket and waved it around like a sword.

They laughed, and then they didn't talk again until they were pulling into the unpaved lot of the clinic. Before getting out of the car, Tula said with more confidence than she felt, "This is a women's clinic, Will. I forgot to tell you that. So they'll probably have you manning the phone."

"What's a women's clinic?" asked Will.

"It's a clinic dedicated to women's health."

"Okay," said Will. "They don't treat men?"

"No, they don't. But sometimes husbands or boyfriends come with the women. And the doctor is usually a man."

"What do they treat the women for?"

"You know," said Tula. "It's women having babies and stuff."

Will rolled the window closed and unbuckled his seat belt while Tula gathered up her purse. "The doctor can be a little gruff, but you'll like the midwife. Her name is Dolly."

"What's a midwife?" asked Will.

Dolly told Will he could straighten the magazines in the waiting room and then the contents of the supply cupboard. "I'd let you answer the phone, but some of our patients hang up if they get a man." Then she passed out smocks and took Tula with her into the back. "I wish I could give your boyfriend something more interesting to do," said Dolly while they waited for the doctor to arrive.

"He's not my boyfriend. He wants to be a doctor, so I invited him to come along, but it wasn't until we were on our way that I realized this probably isn't the best place to bring him." Tula laughed, releasing the tension that had built up during the drive. The two women were giggling over the awkwardness of the situation when the doctor walked in.

"What's so funny?" he asked.

"Will wants to be a doctor, so Tula brought him along. We were just hoping that the sight of all the pregnant ladies doesn't scare him away."

"You just leave your boyfriend to me," said the doctor. "I'll let him autoclave the instruments and show him how a fetal heart monitor works."

"He's not her boyfriend," said Dolly with a wink, and Tula said, "Will's in for a big surprise."

When they unlocked the door at nine o'clock, two patients were waiting on the steps accompanied by their husbands, but a third said her boyfriend was a little freaked out and wanted to wait in the car. "He was in Iraq," explained the woman. "He's on crutches, so it's a little hard for him to get around."

"That sounds like a job for me," said Will. "I'll take him a cup of coffee and see what I can do."

"Men," said Dolly as the door rattled shut. "Always racing off to fix things. I guess you're stuck with cleaning out the cupboard as well as answering the phones."

Will was gone a long time and didn't come back into the clinic with the empty coffee cup until the third patient was leaving. "What were you up to out there?" Tula wanted to know.

"Guy stuff," said Will. "Nothing much."

Toward the end of the day a new mother came in for a checkup. Her hair was unwashed and her husband had to help her fill out the form Tula gave her. "Get away from me!" the woman shouted when Dolly tried to take her blood pressure, so Dolly called in the doctor, who showed Will how to put on the cuff while Dolly and Tula backed out of the room. "It's okay," said Will. "I'm here now."

"Well," said Dolly. "Will you look at that?"

"What happened to her?" asked Tula.

"Her baby was born with severe deformities. It was horrible. Of course they blame me."

"How could it be your fault?"

"It wasn't! But I was there, so they link me to the experience." Tula told Dolly about Will's mother and how she had quit her job at the munitions factory because of something about deformed frogs.

"Interesting," said Dolly, but then she changed the subject to the coming-home party she was arranging for her boyfriend. "His name is Danny. Do you think I should go with a patriotic theme or just keep it simple? A barbecue would be fun, or what about a friendly baseball game?"

"I like the baseball idea," said Tula. "Will's a baseball player."

"I'll send you an invitation once I know when it's going to be." A few minutes passed, and then Dolly asked, "What's her name?"

"Who?" asked Tula.

"Will's mother. What's Will's mother's name?"

"Maggie Rayburn. There was a lot of talk about her at one point—don't tell me you heard about it all the way out here!"

"Interesting," Dolly said again, and then she talked some more about the coming-home party until it was time for Tula to leave.

On the drive back to Red Bud, Will was even quieter than he had been that morning. "Thanks for coming," said Tula.

"I should be thanking you," said Will. "I learned a few things."

"You were really good with those soldiers. What did you talk about with the guy in the truck?"

"Oh, you know. We listened to music and talked about baseball."

"I'm glad they were there, since there wasn't much else for you to do. I guess I didn't think things through when I invited you."

"I never really thought about where babies come from before, about how one minute there's nothing and the next there's a new life. And then when you die, it all happens in reverse. Nothing to nothing."

"They're just talking about the body when they say that. The soul is something else."

"I used to believe in the soul," said Will, "but I don't anymore."

"I think that right at the last second our souls will fly up to heaven and wait for a new body to inhabit. It will be like being born all over again."

"Huh," said Will. "That's just a fairy tale."

No sooner had they turned onto the highway than the clouds turned livid. Lightning forked in the distance, and then, closer in, the sky seemed to ignite. Pretty soon it was raining so hard that Tula had to pull beneath an overpass to wait for the storm to blow over. "We're lucky it's not a tornado," she said.

"Why?" asked Will. "That's something I've always wanted to see."

They sat for a while peering out at the rain, which seemed to be moving in a line across the fields, battering one strip of wheat before moving on to the next. When the windshield fogged up, Will swiped at it with his sleeve. "Did I ever tell you I was shot?" he asked.

"No!" exclaimed Tula. "You didn't."

"It was just a BB, but still. That soldier today had a big ol' hole in his leg." Will's eyes were gleaming as he rattled on about the soldier, about how he knew everything there was to know about radar and military electronics.

Fifteen minutes later, the spongy sky squeezed out the last drops of rain and the sun came out. When they were back on the road, Tula put her right hand on the seat beside her, but then thought better of it and returned it to the steering wheel. In any case, Will was staring out the window and didn't seem to notice. Just before they turned off at the Red Bud exit, Will told Tula he was ready for something. "I just don't know what it is," he said.

"I'm ready for something too," said Tula. She thought Will was talking about kissing her or asking her on a real date. Maybe he was even talking about sex. Dolly had told her that even the nicest boys were always thinking about it, but when she dropped him off at his house, he waved good-bye quickly and didn't ask her to come in as she had expected him to.

"Thanks," said Will. "That was really interesting."

"Men," said Tula out loud, trying to sound both dismissive and admiring the way Dolly had sounded, trying to roll her eyes and smile at the same time. But Will was already running up the muddy driveway to the house.

## 5.5 MAGGIE

Stop buying me presents," said Tomás a few days after Maggie had come to the same conclusion herself, but it was an example of his devious nature that he added, "I don't want to make your husband jealous."

"Don't be silly," said Maggie. "Lyle isn't jealous."

"Or your son."

"My son isn't jealous either." She regretted telling Tomás about Lyle and Will, but there was nothing she could do about it now.

The schoolroom was sunny in the afternoons, and a tree outside the window was filled with chattering birds. "What kind of birds are they?" asked Tomás.

Maggie didn't know, but instead of saying she would find out and tell him later, she said, "They're starlings," even though she wasn't sure they were.

"I wonder what starlings do with the members of the flock they don't like. To the outcasts. I bet they chase them out of the tree. I bet they peck them to death."

"You're not here because people don't like you, Tomás."

Tomás looked at her in surprise, and then he smiled sadly. "Sure I am. That's exactly why I'm here."

Another time Tomás said, "The biggest thing I can give you is my trust. What more do you want from me?"

Maggie didn't want anything, but she suspected Tomás did. He was staring at her in a way that reminded her of a dog that knew she carried a biscuit hidden in her pocket. It was getting harder and harder to think of him as fully human, which was what Valerie had been telling her all along. She knew it wasn't Tomás's fault. She knew the prison system cast them in roles and the roles came with feelings already attached to them, feelings that allowed people to believe that prisoners were getting what they deserved, but she couldn't help experiencing a tiny bit of revulsion, a tiny sense that Tomás could be more respectable if he wanted to be, a little less fawning and servile. A little bit more like George, she couldn't help thinking—if only Tomás were dashing!

"Stand up straight!" she commanded the next time he came slinking into the schoolroom with that expectant hangdog look. It crossed her mind not to give him the slice of cake she carried in her purse. She would hand it over to the old man weeping and wringing his hands at the next table just to teach Tomás a lesson.

But what would she be teaching him? That he had no power in his relationship with her? That anyone who wanted to could give him a command and he would have to follow it? It was something he knew all too well. It was the reason for his servile demeanor in the first place. She took out the cake wrapped in the crumpled wedge of foil and said as cheerfully as she could, "Look what I brought you, Tomás. A nice piece of cake for your dessert."

# 5.6 DOLLY

Dolly had spent the past two years avoiding news about the war, but now that Danny was coming home, people she knew kept calling her up with the latest reports: They were winning the war, they were losing it, they were winning, but at a terrible cost. They were fighting for freedom, or maybe they were fighting for oil—in either case, they were touching hearts and minds. They were winning the peace unless they were losing it. No one was really sure.

She decided the coming-home party would include both the baseball game and the patriotic theme. After all, the Fourth of July was coming up—what had made her think she had to choose one over the other? Once that was settled, everything started to fall into place. She had met Danny at a Fourth of July celebration four years before, and the patriotic theme not only honored his service to his country, but was also a reminder of their history as a couple. She bought a tablecloth patterned like an American flag and tied red and blue ribbons around white candles for the tables and bought boxes of sparklers for the guests and researched brisket recipes and stockpiled cases of beer.

Danny's arrival had been delayed by several weeks so the returning troops could get medical care and finish up their discharge paperwork.

"What medical care?" Dolly asked when Danny told her about it. "I thought you were okay. You're okay, aren't you?"

"It's nothing, baby. Just protocol. Mostly we sit around and wait."

"It'll all be over soon," said Dolly, and Danny replied, "I know it, babe. I know it will."

But it wasn't over, or if it was, something else was beginning. Danny didn't notice the pretty apartment Dolly had worked so hard on; he noticed the smudges on the windows. He noticed a chip in the new floor tile.

"You should get that tile guy back and make him fix it," said Danny, who was speaking in a loud voice and clenching his fists. "Get him back here, and I'll talk to him myself."

Dolly had no one to confide in, no one to tell her, You're worried about nothing! No one to say, They all come home a little agitated and they all get better—all it takes is a little time. No one, that is, except for her sister, who was burdened with troubles of her own, and her friends, who, if she said anything negative, would look at Danny skeptically from then on. And she couldn't call her mother. Her mother would say, You didn't take my advice about your career, and you didn't take my advice about that peach prom dress, so why would I give you any advice now? And then she would give it anyway, and it would entirely miss the point. The person Dolly wanted to confide in was Danny, but Danny was creeping around at night with a cleaning bucket when he thought she was asleep. Or he was chipping out the broken tile and ruining the floor, or he was lying awake and twitching, or he was dozing restlessly and calling out unintelligible things in his sleep.

Danny almost didn't come to the party, which Dolly had scheduled for the second Saturday he was home. "I don't really want to see anybody," he said. "I won't know what to say to them."

"You don't have to say anything," said Dolly.

"Then they'll just talk about me behind my back."

They argued because Dolly thought he should wear his uniform to the party and Danny thought he shouldn't. "It's just what people will expect," she said.

"How am I gonna play baseball in a uniform?"

"Okay, baby. Okay."

Throughout the party, Dolly felt like she was trying too hard. She ran from the picnic area to the car and back again. She found stones to weight the tablecloths against the wind, and when people didn't seem to be mingling, she passed out some of the sparklers. Then she turned on the CD player she had brought with her and danced frantically around. She got one of Danny's friends to make a toast, enlisted Tula and Will to drum up support for the baseball game, and then she pretended to drop the ball when Danny hit a fly right to her. "Home run!" she cried, forgetting for a minute that she shouldn't be rooting for Danny's team.

Danny trotted around the bases and put his arms up in the air, but his heart didn't seem to be in it, and he immediately put them down again. Danny's brother passed out a round of beers between each of the innings, and as the game wore on, it began to seem as if something more than bragging rights was at stake. One by one, the women dropped out until it was only the men winging balls back and forth and stumbling around the bases and whacking aluminum bats at each other in the fading light.

When it was too dark to continue, someone made a bonfire in a garbage can to burn all of the party debris, and then they had a contest involving the rest of the beer until the police came and told them to shut it down. "Park closes at dusk," said the officer. "Can't you read the sign?"

"He's a war hero," said Will, pointing to Danny. Flames were shooting out of the garbage can and turning the assembled faces orange. Now and then someone would throw in a box of sparklers, and bouquets of silver sparks would blossom and hiss. Danny stared into the fire as if he was hypnotized, and later on Dolly saw a girl grab him and kiss him, but she forgave him. She forgave him right away.

"I shouldn't have bought so much beer," she said as the women tried to corral the men and drag them off.

A woman named Kathy, who had come with one of Danny's military friends, said she'd be happy to meet for coffee if Dolly ever wanted to talk.

"About what?" asked Dolly, but in her heart she knew what Kathy meant.

"About what to expect. About making sure you and Danny are on the same page."

Over coffee, Kathy suggested that Danny and Dolly make lists of things like core beliefs and life goals. Then they could use the lists as planning tools for the future. "We also have a house rule that says we have to give two compliments before we say anything critical, so Mike has to tell me the dinner was good and my hair looks nice before he can tell me to shut the fuck up."

"Danny doesn't talk like that," said Dolly, which was one of the things that made her think things were going to be okay, even if one of the things that made her think they weren't was that Danny could go for a long time without talking at all.

That evening Dolly told Danny that even though they had both changed, they still had a lot of things in common.

"Like what?" asked Danny.

"Life goals," said Dolly. "Not to mention core beliefs."

She got two sheets of paper and two felt-tip pens and said they were going to write down ten things that were essential to a strong relationship.

"Nouns or adjectives?" asked Danny.

"We'll start with core beliefs," said Dolly, "so I guess that's

167

nouns." She felt vindicated when many of the words on the two lists matched. "You see?" she said. "We both believe in honesty and love and brotherhood and respect."

"You wrote down brotherhood?" asked Danny.

"I did," said Dolly. Kathy had told her how important brotherhood was to soldiers, which is why she had included it on her list. Besides, anything important to Danny was important to her, so it wasn't a completely dishonest thing to do. But the other words came from her heart. One of the most important words on Dolly's list was "family," and she was disappointed and a little shocked that the word was missing from Danny's list. But perhaps to Danny, family was a life goal, and she had been clear that they were going to concentrate on beliefs first. Still, there was enough agreement that she could use the lists to prove her point.

"What was your point again?" asked Danny, so she repeated her speech about building a future together based on common values. "Our core beliefs are the foundation. Our goals are the engine."

"Are you building something we can live in or something we can drive?" asked Danny, laughing.

"You know what I mean," said Dolly. Then she laughed a little too. "Keep your sense of humor," Kathy had said. "As long as you can laugh together, you have a fighting chance."

"See, honey? Sixty percent of our core beliefs are identical."

"I only put 'God' on my list because I knew he would be on yours," Danny told her the next day. "And 'peace.' I put that down because you look like a jerk if you don't believe in peace. I mean, what am I going to write—that I believe in war?"

But love was first on both their lists, and that had to count for something. Danny hadn't mentioned marriage since he got home, and Dolly was eager to see what his goals list looked like, but she didn't want to rush it. Both Kathy and the counselor at the VA hospital said the most important thing was for her to be understanding and the second most important thing was patience. "We'll work on goals next," she said, "but we have plenty of time for that."

## 5.7 WILL

That summer the big news in Red Bud was that McKnight's was switching to organic, free-range chicken. "There's money in doing the right thing," said Bill McKnight when Will showed up for the first day of his summer job. "So anything you can do to make people feel sorry for the non-organic chickens will be really good for us."

"Okay," said Will. "Sure thing."

"If this doesn't work out, I'll have to contract with a big conglomerate, and half the independents who do that go out of business within three years."

"You can count on me," said Will.

A man with a blowtorch came to cut little holes in the sides of the aluminum chicken barns that ran like barracks over a forty-acre patch of ground on the west side of town. Inside, the doors to the chicken cages were wired open, and if a chicken got up the gumption to exit the nesting box that was all it had known since being moved from the hatchery, it could theoretically hop down to a sawdust walkway and make its way, right or left, to one of the newly cut openings. And, if it found the nerve to step through the opening, it might enjoy a little morning or afternoon sunshine, depending on which side of the barn the chicken found itself and at what time of the day it had chosen to venture out. It might even peck at a piece of honest-to-goodness ground if it didn't first die of fright at its encounter with the unknown, for chickens were not known to be courageous.

In all of June and July, Will never saw a chicken take advantage of this opportunity, but he liked it that the doors were there. It was a poultry version of the American dream, for all that was promised to Americans was the freedom to pursue happiness, not happiness itself, and it gave him a little frisson of excitement to think ahead to graduation, when he and his classmates would file up to the opening in their own lives and some of them would step right through it and a few of them would fly away.

Because he didn't have a car, Will rode a bicycle to McKnight's in the morning, and after work he rode it to practice for his summer baseball league. His afternoon route took him near the Ash Creek part of town, where Tula lived. If he had time, he liked to circle past her little ranch house so she could sit with him while he ate the extra sandwich his mother had packed because it was too far to go all the way home to eat.

Will also liked to visit the stores near the train tracks where the shelves were arrayed with the cheap, exotic things women needed for their lives. He liked the familiar way the shopgirls bantered and the sense of being perched on a hill overlooking a wide valley of choices. He always had the feeling he was invisible to the girls as he sauntered up and down past the tables of jewelry and undergarments, listening to their conversations, until one day a tall, attractive girl called out, "Wachulookinat?" He stayed away for a week, but eventually he crept back, armed with the camouflage of a shopping list and a small wad of cash, and told the girl he was there to buy a present for his mother.

"Your mother! Ainchu the ladies' man." She laughed before leading him to a display case full of cheap jewelry that looked like gold until the coloring rubbed off a week later against his mother's skin.

After the trip to the women's clinic, Will decided he should buy something for Tula too. He was writing his scholarship essay on his experience at the clinic, and he wanted to give Tula something to show his appreciation.

"Another present for your momma?" asked the girl.

Will had inherited from Lyle the ability to make his face blank, a trick that resulted in other people's reading into his expression whatever they hoped to find in it, and now the girl said, "Or are you jes comintasee me."

"It's for my girlfriend," said Will.

"Who's your girlfriend?" asked a second girl, who was sitting at the cash register reading a magazine. "See if I know her."

"Tula Santos," said Will.

This revelation sent the girl with the magazine into peals of laughter. "The Virgin Mary herself!" she cried. "I thought she was into all of that purity 'n' shit. I thought she was saving herself for Jesus."

"Here," said the tall girl. "How about getting her this little cross? This is just the kind of thing she'd like."

Will knew he had made a mistake mentioning Tula's name, but he squinted coolly at the girl and bought the cross. "I'll see you next time," he said, tucking his purchase into his pocket.

"Next time you need a gift, or next time you wantasee me?" she asked, following him to the door. Now she was smiling coyly, and the girl at the cash register gave him a friendly wave.

Will smiled back at them, feeling like he had cracked the code of how to deal with women. At least he felt that way until people at work started coming up to him and saying, "I hear you're dating Tula Santos." A few days after that Tula herself said, "I guess the girlfriend's always the last to know."

"It just kind of slipped out," said Will, trying to make his face a blank. "If you want, you can come by for dinner on Sunday. You can help me with my essay after."

"If I want?"

"I mean, I'd really like it if you came."

On Sunday, Will told his parents to stay in the kitchen while he greeted Tula at the door. The plan was to get a few minutes alone before taking her into the kitchen to introduce her.

"This is a nice surprise," said Lyle, who seemed to think Will wanted him to act as if they hadn't been expecting anyone.

"I'm sorry to barge in on your dinner," said Tula.

"You're not barging in," Will said to Tula, and to his father he said, "You knew Tula was coming, Dad. So it's not really a surprise." He expected his mother to smooth over the awkwardness, but she was bent over a sheaf of papers and he had to tug on her sleeve to get her attention.

Maggie had set the table with candles in special-occasion holders, but it was Tula who lit up the room, sparking off the faded china and transforming the old stories of Will's childhood his parents insisted on telling into fresh and hilarious gems just by listening. "Headfirst into the diaper pail!" cried Maggie, tears streaming from her eyes.

"How do you like working at the prison, Mrs. Rayburn?" asked Tula when the platters of food were empty and the laughter had died down.

"It's interesting," said Maggie. "And I'm working in the prison school, which is rewarding too."

"I'm glad it's working out," said Tula.

"It is for me," said Maggie. "But not so much for the prisoners." She tapped a quilted bag that slouched next to her on an empty chair.

"Okay!" said Will. "Who wants dessert?" But his mother was already opening the bag and spreading some papers across the surface of the table.

"I have evidence that some of the prisoners are innocent," said Maggie. "Others are serving life sentences for petty crimes, and many were forced to plead guilty even if they're not." She took a tiny booklet out of the bag and handed it across to Tula. "And did you know," she said, her voice dropping to a whisper, "that slavery is still absolutely legal?"

"At least you're making their lives a little better," said Tula.

"Am I?" asked Maggie. "That's like saying that the slaves are lucky to have roofs over their heads. If we're the ones who create the conditions, isn't it dishonest to feel virtuous for making them better?"

"You didn't create the conditions," said Lyle.

"No," said Maggie. "We all did."

"You're not the one who took their freedom away," said Will. "They lost it by committing a crime."

"That's only true for the ones who are guilty," said Maggie.

"But how do you know which is which?" asked Will. "I thought that's what the judge and jury were for."

"I've done a lot of research. I have some of the prison files right here, and the evidence is pretty overwhelming."

"Files?" asked Will. "Do you mean you stole something from the prison?"

"Heavens no," said Maggie. "These are only copies. Anyway, which is worse—taking the files or burying the evidence?"

Lyle jumped up from the table and began taking away the plates. "Stealing runs in the family," he said, giving Will a desperate wink. "Does anyone want to hear about the time Will stole third base?"

"I do, Dad!" cried Will. Anything was better than the embarrassing path they were on. But Maggie was already forging ahead with other facts and statistics: the increasingly burdensome laws and enforcement efforts that unfairly targeted minorities, the 33 percent of male African American babies who would grow up to spend some time in prison, the legions who would lose their voting rights for life and be ineligible for housing assistance or college loans, the confiscation of property based not on conviction but on arrest. "And get a load of this!" she cried, holding up a piece of paper with *Witness recants* scrawled across the top.

Will snatched up the ketchup bottle and then the hen salt-shaker, silently mourning the rooster pepper, which had broken long ago. The table rocked on the warped floor, its matchbook shim knocked out of place. The stubby candles slumped into their tarnished holders. In their frail light, everything seemed chipped and frayed, broken or about to break, including, he couldn't stop himself from noticing, his mother.

"Add to that the fact that people are practically forced to plead guilty," said Maggie, "and you can see how the system creates a permanent underclass."

"I don't see what you're going to do about it!" Will blurted out just as Tula said warmly, "There must be something you can do."

"I can see the headline now," said Will. "Red Bud mother orchestrates prison break to free innocent man."

"I'm not going to break anybody out of prison," said Maggie.

"That's what I mean," said Will. "There's probably nothing you can do."

"But what if we all felt that way?" asked Tula. "We're certainly not going to change things if we don't even try." Now she was moving around the table to sit with Maggie so that the women were allied against the men. It was Will who cleared the last of the dishes and Lyle who served up the yellow cake while the women exchanged Rainbow mottos and advice—because they believed in Justice and because Maggie had been a Rainbow Girl too, once upon a time. Dream rainbow dreams! Your smile is your rainbow, and you are the pot of gold!

"Does anyone want ice cream?" asked Lyle. But no ice cream was to be found, so Will poured glasses of milk to go with the cake while Tula told them that the Rainbow Inspiration that year was Sandra Day O'Connor, the former Supreme Court Justice. "Despite graduating third in her law school class, the only job offer she could get was as a legal secretary. But she didn't give up, and look what she accomplished."

"A Rainbow Girl never gives up!" cried Maggie.

"Why don't you contact her?" suggested Tula. "Some of the girls wrote to her a few years back and received a very nice letter in reply."

Will wanted to shout that these two adults had nothing to do with him, that they had only been thrown together by chance— but it wasn't only his parents. He too shared in the blame because he had lured Tula there under false pretenses: Future doctor! Normal family! Raised with love and optimism to believe that good would triumph in the end!

"Why don't you write to her too—one Rainbow Girl to another," Tula was suggesting. "It's a long shot, but maybe she would give you some advice."

"I couldn't," said Maggie. "Why would she care about me?"

"Once a Rainbow Girl, always a Rainbow Girl," said Tula.

"If it's advice you want, there's no one better than Pastor Price," interrupted Lyle. "He's sure to have some thoughts about what to do. What do you say, Maggie? How about we go talk to him and leave these young people alone?"

"Good idea," said Will, trading another despairing look with his dad. "You two go find the pastor, and Tula and I will finish cleaning up." He had expected his mother to protest, but she didn't. He had expected her to issue a set of instructions, but it was Lyle who said, "Don't forget the dishwasher's broken, so you have to wash and dry by hand." Of course it was! "And don't forget you have a game tomorrow evening." He never forgot a game!

"Don't forget that your mother and I both have to work, so you'll probably need to get a ride."

"I won't forget," said Will.

And then the candles were extinguished, replaced by the cheerful brightness of the overhead fluorescents, and Lyle and Maggie were out the door, after which Will crowded in at the sink next to Tula, getting in her way and letting his hands bump up against hers under the soapy water as they both tried to find the sponge. And suddenly he had to admit that in spite of his mother or even because of her, his first dinner with Tula was going pretty well.

## 5.8 PASTOR PRICE

When the doorbell rang, Pastor Price flipped the television to a religious station before opening the door to find Lyle Rayburn clutching his wife by the elbow. Lyle was saying something about how Maggie wanted to quit her job again, and Maggie was saying no, she didn't. "Slow down, slow down!" cried the pastor, ushering them into the living room, where they settled into the chairs he liked to use for visitors.

"Ask her about the stolen prison files," said Lyle, which launched Maggie into a speech about the Constitution and prisoners' rights.

"What is the point of a document that no one ever reads?" she asked.

At first the pastor thought she was talking about the Constitution, so he said, "I imagine the lawyers and judges read it."

"Or ones that people aren't even allowed to see," said Maggie. "Ones meant only for a small, secret audience, even though they affect everyone else. Shouldn't there be an open debate about that sort of thing?"

"I'd imagine that's what the man's trial was about," said the pastor, trying to follow the thread.

"If that's what you'd imagine, then you'd be wrong," said Maggie. "These documents are from after the trial. They were hidden away in the prison basement until I found them."

"Let's all take a deep breath," said the pastor. In order to illustrate, he took one himself. His lungs expanded against his rib cage, which swelled pleasantly against the soft brushed cotton of his shirt. Then he closed his eyes and slowly opened them again, as if he were emerging from a deep and peaceful trance. "I have my ear to the ground, and do you know what I hear?" he asked.

Maggie and Lyle didn't know.

"I hear that Maggie has gotten in over her head and is looking for a graceful way out. If there's anything I know about, it's grace."

Price was pleased with this formulation, but Maggie only stared grimly across the glass and mahogany coffee table while Lyle looked on, bewildered. Tiffany had cautioned him more than once not to start off with abstractions, so the pastor tried a more personal approach and told the couple that in order to become a preacher, he had had to constantly battle his anarchist tendencies, not to mention his libidinous ones. "What I lacked in inner self-control was thankfully imposed from without by the church. I shudder to think what might have happened if I had been allowed to run wild."

"What would have happened?" asked Maggie.

"Praise the Lord we'll never know! But my point is that total freedom is a very frightening concept." Obedience was an under-rated virtue, and the pastor had been looking for an opportunity to work it in when Tiffany stuck her blond head through the kitchen door and asked if anyone wanted a glass of sweet tea.

"Do you have fresh mint?" asked the pastor.

"I do."

"And maybe some of those famous cookies?"

"Coming right up," said Tiffany, retreating back into the kitchen.

The pastor tried to remember where he had left off, but it didn't really matter since all roads led to the same place. "My point is that man-made structures—institutions like the church and the prisons, for instance—exist for a reason."

"I'm sure they exist for a reason," said Maggie. "But it's not always the reason everyone thinks. That's the thing that keeps me up at night." Then she poured out a confusing story about profit motives and someone named Tomás and the ACLU and a woman who was in love with another someone named George.

The television screen filled with a close-up of a preacher, his face uplifted and shining with sweat. A choir began to sing, and the camera panned out to take in their satin robes, their sparkling eyes, their white teeth and open mouths. "Look at that! Will you just look at that?" said the pastor, unable to take his eyes off the screen. His own services were being broadcast on the radio, but he had recently been approached by a TV producer, and he was cautiously optimistic.

"We like what we see," the producer had said when they met. "We also like what we hear about the Red Bud community. We're envisioning a weekly reality feature where you counsel members of your flock."

The counseling feature was in the pastor's mind as he switched off the television set and turned to look at Maggie: she was attractive, articulate, and more than a little misguided. Hells bells—she'd be perfect for the show! He almost said it out loud—praise the Lord he didn't—but this was just the sort of thing audiences would want to see.

A crash emanated from the kitchen. Hells bells! he thought again as Tiffany came scurrying into the room with a tray of drinks. "The cookies—" she said, but the pastor waved his hand and said to forget the cookies. He made a rectangle of his fingers as if he were setting up the frame: Maggie's white face, Lyle's frightened eyes. They'd be filming in the parish hall, so Tiffany's stack of romance novels and the photographs of her in her high school cheerleading uniform wouldn't be in the shot.

When Maggie stopped talking, the pastor said, "All I can tell you is that this might be God's way of winning George and Tomás and their fellow inmates over. Prison can be a powerful force in getting us to reassess our lives. Has George accepted the Word of God? Has Tomás acknowledged the Living Christ? That is where your efforts should be concentrated. What is freedom of the body without the surpassing freedom of the soul? What an opportunity for you to do some good!"

"But how would we feel if we were in their position?" asked

Maggie. "How would we feel if we were wrongly convicted and no one would listen to us?"

"That would feel terrible," said the pastor. He liked to agree with his opponent whenever possible. They expected him to argue, so he peppered his speech with phrases like, "you're right there!" or "one hundred percent correctamente!" Then he'd pause for a moment to reinforce the bond of agreement before executing a quick pivot. He reached out to touch Maggie's arm as he said, "Modern Americans worry far too much about feelings. Besides, what would feel worse, a few years in prison or an eternity in hell?"

"I don't think that's the choice," said Maggie.

Lyle had been sitting quietly, but now he said, "I'm sorry, Pastor, but you can see she's not herself."

"This is who I am, Lyle. For years we've only seen one side of each other, but there's more to both of us—at least I hope there is."

When Price pointed out the opportunity for showing compassion and brotherly love, Maggie cried out, "But I don't love them! To tell you the truth, most of them give me the creeps. But that's not their fault. It's the prison. It puts people in a position where all they can do is take, so why should I feel good about giving? I shouldn't. I should feel terrible about it, and I do."

"Then perhaps you are not ready for this particular challenge, my child." The pastor was remembering his own sense of superiority, his own feelings of—well, "repugnance" was a strong word—but he was quietly glad that he was not alone in his humanity. He was quietly glad of this reminder that he too needed to be vigilant about humility and service. Perhaps God had sent Maggie precisely to remind him of that very thing. "Perhaps you have taken on too big a task," he said. "There are many other charitable venues. Tiffany is a dynamo when it comes to organizing the efforts of the parish. Ask her about her Mothers of Mercy initiatives—MoMs for short. Perhaps you'd be better off choosing one of those."

"It's not about me being better off, and why should I get to pick and choose?" cried Maggie. "This thing chose me, and I should at least see it through."

Tiffany came into the room with a plate of broken cookies. Even though he knew they had been on the floor, Price took one and complimented his wife on the delicate flavor. "Do I detect a hint of cinnamon?" he asked.

Now that the niceties were over, the pastor let his eyes burn into Maggie's until she looked away. They had come to the point of the encounter, and he wanted her to know it. The husband wasn't capable of understanding, but when Maggie looked back at him, Price could see she was. "I'm sure there's an easy solution," he said. One of his techniques was to lull the parishioner with calming adjectives before delivering his toughest judgment. He said "easy" a second time, and then he said "comfortable" and "humble" before telling her, "You'll find that the right thing is usually the one you want to do anyway." Pastoral counseling was like the martial arts, where a combatant used his opponent's own weight and momentum to defeat him or her. "It is my experience that a person's biggest enemy is herself and that seemingly insurmountable obstacles and complications are often self-imposed."

Price could see he was making progress. Lyle's mouth had gone from a thin, grim line to slack-lipped admiration, and Maggie's eyes had gone from glassy and wild to flat and blank. He would eventually get them both to smile, but he wasn't ready for that yet. He had to finish applying the lesson first. "We are the ones who clamp the manacles around our own wrists," he said, letting a note of hollow warning into his voice. "And we are the only ones who can take them off." Now his voice became lighter, optimistic.

"That is true of George and Tomás, and it is true of you as well. George and Tomás got entangled with the law because of their own actions. And they are only wrongly convicted (here, the pastor made a set of air quotes) because you have decided that is the case. It is completely within your power to decide otherwise."

"Maggie doesn't want to be unfair," Lyle began, but the pastor interrupted him.

"How is she being unfair? Is she the one who put those men in prison? Is she now the judge and jury too? It is my view that the problem is not with the American system of jurisprudence; the problem is with Maggie herself. And that is actually very good news, because it is a much easier problem to solve."

Lyle shuffled his feet and brushed the cookie crumbs from his trousers. Then he gave a slight nod.

"The problem," said the pastor, "is one of grandiosity. Maggie thinks she can know more about these things than highly qualified professionals. That's just wrongheaded, and nothing good will come of it."

Now it was time to get Maggie to admit her role in things. Now it was time to draw closer to her and to use what he thought of as his boudoir voice, but the version with an implied threat. Finally, a tear rolled down Maggie's cheek and she admitted, "Maybe you're right."

"It's my business to be right," said the pastor, slipping into the mode he called release-and-resolution. "But I've been at this a long time. I want you to feel the rightness too. Most of all, I want you to be right with God."

Now the pastor turned to Lyle. "I have a little advice for you too, Lyle. It's what I tell my midlife crisis couples. We talk a lot about negotiation. We talk about giving your loved one permission to do something a little crazy. Maggie agrees in advance that it will be just one slightly crazy thing, then back to business. And you agree that there will be no questions asked. Do you think you two could come to an arrangement like that?" Price wondered if he and Tiffany would ever come to the point where they needed to allow each other extra leeway. He hoped not, but he had seen enough couples to know that life was predictably unpredictable.

It was nearly eleven o'clock when he told the joke he liked to close that sort of session with. He had a little store of them that proved he didn't take himself too seriously. "How many New Incarnation pastors does it take to screw in a lightbulb?" he asked.

Maggie stared at him, but Lyle was smiling already, even before the punch line.

"Three!" declared the pastor in a hearty voice. "One to hold the ladder, one to screw in the bulb, and one to ask you if you've seen the light."

# 6.0 SWEAT AND TEARS

*The surge meant going forward—who ever heard of surging back? So I wasn't going to spend a lot of time crying over mistakes we couldn't do a goddamned thing about.*

—Lieutenant Colonel Gordon Falwell

*Now we had the official incident report and a couple hundred newspaper stories called "Heroic Rescue." No one was asking what those men were doing there in the first place. Who was going to go looking for an email they didn't even know exists?*

—Captain Penn Sinclair

*I sent Danny off to war, but I was never quite certain it was Danny who came home.*

—Dolly Jackson

*There was something different about Le Roy. At first I couldn't put my finger on it, but then he started up at the community college, taking a programming class. That's when I realized how much that man had changed.*

—E'Laine Washington

*Suddenly Le Roy was a fucking genius.*

—Corporal Joe Kelly

# 6.1 PENN SINCLAIR

Penn sat across the table from the beautiful Louise Grayson, who had waited for him, who had believed his promises that he would somehow put his trust fund and philosophy degree to work building an empire and that he would marry her as soon as he got home. He had been home for three weeks, and so far neither of them had brought up the subject of marriage. If he wanted to talk, she listened. If he wanted to be alone, she went out for dinner with a friend. Night after night he lay in bed, sweating next to the cool Louise, and night after night she brought him a glass of orange juice and a scented cloth for his forehead.

But now Louise had arranged a lunch so they could talk about his future. When her cell phone kept clamoring for attention, she held up a finger and rolled her eyes. "Did I say ivory?" she said into the phone, tapping a polished nail on the tablecloth for emphasis. "I absolutely meant ecru."

Penn found it hard to follow the conversation—what was the difference between sautéed and braised? Would the vegetarian stuffing work for the gluten intolerant? Did they need one bartender or two? Three servers or four?

As Louise talked, Penn watched the waiters hurry back and forth from the kitchen carrying aromatic dishes and tried to imagine what their lives were like. Across the room, a thin glass window looked onto a SoHo street, with its scaffolding and construction workers and honking taxis and harried pedestrians, all living lives that were opaque to him. It was as if he had crossed into a parallel universe and was searching for a way back. He had assumed the disconnection must have happened in Iraq, but now he realized he had been looking out the window all his life and only rarely making contact: the night he had first slipped the straps of Louise's camisole over her ivory shoulder blades, the philosophy and Latin classes at Princeton, the small brick caretaker's cottage he pictured when he thought of home, even though the tiny building occupied only a forgotten corner of the sprawling Greenwich estate that had been in the Sinclair family for more than ninety years.

"Brides," said Louise, finally hanging up, and it occurred to Penn that the real point of the lunch was to demonstrate how busy she was, how opposite of needy and grasping, how far from ready to be a bride herself.

"I'll take your word for it," said Penn, who had a sense that if one of the passersby pulled out a gun and shot through the glass into the restaurant, the bullet would pass right through him, as if he wasn't really there.

"Someday you'll find out for yourself," said Louise with a laugh to show that she wasn't being serious even though she was.

Louise's happily-ever-after included two cherubic figments of her imagination named Joseph and Jules. Their pink and blue nurseries were oft-visited rooms in her consciousness. She could describe the darling gingham furniture and soft cotton clothing and daily routines with the precision of an event-planning professional, which was what she was, and because she could imagine those things, Penn could imagine them too: the orderly closets and brightly colored educational toys and the children themselves, beautiful and well-dressed, of course, miniature versions of Louise. The event that held the least reality for her was the explosion of a short string of IEDs that had blown five of Penn's men to kingdom come and left two others wandering in a wilderness of misfiring neurons and brain chemicals run amok. While they waited for the main course to arrive, he spoke the sentences he had committed to memory as he was lying awake in Louise's big four-poster bed the night before.

"But that doesn't really change anything," sniffled Louise, who started to cry before he came to the second clause of the second careful sentence, before he got to the reassurances that he still loved her but that the thing he was had changed so profoundly that the only way to express his love was to leave her.

"Someday you'll see I set you free."

That had been sentence number four. It had sounded convincing in Penn's imagination, but now it seemed hollow and contrived. He hurried on. "In an ideal world ... " he started, but before he could spit out the rest of sentence number five, the red-faced Louise mumbled, "But I don't want to be free!"

Penn wanted to shake her. Freedom! Wasn't that the casus belli that had remained like a golden nugget in the sieve of official excuses once all the silt of lies had washed away? If people like Louise didn't want freedom, what had everything been for?

"I have to do what I think is right," said Penn, the carefully planned speech forgotten. He was crying now too. He was picturing the life he might have had with Louise. And he was picturing the men he had sent on the mission—proud and insubordinate and radiating energy and health. And then he was seeing the men who had come back from it—shaken men, men who were bloody and frightened and changed. "I made a mistake," he told her. "I have to try to make up for it."

"It's not as if you can undo it," said Louise. Across the street, a man slipped on the scaffolding and caught himself.

"Of course I can't make up for it, but I have to do something. I can't pretend nothing happened."

A taxi discharged a woman who carried a small dog in her purse. A businessman strode past, talking angrily into his phone. A girl in a yellow dress thought better of crossing against the light.

"It was a war, Penn. Everybody makes mistakes in war—frankly, it's kind of a cliché. And what about the mistake you're making now?"

"It isn't an easy decision—I think you know that."

"At least you get to make it," said Louise slowly, testing the implications of casting herself in the victim role. "I just have to live with the results."

*"Id est quod est,"* said Penn. "It is what it is." He was going over the insubordination incident in his mind. What had made him so sure it wouldn't burn itself out? What had made him think getting the men off the base was critical to preventing trouble? But the supplies had to go eventually—the colonel was right that no time would have been safe. And since the men had been eager to finish the school—at least he thought they were—he had decided he could kill three birds with one stone. If only all he had killed were birds.

"We don't have to decide now," Louise declared. "Anyway, you're better off staying with me than with your parents. At least until you get settled. At least until you find a job and a place of your own. Then we can talk about this again."

Settled, thought Penn. How would he ever be settled? He felt like a stranger washed up on a foreign shore, and Louise was either a towrope back to the world he had come from or an anchor preventing him from fully escaping. One day he felt one way about it and the next another. And then it seemed to him that the colonel was right that worrying about such things was misguided. Why did it matter what a thing was like? Why wasn't it good enough just to name it in the usual way without thinking you'd find something else if you peeled away the layers? Sometimes he wished the colonel were there to tell him what to do. Then he would just do it, no questions asked.

## 6.2 DANNY JOINER

Danny came home from the war with angry conversations taking place in his head. Whenever he closed his eyes, he saw Pig Eye's body disintegrating in a volcano of blood and guts, and whenever he opened them, he heard a voice say, Why didn't you see him? What are you, a fucking moron? Sometimes the dominant voice was his own, but other times the voices belonged to strangers who were criticizing him for things he did or didn't do. He thought one of the voices might belong to an old drill sergeant, a gruff man no one really liked but they all respected. All of the voices made good points, but the things they were upset about were all things Danny couldn't control.

"You can't control them, but you can write them down," said the therapist at the veteran's hospital where Danny went when the voices got too loud, when he had to shout to be heard above them, and when Dolly went to stay with her mother for another night. "Writing is as good as therapy, you'll see," said the therapist.

Danny was already starting to notice things he hadn't seen before. He was already starting to find words for them. The reception desk was gunmetal gray and the sun exploded in at the window and the therapist's eyes were bombed-out black and the atmosphere in the room was riddled with tension. When Danny started paying attention to the words, some of the tightness went out of him. It was like putting the safety back on in order to smoke a cigarette or take a piss.

"Writers aren't the same as other people," said the therapist. "They use their pain as material. When life deals them lemons, they make lemonade."

Danny didn't think he was dealing with lemons, but instead of arguing about the exact nature of his hand, he said he'd like to write a play, or possibly a television series. He had an idea for a show where some returning soldiers banded together to stop the war. For the first time since coming home, he was hopeful. For the first time it seemed like he could give the voices a useful task to do, but the voices had ideas of their own.

—I'd like to see you try! one of them said, and another one called the therapist a quack.

—Don't listen to that quack, said the voice.

In any case, appointments were hard to get, and after three months of shuttling between therapists and prescribing doctors, Danny had a diagnosis, but no real understanding of what was wrong with him or how to fix it. He purchased a spiral-bound notebook, and instead of blocking the voices out, he listened closely to what they were saying. At first they berated him for everything he had done wrong in his life, and then they started in on the things he thought he'd done right.

—What are you doing with Dolly, anyway? they asked. Are you trying to ruin her life as well as your own?

Occasionally he heard his own voice rise in explanation or defense, but just as often he silently acknowledged that no defense was possible and merely sat with the sand-colored notebook in his lap and watched the volcano of exploding body parts and wrote the ranting down.

# 6.3 LE ROY JONES

Le Roy aimed his weapon at the mouse-shaped target on the screen. It was tempting to neutralize it, but no, he'd save it for later—let it almost reach the safe house and get it then. He was creating the game for his programming class, and already he had five levels of complexity when only two had been required. He liked it that in the game world, he could have purple dreadlocks and tattoos and an ability to show mercy but also to make instantaneous life-and-death decisions. He strode across the virtual landscape pushing trees and boulders out of his way and gaining strength and speed by capturing targets. Five points for the square blue ones, fifteen if they were round and red—more if they had little ear buds and a tail.

"What are you up to?" asked E'Laine when she came home from work. "How was the shop today?"

"Good," said Le Roy. He was surprised to see E'Laine. If he didn't want to be surprised, he had to read the list they made together each evening and he had to set the alarm and he had to take off his headphones and turn his chair so it was facing the door. He knew he'd hit his head and it had changed him, but he liked the way he was now even if certain things caught him unawares. He liked working at the shop's computer repair desk and he liked his online classes and he liked creating games and playing them. He liked the Boolean universe, where things were true or false, yes or no, one or zero—everything logical and ordered according to rules he was learning in his classes.

While he was distracted by E'Laine, his avatar rounded a corner, smack into two of the crosshatched monsters who roamed the hills of his online universe. Luckily for him, a roving robot programmed to annihilate enemy forces saw them and fired, saving his avatar from a serious loss of power. He panned the screen out, saw that the mouselike target was almost at the safe house, took a reading, and punched in the coordinates. Then he hit the enter key and blasted it to smithereens.

"What should I get for dinner?" asked E'Laine.

Le Roy didn't know. "What do you want?" he asked.

"Shall I make lasagna?"

E'Laine was learning. He liked questions where he could say yes or no, either of which would flip open the gate to the next decision point, the one about helping with the dishes, for instance—yes, of course he would! He was learning too. And the one about walking down to the ice cream store and the one about strawberry or fudge brownie swirl. But sometimes she said a lot of complicated things about their relationship or asked the love question, and who knew what that door would lead to. Marriage, E'Laine said, and children and things Le Roy used to care about but couldn't even imagine now.

"Do you want to make the salad?" asked E'Laine. It was a funny question, but he said yes, and then he did want to. He wanted to dice the tomatoes into one-inch squares and measure out the oil and salt with the blue plastic measuring set, everything in proportion, and later, when she was licking ice cream from his chin, it seemed fine to say he loved her even if he couldn't quite remember how love was supposed to feel.


## 6.4 JOE KELLY


Joe Kelly arrived home to a parade. He was ushered into a light-blue convertible next to a man in uniform he had never seen before and driven through the streets of Hoboken in a long line of cars on loan from a local dealership. The cars in front and behind were full of people with pressed uniforms and stunned eyes just as he himself was stunned and pressed. They stopped frequently, and every time they stopped, someone would lean in at the window to kiss him, the unexpected proximity triggering his adrenaline button and causing the sweat to pool in his armpits.

"What's the matter, man? Doncha like girls?" asked the soldier sitting next to him in the back seat.

The breeze was cool on Kelly's brow, but he felt hot, as if the desert heat were trapped inside him or applied like a compress to his body, as if it were a feature of the cloth the uniform was made of or maybe stitched directly to his skin. Sometimes it was a child who leaned in to kiss him, held aloft by a relative who grinned and yammered at him, and sometimes it was a pretty young woman Kelly would have liked knowing before the war. Back then, he would have enjoyed sitting in the shiny car. He would have enjoyed imagining he owned it. He would have imagined one of the women was sitting next to him instead of the soldier and that she was kissing him for real. He wouldn't have minded sitting in the car now if he hadn't had to take a leak so badly, so at the next stop, he jumped out without opening the door and relieved himself at the side of the road.

"Hey! Hey!" shouted the bystanders. "Cut it out!" But Kelly paid no attention to them, looking instead at the glittering sidewalk and imagining a line of ants were enemy forces and he was the mighty rain god, dispatched to do them in.

"What did you do that for?" asked the other soldier when Kelly hopped back into the open car, and Kelly told him he had had to take a leak. He enjoyed kissing the girls a lot more after that.

## 6.5 DANNY JOINER

—And what do you say to the charges?

—Charges?

—Of burning the American flag. Let's start with that.

—I didn't burn the American flag.

—Fourth of July picnic? Coming-home party not so long ago? You have to remember that at least.

—I went to a lot of picnics. I can't be expected to remember them all.

—You met Dolly at a picnic. She was with that tall guy. The guy with the white truck. She came with him, but she went home with you. Surely that must ring a bell!

Of course he remembered meeting Dolly. She had been wearing a cowboy hat and a denim skirt. But there had been so many Fourth of July picnics, so many bonfires, so many flags and banners and garlands and bunting—did garlands and bunting count as flags?

—Is it an American flag if it doesn't have fifty stars?

—Why do you want to know?

—If it's just a paper decoration, is it an American flag then?

—Why the fuck do you want to know?

—Because it makes a difference, doesn't it?

The memory coalesced and then disintegrated: Dolly when she graduated from the nursing program. Dolly back when she was happy and he hadn't yet gone to war. Dolly kissing him and waving. And then the coming-home party, which had taken place two nights before: a bonfire, some bottle rockets and sparklers, plenty of beer and old friends and the baseball game, which started off friendly and then got a little heated. He remembered hot dogs and grilled corn and some little white paper dumplings that exploded on contact when they hit the ground. One of the guys had brought a gun. Danny hadn't touched the gun. He knew he hadn't touched it.

—I didn't touch the gun.

—Did I say anything about a gun?

The napkins had been printed with a holiday motif, but whether there had been thirteen stripes, starting with red, he couldn't say. He couldn't say if there had been fifty stars or some other number. The tablecloths had been red, white, and blue—he was sure of that. And they had stars. He hadn't counted them, but he definitely remembered stars.

He remembered long-ago bonfires and also more recent ones, including one where he had gotten drunk and kissed a girl who

197

wasn't Dolly, something he regretted now. The girl had laughed and said she had to help clean up, so he said he would help her, which is when he had pulled the spangled cloth off of the table and thrown it into the fire, which had flared gloriously toward the heavens. He had thrown the bunting into the fire too, and the paper plates, and the little dumplings and the corncobs and the sparklers—anything that would burn. Anything that would explode. He threw in the napkins, and when the older people had all gone off, the younger ones turned up the music and started to dance.

—Now let's talk about those two boys.

—I wasn't there.

—But you knew about it. You could have told.

—You don't tell on your buddies. No matter what, you keep your buddies safe.

—Then how do you explain Pig Eye?

He couldn't explain Pig Eye. Pig Eye hadn't even been there, and then, suddenly, he was.

## 6.6 PENN SINCLAIR

Summer was almost over, and Penn was still living with Louise. Every time she smiled at him or called him Huggy Bear, he wondered if he had imagined the conversation in the SoHo restaurant. Or maybe Louise had just forgotten it, for whenever the subject of the future came up, she talked as if they were in agreement on what it would look like. He should have gotten a job by now, but interviews made him sweat and stumble over his words, and if he got a call back, he didn't return the call.

"You just hang in there, Huggy Bear," said Louise. "Something is sure to pop." She liked to use words that sounded like their meaning. "Buck up," she would say. "Worse comes to worst, you can always work for my dad. That would be a total hoot."

Louise threw out the offer like a rope to a drowning man, but Penn knew what was on the other end of it. Louise's father, for one thing, and for another thing, Louise herself. But he also knew that none of it was Louise's fault—the rope alone would drag him under. "Okay," he would say whenever she mentioned it. "I've got something on the line, but if it doesn't come through, I'll seriously consider it."

"How seriously?"

"One hundred percent."

Ever since arriving home, Penn had been glued to the Internet, trying to figure out the depth of his mistake—its meaning and historical context, and if it had been avoidable or fated. If it hadn't happened to him and his men, would it have happened to someone else? This led to questions about the role of an individual tasked with acting decisively and even brutally in service of the state, which fashioned itself guardian of ethics and morality—inwardly for the benefit of its own citizens (and along the way squeezing out outliers and misfits)—but also outwardly, forcing its superior vision onto others who were less enlightened. And what did the use of force say about the possibility of peace and also about the common good?

After studying every aspect of the current wars, he started on the wars of history. He was researching the Gulf of Tonkin, a false flag incident that was used to precipitate the last unwinnable war, when Louise came home with a bottle of wine and two noisy friends.

"I'll introduce you," he heard her say, but when she called out to him, he didn't respond. "He must be sleeping," said Louise. And then she added, "I swear, it's like he's living in a different world."

The women chattered about china patterns and how to deal with overbearing mothers-in-law before the talk turned to J-Lo's skin-care secret. Penn waited until the group stepped out onto the patio to admire the view before slipping Louise's library card out of her purse and leaving the apartment. He walked to the big downtown branch where he had been working his way through the history section instead of looking for a job. It was cool in the library. The shelves of books muffled the sounds.

By the time he had finished with the strafing of London and the Nazi death chambers, he had started to ask silent questions about the meaning of life. He didn't necessarily need to know what that meaning was; he only wanted to know if it had meaning or if it didn't. If it did, how did he explain the Srebrenica massacre or the shooting of Russian soldiers by German generals for sport, and if it didn't, why did he feel so sure it did?

"The answer's here somewhere," he said to himself. He didn't realize he was speaking aloud until a homeless man who had been dozing in a corner by the restrooms said, "Man is warlike." The man raised a grizzled hand, using a copy of Sun Tzu's *The Art of War* to shield his eyes from the bright egg-crate lights. "You can read any damn book you want, but that's what it comes down to."

"What?" asked Penn, startled to find he wasn't alone.

"Peace is an illusion. War is inevitable. That's fairly significant, don't you think?"

The two men stared at each other, the older man seemingly

stunned that it was taking Penn so long to absorb what he was saying, and Penn stunned by the realization that the answer he was seeking could be packed into three words. "Man is warlike," he repeated as the homeless man beamed at him and nodded his head.

Penn pulled out a foil-wrapped bagel Louise had put in his pocket that morning and offered the man one of the halves.

"I started out the same as you," said the man between bites. "I was home from Vietnam and looking for answers, so I came here. Of course, we didn't have the Internet back then, but I still found what I was looking for even if it took me a very long time to find it."

"How long?"

"Fifteen years, which is better than never, I guess. Which is how long it takes some people. Maybe even most people, but then again, most people never look. Believe me, I wasted a lot of time searching in the wrong places—bars, mostly—ha! But I finally found what I was looking for."

"In here?" asked Penn, picking up the volume with the warrior on the cover and weighing it in his hand.

"Yes, but also in here." He tapped his head. "Man is capable of nobility and high achievement, but the very same man has primitive impulses that can never be eradicated and will emerge full-force under the right conditions. It's useless to ask yourself if human beings are fundamentally good or not. They are fundamentally a lot of things. But death is the thing that gives life meaning. By extrapolation, then, war intensifies life and gives it meaning too."

A librarian rolled a reshelving cart past and peered at them over the tops of her glasses. "Excuse me, Professor," she said, "but you and your friend are in the way."

"Professor of what?" asked Penn.

"Ha!" said the professor. "Life, I guess."

Penn rolled the foil into a ball and lobbed it at a nearby trash can. "Three points," he said when he made the shot.

"You owe me more than half a bagel, seeing how I've saved you years of trouble," said the professor when he had finished eating.

Penn dug around in his pocket for his wallet. He took out all of the money he had and held it out to the professor, whose hand reached for it and then disappeared into his pocket with astonishing speed.

"Thank you," said the professor, saluting with fingers that wouldn't straighten. "Now, do you want to know what I learned in the next fifteen years?"

"Sure," said Penn. "Lay it on me."

"I learned that the system is designed to preserve itself, even if it has to grind you and me up into little pieces."

"That sounds bleak," said Penn.

The professor picked up a walking stick that was lying on the floor and started to get to his feet. "They don't really like me in here," he said. "The mayor is cracking down on homeless people. We give the city a bad name."

"Where will you go?"

"There's a shelter a few blocks from here, but they don't open 'til five. A better question is, why am I homeless?"

"I'll visit you again," said Penn, but he knew he probably wouldn't. Man was warlike. How could he have been so naïve as to think he had been fighting for peace? It was only the terms of the next war that were being decided. Everything had happened before. Everything would happen again.

Unless, he realized, someone did something to stop it.

# 6.7 DANNY JOINER

The doctor at the clinic abruptly changed Danny's diagnosis from post-traumatic stress disorder to personality disorder. "What's the difference?" asked Danny. "Why the change?"

"I'll give you this brochure to take home with you," said the doctor. "It should answer all of your questions, but if it doesn't, please don't hesitate to call."

When Danny called, he was informed that if he wanted to talk to the doctor, he would have to make another appointment, and if he made an appointment, he'd have to make it quickly, before he was discharged from the outpatient program and his benefits were stopped.

"Why would I be discharged? And why would my benefits stop?"

"Don't you have a brochure?" asked the pleasant female voice. "I can send you one if you want."

"But the doctor was already treating me. I'd like to speak with him."

"Hmm," said the voice. "They were already treating you? That would be unusual, given that personality disorder is a pre-existing condition, but give me your name and I'll see what I can do."

Danny told her his name and she relegated him to hold, where a British voice was announcing the news. Just when he was about to find out whether or not the trailers that had been donated to house refugees from Hurricane Katrina were toxic, another voice came on the line to tell him that in cases of personality disorder discharge, benefits were always discontinued.

"Discontinued!"

A broom handle was sticking out of one of the garbage cans that had been set out for morning pickup, and now he used it to whack at the lid of the can. "We're just like one of these garbage cans," he said into the phone.

"What?" said the voice on the other end of the line.

"We're not as useful," said Danny. "We're like the garbage in the cans."

—Don't take no for an answer, said the voice of the old drill sergeant.

"I'm not taking no for an answer," said Danny.

"I'm sorry, sir. It's Regulation Six-thirty-five dash two hundred, chapters five to thirteen. There's really nothing I can do."

—So you're quitting? I think you should march yourself back to that doctor's office and demand your rights. A soldier never accepts defeat.

The doctor had a bristly mustache and a black Mustang. "Do I know you?" he asked when Danny, who was holding the broom handle as if it were a rifle, stepped from behind a line of parked cars and said, "Hey, Doc.

"Apparently you know me well enough to tell me I have personality disorder."

"Oh, yes, yes." The doctor seemed defenseless without his white coat and hospital badge.

Danny's arms were nearly as big around as the doctor's thighs. If he and the doctor had met in a parking lot in downtown Baghdad, Danny could have ordered the doctor to drop his weapon and put his hands in the air. He considered doing it now, and then he did it. What the fuck? he thought. "Drop your weapon and put your hands in the air," he said.

"What? What are you talking about?" The doctor looked like a beaver. Behind the mustache his teeth were an unprofessional yellow. "I don't have a weapon," he said.

"Hands up," said Danny, moving in closer and tensing his biceps and causing the doctor to take a step backward until he was leaning against the faded fabric top of the Mustang.

Slowly, the doctor put his thin white hands in the air, dropping his keys to the pavement as he did so. "What do you want? Money? I don't have much, but you can have it." He was wearing a light blue shirt and a striped tie. His sleeves were rolled to show pale forearms and a gold wristwatch. It all made a nice picture against the black car, pleasing somehow.

—What do you mean "nice"?

—It's easy to distinguish the details, that's all. The black sets everything off.

—Then say that. Don't use some mealy word like "nice."

—Vivid, then. The black-as-petrified-shit background enhances the vomit-and-blood colors of the tie.

When Danny's eyes lingered on the watch, the doctor seemed relieved. "Do you want the watch?" he asked. "Do you want the car?"

"I want to know the difference between personality disorder and post-traumatic stress disorder," said Danny. "I want to know why you changed my diagnosis."

The doctor let his hands drop to his sides. "The medical review board is pressuring us to give lesser diagnoses," he said.

—Tell him to put his hands back in the air.

"Put your hands back in the air," said Danny. And then he said, "Shut up!"

"I didn't say anything," said the doctor.

"What's a lesser diagnosis?"

—Tell him to look you in the eye when he talks to you.

"What's a pre-existing condition?"

—Tell him to lie on his belly. Tell him to eat dirt.

"Lie down and eat the dirt!" shouted Danny.

The doctor dropped to his knees, hands shaking. "It means that you were already damaged when the army got you, so you're not their problem anymore. It means that every dollar they spend on you means less money for bullets and able-bodied soldiers." The doctor squeezed his eyes shut after he said it, as if Danny was going to hit him with the broom handle, but Danny figured that's what they wanted him to do. He might be damaged, but he wasn't a fool. He knew the rules that allowed sending someone off to war and then failing to help him didn't allow hitting a doctor. He knew that because one of the voices was shouting at him.

—If you hit him, they'll arrest you, asshole! Now tell him to stand the fuck up.

"Stand up!" shouted Danny, and the doctor stood up, holding the keys he had dropped and pressing a button on his key ring that started a horn blaring.

The commotion scared Danny so much that he raised the broom handle and brought it down on the Mustang's fabric top as close to the doctor's shoulder as he could without touching him. The breeze from the stick riffled the doctor's hair. The sound made him jump and his eyes popped open, bugging out almost comically as the car's emergency horn ripped through the sultry air until someone shouted at the doctor to shut it off and Pig Eye exploded in the distance for the thousandth time.

"I don't make the rules," said the doctor in self-defense, but the words sounded as puny and untrue as the doctor himself.

—Yes he does!

206

"Yeah, you do," said Danny.

"I don't. I swear to you I don't. There are rules and regulations." The doctor looked hopeful now that they were talking and the physical threat had receded somewhat.

Danny thought about using the broom handle to wipe the look off his face after all.

"There's a rule book," said the doctor, "but there are also monthly updates. My folder of updates is this thick." He stretched his thumb and fingers to illustrate.

—Tell him he's a fucking liar.

Danny was tired. The notebook was in his pocket, along with a mechanical pencil that had a reloadable cartridge for pencil leads and a retractable eraser. They all thought words could acquit them, when Danny knew that words could also be used to trick people and to control their thoughts. For instance, Danny had always considered America a place of equal opportunity because of words that had been drilled into him, not because of anything he observed. There was probably an evolutionary reason for this, but he didn't know what it was.

—Repeat after me, asshole. Say "equal opportunity." Fucking say "American dream."

Danny raised the broom handle in the air and brought it down again. "American dream," he said, but his heart wasn't in it. He was tired. He wasn't a violent person. "Here," he said to the doctor. "Take this stick, and next time you want to destroy someone, be honest about it and use this."

Then Danny sat on the curb and took out the notebook and wrote down what he could remember of the encounter. He didn't look back at the doctor, but he could imagine him taking up the broom handle and holding it over Danny's head.

—Never take your eyes off the enemy.

"Who's the enemy?"

"I don't know, but it's not me," said the doctor. "I hope you can find what you're looking for somewhere else."

The somewhere else was the army recruiting station where Danny had enlisted almost three years before. The soldiers there joined the chorus of voices shouting, "Who the fuck do you think you are?" at Danny. They must have called the police because a squad car roared up, followed by what seemed like a whole squadron of cars with sirens and loudspeakers.

"Come out with your hands up!" roared the speaker, but Danny's voices laughed and turned their venom outward.

—Who the fuck do they think they are!

For one blissful moment, Danny had the illusion that he was leading his old company in a daring attack against the enemy. Armed with nothing but a U.S. Army ballpoint pen he had picked up off the counter, he charged at the first policeman to come through the door. He held his pen like a rifle, took aim, and then he tossed the pen to the officer and laughed.

BE ALL YOU CAN BE, said the pen.


# 6.8 JOE KELLY


Kelly's parents had moved to New Jersey while he was overseas, and even though they greeted him with a banner over the door and arranged a gathering of neighbors, Kelly knew he didn't belong there and the sooner he left, the better.

"I'll bet you're glad to be home," said the people who came in the door carrying fragrant dishes and bottles of beer, and Kelly nodded and said he was.

"I'll bet you're glad to be home," said a strong-looking girl who lingered in the entry, primly settling a cardigan around her shoulders and assessing the crowd.

Kelly was about to say he was, but then he changed his mind. It was one thing for a bunch of old people to drop by to have meaningless conversations with him, but the only reason a girl like that would do it was because someone had told her to or because she was desperate. He kind of liked the desperate ones. They made him feel like a trained sniper at an arcade game. When she started to walk off, he said in a low voice, "Scared of soldiers?"

"Not really."

Game on, thought Kelly. "Well, I'm scared of big girls," he said, smiling to show he was playing with her, drawing it out a little—respectful, but sure of himself, like if she didn't want him now, he hoped she would change her mind. If he brought his A game, she might even end up thinking it was her idea. But where Kelly used to like to play the game straight through from "Hi, my name is Joe" to "Why didn't you warn me you're part tigress," an inner restlessness prompted him to make the game more challenging by cutting right to the chase. He couldn't see himself asking about her job or her family situation or giving her a bunch of meaningless compliments or making up some bullshit about his ambitions and goals, so he said, "You must be bored. Can I get you a drink or do you want to get straight to the sex?"

"What do you say we skip the drink and the sex and the wedding and the two kids," said the girl, "and we go straight to where I run off with another man."

"Shee-it," said Kelly. She wasn't desperate after all. "I must be losing my touch," he said. He smiled, and the girl cracked a smile too, at first like she was humoring him according to the rules of her own game, but then with her eyes too, smiling for real. Just when they were beginning to understand each other, Joe Senior limped over with a bowl of chips and introduced them.

"This is Rita. She works down at the U-Haul with me. Her uncle runs the dealership."

It was more than Kelly wanted to know. "Rita," he said. "Ri-ta."

"Joe," she said.

Now that she had a name and a family and a reason for being there, the game was less interesting, and he started marking the exits and keeping his back to the wall just in case. Just in case a fire-fight broke out. Just in case insurgents stormed the living room. He laughed and said, "For a minute there, I thought I was back in Iraq."

"That must be kind of weird," she said.

It was the conversational cross talk that did it, and the crowded room, and his father, who was wobbling around grinning and making sure people were enjoying themselves. And it was New Jersey, with its potholes and smokestacks and rows of shabby brick houses, one of which was his home now even though he had never been there before in his life. Even the army was better than New Jersey. Even the fucking Bronx.

"I see you met Rita," said someone Kelly didn't know, and Kelly said he guessed he had.

"She works down at the U-Haul with your dad."

A few minutes later someone else came by and said, "Say, Rita, have you met Joe?"

"What's your name again?" asked Kelly, leaning in close enough to smell the musk of her hair. They had been introduced three times and he meant it as a joke, but Rita backed up a step and regarded him as if he was slow on the uptake or dangerous or possibly both, which was when he noticed she was marking the exits too.

"This isn't a required event," said Kelly. "Feel free to leave if you want to." He had to admit he said it a touch brusquely, so to make up for it, he blurted out, "It's just that you're very, very hot." But the sentences were out of sequence now, and lines that had always worked to flatter and spark now came off as aggressive and a little, well, desperate. "I knew I shouldn't have worn the uniform," he said in an obvious play for sympathy. "It changes things. It changes how people look at me."

"I can only imagine," said Rita.

"I can take it off and you can tell me if there's a difference."

"That's a nice offer," said Rita, "but maybe some other time."

"I didn't mean . . . I just meant I could change into jeans."

Kelly's mother came up with a tray of drinks, and Rita used the interruption to move toward the door. When Kelly turned around a moment later, she was gone.

"Shit, Mom. There you went and chased her off."

"I'm sure you'll see her again," said Kelly's mother. "Her name is Rita and she works with your dad down at the U-Haul."

Kelly took one of the drinks and then another. It was some concoction his father had whipped up. It tasted like pineapple and coconut with something pink mixed in, but it carried a kick. By his third drink, the shabby house seemed to be disintegrating around him. What was he doing sleeping in a dingy little bedroom off the kitchen of his parents' house? He was twenty-two years old. He was a man. He was a warrior, for Chrissakes. He could take any man in the room with his hands tied. Blindfolded with

211

his hands tied. Blindfolded with his hands tied and bowling balls chained to his legs.

"How about tomorrow you look for a job," said Joe Senior when everyone had gone.

Yeah, he could do that. Or he could hold up a bank and take what he needed without bungling the job the way his father had done. Or he could bungle it in the family tradition and go off to prison and come back fifteen years later and pretend everything was A-OK. He could vanish into thin air, kind of the way he had come. He could do all of those things or none of them. Suddenly he wanted to cry like a baby, and then crying was the last thing he wanted to do. Instead, he took a twenty out of his mother's purse and headed out to see what people in the great state of New Jersey did for fun.

## 6.9 PENN SINCLAIR

When Penn left the library, the air was fresher than it had been, as if a storm had blown through or an oppressive haze had burned away. The sun was sharp and clean and the shadows were cool and blue, reminding him of his boyhood and hiding from the heat beneath the long veranda of the Greenwich house. Two privates were walking along the sidewalk smoking cigarettes. Every now and then one of them would stop to look around as if he wanted to take it all in: the traffic, the sooty buildings, the girls in summer dresses, the street vendors, the city smell. Recognizing military, they saluted when they saw him, and Penn saluted back.

"Where're you headed?" he called out after them, but he said it too late and they didn't hear him.

When he got back to Louise's apartment, he was relieved to find it empty. After he showered and shaved, he stood in front of a long gilded mirror, dressed in a black T-shirt and new jeans, and tried to see himself as other people saw him, but he couldn't. For the first time in months, hope stirred within him. Gone was the shame that had followed him everywhere since the incident and along with it, the impulse to study theories and avoid life. Gone too was the dense flock of misgivings that had pecked steadily at his insides as if he were Prometheus, sentenced to have his liver devoured by a giant eagle for bringing the fire of the gods to undeserving mortals. This was the way he used to feel after the snow began to melt and the crocuses and little stubs of grass poked through. He had been waiting for months for someone to tell him that everything was going to be okay, and now the news about redemption was his to tell and spread.

Louise came home a little while later. "Did you get the job?" she called down the narrow hallway. He could hear the liquid rustle of her jacket against the silk of her blouse as she took it off and hung it on a hook in the vestibule. "I've just discovered something. Do you want to know what it is?"

"I've discovered something too." Penn could hear her opening the refrigerator and setting something on a shelf.

"It's actually really good news for you," called Louise.

After considering whether to share his news or listen to hers first, Penn said, "What did you discover?"

"Come out here and I'll show you."

"In a minute. Just tell me." He had left the television tuned to CNN, and in the background, the six o'clock anchors talked crisply of world events. For days the news had been filled with the case of Ehren Watada, who was the first commissioned officer to refuse to deploy to Iraq on conscientious grounds and whose case was making its way through the military courts. Penn strained to listen to the story over the sound of Louise's heels clicking against the polished floor, but he lost the thread.

"I've discovered costume jewelry!" she called from the bathroom. "I never understood it before, but now I do."

The next story was about collusion between the government and the media and the blurred line between news and propaganda. Was his crime not just that he had failed to properly lead his men but that he had thought he could lead them at all in such murky circumstances? Was Watada a coward or was he insanely brave to risk being called about the worst thing Penn could think of? The questions swirling through Penn's mind had given him the idea that he could partly make up for his mistakes by helping Watada or someone like him. That he could do something to clear away the fog and tell the truth about the war. Louise's voice floated toward him: "Just wait until you see!" He would help Watada, and if he could help his men in the process . . . He didn't know yet what he would do, but it wouldn't be theoretical help. It would be practical and real, and nothing Louise or anyone else said or did would stop him.

When Louise walked into the bedroom, his clothing was stacked in neat piles on the bed next to his open duffel, but she didn't see it at first. "It's really fabulous, and it's so cheap," she said, striking a pose that showed off the strings of colorful baubles draped around her neck. "You'll never have to give me anything measured in carats again!" She caught herself and laughed. "Or, well, almost never." Then her eyes swept the room and she saw the piles of folded clothing.

"It's not you, it's me," said Penn when Louise sat down next to the duffel and started to cry. He was reminded of what he loved about her—her sincerity, her elegance, her pleasure in new things. Even when she was crying, her skin was like porcelain, her eyes like glass. But he and Louise were like trains traveling in opposite directions—either they passed each other safely by or they met and destroyed each other.

"Obviously it's you," she said.

The tears threatened to give way to anger, but Penn had nothing more to say. The knot in his stomach was back, tense and ticking. He knew it wouldn't go away as long as he and Louise kept each other trapped inside old versions of themselves.

Louise raised her damp eyes. Behind the tears was a smoldering clot of questions, as if she too housed a ticking mechanism and she was waiting for him to either set it off or snuff it out. Penn was sorry for so many things. "I'm sorry, Louise," he said. "I'm so, so sorry." He could see her deciding whether to continue to cry or to shout at him, but her indecision lasted longer than usual, as if she finally understood about more than costume jewelry. He felt sorry for her, but the good thing was, he no longer felt sorry for himself.

Penn tracked Le Roy Jones down at a computer repair shop. Le Roy found Hernandez in a veterans' database, and Hernandez had the number for Kelly's parents' house in New Jersey. Kelly had Danny Joiner's number, but Danny wasn't answering his phone.

Penn explained his idea of going to Seattle to support Watada. "Or we can do something else that will expose some of the lies about the war."

"You can count me in," said Kelly. "I don't have anything better to do."

"Or there's a protest in Washington, DC," said Penn. "What do you say we go to that?"

## 6.10 DANNY JOINER

Danny arranged his uniform carefully on a hanger. After everything was in order, he noticed a thread hanging from the sleeve of the jacket, so he rummaged through the kitchen drawers for a pair of scissors, worried that Dolly would come home for lunch and surprise him. It was nearly noon. He had hidden the prescription bottles deep in the bathroom trash. If she thought he was sleeping, she would leave him alone, but if she saw the contents of the kitchen drawer in disarray, she might come into the bedroom to wake him up. He shouldn't leave the uniform out either. If she came into the room, it would arouse her suspicion. He could put it on, but he worried that was disrespectful. Instead, he straightened the kitchen drawer. He tipped over the trash to make sure the two amber pill containers were all the way down at the bottom. Then he looked under the pillow to see if the locket his mother had given him was there.

—Why wouldn't it be there?

He didn't know why, but why had he been diagnosed with personality disorder? Why were Iraqis killing Americans, or was it the other way around? Why was Pig Eye dead and why didn't he stay that way? Why did the postmaster insist on saluting whenever Danny went into the post office, and why did poor people keep voting to give rich people all of their money and their lives?

It seemed a shame to hang the uniform in the closet where he couldn't see it, so he hung it on the back of the closet door. Then he pushed the discarded toothpaste tube and the wads of Kleenex aside to look for the two pill containers—just to make sure they were there—and then he covered them up again so they couldn't be seen by anyone who was casually glancing in the direction of the wastebasket.

The contents of the kitchen drawer were as neat as a pin, but were they too neat? Before joining the army, Danny had been the messy one, but now it was Dolly who scattered things here and there. He decided that the neatness of the drawer would worry her. Just the other day she had called him a neatnik and made a comment about obsessive-compulsive disorder. "If only I had that," he had told her. "Maybe that would be covered by the plan."

Yes, the locket was there—at first he didn't see it because it had slipped inside the pillowcase, so he slid it out again and tucked it farther toward the middle of the bed before fluffing the pillows over it. Then he went into the kitchen to mess up the drawer slightly—just enough so that it looked like Dolly had straightened it instead of him. Dolly didn't care if the knives with the red handles and serrated blades were mixed in with the butter knives. Then he switched on the closet light to check the uniform for dust and stray threads and the bathroom light to check the wastebasket again before turning both lights off. Off or on? It hadn't occurred to him to consider which was better. It was possible neither was better, but if one had even the slightest advantage, then that's the way he wanted it. Everything as right as he could make it, even if he couldn't make it perfect, which he realized with deep regret that he couldn't. He knew that sometimes both options were good and sometimes neither was, but in either case, you had to choose.

As Danny considered this, his eyes strayed to the window, which admitted a rich band of late-summer sunlight into the room. Everything happens for a reason, he thought, for the sideways glance at the window was enough to convince him that natural light was eons better than artificial light, especially since

217

Dolly had switched all of the lightbulbs over to compact fluorescents, which weren't as soothing as incandescent. Not that he really believed everything happened for a reason. Some things just happened— what possible reason could he give for what he had done to Pig Eye and what he was about to do to himself? He believed in chaos, which might partly explain the OCD, which he decided he probably had, not that it made a difference now.

The ice had melted in the glass of water, so he thought about going to the kitchen and replacing it. Cold water would taste good, but why did it matter? He should get a fresh glass because he wanted to do things right. He also wanted to be kind to himself the way everyone he talked to said he should. It was too bad the melting ice made the glass sweat. The condensation would drip on the table and leave a stain. But then he told himself that nature wasn't bad or good and that if he was going to try to change the actual physics of things, he was setting himself up for failure. Failure, he thought, and then he laughed.

It was 12:30. If Dolly were going to come home for lunch, she would have been there by now, so it was a pretty safe bet that she wouldn't be home until after five—later if she stopped at the store. He had plenty of time to check for the two amber pill containers, but this time he found, buried underneath a folded piece of cardboard that he had thought was the bottommost piece of trash, a receipt from an expensive shop and a third container, the little round dispenser of the birth control pills Dolly used. When he peered down into the very depths of the trash can, he saw that the dispenser still contained some of the little pink pills, so he removed it, thinking they must be the placebos the manufacturer added on to the end of the month because it was easier to take a pill every day than to take them three weeks on, one week off. Just in case she had thrown it away inadvertently, he set it on the countertop where she would see it. As he did so, he counted more than seven days of sugar pills—almost half the pills were there. Why would Dolly throw away the medication she relied on? Was she trying to deceive him by getting pregnant without asking him first? Was she already pregnant, and if she was pregnant, was the baby his?

He rearranged the garbage in the can the same as it had been, exactly the same except that now the two amber containers with his name on them were wrapped together in a thick cocoon of tissue. He didn't know if that was better or worse than wrapping them separately, but he couldn't decide because now he was distracted by the new mystery of Dolly's intentions regarding the birth control pills. Not that it mattered. He had already decisively concluded that Dolly would be better off without him, which meant that she would be better off without him with or without a baby and that he would have to trust her to make her own decisions from then on.

In the bedroom, the pillows were perfectly arranged. With the new quilt Dolly had bought, it looked like a bed in a magazine. He hated to disturb anything, but he picked up a corner of the pillow and peered underneath it, just to make sure the locket was there.

It made Danny sad to think that he would never see the locket again, that he would never see his mother even if he didn't kill himself, because his mother was already dead. "Never forget who you are," she had told him the last time they talked. But he *had* forgotten, and maybe he had never known.

He was wondering where dead people went when he heard a sound on the roof. It was probably a squirrel. He liked squirrels. He liked all animals. If he hadn't been going to kill himself, he'd get a dog. He didn't think they went anywhere, at least he hoped they didn't. He didn't want to go to all this trouble merely to wind up somewhere else. He checked the drawer again, separating the knives by color because that's the way he liked them and then

219

mixing them together again because that was more realistic. What was real? What did realistic even mean?

He backed down the hallway toward the bedroom like a floor-waxer making for the exit. The glass of water with fresh ice in it was already sweating. A handful of bullet-shaped pills spilled across a magazine, covering Condoleezza's face. He had scooped half of them into his cupped hand when the phone rang. What if it was Dolly? He should answer it. He should answer it just to say good-bye—not that she'd know what he was doing. He would make sure the conversation went well—he wouldn't say anything about the discarded birth control pills or the receipt from the expensive shop. He picked up the phone, practicing the perfect tone to use in his head, but before he could say anything, he was surprised to hear the voice of his old company leader, Captain Sinclair.

"Yes sir," he said when Sinclair asked him if he was doing okay. "Yes sir," he said when Sinclair asked him if he thought much about the war.

"I owe you an apology," said the captain, to which Danny replied, "Yes sir."

Danny was so surprised he sat down on the bed, but then he jumped up again because he didn't want to rumple the new cov-erlet. He still didn't know why Sinclair was calling.

"Guess what?" shouted Sinclair. "I'm here with Joe Kelly and Le Roy Jones."

"Here with Kelly and Le Roy? Where's here?"

Captain Sinclair had never really liked Joe Kelly, and Danny hadn't really liked him either. Danny didn't like hotheads, but perhaps Danny would like him now, since now Danny was a hothead too.

"I'm here in Oklahoma with Kelly and Le Roy. We've got a plan and we're headed over to pick you up."

# 7.0 THE LINE

*She told me my clothing was made by Indonesian child-slaves. I said, "Good lord, Maggie. And where do you think that cup of coffee came from?" That stopped her in her tracks. That's the closest I ever came to making her cry.*

—Valerie Vines

*I saw her the day she came up to the house to talk to Houston, and right away, I knew I was looking at someone special. That's when I decided to kick my MoMs group into a higher gear.*

—Tiffany Price

*All of a sudden Maggie stopped talking about saving the world. She talked about weeding her garden. She talked about cleaning her house.*

—Misty Mills

*That's when I knew she was up to something. I have a sense about these things, and that was a surefire sign.*

—True Cunningham

*At first it was only rumors: things were missing; prisoners were innocent. And then, as you very well know, some fresh-faced reporter started nosing around.*

—Lucas Enright, proprietor of the Main Street Diner

*That first newspaper article didn't mention Maggie by name, but it was only a matter of time before they found out who it was.*

—Jimmy Sweets

# 7.1 MAGGIE

By August, Max Gray's file was so full of documents that Maggie had to create another, which she labeled "Mickey Grant." And her dresser drawer was so full of what she called evidence that she had to move the sweaters to a shelf in her closet. "Spring cleaning!" she announced when Lyle asked her what she was doing.

"It's not spring, it's summer," said Lyle.

"My goodness," said Maggie. "I'm behind." But something had shifted, and inside Maggie, it was spring. It was as if she had spent the past twenty years not only keeping house and mothering, but also training for some clandestine project that was so top secret, even she hadn't been told what it was. Still, her intuition told her that a revelation was coming and that she had better be ready when it did.

She received a letter from George's lawyer saying that Tomás's documents had been received and forwarded to an attorney in another state, since cases had to be handled in the correct jurisdiction. Every time she tried to write a letter to Sandra Day O'Connor, the words sounded inadequate or easily dismissed. Finally, she wrote about Tomás's innocence and about how George was the victim of a prosecutorial vendetta for failing to inform on others, only mentioning at the end the cover-up concerning toxic munitions. Finally, she wrote that she too had been a Rainbow Girl, which had instilled in her a desire to work for the greater good, and that she would welcome any advice on how she should proceed. Then she signed her name and dropped the envelope off at the post office before she could change her mind.

One oppressive day in the middle of a week when the temperature had reached 100 degrees for five days in a row, Maggie returned from lunch to find a report titled *Prisons and Profits* sitting on Valerie's desk. Since Valerie was nowhere in sight, Maggie carried it with her to the cool dungeon of the file room, where she could read it undisturbed. The article talked about the revenue generated by three-strikes laws, where offenders would get mandatory sentences of twenty-five years to life for their third criminal conviction.

The first such law was enacted in Texas and was upheld by the Supreme Court in 1980. In that case, the defendant's offenses amounted to a total of $230 worth of fraudulent activity. More recently, the Supreme Court held that harsh sentencing and three-strikes laws are not cruel and unusual, even in the case of minor offenses such as stealing golf clubs or videotapes or, in one case, a piece of pizza. It is interesting to note that in some states the first and second strikes can refer to individual charges rather than convictions, so that a defendant can accumulate more than one strike from a single illegal act.

The implications of three-strikes laws for private prisons is intriguing. Besides bringing in revenues upwards of thirty thousand dollars per year, each new prisoner increases the pool of available labor. This is a workforce that is available full time. Absenteeism due to vacations and family problems is nonexistent, and expensive benefits need not be paid. If workers don't like the pay of twenty-five cents an hour, their attitudes can be adjusted by withholding educational opportunities or the use of isolation cells. To date, twenty-six states have such laws, leaving ample room for growth both by adding new states to the list and by strengthening existing laws.

Private prisons not only bring high-quality jobs to the state, but they also fuel growth in secondary sectors, such as prison construction, uniform manufacture, and food service. And they keep businesses at home that might move overseas in search of less expensive labor. Effective phrases to keep in mind when communicating with legislators and voters are *public safety, job creation,* and *tough on crime.*

Attached to the article with a paperclip was a newspaper story about the Supreme Court Ruling referred to in the article, the one that upheld the harsh laws and sentencing. The majority opinion had been written by Sandra Day O'Connor.

There must be some mistake, Maggie told herself as she copied the set of documents and made her way back to the basement to add them to Mickey Grant's file. Sandra Day O'Connor was a highly educated woman of the world. She was a wife and mother of three who was revered by many and respected by all. How could she have upheld such draconian measures? There must be some vantage point from which things would be clear— if only she could find it! But then it occurred to Maggie that the justice had been duped and used. But duped and used by whom? Despite the August heat and the flagging air conditioning and the blazing inner furnace that had powered her up and down the stairs to the file room five times by one o'clock, her blood ran cold and a rush of adrenaline caused her heart to thump and her muscles to tense in preparation for confronting … but what exactly was the threat? And why did she think she could do anything about it?

Just as Maggie was deciding she should put all of the original documents back where she had found them and shred all of the copies she had made, she heard a rustle of fabric somewhere in the vastness of the file room. She hadn't turned on the lights when she entered and whoever had come in after her hadn't turned them on either, so the only illumination came in thin, mote-speckled shafts from the windows high above her. Was she being followed? Had someone discovered she was stealing documents? And was that person trying to keep her from passing on the information she had learned?

The rustle of clothing came again, and with it, the slightest tap of a shoe against the concrete floor and the soft hiss of air being sucked in and then expelled again. Should she continue to hide, or should she start to whistle, as if she were happily engrossed in some minor secretarial task? Filing—she'd say she was filing. But who in tarnation would she say Mickey Grant was if whoever had just entered the basement grabbed the fictitious file out of her hands and demanded an explanation?

Slowly she tensed her muscles and straightened her knees until she was standing. Slowly she slipped the article into the incriminating file and replaced the file in the drawer and eased the drawer shut. As she did so, she hummed a hymn from church, softly at first, and then a little louder: *If I get there before you do, Comin' for to carry me home. I'll cut a hole and pull you through, Comin' for to carry me home.*

Cut a hole in what? she wondered. Even getting to heaven seemed like a prison break.

The shaky notes covered the sound of the file drawer, but also the sounds coming from other parts of the room, so she wasn't expecting it when Hugo suddenly put his arms around her from behind and spun her into his arms, stifling her cry of surprise with a forceful kiss. Before she could stop him, his hand was up underneath her blouse and he was whispering in her ear, "You knew I was following you, didn't you? You wanted to find a place to be alone."

"Oh my goodness, Hugo. I didn't . . . You startled . . . I can't . . . "

"Oh, yes," breathed Hugo. "Oh, yes you can."

"I have to go!" cried Maggie in alarm.

"What's the big rush?"

"The director has asked for these files ASAP. If I don't get them back to him quickly, Valerie will come looking for me, and you know how Valerie is."

"What files?" asked Hugo, nodding at Maggie's empty hands, which were pushing against his chest.

"The ones I've come to get!"

"Why? What does he want them for?"

"I don't know, and I wouldn't tell you even if I did. What kind of assistant would I be if I gossiped about my supervisor's business?" Maggie felt on surer ground now, and her air of authority seemed to be having a good effect because Hugo took his hands off her breasts and moved a step away from her.

"Well, don't keep me waiting too long," he said. "I'm not what you'd call a patient man."

It thrilled and repelled Maggie that Hugo was the sort of man who took what he wanted and that he wanted her. All the way home, she tried to shake off the notion that she had a dark side after all, and when she was unsuccessful at that, she told herself that all people had a dark side, but they had a noble side too, and it was how they used their various sides that mattered. She told herself that it didn't take anything away if doing a good thing entailed a few thrills and indiscretions along the way. And then she told herself that people with no experience of the underbelly of existence would have none of the tools needed to fight against it.

That evening she arrived home to find two letters in the mailbox. One was her letter to Sandra Day O'Connor, which had been returned unopened. The second was from the new appellate attorney, saying he had received Tomás's documents from a colleague and asking her to call. It was only when the two envelopes were lying side by side on the kitchen counter that she noticed that both the lawyer and the former justice were in Phoenix, Arizona.

Phoenix, she thought as she dialed the attorney's number.

"First the good news," said the attorney, who answered the phone himself. "The arresting officer in the case was later investigated for a string of false arrests. That's very good for your man Tomás. The bad news is that I'm overworked and understaffed. And I'm going to need to hire a private investigator. All of which means I'll take the case if you can foot part of the bill."

"I don't know how I'll do that," said Maggie.

"How about we trade services, then? You could come to work for me to offset some of the cost. Just until I find someone else."

"Can I think about it and call you back?"

"Absolutely," said the attorney with a chuckle. "It's not as if Tomás is going anywhere."

Phoenix, Maggie thought again. Sandra Day O'Connor was in Phoenix, and even if the idea of meeting the justice in person was farfetched, once it had occurred to her, she couldn't get the notion out of her mind. Besides, a letter wasn't the right form of communication for her message, which had grown far beyond the individual cases of Tomás and George and even beyond the fact that radioactive substances were putting soldiers and munitions workers at risk. Human beings were being trafficked for corporate interests right underneath everyone's noses! The judicial system was being used for private and political ends! Slavery was legal, at least in certain circumstances! All of which was far too much for a flimsy letter to convey. She would go to Phoenix, but first she had to get the rest of her evidence out of the prison, which, given the tight security and Hugo's increasingly aggressive state of mind, wouldn't be so easily done.

## 7.2 LYLE

Lyle had driven the forklift for four years, and whenever MacBride, who was the deputy director of fulfillment and shipping, said, "You're doing a great job, Rayburn. Keep it up and there's bound to be a promotion in it," Lyle always said, "Yes sir" and felt pleased even though he never really expected anything to come of it. But now he wondered if he should knock on MacBride's office door and ask more about the promotion. When he mentioned it to Jimmy Sweets, Jimmy encouraged him. "Hell yeah," said Jimmy. "What are you waiting for?"

After that, Jimmy would bring it up whenever they were alone. "Did you do it?" Jimmy would ask, and then he would say, "Try it on me. Pretend I'm MacBride and see if you can convince me to give you a raise."

"Not a raise," said Lyle. "A promotion."

"The only reason anyone wants a promotion is to get a raise," said Jimmy. "Otherwise there wouldn't be any point."

"I'm waiting for the next time he stops by the floor."

But when MacBride came through ten minutes later, he said, "He's always in a better mood after he turns in the monthly report. I'll ask him after that."

"Don't wait too long," said Jimmy, "or he'll give the promotion to someone else."

Lyle could imagine himself saying, "About that promotion, sir," but he wouldn't know what to say next. Jimmy could probably give him an idea of the words to use, but Jimmy was fond of pulling people's legs, and it might be hard to tell if he was being sincere in his advice or setting Lyle up as part of a joke. And it wasn't as if Jimmy, who had worked as a supervisor in the shipping operation for fifteen years, had ever gotten a promotion himself. When Lyle finally said, "How would you ask him? Let me hear you do it," Jimmy replied, "First of all, it isn't about what you want. It's about what MacBride wants. You don't catch a fish by dangling pretty girls or chocolate cake under its nose. You use worms."

"Sure," said Lyle. "But what does that have to do with it?"

"Once you figure out what MacBride wants, you tell him how you can help him get it. You make him believe he can't get it without you."

"How do I do that?"

"The particular words aren't important, but you have to make yourself seem indispensable to the operation at hand."

It sounded very complicated to Lyle, and he almost gave up on the idea altogether. "Heck," he said. "I'm happy where I am."

"But underutilized," said Jimmy. "Not to mention underpaid."

When Lyle saw Jimmy in the break room the afternoon the monthly report was due, Jimmy winked at him and said, "It all boils down to tactics and execution." Then he told Lyle that above everything else was strategy and goal-setting. "There are only a few real goal-setters in the world, and most of them are CEOs and generals. They set the agenda, and then it's up to the rest of us to get things done. MacBride is in tactics, and you," he said giving Lyle a poke in the chest, "you're in execution."

It sounded like a death sentence to Lyle, who had never asked himself any of the large questions Jimmy not only asked, but seemed to have an answer for. But once the idea of a promotion had occurred to him, it was like standing on a cliff looking down at a swimming hole. The only way to shut the cycle of indecision down was to jump.

Finally, Lyle could stand it no longer, and he made his way to MacBride's office just so the imaginary harangue would stop. He reminded himself not to demand anything, only to ask politely, but first he washed his hands carefully with grease-cutting soap so he wouldn't leave black smudges on any of the papers that always littered MacBride's desk. He waited until most of the men had gone home for the day before knocking gently at the office door.

MacBride sat Lyle down and gave him his choice of a Dr Pepper or a Sprite. Then he went through the various job openings with him. It was a shock to Lyle to find out that all of the positions were paired with complex personality profiles. Managers were supposed to be *highly self-reliant* and *strongly pragmatic by nature*. They should *emphasize realistic goals* in the *development of workable plans*. They should be *assertive* and *forceful* and *persistent in the face of frustration*. None of the listed attributes were ones Lyle possessed, but Jimmy's voice was in the back of his head, egging him on. "I think I can be indispensable to the accomplishment of your goals," he told MacBride.

"And you are, Rayburn. You have a spotless record. On time every day. No accidents with the equipment."

Lyle rubbed the place where the metal filings had gone in, but thought it better not to mention it.

"All this tells me that you're right where you need to be," said MacBride, who rambled on a little longer before telling Lyle he could take the rest of his Dr Pepper with him.

"He said I wasn't a visionary," Lyle told Jimmy the next day.

"That shows how much he knows," scoffed Jimmy. "Being a visionary is only important for goal-setters and strategists."

The next day Jimmy gave Lyle a dog-eared book. "This here is the bible on this sort of thing," he said.

"What sort of thing?" asked Lyle.

"Getting what you want."

"I thought it was about MacBride getting what he wants."

"Jeezus, Lyle," said Jimmy. "That's only what you want MacBride to think."

It was the first book Lyle had read in years. The table of contents wasn't too bad—short phrases, one per line. But the rest of the book was a different story. Even though he read the first chapter over and over again, he couldn't understand the point of it. The author told some amusing stories about gangsters who couldn't see how all the terrible things they had done were wrong, but Lyle wasn't a gangster. And he didn't see what gangsters had to do with becoming a supervisor on the floor. The book said, *The only reason you are not a rattlesnake is that your mother and father weren't rattlesnakes.* And it said a person usually had two reasons for doing something, *one that sounds good and the real one.* And it said to smile and talk about the other person's interests and to let the boss think the idea of the promotion was his and also that it was Lyle's job to keep MacBride from saying "no" because no was hard to overcome. Okay, Lyle told himself. I guess I can do that.

The next day he went back to MacBride and chatted with him

about fishing and about MacBride's grandson while MacBride showed him a few photographs he had taken at the lake. When the time seemed right, Lyle said, "About that promotion," but MacBride, who had never been anything but friendly to Lyle, hardly looked at him as he said, "We're in a holding pattern, Rayburn—especially considering the economy is in the tank. Not to mention that business with your wife."

"What business?" asked Lyle.

"All that talk about how what we do here is harmful got some of the other employees upset, and now I hear she's causing trouble up at the prison."

"How is she causing trouble?" asked Lyle. Maggie had promised him that the prisoner records were only copies and no one knew she had taken them.

But MacBride just said, "That's probably something you should ask her yourself."

Lyle tried to find out what MacBride meant, but whenever he asked about work, Maggie said things were fine, and when he asked her about making a difference in the world, she said she wasn't thinking about innocent prisoners or freaks of nature anymore. He wanted to believe her, but something about the way she was whacking at the lawn worried him.

"The trick is to get the clover without pulling up all of the grass," Maggie told him.

"Wouldn't it be easier just to poison it?"

"Easier for me," said Maggie, "but lethal for the insects."

Fall was coming, and soon Will would be back at school. The leaves on the Japanese maple were already tinged with orange, and the beautyberry bush was covered with fat purple berries. Maggie showed Lyle how to water the petunias she had planted in pots by the back door. "Just in case," she said.

"Just in case of what?" Lyle wanted to know.

"Just in case I'm hit by a truck," said Maggie. "Just in case I run off with the mailman."

"The mailman?" asked Lyle.

"Remember what the pastor told us. One crazy thing, no questions asked."

They had a good laugh, and then she showed him the drawer in the desk where she kept the passwords for the checking account and the health insurance card.

"Just in case you're appointed ambassador to Japan?" asked Lyle.

"Yes," said Maggie. "Just in case of that." But Lyle could tell she wasn't really listening. An army of sugar ants was making its way from the windowsill to a blob of goo that had been spilled by the kitchen sink. "Sugar is really bad for you," said Maggie. "It's worse for you than fat. And mostly it isn't even sugar. It's high fructose corn syrup, which is subsidized and overproduced, so they have to come up with more and more ways to use it. They put it in everything and then they make the portions bigger, which leads to obesity and diabetes. I don't think any of us should eat it anymore."

After dinner, Maggie sat at her desk to sort the mail while Will and Tula cleared the table and washed up. Lyle smiled to recall how he and Maggie had washed the dishes together all those years ago. He walked over to where she was bent over her papers in a warm pool of light from the desk lamp. He wanted to touch her that way again. He wanted to be young, with everything before him. He wanted to sit down beside her and ask her advice on how to handle MacBride, but when he stooped down to look over her shoulder, she said, "This is where I keep the checkbook, Lyle. Right here in the top drawer. And this is where I keep the stamps."

Lyle backed away. He could see how the little pool of lamplight was just big enough to contain Maggie and the desktop and how there wasn't any room in it for him.

## 7.3 MAGGIE

One day while Valerie was out of the room on an errand, Maggie answered the telephone to find a Mr. Pickering calling to speak with the director. "Please hold while I see if he's available," she said, but she was thinking, Pickering! Wasn't he the author of the report called *Prisons and Profits* she had found on Valerie's desk? When DC came on the phone, she disconnected her extension, and then, as quietly as she could, she pressed the button to connect again, ready with an excuse in case either of the men could hear her muffled breathing. But the two men were talking excitedly, and if the open line whooshed or echoed, they didn't seem to notice. The ACLU woman had been right about the sense of urgency and importance. Right about the adrenaline rush. Right that the line was not wide and heavily patrolled but thin and alluring, as much a mirage as an identifiable boundary between what was acceptable and what was not.

"There's a precedent for using prison labor if the business serves a public purpose," Pickering was saying. "And what's more important to the public than a safe supply of inexpensive food? What's more important than keeping jobs right here in Oklahoma?"

DC sounded unsure. "I don't know. The munitions factory is a government facility. We're authorized to provide labor to government entities and even to some private businesses, but not to farms. How would we keep the prisoners from escaping? I don't think chain gangs are a modern-day solution. I'd like to help you out, but my hands are tied."

"What are they tied by?" asked Pickering. "Realistically, I mean."

"Laws, for one thing," said DC.

"And who makes the laws?"

When DC didn't answer, Pickering said, "We're not talking about Moses and the stone tablets, here. We're talking about laws made and changed by human beings. Human beings who are a lot like us. Who could actually *be* us if you think about it. A few persuasive arguments are all we need—that and a tiny bit of access to the people in charge. That's what the draft legislation group is all about."

DC promised to keep an open mind.

"Just so you know," said Pickering, "it's projected that soon one out of every three African American men will go to prison at some point in his lifetime, and seventy percent of all released inmates will be re-arrested within three years. But it can't just be the African Americans who are breaking the laws, even if they're the ones getting caught. My point is that the industry needs to adopt a two-pronged approach: on the one hand, we need stricter laws and sentencing; on the other, we need better enforcement. Yours is a growth industry, anyway you slice it."

"Hmm," said DC. "Growth is good."

"My firm leverages your clout with the movers and shakers. We place people in think tanks that draw up model laws. We help sell those laws to the public. That's what I can do for you. What you can do for me is to review that draft legislation I sent you. The material is highly sensitive, so your eyes only and all that. And if you can provide some relevant statistics or any other supporting information, I'd be very grateful. I promised my clients I'd get it to some influential members of the state legislature next month, and time is running short."

"I guess it wouldn't hurt to take a look," said DC. "I guess I can do that for you."

As soon as Valerie stepped back in the office, DC stuck his head out of the door and asked, "Did that missing document ever show up?"

"No," said Valerie. "It never did."

"Damn it," said DC. "Damn it all to hell."

"DC seems awfully grumpy lately," Maggie remarked in an attempt to elicit information, but Valerie merely grunted and said, "You would be too."

"I would be when?"

"DC is under a lot of pressure. The rest of us assume it's all wine and roses for the people with the important jobs, but they take on a lot of responsibility. We're lucky they're the ones making the decisions so we don't have to."

"What decisions?" asked Maggie.

"Important ones," replied Valerie. "Decisions that benefit everybody else."

Maggie tried not to let Valerie's air of superiority bother her, but more and more she found herself thinking, Why should I always take a back seat to Valerie? But then she told herself, My job is only a means for accomplishing my real work, anyway. What Valerie and DC do on their own time isn't my affair. Then she laughed at the word "affair," and then she stopped laughing. Nothing was as it seemed!

During her last days at the munitions plant, Maggie had become progressively certain that Mr. Winslow was monitoring her movements, and now she had the same feeling about Valerie, who would quickly avert her eyes when Maggie looked up from her desk. And sometimes Maggie heard strange patterings in the hallway, as if she was being followed by someone wearing soft shoes. She knew from the movies that a guilty mind could play tricks on a person, but should a person feel guilty for defying convention or even breaking a few laws in order to do right? The sense of being watched was exacerbated by Hugo, who leered at her when she walked by the security desk and who had started to loiter in the hallway outside the director's office at lunchtime or when he was on his break. Even when he was safely on duty, Maggie couldn't help feeling he was lurking around the next corner about to burst into sight, which set her nerves on edge. "There you are!" she would cry whenever she saw him.

"Waiting for me again," Hugo would reply, and even though she did her best to avoid him, Maggie found herself saying, "There you are!" several times each day.

Once, soon after she had given her notice at the munitions plant, Winslow had passed Maggie in the hallway and said, "I've got my eye on you," but he had said it so quietly that Maggie wondered if she had only imagined it. Now it occurred to her to turn the tables on Hugo by making him think she was the one watching him. She found her opportunity the next day, when she happened to be walking back from the restroom just when Hugo was starting his lunchtime patrol. She fixed her eyes on the waxed linoleum floor tiles and tried to appear preoccupied with her own thoughts. As the hard soles of his boots clipped toward her, she almost lost her nerve, but at the last second she whispered, "I've got my eye on you," very quietly, under her breath.

"What? What?" asked Hugo, stopping in his tracks and giving her a piercing glare.

Maggie raised her eyes and smiled as brightly as she could. "I didn't say anything," she said. "Don't tell me you're hearing things now!"

This little act of aggression came seemingly out of nowhere. It gave Maggie confidence, but it also worried her, as if she had taken a step closer to the line the PATH woman had talked about. The trick was to use Hugo's stubbornness to her advantage, for he was too big and too smart for her to make him go against his nature. Still, she could feel events gathering momentum, and when she approached the exit that evening, she looked at Hugo in a new way—not so much as an adversary, but as a tool. He might have a shiny badge pinned to his uniform and muscle-bound shoulders and a gun strapped to his hip and a savage glint in his smiling eyes, but she had the element of surprise. I know what you are, she thought, but what do you really know about me?

## 7.4 MAGGIE

Every year, DC took his family on a camping trip at the end of the summer, and as the date approached, Valerie became more and more irritable. She huffed and moaned and made cryptic gestures in the direction of the office where DC sat with his hands clasped together and his head bowed over his work. When Maggie asked what was wrong, Valerie said, "I'm going to be ill. I'm going to be physically ill." Once DC left for his vacation, she started to miss work—first it was a broken alternator and then it was a summer cold.

With the director away and Valerie in and out, the office echoed with absence. Maggie's eyes strayed to the bank of locked files in DC's office, and when a bumblebee lit on the tall steel cabinet, it seemed an invitation to search for Valerie's keys, which were easily found in her desk drawer, to stand on a chair, and to crush the brittle body in a scrap of paper from the waste bin— and, while she was at it, to slip the key into the lock on DC's personal file cabinet and slide open one of the heavy drawers. She was so preoccupied she didn't remember until too late that bees were dying left and right and that if people wanted fruit crops to exist in the world of the future, they needed to protect pollinators and not annihilate them. She rushed to the waste bin, but the bee was a smear of body parts. It was impossible to think of everything at once!

Maggie's heart was thumping in her chest as she climbed back up on the chair. She had let the bee distract her, and she knew that lack of focus could lead to fateful mistakes. The hair on her arms stood on end as she opened the second-to-top file drawer and finally the top one. The air was buzzing as if it were full of bees or as if a warning bell was warming up for a full alarm. She knew Valerie wasn't really sick and might show up at any moment. She even imagined DC might hear his own buzzing, leave his family zipped in their tent beside the Red River, and come rushing back to the office to catch her in the act. When someone dropped a stapler in the copy alcove, Maggie froze on the chair, swaying slightly and cocking her head toward the door, but no one appeared. Footsteps clumped down the hallway. Someone laughed. A minute later, the copy machine chugged to life.

The topmost drawer was the one she had seen Valerie open the day she had worn the inappropriate blouse and Maggie had watched her from the hallway. Right at the front of the drawer was a training brochure on prison discipline and a pamphlet called "You and STDs," both of which she skimmed before slipping them into the waistband of her skirt. The PATH woman had been right about solitary confinement: among other things, prisoners had no right to question their confinement and the term of such confinement should not exceed ten years, although that was not a hard-and-fast rule. Ten years! thought Maggie. The idea of it was enough to break a person's heart.

At the very back of the drawer was an unmarked accordion folder, and in the folder was a heart-shaped card from DC to Valerie that said, "Be good while I'm away." Scrawled beneath the message was the address of the River Motel. And there, fallen down behind the unmarked folder, was the missing draft legislation.

A printout of a series of emails was tucked inside the cover, with a subject line saying The Safe Neighborhoods Act: Draft 3.2. The email exchange started off:

The fact that spending on prisons has now surpassed spending on education has directed an unfortunate spotlight on our entire industry, but should community safety be sacrificed for budget constraints?

Maggie's hands were trembling as she put the document into the top drawer of her desk. More people stuck to the flypaper, she thought. More money lining the pockets of the people in charge!

She spent the rest of the day devising ways to smuggle the draft legislation and her other files out of the prison and shuddering to imagine what would happen if she was caught. All personnel were subject to random searches, and there was never any telling how thoroughly the exit guards would search an employee's purse and bags. She decided to start with something small, so as a trial run, she tucked the pamphlet on STDs into the bottom of her purse. Then she zipped the one on prison discipline into the side pouch where she kept her sunglasses.

She had wanted to leave with the five o'clock rush, but without Valerie to do her share of work, it was almost six by the time she reached the exit. Her heart sank to see that no one else was waiting in line for security—only Hugo was there, twiddling his thumbs and grinning at her. "Good evening, Hugo," said Maggie, hoping she didn't look as nervous as she felt.

"ID, ma'am," Hugo replied.

"Oh, Hugo! You know who I am!" exclaimed Maggie.

*"When a guard asks for documentation, the employee must immediately produce it,"* said Hugo, reciting from the handbook.

Maggie opened her purse and fumbled around in it, finally producing both her ID badge and her driver's license.

*"Employees must wear the ID badge at all times while on prison premises,"* recited Hugo.

At first Maggie had regretted the kiss, but now she wondered if she could use it to her advantage. "Any plans for the weekend?" she asked in an insinuating tone of voice.

"Maybe I'll get lucky," said Hugo.

"Luck comes in two flavors," said Maggie. "Good luck and bad."

Hugo made a show of starting to open the electronic door, but then he tapped his temple as if he had just remembered something. "I can search you or your bag, ma'am—your choice," he said with a nasty smile.

None of the women wanted to be searched, so if Maggie opted for a pat down, it would be obvious she had something to hide and Hugo would search her bag anyway. Sweat was breaking out on her forehead and under her arms, but there didn't seem to be a good alternative to continuing on the course she had started. As she held the bag open, she said, "You naughty boy," all the while hoping the scarf and the sweater and the homemaking magazine that were stuffed into the purse would provide ample cover for the pamphlet hidden beneath them. Then she winked and said, "Search away." But it made her stomach turn to watch Hugo's beefy hands push the sweater aside and pull carelessly at the delicate scarf.

"*Good Housekeeping*," said Hugo, sliding the magazine out of the bag. "My mother reads that."

"Tell her there's a fabulous recipe for lemon bars in the July issue. I'd tell you the secret ingredient, but then it wouldn't be secret." As soon as the words were out of her mouth, Maggie regretted them. Why had she said the word "secret"? It was almost as if she wanted to get caught.

Hugo dug out Maggie's pink pearl lipstick and her baggie of emergency tampons and finally the pamphlet on prisoners and sexually transmitted diseases. "What's this?" he asked.

"It's a pamphlet on STDs," said Maggie, trying not to look at the zippered compartment where the pamphlet on prison discipline was concealed.

"I mean, what are you doing with it?"

"It's very well written. And as you might or might not know, I have a teenaged son."

"Hmph," said Hugo, leering again as he stuffed the items back into her purse. "So you're going to talk to him about the birds and the bees, are you? What, exactly, are you going to say?"

All Maggie could think of was the bee she had killed earlier in the day, so she was late in replying. "Yes, I am. I'm going to tell him that love and sex are two different things and that he should be aware of the risks and take steps to protect himself."

"Protect himself from love or from sex?" asked Hugo, belching out a laugh. Then he pushed the purse back at her and let her pass.

Maggie took her time walking across the baking asphalt to the bus stop, swinging her hips and wishing an evening breeze would break through the unrelenting humidity and cool her burning cheeks. The good news was that she had successfully gotten the two pamphlets out of the prison, even if the bad news was that Hugo had found one of them. But she had learned something, and she had to be happy about that. When she got home, she added the pamphlet on prison discipline to her stash of evidence before making her way to the kitchen, where Will and Lyle were eating the last of a chocolate cake.

"We're spoiling our dinner," said Lyle.

"I guess I can't stop you," said Maggie. Then she put the pamphlet on STDs on the table and said, "I got this up at the prison, Will. You might want to take a look."

"That's really embarrassing, Mom."

"You're going to have to make a lot of decisions for yourself at some point, so you might as well have the facts."

"Gosh, Mom. What's going on?"

"You're growing up, that's all," said Maggie.

"She just wants you to be prepared," said Lyle. "In case she's abducted by Martians or whisked off to Hollywood to star in a film."

# 7.5 WILL

When the weekend came, Lyle drove Will to Glorietta for the first game of the summer play-offs. If they won, they moved on to the next bracket. If they lost, they were out. The mayor was standing at the entrance to the ballpark, handing out campaign buttons that said Call Me Buddy even though his name was Robert Hutchinson and up until then, everybody had called him Hutch.

"I guess he wants the citizens of Red Bud to think of him as inseparable from the town," said Will.

"It's all about winning friends and influencing people," Lyle said. "I read about it in a book."

"When did you ever read a book?" asked Will.

"Jimmy gave it to me. It said you have to make people think that whatever you want them to do is actually their idea."

"Hmmm," said Will. "That sounds like something the teachers up at school would do."

It seemed that the whole town had driven up for the game. Jimmy charged past, headed toward the stands with Lily De Luca in tow. "Pre-med!" Jimmy called out. "That's pretty heady stuff!"

"That's an example of your theory right there," said Will, but Lyle only beamed and called back to Jimmy, "Tell me something I don't know!"

Mr. Quick waved over the heads of his wife and baby, and Lucas Enright, who had owned the diner for as long as anybody could remember, wished Will and Lyle both luck as if Lyle were on the team too. By the time Will hurried off to find his teammates, he was seething with an unfamiliar rage. When Stucky Place slapped his shoulder and said, "Here comes our secret weapon," it took him a few seconds to respond, and during the warm-up, it seemed to be pure chance that determined whether he caught the ball or dropped it. Only the sight of Tula sitting in the third row eating a candy bar calmed him. From that distance he couldn't tell what kind it was, but he could imagine the crinkling sound of the paper as she pulled it back to take a bite and the soft wet sounds as she chewed and swallowed.

"Rayburn, get your head in the game!" called the coach.

Will mouthed, "Yes sir," but all he could think about was Tula. He could almost taste the chocolate and feel the crunch of the peanuts and the pulling of the caramel when it stuck to her molars.

Ever since breaking his arm, Will had felt that something else in him had broken. Where he had once done things without thinking too much about them, his head was now bursting with all of the advice his coaches had given him over the years: keep your weight back and your head down, square your hips, stay inside the ball, choke up on two strikes, make sure to follow through. And now there were advice and expectations on the academic side of things as well.

"You're trying too hard," said the team captain just as the coach interrupted to say, "Try a little harder, Rayburn. Give it everything you've got."

"Muscle memory," said Stucky. "That's the way to go."

Will was thinking about Tula, but also about his life goals, which didn't seem to fit him right, as if he had put on somebody else's uniform. The test scores hadn't helped. Now there were college applications to fill out and essays to write. Mr. Quick had agreed to help him over the summer, but when Will had shown him a draft of his overcoming challenges essay, the effort had been greeted with a frown. "It sounds like the soldier you met at the clinic is the one who is overcoming the challenges," said Mr. Quick. "The essay is supposed to be about you."

Mr. Quick, who had once insisted learning was the point, started to go on about commitment and excellence and the importance of grades. "If a thing is worth doing," he said, "it's worth doing well." So now Will was adding a paragraph about his broken arm and baseball, but he worried it sounded like he was comparing his injury to a war wound and a baseball game to war. If only something significant had happened to him, but it hadn't.

A ball whizzed past Will's ear. He hadn't even seen it, but he recovered enough to relay the ball home, where the runner was tagged out. That left a man on second. The next batter grounded to the shortstop, who pitched the ball to third. The ball made a soft thud in the pocket of Will's glove, but just as he stepped back onto the base and reached out to tag the player who was hurtling toward him, his wrist went limp. The ball fell to the ground, and the umpire shouted, "Safe!"

"Libby, go in for Will," called the coach.

Will's ears burned as he walked off the field. He didn't look at the stands where he knew his parents and Tula were sitting and worrying about him. He chewed a piece of Juicy Fruit gum and tried to empty his mind the way it used to be empty. He shrugged his shoulders and tried not to care the way he used to not care. He tried to feel like Derek Jeter coming back from a dislocated shoulder to help his team make it to the World Series. Of course, all of that was in the future for Jeter as he faced Martinez in the eighth inning with his team trailing the Red Sox 5-2, hoping against hope that his shoulder would hold up and not knowing he was about to hit a double that would start an epic rally because no one, not even Jeter, could know what the future would hold.

# 7.6 MAGGIE

Maggie planned to move the files on the last day of DC's vacation. While Lyle and Will chattered over breakfast about Stucky Place's lucky homer and the upcoming championship game, Maggie put on a blouse she had bought for the occasion. It consisted of a sheer shell and a lacy undergarment and was exactly the sort of thing Valerie might wear. Although the day was bound to get hot, she covered the blouse with the bulky birthday sweater and packed two double-thickness grocery bags with magazines and party snacks. "They're for the team," she said to Lyle as she loaded them into the back of the truck.

When they reached the prison parking lot and she went to take them out again, Lyle said, "Why don't you just leave them in the truck. The game's not until tomorrow."

"No, no," said Maggie, trying to think of a reason why this wouldn't work. "Some of the cookies are for the prisoners, and I haven't sorted out which is which."

"Can't you do that now? No sense having to carry everything home again on the bus."

"No, no," Maggie said again. "If I do that, I'll be late."

"Really, Maggie. It'll save you ... "

"I said no! I really can't!" Maggie tried not to look as if she was struggling under the weight of the bags, and after a moment's hesitation, she added, "You can't say anything to anyone, Lyle, but I might not be working at the prison much longer. I've been offered a job in Phoenix, and I'm considering taking it."

"Phoenix!" cried Lyle. "What would you go to Phoenix for?"

"There's an attorney there who can help Tomás, but he needs an assistant. It would just be for a little while."

"Are you in trouble?" asked Lyle. "Jimmy mentioned something that day at the lake, and MacBride said something too."

"Lots of people are in trouble," said Maggie. "That's the entire point."

She watched from the sidewalk as Lyle slammed the truck into gear and roared off, before making her way up the steps to the employee entrance.

"That looks good," said Louis, who was manning the scanner.

"Snacks for tomorrow's big game," said Maggie.

"Well, save some of those cookies for me."

When everyone had left at the end of the day, Maggie made her way to the basement to clear out the two burgeoning fictitious files. She stuffed the folders into the paper grocery bags and covered them up with some of the snacks. She felt like a secret agent as she used a box cutter to remove the pages of a magazine she had bought to use as a false cover for the draft legislation. But first she had to copy it. The copier had already been turned off for the weekend, so she went into the alcove and flipped the switch. Since the machine was slow to warm up, she decided to make one last visit to Tomás. It took her almost no time at all to clear security, so she was already sitting on one of the folding chairs when Tomás shuffled into the visitors' room.

"What's going on?" he cried. "This isn't your usual day!"

"I wanted to tell you I won't be here next week," said Maggie.

"Are you going on vacation?"

"Yes," said Maggie. "I am." She had brought a package of cookies with her, and now she held it up. After that, there seemed to be nothing to talk about, partly because there were no math problems to solve and partly because Tomás didn't launch into his usual litany of complaints. He looked sheepish, almost like a schoolboy in front of a new teacher, causing Maggie to wonder what was up. Soon enough, however, Tomás peered out from under his eyebrows in the wheedling way he had, but instead of wincing as if someone was about to kick his shin or pull his chair out from under him, he seemed to be trying to hide how happy he was.

"What is it?" asked Maggie. "You seem happy today!"

"I brought you something. You're always giving me things, and I wanted to give you something in return."

Maggie had noticed that Tomás was sitting with one arm behind his back, and now he swung it around with a flourish. "Ta-da! I made it!" He set a lump of glazed clay on the table between them and grinned expectantly at Maggie. When she only stared at the object in confusion, Tomás carefully took the halves apart to reveal a hollow where some very small keepsake could be hidden. "It's for your dresser at home," he said. "I'll bet Lyle has given you some piece of jewelry you cherish. Now you have a place to keep it!"

Maggie was not sure what to say, but Tomás was rattling on. "It's not obvious that this is a container, so if thieves come into your house to steal your valuables, they probably won't notice and your present from your husband will be safe."

Maggie was speechless and a little appalled, but Tomás jabbered on about possible uses for his gift.

"Or it could hold a lock of a loved one's hair," he said. "Who would you choose—Lyle or Will?"

Maggie didn't like it when Tomás mentioned her family, and now she interpreted his gift as a means of inserting himself into their home—into her very bedroom—by enveloping a present to her from Lyle with a present of his own.

"Thank you, Tomás," she said, but she knew the words didn't sound heartfelt, and when she dragged her eyes up from the ceramic object to meet his, it took her an extra second to make them sparkle with the delight he was expecting and she wished she could feel. She recalled how she would set the treasures Will brought home from school in a place of honor and how she would tell him they were the most remarkable things she had ever seen. It was clear Tomás was expecting something like that now, and there was an awkward silence while she tried to think of what to say.

As she was deciding between the words "imaginative" and "unique," Tomás said, "I like your sweater."

"Thank you!"

"Where did you get it?"

"My goodness," said Maggie. "I can't remember." The birthday sweater was far too big for her, and she had only worn it because it covered up the sexy blouse she was wearing in order to distract Hugo when she left with the files. But now she felt defensive on her family's behalf and didn't want to let on to Tomás that they would buy her something so ill fitting and drab.

"I wish I had one like it," said Tomás.

Tomás was small. The sweater wouldn't fit him any better than it fit Maggie, and it was rude of him to basically ask for it outright. Still, she knew she wouldn't be seeing him again, and she would be taking the sweater off in a few minutes anyway in preparation for her confrontation with Hugo. Perhaps it would be a way to buy him off—though exactly why she needed to buy Tomás off, she wasn't sure. Adding to her guilt was the knowledge that in all these months at the prison, she hadn't accomplished anything significant—all she had succeeded in doing was to flirt with a security guard and develop the same sense of superiority she had criticized in Valerie. So she unbuttoned the sweater and said as solemnly as she could, "I want you to have it, Tomás. It's obviously too big for me, but I think it would fit you just fine."

Tomás didn't smile very often, but now it looked as if his cheekbones would pop right through the skin. He hugged the sweater to his chest and beamed at her over the plastic tabletop.

"I'm glad you like it, but that's not even your real present," said Maggie. "The thing I wanted to tell you is that I've sent your file to an appellate attorney who is going to review all of the evidence. I can't promise that anything will come of it—in fact, it probably won't. But at least we've taken the first step. We'll just have to wait and see where it goes."

Tomás fidgeted in his seat, taking her words in. "That's a pretty big present," he said. "But you know, don't you, that if they hadn't gotten me for running away that day, they would have gotten me for something else."

"You might as well give up right now if you're going to think like that. Promise me you'll practice being optimistic."

"Okay," said Tomás. "Anything for you."

"There's one thing you *can* do for me," said Maggie. "You can tell me about solitary confinement. Do they even do that here?"

"I'm not allowed to say."

"Why ever not?" asked Maggie.

"It's the rules, that's all."

"But who would know if you told me?"

For an answer, Tomás made a zippering motion by drawing his finger across his lips.

"Have it your way," said Maggie. Then she repeated that she

was going away for a little while, but she'd come to see him when she got back.

When she left him, Tomás was staring straight ahead with his mouth open and tears leaking from the corners of his eyes. He raised one of his hands in her direction before letting it fall back into his lap. Maggie knew from the PATH woman that appeals were a long shot, but it was something, and probably the best she could do for now. As she walked back to her office, she was filled with a kind of love for Tommy. But then she thought about the flypaper and the thousands of human flies who were stuck to it, and she hurried back through security to finish what she had started all those months ago.

Her thoughts were racing as she turned down the corridor that led to the director's office, so it took her a moment to realize that the office wasn't empty. Valerie was standing in the open space between the desks. Her hands were on her hips, and her eyes were fixed on Maggie's desktop, where the draft legislation was waiting for the copy machine to warm up.

"You found it!" cried Valerie. "The missing document!"

"It was misfiled," said Maggie quickly.

"Where?" Valerie wanted to know, but Maggie couldn't tell her without admitting she had snooped in the director's office and found the file in the drawer where he and Valerie left notes for each other.

"It was in the wrong folder," Maggie said, hoping she wouldn't be pressed for a better answer, but Valerie seemed preoccupied with other things.

"I just came by to make it look like I was here at least some of the time DC was away. You'll cover for me, won't you?"

"Sure," said Maggie. "Of course I will."

"I don't want him to know I followed him downstate."

253

"You what?"

"Well, he knows I followed him, but I don't want him to know I stayed."

"I won't say a word."

"You'll let me tell him I was the one to find the document, won't you?"

"Of course," said Maggie. "That's no problem at all."

"Okay, then," said Valerie. "Close your eyes for a teensy sec."

Maggie looked out through her lashes as her co-worker took the key to DC's office out of her drawer and filed the report in the gray steel filing cabinet. As soon as Valerie clattered down the hall to the restroom, Maggie took the key from its hiding place, unlocked the office, and removed the file again, along with two other important-looking documents. There was no time to copy them. There was barely time to stuff everything into the grocery bags and hurry out of the office. Valerie would tell the director she had found the missing document, but when he went to look for it, it wouldn't be there. It was Friday, and Monday was a holiday. At most, Maggie had until Tuesday before they figured out what she had done.

"Whoo-ee," said Hugo when he saw her. "What's the special occasion?"

As Maggie put the two large grocery sacks on the table, she told Hugo about the play-offs and the snacks for the post-game party, all the while batting her lashes and thrusting her hip provocatively out to the side. She tried not to think about the smuggled documents in case Hugo could pick up on thought signals, but sweat was pouring down her back and she was sure he could see that she was hiding something. He looked her up and down appreciatively before turning his attention to her things. "Whoo-ee," he said again, running his hands up and down the first of the two bulging brown paper sacks as if it were a woman. "I have a bit of a sweet tooth myself."

Maggie pretended to be worried that their conversation might be overheard by another guard who was standing by the exit. "Shshsh," she said. "Anyway, I can't talk now or I'll be late."

"You're already late," said Hugo ambiguously.

"You're right," said Maggie. "The last bus has gone, so I'll either have to call Lyle to pick me up or catch a ride to the ball field. I'm sure one of the other parents can take me home."

A tiny push was all Hugo needed. A tiny redirection of all that muscle and attention so that Hugo wouldn't even notice she was the one controlling things.

"That's an idea," said Hugo, removing a package of cookies from one of the bags. "But I'm not sure you should wear that blouse in front of a lot of teenaged boys."

"I didn't wear it for the boys," said Maggie.

"If you can wait until the end of my shift, I can take you home."

There was no time to look too far down the possibility paths before choosing one of them. No time to imagine Hugo's hot hands on the curve of her hip or the cold concrete of the basement floor against her skin or the twin shafts of slanting light from the too-high windows making their way up the wall as the sun sank in the vacant, distant sky before closing her mind to further thought and willing her features to radiate frailty and indecision. She reminded herself that doing good occasionally entailed actions that in other circumstances might be considered questionable and that love and sex were entirely different things. She said, "Or . . ." as if an idea had just occurred to her. All she needed was for Hugo to think he was the one giving the final push, so she added, "Silly me. No, never mind."

"What?" asked Hugo. "Never mind what?"

"I was going to say, how about you search me instead of that bag?"

## 7.7 PASTOR PRICE

Red Bud's annual Glory Dayz festival coincided with the last game of the summer play-offs, and this year most of the town had turned out for the evening barbecue and baseball game. Pastor Price steered Tiffany toward the welcome tent, where three Rainbow Girls were selling raffle tickets to fund their annual project.

"What's the project this year?" asked the pastor.

"We'll know in a few hours," said a girl who was wearing the kind of short shorts and cropped top that would have shocked the pastor only a few years before.

"That one's going to be trouble," he whispered into his wife's ear as he tucked a raffle ticket into her pocket.

Tiffany stood on tiptoes to whisper back. "Does she remind you of anyone in particular?" she asked.

"As a matter of fact, she does."

Tiffany drifted off to join some women she knew while the pastor lingered in the shade of the tent, watching the girls. He missed being outraged by female sexuality, but he guessed he had moved on to other, thornier, provocations, and after a few minutes, he made his way to where the mayor was holding court and passing out campaign promises even though the election was more than a year away.

"What's this?" asked Price. "No one ever runs against you!"

"There's always a first time," said the mayor, poking his head into a nearby tent where Helen Winslow, who was dressed as a fortune-teller, was jangling her bracelets over a crystal ball. "What do you say, Helen?" he asked. "Will there be stiff competition in the mayor's race next year?"

"Not unless that young Fitch boy is thinking of running."

"The Fitch boy!" exclaimed the mayor. "Surely you can't be serious!"

"He attracted quite a following among the younger folks with that article about government overreaching," said Helen.

"Oh, that," said the mayor. "I don't see how encouraging a developer to give us a badly needed office building can be described as overreaching."

"I don't think 'encouraging' is what he called it," said Helen.

"'Kickback' is a strong word," said August Winslow, who was sitting next to his wife, drinking a lemonade. "I'll bet you could get him for slander."

"One hand washes the other," said the mayor. "Anyway, let's not go poking our sticks into the hornet's nest after we've sprayed it with Raid."

"Who did you spray with Raid?" Lex Lexington slid out of the crowd and entered the backwater created by the fortune-teller's tent. "Don't tell me Martin's nephew is causing trouble again!"

"Why hello, Lex," said Helen. "I've just been telling Buddy that young Fitch is going to make a name for himself by exposing all of Red Bud's secrets. Then he'll throw his hat in the ring and run for mayor."

"You see all that in there?" Winslow leaned over his wife's shoulder and squinted at the glass ball.

"Of course not, darling. I made it up."

"You nearly gave me a heart attack," said the mayor.

"You and me both," muttered Lexington.

"It would serve you all right," said Helen, glancing sideways at her husband. "You of all people should know that trying to shut someone up is the surest way to prolong an argument."

"Let's not tell these good people all our secrets," said Winslow with a hollow laugh. "We have a reputation to uphold." He turned to Lexington and said, "How was your vacation?"

"If you don't count the fire ants and the heat and the bad fishing and the spoiled kids and all hell breaking loose back at the office ... " Lex mopped at his forehead with a limp bandana and blinked several times in succession at the pastor, who finally caught on that Lex wanted to speak privately. When the notes of the national anthem floated to them from the ball field, the mayor said, "Okay Helen, now tell us who is going to win."

"You'll have to wait and be surprised," said Helen. "The first Rainbow assembly of the school year is tonight. I just have time to go home and change out of this gypsy outfit. August, you're in charge of the crystal ball."

As soon as Helen and the mayor were gone, Lex sat heavily in the chair Helen had vacated, and the pastor sat down across from Winslow, as if his fortune were being told. "What do you say, August?" he said, making a joke of it. "Tell us what the future holds."

It was a hot day, and Lex was sweating so profusely that patches of his polo shirt had turned clinging and translucent. "Good God, man," said Price. He was proud of his ability to stay cool in most circumstances, and although it was probably a genetic trait and not technically something he could take credit for, he couldn't help feeling slightly superior to the man who was practically melting in front of him.

"I need a little advice from you two," said Lex. "I misplaced a confidential document at work—something given to me by a lobbying group—and while I was away, my assistant found it. So I dropped by the office to get it on my way over here, but it wasn't there. Valerie tells me that the only person who could have taken it is Maggie Rayburn."

"Maggie Rayburn!" exclaimed Winslow, his face turning purple. "Don't tell me she's at it again!" He slammed his fist on the table and stormed out of the tent into the crowd that was still streaming toward the stands, only to immediately turn back again.

"What? What?" asked Lex. "If there's something you can tell me about that woman, I'd like to know about it!"

Winslow sat back down. "This goes no further," he hissed. "Do you understand?"

The pastor nodded coolly, but Lex looked like he was about to explode. "For Chrissakes, man. What goes no further?"

"A top-secret document went missing from my office too. Back in the winter, just before that Rayburn woman quit working up at the plant. I haven't told anyone because ... well, because it wouldn't look too good for me if anyone knew. But this is just a little too much of a coincidence, don't you agree?"

There was no disagreement.

"That's not all," said Price. He was thinking back to the day Lyle had brought Maggie to his house for counseling. "She also admitted to stealing prisoner records. At least her husband said she did. He said so right in my own living room, and she didn't deny it."

"What if we turn her in?" said Winslow. "What if we turn the little hussy in? Lex and I will just have to take the heat and hope it doesn't get too ugly."

"We can't do that," said Lex. "There's too big a downside."

The pastor's mental wheels were already turning—another trait he was proud of was the ability to see solutions while others were still poking at the problem like sad sacks with a sore tooth. "I'm wondering if there's some way we can use this to our advantage," he said.

"To our advantage!" cried Lex. "This is a disaster. How could it possibly work to our advantage?"

"Using a person's momentum against him—or her—happens to be one of my specialties." Price put his hand up to forestall interruptions. "Do you remember how young Fitch wanted to write an article about Maggie back when she left her job at the munitions plant and how we told old Martin to shut him down?"

"I do," said Winslow. "No sense giving the woman a megaphone is what I said at the time."

"Well, what if we give her one now?"

"Are you joking?" asked Lex. "That's a sure way to get me fired."

"I don't mean we say anything about the top-secret documents. I mean we create a distraction. We tell Fitch that someone is stealing prisoner records—nobody cares much about those, do they? We say she's got the best intentions, of course—peace and justice, et cetera, et cetera—all the same reasons that caused her to leave her job in the first place. We get Fitch to ask himself questions—for instance, can do-gooders carry a thing too far or does a good outcome justify illicit means? That's exactly the kind of high-minded stuff he likes. Meanwhile, the Rayburn woman comes under scrutiny for theft—only of the prison records, mind you—which makes her think twice about making any other stolen documents public. Everyone is entertained by a local scandal, and young Fitch is happy because he has a story. All the better if the prisoner is actually innocent, frankly—then Fitch can go off on a tear about injustice and all that. There's a good chance we can even leverage this thing to get your sensitive documents back."

The three men were silent as they contemplated the proposal. A breeze had sprung up while they were talking and the sun had slipped past the topmost branches of a stand of cottonwood trees, leaving the day ten degrees cooler than it had been. Price moved Helen's crystal ball closer to him, noting how it turned everything upside down. "You see that?" Price asked the two other men. "Crystal balls might not tell the future, but they can get you to look at things from another point of view."

A roar erupted from the stadium, and the pastor took the opportunity to excuse himself. "If you're both in agreement, I'll get things rolling by contacting Fitch—anonymously, of course. And Lex, wipe that frown off your face and go get a plate of barbecue. You too, August. Things will work out just fine."

The empty tents were flapping in the breeze as the pastor made his way up the path toward the bleachers, stopping first at the food court to treat himself to a lemonade. Two girls eating ice cream out of paper cups waved their spoons at him. A man bought his son a hot dog and hurried back to watch the game. A vendor refilled his ice chest with soft drinks and fitted the strap around his neck. "Who's winning?" asked Price.

"Dr Pepper," said the vendor. "It's not even close."

Price smiled, amused by the misunderstanding. That just goes to show, he thought, and then he let his mind drift away from lessons about human nature. The leaves on the sycamore trees were already turning. For once, no one was tugging at his sleeve asking him to slice a baby in two so they could each have half of it. One time, he had asked a divorcing couple, "Okay, folks, heads or tails?" But he had mellowed since then.

Just when he was thinking that fall was as good as spring for the way it made a man feel, Maggie Rayburn burst into view, running along the sidewalk with a paper grocery sack clutched in her arms and her hair falling from its clips. Their eyes locked for an instant, and the pastor zigged backward as though some high-voltage connection had been made and quickly severed. He stumbled on the edge of the pavement and almost fell before zagging forward again. Hells bells, he thought. She'll think I've been drinking something stronger than lemonade! In order to cover his awkwardness, he called out, "Happy Glory Dayz," but he said it too late, for Maggie was already scurrying toward the bleachers like a frightened rabbit.

She was definitely guilty. Chickens had a way of coming home to roost even if they needed a little encouragement now and then. "Encouragement." That was the word the mayor had used when he meant "graft." Tiffany would be wondering where he was, but the strange force of the encounter with Maggie had knocked him off course, and now, instead of following the stragglers into the stadium, he let his altered momentum carry him down a steeply cut embankment to the creek.

He'd swum in a creek just like this one as a boy. He and his friends had caught tadpoles and put them in jars so they could watch them turn into frogs if they didn't die first from lack of oxygen. But now a slick of green slime covered the rocks, making the going treacherous. He thought how, if the theory of evolution was true, man's ancestors must have crawled out of the slime and up the banks, their gills turning instantly into lungs. Of course, there were mutations not only of physical features, but also of outlook and character. How else had people emerged from the

Dark Ages, and how else had tyrants given way to more enlightened rulers? But, like anything else, enlightenment could go too far. It was a strange world, and he didn't pretend to understand it. Strange and wonderful, he told himself, shaking his head over an image of the cute little Rainbow Girls and only belatedly adding a thought about the glory of the Father and of the Son and of the Holy Spirit. Amen! He sat on a fallen log and peered into the water, but it was sluggish and opaque, and if there were frogs or tadpoles hiding there, the pastor didn't see them.

## 7.8 WILL

The team was behind by two runs, but things were finally clicking for Will. His arm was smoking. His legs were on fire.

By the time he thought to glance up at the stands, it was the fifth inning. His parents were sitting on a high tier behind third base. Tula had another engagement, so she wasn't at the game, but they had plans to meet up after. He wished he had a car. If he had a car of his own, he could take her out when the game was over. But he didn't, which meant he'd have to go home with his parents, and if he couldn't persuade them to let him have the truck for the evening, he'd have to ride the bicycle or walk the two and a half miles to Ash Creek Circle on foot.

Don't let the future interfere with the present, his coach was always saying, so Will forgot about Tula and the truck. He excised the present from everything that had come before it and everything that would come after. He was coming from and going nowhere. He said his cue word, which worked to center him. "Spider-Man," he said. He immediately felt a contraction of his body mass, as if his mind and body were undergoing a kind of cold fusion before releasing a blast of focused heat. As he approached the plate, the coach called out, "Okay, killer. Knock it out of the park."

Will let the bat slide through his hands and settle into place before he tightened his grip around it, stepped up to the plate, and pounded the bat against it. Then he sized up the pitcher, who was pivoting to hold Stucky Place on second. Stucky gave a nonchalant shrug and spat in the dirt. When the pitcher turned back around, he squinted into Will's eyes and Will squinted back, both eyes together and then each eye on its own. He refocused on Stucky. Then he let Stucky go and narrowed the universe until it contained only Will and the pitcher and then only the ball and the bat. He ran his left hand and then his right hand between his ear and his cap, as if to push a lock of hair out of his eyes. He swung the bat loosely in a figure eight before locking his wrists again, this time for real. Now when he said his cue word, the power surged from his hands up through his elbows and shoulders and down through his core, where it connected with a countering surge that started at the ground and ran up through his legs and groin. The forces met in a tightening of his abdominal muscles and culminated in what the coach called the resonating moment—a snapshot of approaching time showing only the smack of the bat and the sweet spot of the ball. When the pitcher wound up and released, Will's muscles took over, transferring the blast of pure thermonuclear energy into the ball, converting the vision into reality, and sending the baseball out of the park.

# 7.9 TULA

Tula and the other rising juniors had drawn lots to determine the order of their presentations. As luck would have it, Tula was to go third, after Sammi Green and a tall, composed girl named Wanda Wallace who had moved from Oklahoma City the year before. Most of the presentations were predictable—only Sammi's plan for honoring the heroes of Red Bud and Tula's idea of a new bow station had never been done before.

Wanda had made a PowerPoint presentation with captions that said HELP FOR WORKING FAMILIES AND GIVE A KID A BREAK. Each year someone presented a version of the same idea. Tula herself had played kick ball and consumed sugary snacks at just such an after-school program while she waited for her mother to finish her shift at a local motel. "Role model" was an enduring Rainbow concept, and the older girls who staffed the program competed vigorously for the title of most energetic and most sincere. They were the reason Tula had become a Rainbow Girl, so while the idea wasn't original, it had a proven track record of making a difference in actual lives.

Sammi's presentation featured a series of slides showing men in uniform and other slides showing wealthy donors handing over giant checks to the previous year's Worthy Advisor, who beamed and blushed from her chair on the stage when her picture went up on the big screen. Sammi and Wanda sported broad smiles and gleaming teeth and paused confidently when their presentations were over to have their pictures snapped shaking hands with the people on the stage.

By the time her name was called, Tula was nearly faint with excitement. She had called her proposal Project Purity and had made a rainbow-colored banner modeled on the banner that hung on the wall of the meeting room. But where the traditional banner comprised seven bright swaths of color, hers consisted of eight, with the eighth made of the purest white silk her little stash of savings could buy.

When Tula stood up and tenderly unfurled the banner, she was greeted with an intake of breath. "My project is to expand the Rainbow principles to include an eighth bow station, represented by white to symbolize Purity," she began. "Purity is not only the highest female virtue, but it also represents cleanliness and health." When she said the word "cleanliness," she had an unwelcome vision of her mother swabbing out a toilet at the motel, but she shook the image off. She explained that white was not an absence of color but included all wavelengths within it, thus symbolizing the very essence of the Rainbow tradition. Then she paused to gauge how the audience was receiving her presentation. People had clapped in the middle of Sammi's presentation, and the tall girl had made everyone laugh when she told them that of course they could donate money instead of snacks and toys for the disadvantaged children. But now, except for the tick of acorns falling on the metal roof of the meeting hall, all was silent and blurred, the audience an undifferentiated flotilla of oval faces bobbing on a sea of frothy dresses and not even Sammi beaming out encouragement from the front row.

The silence was broken when someone coughed. Another person shuffled her feet. Tula tried to think of something funny to say, but she couldn't. Tula's strength wasn't humor, but passion, which she hoped would come through when she talked about saving up her money for the silk, about borrowing the motel sewing machine to stitch the panels together, about her plans for rewriting the Rainbow Handbook to include the new station. But instead of emitting sparks of passion and enthusiasm as she rushed through the second part of her speech with the banner hanging limply in front of her, she found herself stuttering and blinking back tears.

That year's Worthy Advisor had been elected by her classmates the previous spring, and presiding over the autumn assembly was her first official act. She was wearing a long white dress for the occasion, and when she got to her feet right in the middle of Tula's presentation, the layers of fabric sprang away from her body and shimmered with subtle iridescence. "I'm not sure we understand," she said, the words crisp with new authority. "Please tell us exactly how this is a project for the entire junior class to work on over the course of the coming year. It seems like you plan to do it all yourself. It seems, frankly, as if it's already done." She held her ivory arms out like a queen addressing her subjects, who were fanned out before her and beginning to whisper behind cupped hands.

Tula had thought of this. How purity translated into action was outlined in the last section of her presentation, but she jumped ahead to cover it now. Will had given her a pamphlet on STDs that his mother had found at the prison, and she had adapted it and added cartoon drawings so that it would appeal to middle schoolers. She had been pleased with the final product, but when she held it up, it looked like a piece of folded scrap paper the size of a business envelope. She should have made a giant version of it the way Sammi had done with the checks. "This is a pamphlet I made," she said. "I thought we could go into the schools and talk to the younger girls about Purity, and also about abstinence and sexually transmitted diseases. I learned at the clinic where I work that this is a big problem in our area and that we need to target kids before they reach high school age."

"So your project is about sex education?" asked Mrs. Winslow, patting a stray lock into place.

"Really, it's about Purity. But it's a multifaceted approach."

"So you made a banner and tampered with chapter literature," said the Worthy Advisor.

"Oh, no! I won't change anything. I only plan to add ... "

"Yes, yes. I understand that you want to add a new Rainbow station. But by what right? Who authorized this desecration of tradition? That is what we're trying to find out."

"I'm presenting it now, with the idea that the chapter can vote on it and adopt it according to official procedures," said Tula. "I should have explained that right up front."

But the word "desecration" said it all. Tula barely managed to sit through the rest of the presentations, and as soon as they were over, she slipped out the door into the darkening parking lot. She didn't stay to see whose project would win the vote and the Rainbow scholarship that came with it. Sammi would win it, or the tall girl. In any case, neither the position of trust nor the scholarship would be hers, and without the scholarship ...

Above her, the first stars blasted across the universe, and closer in, the dry leaves of an old oak tree rustled in the breeze. Acorns cracked like tiny skulls under her feet, so she stepped carefully, but she couldn't avoid them all. She had hoped Will would be waiting for her, but he wasn't, so she gathered the skirts of her long dress in both hands and started up the road toward home. She was halfway there when Will came laboring up the hill on his bicycle, calling out to her that his team had lost the game. They walked together, the bicycle between them, and talked about shattered dreams and contingency plans and how if the world had a place for them, it wasn't at all clear what it was.

## 7.10 DOLLY

Dolly took her feet out of the stirrups and used a tissue to wipe between her legs. Then she slipped her skirt over her hips and buttoned her blouse.

"Well," said the doctor, coming back into the room. "Well, well, well. We'll need to start you on prenatal supplements and schedule a sonogram."

"What if there's something wrong with it?" asked Dolly, who envisioned growing within her not a baby, but a misshapen clot of all the terrible things that could and did happen in the world.

"Why would anything be wrong with it?" asked the doctor. "You know as well as anyone that most new-parent fears are unfounded."

"But Danny was in Iraq."

"Lots of our patients were in Iraq or are married to people who were there. Was your boyfriend exploding unused munitions? Was he cleaning up blast sites or burned-out Humvees?"

"Not that I know of," said Dolly. "But it's not just my own baby I'm worried about. You know I've been thinking about this ever since those poor babies were ... you know the babies I mean."

The doctor tapped a sheet of test results. "Your hormone levels are good and high. It's common to experience mood swings, so let me know if things don't improve in that regard."

"And I've been thinking about those two reports . . ."

"What two reports?" asked the doctor.

"The ones you told me about—the original and the one that was altered."

"Those studies are to do with the First Gulf War, so I wouldn't worry."

"But why would this war be any different?" Dolly removed the package Maggie Rayburn had sent her from her purse and thrust it toward the doctor. "You told me that a report had been altered," she said. "Well, this is more evidence that the government knows what's going on."

"I'll look it over," said the doctor. "Now if there's not anything else, our first patient will be here in a few minutes. We don't want to keep her waiting."

When Dolly got home that evening, she poured herself a glass of lemonade and sat out on the porch to drink it. After Labor Day the temperature was supposed to drop, but the backs of her knees were sticky and her thin cotton dress was plastered to her backside. Maybe the doctor was right about the hormones, which would explain not only her discomfort, but also her fears for the little tadpole growing in her belly. Of course fears were normal. And despite the fears, or because of them, she gradually became aware of an inner starburst of hope and significance. Things that had seemed only moderately important before seemed absolutely critical now. How much to eat? Whole milk or skim? Exercise, but not too much. Stop whoever was poisoning the world! But how? How did a person accomplish a thing like that? One moment she was optimistic and the next she was on the verge of despair. What if Danny never got better? Oh, what did she need Danny for!

She called Kathy, the woman who had advised her about making lists of goals and core beliefs. "Guess what?" she said when Kathy came on the line and said hello. But Kathy had news of her own. Her husband had a new girlfriend and had filed for divorce. "It's good you and Danny aren't married," she said. "Marriage just makes everything more complicated. Enjoy your freedom while you can."

Dolly's mother wasn't much better. "It's a terrible time to bring a baby into the world," she said. "So much uncertainty. Why, just the other day my friend Mabel was let go from her job, and the O'Haras are losing their home to foreclosure, and Selma Drew's husband dropped dead of a heart attack—and you remember Hattie Lane? Three hundred pounds and diabetic ... no wonder she's losing her eyesight! To say nothing of all those Middle Easterners trying to blow each other up. Still, it's important to think happy thoughts so the baby can have a normal life. Not that he'll have a normal father, but I suppose it's a little late to think of that."

Her mother dragged her off to church on Sunday. "You're praying for two now," she said.

"Why are we driving all the way to Red Bud?" asked Dolly.

"I've been going there for nearly a year," said her mother. "Pastor Price is really good."

After the service the pastor said that even an out-of-wedlock baby was part of God's plan for Dolly, a comment that served as a springboard for sharing the story of how, way back when, his eyes had been opened to his own life plan.

"There I was, walking home from my job at an insurance agency and minding my own business—at least as much as I usually mind it—when a pure white cat crossed the path in front of me. Pure white, mind you. I didn't think anything of it, but the next day the same thing happened, and it happened again the day after that. On the fourth day, a woman who had lost everything in a tornado came into the office. I told her that the policy she had in her hands had been issued by another insurance company. 'No, you are the one,' she said. If she had said anything else, I would still be an insurance agent, but she poked me in the chest and said, 'You are the one.' I know what you're going to say—that I should have known that the three pure white cats were the Holy Trinity even before the woman drove home the point in such an obvious way. But I was a numbskull back then, too thick to see it until I was driving home a few nights later and passed that sign to the Choctaw Casino—the one that says Turn Here to Change Your Life. So I slammed on the brakes and bless me if I didn't make the turn and stay there half the night—first losing my money and then making it back and then losing it again—so that when I finally went home, I was flat-out broke. I thought a lot about that casino sign, and I have to admit that at first I was bitter. 'It changed my life, all right,' I said when my own pastor pried the story out of me and proceeded to show me how everything fit perfectly together and how the Lord wasn't just calling me, he was grabbing me by the hair. And my life kept right on changing. Eventually I became a pastor myself, and that never would have happened if all of those other things hadn't happened first."

"What happened to the lady?" asked Dolly.

"What lady?"

"The one who lost everything in the tornado."

"I've often wondered that myself," said the pastor. "I'm guessing she went on down the street to the State Farm office and got things sorted out with them, but I suspect she has her own story to tell. Wouldn't it be a hoot if it included me! By all rights, though, we never should have met. She was in the wrong darn place. The wrong place for her, that is, but exactly the right place for me. That's what you have to do, Dolly. God puts people into your life for a reason. Making sense of it is up to you."

"I've been getting signs now too," said Dolly. She told the pastor about the damaged babies and how she had felt called on to help them if she could. "Not that I can help those particular babies, but I want to do something to prevent other babies from suffering a similar fate."

"Don't you wait another minute," said the pastor. "Those damaged babies are signs from God."

Dolly's sister was the worst of all—she was genuinely happy about the baby, which was so unexpected that it plunged Dolly into a cycle of guilt and self-recrimination. How was having a baby anything but selfish, particularly when she hadn't provided it with the most basic of requirements, like a stable family and genetic health? How had it happened? But she knew how it had happened. Danny's homecoming, the lapse of a single night, the burst of love and optimism and indiscretion. She tried to remember the optimism—and then she did remember it. She remembered the love too, but the love came wrapped around a bundle of sorrow and inside the sorrow was the unavoidable fact that the Danny who had come home was not the Danny who had left, which caused her teetering high spirits to plummet into yet another chasm of despair until she thought, A baby! A baby of my very own!

The next week the doctor handed Dolly an envelope. And there, tucked inside, were the two scientific reports. "Here you are then," he said. "Let me know if you need more help."

Dolly remembered the story the pastor had told her, and her scalp tingled to think that God was pulling her by the hair too. She had the information she wanted. Now she just had to decide what to do with it.

# 8.0 WARTRUTH.COM

*There was a series of anti-war protests coming up, so the captain bought a used minivan, and after we picked up Le Roy and Danny, we headed to DC.*

—Joe Kelly

*The protest was a disaster, but I just said, Fuck the protest, and posted some pictures online, and that's when we had the idea for a website that would support the soldiers and tell the truth about the war.*

—Le Roy Jones

*So it was still us versus them, but now "them" was the politicians. "Them" was the employers and the bureaucrats and the doctors at the VA hospital and sometimes just the regular people on the street.*

—Joe Kelly

*After the trip to Washington, everything happened really fast.*
—E'Laine Washington

# 8.1 LE ROY JONES

Le Roy liked to find clues in his environment for where he was and what he was doing there. Now, he was surprised to see so many people with missing limbs. Some stomped haltingly on artificial prostheses, while others occupied wheelchairs or hobbled along with the assistance of friends. He looked down at his own feet just to make sure, but they were laced up in their imitation Ice-Ts and he could wiggle his toes just fine.

"What are you protesting?" asked a bystander who was wearing a souvenir T-shirt with a silkscreen of the Lincoln Memorial on it.

"The war," said Le Roy. "We want the president to stop the war."

Penn Sinclair was there, and so were Danny Joiner and Joe Kelly. It seemed like an astonishing coincidence until the captain reminded him they were staying together at a motel out by the airport. Of course he remembered that. Of course he remembered the trip down in the minivan and the free Wi-Fi at the motel. "Oh, yeah," he said. The moments after he hit his head could get mixed up, but the moments from before were crystal clear. He could picture himself riding in the truck with Rinaldi and Summers and their medic, Satch. He remembered trying to get the radio to work and telling the recruiter he was good with electronics and waking up in the hospital with bandages around his head that felt like reinforced concrete. He remembered the blood pounding in his ears and the doctor saying, "Hey there, cowboy. You've got a pretty hard head," which was what the doctor said every time he saw him. He remembered the rehab guy hauling him out of bed long before he was ready. He remembered fiddling with the volume on the radio and the captain saying the convoy was doubling back and heading west and someone asking how much farther to the school, and then the blood was pounding in his ears and the doctor was saying the thing about the hard head and the rehab guy was hauling his ass out of bed.

"Let's all stay together," said Danny. "But just in case we get separated, do you still have the address of the motel?"

"Twenty-two twenty-one Arlington Boulevard. Room two-thirteen," said Le Roy, tapping his pocket. He could remember certain things just fine. "But yeah," he said. "I have the card."

"If you lose us, just go to that address."

Le Roy liked to have a routine, but not having a routine could be good too, so long as he felt safe. He felt safe when he saw the captain and Danny, but he didn't feel safe when someone in the crowd started shouting and two officers on horseback started to ride straight at a group of people holding placards. He liked horses, but he didn't feel safe when one of the big animals got too close to him or when the policeman waved his baton or when the Lincoln Memorial T-shirt guy was knocked to the ground.

Le Roy helped the man to his feet and said, "Fuck this shit." He solved the horse problem by turning his back to it—out of sight, out of mind—before flipping the bird at the yellow police tape and the official-looking signs that said PROTESTERS HERE. Then he turned his back on those too and walked up to a man with a megaphone and then to a police officer and then to someone wearing a Ranger beret, and each time, he looked the person in the eye and said, "Fuck this shit." Soon he and the Ranger had a small following and he had forgotten to remember about Kelly and Sinclair. The group walked as a unit when the crowd began to move down Pennsylvania Avenue toward the Capitol building—except for the guy in the wheelchair, who wasn't technically walking. Le Roy put his hand on his heart and gaped at the majestic building with its iconic marble dome gleaming in the sun. A flag streamed out from its pole. "This is Washington, DC?" he asked, even though he knew it was.

"Yeah, man," said the Ranger. "This is it."

Le Roy stood with his hand on his heart until the officers on the horses told them to move along. Le Roy wanted to stand just a little longer, so when the horse shouldered into him, Le Roy shouldered back, but the horse easily stood its ground. He liked horses. He didn't blame the horse, but what the fuck? The Ranger put a hand on his shoulder and said, "Chill out, man," but Le Roy couldn't process what he was saying because the officer was shouting into his other ear. Easy does it, he thought. One at a time. He wished he had his computer, but it was back at the motel. The motel card was in his pocket, but he didn't need it because the address involved numbers. Numbers and codes— that's what he was good at.

The Ranger had taken one of the signs that had been planted in a soft patch of ground and was thrusting the rough wooden stake in front of him like a sword. When someone grabbed his shoulder from behind, he reacted the way he had been taught to react, and soon his assailant was on his back, head lolling like a football in the gutter, which was all it took for the policemen stationed at the perimeter of the zone to pull Tasers and pepper spray out of their belts.

"Stop right there!" shouted one of the officers, and the other fired his pistol into the air, which caused most of the assembled veterans to dive to the ground and two of them to storm a row of metal barricades and tear away the yellow tape.

"Halt!" shouted the police, but they didn't halt, so the mounted officers rode forward into the crowd, knocking down anyone who was in their way. Le Roy was in their way, and he fell to the ground just inches from a big black hoof with a cleated iron shoe. He turned his head slightly and forgot about the horse, but blood was trickling from his forehead into his eyes and spattering the back of his hand. What the fuck? Where the hell was he, anyway?

"Follow me!" shouted the Ranger, dragging Le Roy to his feet. "Run!"

Le Roy started running. He ran and ran and didn't stop until his lungs were on the verge of collapse, and then he ran a little farther, even when the reason for running got lost somewhere far behind him. He had gotten soft and, he had to admit, a little flabby, but he hadn't forgotten how to find escape routes and assess a crowd for potential threats. He hadn't forgotten how to stick to the shadows and double back on his trail. He hadn't forgotten to be suspicious of males with skin that was darker than Danny's skin but not as dark as his own, of people in flowing clothing, of people wearing backpacks, of people in beat-up cars.

As he ran, a space in his brain opened up, and he remembered something he'd forgotten—E'Laine lacing up her jogging shoes and shouting, "Come on, track star. Catch me if you can!" It was a small thing, but it served to power one last burst of speed.

# 8.2 JOE KELLY

Kelly had expected something more dramatic than running away from the police. He'd expected a mission-accomplished sense of satisfaction or at least some outlet for the tension that was mounting in his brain and muscles and demanding some sort of release. He'd like to have sex with a girl. He'd like to have sex with a girl he didn't know—not the kind of sex where they lit candles or talked before and after or fit it in around a practical activity like cooking dinner or gassing up the car and not the kind where he had to take her out to a nice restaurant and feign interest in her life goals. Kelly no longer had any life goals—if he had ever had them—and the idea that other people might want to talk to him about theirs made him want to smash his fist through a piece of glass. "I'll see you back at the hotel," he said, but the captain put a hand on his shoulder and said, "How about we all stay together?"

Kelly twisted his body out of reach and thought about slugging the captain in the face. "Who's coming with me?" he asked. But Le Roy had run off somewhere and Danny would only slow him down.

"I think we've had enough excitement for one day," said the captain, but Kelly said, "I'm just getting started," and slammed his shoulder into the captain's as he walked past him and felt the captain slam back. "Why isn't Hernandez here?" he asked, but he knew where Hernandez was. Hernandez was home in Texas with his wife and kid.

Kelly started walking. He passed a lot of official-looking buildings and restaurants—nice enough, but the exact wrong kind of nice. He checked for telltale bulges in people's clothing. He watched a nondescript car drive slowly up the block. He envisioned a beautiful girl, one who would take pity on him, but not the kind of pity where she felt sorry for him. Maybe "pity" wasn't the right word for the attitude she would have. Empathy or respect would be better, or, best of all, she wouldn't have any kind of attitude toward him, just some inscrutable need of her own, a need he didn't want to hear about but that would sync her up with him in just the right way.

After a while he came to a strip of trees, and beyond the trees, a river, and there, standing on a bridge over the river, were two teenage boys. There was Harraday, aiming his rifle at them. There were the boys, stepping into thin air. Nah, he was just imagining it. No boys, no Harraday, just a bridge over a river, and on the bridge, a stream of shiny late-model cars.

The good news was that he found an area of seedy bars and restaurants on the other side of the bridge that were just the kind of nice he had in mind. He went into one of them and ordered a beer, but when he put his hand in his pocket, he drew out his cell phone and some loose change, but not his wallet. It was then he remembered knocking into Sinclair. The captain had picked his pocket. Jeezus, he thought. Christ.

He put the change on the table and counted it by separating the coins into little piles depending on denomination. Then he knocked them over and arranged them again, this time where each pile equaled twenty-five cents. "Shee-it," he said out loud, just as a smoky voice said, "Don't worry about it. The beer's on me."

It was and wasn't what he wanted. He wanted the beer, but he didn't want the charity. He wanted the smoky voice, but he didn't want the intelligence behind the eyes. He wanted the female body, but he didn't want the pity or the story the woman would be making up to explain the piles of coins to herself. He should be buying her a drink. He should have a wallet in his pocket and a nice car parked outside. But the deck was stacked against him. War or no war, he was never going to have those things. His father hadn't had them and his father's father hadn't had them, so why should it be any different for him?

"Okay, thanks," he said.

The woman smiled again. The bartender thunked the mugs on the table. Kelly could feel the anger clenching up inside him. His hands were shaking, so he took a quick slug of beer before hiding them in his lap. "Shit," he said again, and then he gave the girl a friendly smile. When she smiled back, her face caught the light from the beer signs hanging above the bar and he noticed her eyes had a hint of yellow in them. "Why didn't you warn me you were part tiger?" he said.

# 8.3 LE ROY JONES

When Le Roy finally stopped to rest, he was surrounded by unfamiliar buildings and the members of his impromptu unit were nowhere in sight. He ducked into an alley and hunkered down against a grimy wall. All he could see from there were the back doors to a row of commercial buildings and a clutch of rusting dumpsters, and when he put his hands over his eyes, he couldn't even see that. Every now and then he would peek out at the changing color of the clouds as the sun shifted in the sky, and then the world would stop spinning and his heart rate would even out. A flock of birds startled and then went back to scavenging for garbage. He liked birds. He liked birds even more than he liked horses, and he liked horses quite a lot.

After watching the birds he started walking again, now and then picturing the map he had seen over the captain's shoulder and adjusting his course accordingly until the only thing that separated him from 2221 Arlington Boulevard was a six-lane highway. Hernandez had taught him a trick for making time slow down. "Guaranteed," Hernandez had said, so Le Roy decided to try it. But first he tried the rehab guy's checklist trick. He visualized success and thought, I am an American soldier. I will not accept defeat. Then he crouched at the side of the road in starting position, watching for a gap in the traffic. "Okay, Hernandez," he said aloud. "I hope the fuck you're right."

He pushed off with his right leg, aiming for the gap, dodging through it, breaking and dodging again before diving left-thenright, behind a shiny panel van. The trick almost didn't work, but instead of hitting him, the car in the last lane swerved and almost hit the guardrail. It was quite a sight to see the look on the driver's face as the car fishtailed and almost spun into oncoming traffic before straightening out again. "Hey!" shouted the driver from behind the glass. "Hey, you!"

Le Roy hurdled the guardrail and rolled down the bank. He sprang to his feet and then he was running again. It felt good to run, with the motel shimmering in his imagination and then rising before him as if he had conjured it up and, when he got there, his buddies sitting on the couch drinking beer just like he could have predicted. They all jumped up when he walked through the door and said they were glad to see him in a way that made time slow down again, just for an instant. He was glad to see them too, but he didn't think to say so.

"Did you get arrested?" asked Danny.

"No," said Le Roy. "Did you?"

"Nah," said Danny. "But Kelly's still unaccounted for."

"I guess we're not cut out for demonstrations," said the captain. "We'll have to think of something else."

"What kind of something else?" asked Le Roy after chugging a can of beer.

"The sky's the limit," said the captain, handing Le Roy his computer, which he had put underneath the bed so no one would step on it. Le Roy's heart was still beating double time, but with his computer in his lap, he started to calm down.

"Who else is hungry?" asked Danny. "I'll order a pizza and some more beer."

It sounded good to Le Roy. Meanwhile, he put on his headphones and started working away at some code. By the time the pizza came, he had found some photographs of the demonstration that other people had posted online, and by the time everyone finished eating, he had uploaded them to a website he'd created for Watada. He liked having all of the photographs in one place where he could access them or even delete them with the tap of a finger. Tap, there were the police on horseback. Tap, tap, they were gone.

# 8.4 DANNY JOINER

Danny wanted to borrow the computer so he could email himself some notes for the television pilot he was working on, but each time he asked, Le Roy said, "Just a sec," and then ignored him. A few minutes would pass and then Danny would ask again and get the same response, which was why he was sitting next to Le Roy when the captain said they needed a different outlet for their efforts. Protests didn't seem to be their thing.

Le Roy was flipping through YouTube videos from Iraq and saying, "Sweet. Swee-eet," whenever he found one he liked. Danny looked over to see an explosion, and when Le Roy noticed him, he rewound the film to show a road-clearing crew setting a charge and unrolling wire from a spool until they were at a safe detonation distance. "That's what Pig Eye needed," said Le Roy. "That's what Pig Eye needed in his kit."

The season was changing, and the light outside the dingy motel room window was already thick and fading. When Danny was a schoolboy, autumn had always been rich with promise, as if the bus he and his friends boarded every morning would blow right past the school with the chain-link playground patrolled by grim disciplinarians and deposit them in other lives. But lately it seemed that possibility was a thing of the past, that what lay ahead of him was dark and dreadful. He didn't know if he would ever shake the sense of impending doom he had brought home with him from the war. "Can I check my email?" he asked again, but he wasn't in a hurry yet. Urgency was something that waxed and waned in him, something he could no longer predict, so when Le Roy said, "Just a sec," Danny was happy to wait a little longer, happy to look over Le Roy's shoulder to see a tank mowing down a row of trees, happy to see Pig Eye unrolling a spool of wire and this time surviving the blast, although he knew from experience that patience could evaporate and become impatience in the blink of an eye.

After a while Kelly came in and said, "Fuck you," to the captain for taking his wallet, but he was in a good mood.

"We could interview soldiers and write a book," suggested the captain. "We could work for anti-war political candidates. We could ... "

They talked about it for a bit. Kelly made another beer run, and pretty soon they were whooping and laughing so hard that beer was spraying from the cans and the people in the room next door started banging on the walls, and pretty soon after that the motel manager knocked on the door. "Can you keep it down?" he asked. "You're not the only ones staying here." The captain tossed him a beer, and before too long the couple next door had joined them too.

"Hernandez should be here," said Kelly. "Let's get him on the phone."

"What are you all doing in town?" asked the wife from the room next door while the captain took out his cell phone and started dialing. "Are you here on business?"

"We're here to protest the war," said Le Roy.

"You've come to the right place," said the wife. "The national cemetery is right across the street. Seeing all those graves always makes me wanna cry."

"But we kind of suck at protests, so we're trying to figure out what to do instead."

"You should start a blog," said the wife, tapping a red fingernail on the computer screen. "A memorial or something—kind of like the cemetery, but on the Internet."

"Yeah," said Le Roy. "A blog would be good."

While the captain tried to reach Hernandez and Le Roy showed the wife videos of the war on his computer, the husband turned to Danny and asked, "Did you kill anyone? In Iraq, I mean."

"That's none of your business," said Danny.

"Sure," said the husband. "But did you?"

Of all the answers Danny could give to that question, the simplest one was both a lie and the truth. "I was in a forward support unit," he said. And there he was again, riding the train of thought that always ended in watching Pig Eye explode.

"I heard that about two percent of people—of guys, anyway—are natural killers," said the husband. "The kind who can kill without feeling any remorse. Did you run into any fellas like that?"

"Hey, Captain," said Danny, thinking of Harraday. "Rube here wants to know if we're natural killers." Once Harraday's switch got flipped, it was like he couldn't turn it off. Danny's switch was different, but he couldn't turn his off either.

"No, no." The man laughed, deep in his throat—a genuine laugh, Danny thought at first, but then he changed his mind. There was something not quite right about him, like he was laughing to cover up how deadly serious he was.

"That's not what I asked," said the husband slowly. "I just asked if you knew any. And my name's not Rube."

"My mistake," said Danny.

"I'm wondering if I'd be a natural killer, that's all."

"You are, honey," said the wife. "You've been killing me for years."

"In a good way, I hope," said the husband. Then he turned back to Danny and said, "I'm just wondering if it comes more naturally to some people than others and if those people make better soldiers and if I'd be one of those."

"They teach you what you need to know," said Danny.

The husband was leaning forward now, a little too close for Danny's liking. Over by the window, Kelly was talking to Hernandez on the captain's phone. "I love ya, man. Wish you were here."

"How do they teach you?" the husband wanted to know.

"They teach you to work as a unit. They teach you to be really good at what you do."

"I heard they teach you to hate people," said the wife, who had plopped down on the bed beside Le Roy, her mouth open and her eyes wide.

"Nah," said Danny. He was thinking he might hate the husband. And he might hate the wife. Her hand was on Le Roy's thigh, and Danny could feel the heat of it just by looking.

"To be honest, I'm kind of jealous," said the husband, ticking down a level in intensity. "Sure, I have a family and all, but I don't have any buddies anymore."

"I can believe that," said Danny. On a whim, he thrust his face forward so that he was almost as close to the husband as the wife was to Le Roy. "I did kill someone," he said, trying it on. "I wasn't going to tell you, but you seem like the kind of guy who can handle the truth. Do you want to hear about it?"

The husband dipped his chin in a wary nod.

"This is something I haven't told anyone else."

The husband took a sip of his beer and nodded again, his slack lips flapping a little against his teeth.

Danny was about to say something about shooting the driver of the pickup, but then he was overcome with a wave of nausea and changed his mind. "There were these two Iraqi boys," he said. "They were throwing stones into the long grass below a bridge near where we were on patrol, trying to make us think there was something there. Could be there was, I don't know. But we were jumpy and those boys were annoying the hell out of us." Danny tried to recall what he had heard about the incident. Then he tried to imagine what he might have done if he had been there—if he were Harraday, for instance, instead of who he was. He could feel the tense ratcheting up as Harraday's knot of irritation gave way to fear and the fear gave way to anger. He could see the clobbered look on the boys' faces as they realized what was happening, the panicked flailing of their arms as they jumped, the one boy slipping beneath the oily surface of the water and the other boy reappearing again and again, fighting against the current. And then the water was sliding up Danny's nose and pouring down his throat as surely as if he were imagining he was one of the boys instead of imagining he was Harraday, who was standing on the bridge and shooting into the water—just for fun, he bragged, but it was never just for fun. Because of the 360 degrees and because a person's eyes couldn't be everywhere at once and because maybe there was something hiding under the bridge and also because maybe was the same as maybe not. The words came easily to him, and he could see the gears grind behind the couple's eyes as they tried to make sense of something that was senseless. "But you were frightened, right?" asked the wife. "And they were the enemy. They might have killed you."

"Maybe I was," said Danny.

"Of course they were the enemy," said the husband. "These guys here could have been killed at any moment."

"I guess we'll never know," said Danny. "But they were teens—fifteen or sixteen years old."

"Teenagers can be vicious," said the man. "You did what you had to do."

Over by the window, the captain grabbed the phone away from Kelly. The plate glass was a sheet of orange now, the dust refracting the last rays of light and obscuring the view of the highway.

"Their brains haven't developed yet."

"Yeah," said Danny. Harraday had been hardly more than a teenager himself, and it was mostly because of him that more of the unit hadn't died after the IED attack.

"Hey, Hernandez," said the captain into the phone. "You should be here with us. We've got something going. We're not sure what yet, but whatever it is, it's going to be great." He was silent for a minute, listening to Hernandez, and then he said, "Hernandez wants us to know he's on an emergency diaper run and Maya is waiting for him at home."

"Pussy," said Kelly, looking the man from next door up and down.

"Do you want to see something really sick?" Le Roy asked the wife, who was almost draped across him on the bed, clutching a pillow to her chest. Her blouse and jeans had separated to reveal Jesus tattooed in muddy ink on the small of her back.

When Le Roy opened a video clip showing hooded American soldiers getting their heads cut off, she let out a puff of air as if she had been punched in the gut, quietly, through the pillow. "Those are the guys we were fighting," said Le Roy.

"That's crazy," said the wife, and the husband said, "Makes me want to join up right now and kill those motherfuckers with my bare hands."

"Rube here wants to know if we killed anyone," said Danny, looping the captain and Kelly into the conversation now that they were no longer talking to Hernandez. "He wants to know if he's a natural killer."

"How about we find out," said Kelly, rising from his chair and blocking the window so that the room became a shade darker and a size smaller because Kelly was pretty tall.

"Whaddya mean?" asked the man.

"There's a way to test for it," said Kelly. "We get the guy in a chokehold—like this—and another guy punches him in the gut and we see what he does about it, right Danny?"

"Right," said Danny.

Kelly had the man's neck in the crook of his elbow and was hauling him to his feet and the captain was tipping his head back to drain his beer and Le Roy was tapping his computer screen and saying, "You can check your emails now," when the urgency kicked in. Danny landed a punch in the softness of the man's abdomen and then he wound up for another one as Le Roy and the wife rolled onto the floor and the captain dove across the room so that the four men were thrashing around on the bed and it was unclear who was fighting whom. Someone was screaming in the background. Then the fight went out of Danny as suddenly as it had come.

"Sorry, Rube," said Kelly. "You didn't pass the test."

"What the hell!" cried the husband, jumping up from the tangle of bedcovers and rubbing his neck and looking around for his wife, who had flung herself into a corner when the fighting started. "What test? That didn't seem like any kind of test!"

"The natural killer test," said Kelly. "You're not a natural killer after all."

"Jeezus," said the husband. He and the wife and the motel manager had succeeded in getting the door open, and now they were backing out of it into the hallway. "What the hell," the husband said again, and the motel manager said, "You all keep it down in here. Other people are trying to sleep."

# 8.5 PENN SINCLAIR

Penn followed the manager into the hallway and tried to smooth things over.

"I'm only letting you stay because you're soldiers," said the manager. "But no more trouble. If you promise to check out first thing in the morning, I can probably convince that couple not to call the police."

"Thanks," said Penn. "I owe you one."

When he returned to the room, Danny and Kelly were laughing over the incident and Le Roy was posting links to some protest videos onto the website he was in the process of expanding.

"It almost wasn't funny," said Penn. "It still won't be if they file a complaint."

"Natural killers," said Kelly, which set Danny laughing again.

Le Roy said, "The wife suggested we make a website dedicated to the soldiers. Some kind of memorial or blog. That way we could support the protesters from afar."

"The wife suggested that?" asked Penn.

"Yeah," said Le Roy. "The husband was an asshole, but the wife was okay."

"Here's to the wife," said Danny, draining the last of his beer.

"What will we call it?" asked Le Roy.

Danny suggested wartruth.com, and the captain asked, "Shouldn't it be dot o-r-g instead of dot c-o-m?"

"We want to make money," said Kelly. "Whatever we do, I don't want to take charity."

"How are we going to make money on a website? We'd be doing it more because it's a good thing to do than because it would pay anything," said Penn.

Kelly said he didn't know anything about websites, but he knew that some of them paid off. Le Roy said he didn't know about money, but he knew about websites. Danny talked about bringing their brothers home and helping with their transition to civilian life. "I could have used something like that," he said.

Penn was more and more excited by the idea. "Everybody's bringing something to the table," he said. Then he gave a speech about how it had taken Odysseus ten years to get home and how Agamemnon was murdered by his wife's lover when he finally returned from Troy.

"Not that that's relevant," said Kelly, but Danny wanted to know what had taken Odysseus so long.

"It's not that he couldn't get home," said the captain. "It's that he didn't want to. He knew he couldn't be a hero sitting around at home."

On the drive north the next day, Penn was acutely aware of the three big men with him in the van—of the body odor and the restlessness. It was as if the vehicle contained live but quiet rounds. They had been driving for an hour when Kelly asked where they were going.

"We've got to establish an outpost," said Penn. "The question is, where should it be?"

Instinct was taking him north, toward Louise in New York and his family in Greenwich as if that was his destiny, but he couldn't decide if he was trying to become something he wasn't or trying to avoid being something he was. Then Le Roy was hungry, so they stopped and bought sandwiches, and then they stopped for gas, and a little while after that Danny said he wanted to get out and walk around. Kelly wanted to keep going, but Le Roy had to take a leak.

"We were just at the gas station for Chrissakes," said Kelly. "Why didn't you do whatever you had to do there?"

"Anybody got an empty bottle?" asked Le Roy, which caused Penn to declare, "We're almost there," even though he still had no idea where they were headed.

WELCOME TO NEW JERSEY said a sign. "New Jersey," said Penn. "Why the hell not?"

He parked the car on a street lined with dilapidated buildings, which, on closer inspection, showed small signs of improvement: a repaved driveway, windows with yellow stickers in the corners, a fresh coat of whitewash on the brick, a woman pushing a stroller along the sidewalk, a sign that said GROW WITH TRENTON! LOCATE YOUR BUSINESS HERE!

"This could be it," said Kelly, and Penn agreed that it could be. It was as if Louise's magnet had been turned around and what he felt now was its strong repellent force, a sensation that caused him to view the railroad tracks that divided the neighborhood and the litter caught in the uncut roadside grass and the boarded-up community pool and the men loitering on the corner as selling points, at least in an enemy-of-my-enemy kind of way, so that even if Louise was hardly his enemy, he knew that by saying yes to the neighborhood, he was taking a stand against some of the things she stood for—unearned privilege, for instance, and willful ignorance of how most people lived.

They spent the night at a motel near the highway, and the next day Penn rented space on the first floor of a warehouse and the group dug in. In anticipation of winter, they purchased a portable space heater and weather stripping for the windows. They bought a mini fridge and a microwave from Best Buy, cots and plastic storage lockers from Target, and heavy-duty sleeping bags from REI. They arranged the cots and lockers along one wall and set up folding tables and chairs and computers from an office supply store along another. They bought desks off of Craigslist and argued about who was responsible for which chores and what were the consequences for laziness or dereliction.

"This ain't the army, man," said Kelly.

"I know, I know," said Penn, backing off.

But a natural discipline seemed to take hold of the men according to their interests and abilities. Penn went out early and came back with breakfast. Then he set to work identifying donors to solicit and causes to promote. Danny installed the weather stripping and cleaned because he had the strictest standards for how those things should be done. Le Roy ran five miles every morning before gluing himself to his computer for the rest of the day. And Kelly set up the office space and worked the longest hours, making spreadsheets and organizing files and researching how Internet advertising worked. "Who said I can't be a businessman?" he asked when the first check arrived in the mail. "Who said we can't make this sucker pay?"

The room had barred windows on three sides, and to the north, it looked out onto a railroad track. Every hour or so a train rumbled through, shaking the glass in the windows and causing Danny to dive for cover behind a couch they had found discarded on a curb.

"Hit the deck, Danny!" Le Roy would say if Kelly didn't say it first, and then Kelly would say, "New Jersey! At least it ain't the fucking Bronx."

The neighborhood was just squalid enough for Penn to imagine that they were still fighting for their country—particularly at night, when the businesses were shuttered and feral cats ransacked the garbage cans and the only light came from a lone streetlamp half-way down the block. Every now and then Penn would shout, "Into the breach, boys. Let's stop the goddamn war!" He was mostly play-acting, mostly putting on a personality he had first observed in his father at the yearly picnic he held for the families of his employees on the sweeping grounds of the Greenwich estate. "Who's ready for the sack race?" the old man would call out. "Who wants to win a prize?" And the children would flock to him as if he were good with children, which, on that one day of the year, he was.

One evening, something unusual in the cocoon of nighttime stillness drew Penn outside, where he walked up and down the block, checking that the grilles on the ground-floor windows of the businesses were secure and across the tracks to a dilapidated apartment house where a woman was sitting in the darkness smoking a cigarette and sobbing.

"I thought I heard something," said Penn.

"It's just them cats," she said.

"Is everything okay?"

"Yeah," she said. "Ever'thin's okay."

"We're just down the block if you need anything."

"I'll remember that," she said, but she never came asking for anything, only waved at Penn when he walked up the street now and then on what he called "patrol" or when he went the long way around on his morning coffee run so he could see her sending her three kids off to school. Each time, she waved to him before going back inside the building, and one day Penn realized that what she needed wasn't him patrolling the streets at night. What she needed was a job. "Hey," he called out the next time he saw her. "You don't know anybody who wants to cook and clean for a bunch of ex-soldiers, do you?"

"I jes might," she said. "I jes might know someone like that."

Meanwhile, the upstairs tenants clomped up the warehouse stairs to their office in the morning and down again in the afternoon in pursuit of their own entrepreneurial dreams, and now and then they said, "How ya doin'?" when Penn ran into them on the front walk, where some faded hydrangeas from an overgrown bed spilled onto the pavement. Across the street, a car parts salvage business had taken over an empty building, and two months after the soldiers moved in, a commercial laundry service opened up. In the white-gray light of early morning when he was on the breakfast run, Penn allowed himself to think that something good was starting up—the website of course, but also the little neighborhood near the tracks.

## 8.6 JOE KELLY

The first thing they put up on the site after the pictures from the protest was a schedule of other protests. Then they created a message board where returning soldiers could post their stories of the war. In the back of his mind, Kelly was wondering how they were going to make a bunch of stories pay, but for the time being he was happy just not to be living with his folks.

"I'm going to post something," said Danny, who had put aside the television pilot and was working on an epic poem. "Think of the *Odyssey*—if it was written by Eminem."

Kelly was still working out the angles of the site. "How do we know if the stories are true?" he asked.

"What's true?" countered Danny. He stood up in the open space between the desks and read from his notepad:

> *News, news, fact or ruse,*
> *Raise the flag and light the fuse*

"I'm not sure the personal stories need to be true," said the captain. "The idea is for soldiers to share their experiences. It's how they see what happened that counts."

"The documents don't need to be true either," said Le Roy. "They only need to be authentic, so I'm studying up on that."

At a pause in the conversation, Danny continued reading.

> *"The war will be over before it starts,"*
> *Goes the official pronouncement*
> *(While PhDs using proven marketing techniques send*
> *Catchy slogans into the ether)*
> *And military contractors ramp up production,*
> *Turning depleted uranium and enlisted men*
> *Into dollars and cents.*
> *Coincidentally, it is the Congressional naysayers*
> *Who receive anthrax-laced letters in the mail.*
>
> *Meanwhile, by the waters of Babylon,*
> *A car laden with explosives*
> *Approaches a convoy on a lonely desert road.*
> *A soldier makes a lucky shot, and . . .*

The train went through, blaring its whistle at the crossing and startling even Kelly. "Man, that sounded like incoming artillery fire," he said.

When the glass had settled back into its wooden frames, Danny climbed out from behind the couch and said, "Anyway, I figured that since it's impossible to forget, maybe I should be trying to remember."

"You didn't know about the grenade," said Penn. "There's no way you could have known."

"That's the point," said Danny. "What do any of us know—me or anybody else? We run around with guns and battle plans and grandiose statements about liberation, but we might as well be kids running around in the dark. So now we post the stories and we write the poems and we dig through the official record for shards of truth or evidence of wrongdoing—and what? It doesn't change anything we did. The damage is done."

"The blast was going to kill him anyway," said Kelly. "Even if you hadn't stopped the truck."

"He might have had a chance," said Danny. "He might have had a fighting chance."

"He had zero chance," said Kelly. "Not even one in a million."

"And those shards of truth might change things," said the captain. "Not the past, but the future."

"What's true?" Danny asked again.

"I'm thinking it's all of the personal narratives together," said the captain, "each of them a tiny pixel in the bigger picture of what is what. And then the documents tether the narratives into some kind of objective framework. They allow people to look behind the personal accounts and the news stories to see if what we're being told is true."

Le Roy was still going on about authentication. "I've got a good guy working with me on that, but he tells me we need some kind of anonymous drop box. People can't just email us top-secret documents. And we don't want to know who the leakers are—we need a system where they can't be traced."

Kelly noticed how everyone occupied his own boxcar of thought: The captain had some theory of journalism in mind. Le Roy was obsessed with the mechanics of collecting and disseminating information. Danny was interested in stories as catharsis and art. Kelly wasn't sure yet what he was interested in, but money was never far from his mind. "Speaking of stories," he said, but just then the single mother from down the block arrived with the dinner she had cooked for them, and Kelly didn't finish what he was going to say.

"You boys are in for a treat," she said, putting a pan of lasagna on the table. "Mmm–mm. I outdid myself today!"

The first document to go up on the site was Penn's old email to himself describing what had happened with the convoy and the IED, juxtaposed to the official version of events.

"Are you sure you want that up there?" asked Kelly.

"Yeah," said the captain. "I do."

"Kind of like a confession?" asked Kelly.

"Yeah," said the captain, "kind of like that."

The captain was headed out on his evening patrol, so Kelly pulled on his jacket and followed him down the walk, kicking at the hydrangea heads, which had turned brittle and brown as the season deepened. He was surprised to see that night had fallen and the cloud cover had given way to a clear blackness that dissolved at the edges where lights from the city center fought back the dark. "I was thinking," he said. "Could be it's better to leave the ghosts alone."

"How does that help?" asked the captain. "Ghosts are creatures of darkness. They might not ever disappear completely, but they lose some of their power in the light."

They walked across the tracks and turned down toward the river, past the boarded-up community pool. "We should get that pool reopened," said Penn. "That's something the neighborhood kids would like."

"Every kid should know how to swim," said Kelly, but he wasn't thinking about the neighborhood kids, he was thinking about the two teenagers on the bridge. Danny hadn't been there, but he had. "The thing is, those boys didn't do anything but throw some rocks into the weeds, but it didn't matter. I remember saying, 'Wait a minute,' but I wasn't thinking, Let's not hassle those kids. I was thinking, I hate fucking hajis. And I was curious about what Harraday would do and also kind of detached, as if none of it was really real." And then he laughed and said, "What's real?" the way Danny would have said it.

"Let it be, Kelly," said Penn. "Whatever it is, there's no sense dredging it all up again."

"I thought you wanted to let the ghosts out."

"Only if it helps, man. Only if it helps."

"They wanted us to be afraid, and so we wanted them to be afraid too."

They stood smelling the coming winter and listening to the wind moving through branches that still held a few papery leaves and watching the river roll underneath the railroad bridge. Then Sinclair said, "What's to say that the stars above us aren't the bright points of swords aimed at the earth by alien forces."

Kelly thought he was joking, but the captain just eyed him in the steady way he had when he was being serious or when the joke went over his head. "Hey, man," said Kelly. "We've got scientists 'n' shit, so we know those are stars, not the points of any swords."

"We *had* scientists," said the captain. "We had weapons

302

inspectors. We had the biggest intelligence agency in the world. Anyway, I'm just saying that if they told us those stars were cosmic swords hurtling toward us ready to attack the earth, we'd man the rockets and blast the stars to smithereens."

"If," said Kelly. "If that's what they told us, I guess we would."

"I'm just saying that we wouldn't know not to. I'm saying that once you believe certain things about the world, other things become possible, even inevitable."

Kelly didn't say anything.

"I guess my point is that we all did stuff over there. We all did stuff we're proud of and we all did stuff we regret and maybe you don't get one without the other in this life. It was stubbornness and vanity that made me send that convoy ... I wanted to finish the school. I wanted to be in charge and to think I could know what the best course of action was, given the circumstances. Danny's right about that—none of us knows shit."

"We regret it, but that's only because we're back here. If we were over there, we'd do it all again."

"Could be," said Penn. "Could be you're right."

The two men stood for a while contemplating the night sky before resuming their patrol. Kelly said, "The other thing I think about is if Pig Eye killed himself on purpose. The blast was going to get him whether or not Danny stopped the truck. So my question is, did he sacrifice his life for ours?"

"Knowing him, he probably thought he'd come through it just fine. He liked to imagine escape scenarios."

Kelly laughed. "Yeah. He prided himself on that."

They had circled around past the car parts shop. Penn went back inside, after which Kelly spent a little longer mourning Pig Eye and the other men and what he had always thought

303

of as stars but now imagined were swords from a murderous extraterrestrial race. And then for some reason he was thinking there must be pretty girls in New Jersey, girls who wouldn't fall apart too easily when things got rough. He didn't know where to find them, but somewhere out there, the love of his life was standing in the moonlight wondering what was taking him so long to find her.

# 9.0 FREEDOM

*And then one day she was gone. We found out later that she got a job in Phoenix, but Lyle wasn't talking. He said she disappeared and he didn't know where she was.*

—Jimmy Sweets

*I think she fell in love with another man. Why else would she run off like that? And then Lyle started sniffing around Lily De Luca, and the son had that little dark-skinned girl. The apple doesn't fall far from the tree, if you know what I mean.*

—Mrs. Frank Farnsworth

*When DC started saying Maggie's prisoner friend might be innocent after all, you could have knocked me over with a feather. Of course, that didn't make stealing his records right.*

—Valerie Vines

*People started using Maggie as an example. They started asking themselves, What would Maggie Rayburn do?*

—Lucas Enright, proprietor of the Main Street Diner

*It was like trying to put out a brush fire. You'd stamp it out in one place, only to turn around and find some other parent using her as an example to her kids.*

—Pastor Houston Price

*What did she think she was saving us from? She was the threat to our way of life.* —Mrs. August Winslow
*Without the plant and the prison, Red Bud would dry right up and blow away. And if there were no jobs for us, we'd probably be the ones breaking the laws and going to jail.*

—Hugo Martinez, Prison Security

# 9.1 MAGGIE

Maggie pulled a map of Phoenix out of its cellophane pouch, and after consulting it, she headed north. The bus station was located next to a busy airport. Planes were skirling overhead, and cars rocketed in all directions on roads that hadn't been built with pedestrians in mind. When she finally succeeded in detaching herself from the airport's grip, it was the pedestrians who surged around her with nearly lethal force, who knocked into her as they chased after unruly children or shouted into their cell phones or waved placards in her face and hissed, "Why are we rescuing animals when so many babies are being killed?"

Oh, for heaven's sake, thought Maggie. Why can't people get along!

A red-faced woman thrust a pamphlet into her hand. A bearded man stood on the corner shouting, "Half the people entering an abortion clinic don't come out alive!" Someone else said, "Let the baby choose!" while across the street, an equally enthusiastic band of counterprotesters carried competing signs and shouted slogans of their own.

A smile is like a rainbow, Maggie told herself. So she smiled at the bearded man. She smiled at the red-faced woman. She smiled at a girl who rushed after her spouting a complicated story and causing a narrow miss with a panel van. "I'm sorry!" Maggie called out to the driver, who waved a fist at her. It didn't help that she hadn't slept in over a day. It didn't help to be sweaty and hungry and short of breath or that the heavy backpack was cutting into her shoulders and neck.

When a man in a Hawaiian shirt called out, "This way, this way," she allowed herself to be swept up in a swarm of cheerful vacationers and into a large arena that smelled of freshly dug garden soil and sour beer and doughy concoctions frying in deep cauldrons of hydrogenated fat. Instead of asking to see her ticket, the ticket-taker opened the gate for her when her duffel caught on the turnstile. "Come on, come on," he scolded. "You're holding up the line!"

Inside the building, people were crowded around a railing stuffing food into their mouths and cheering on a pack of frantic-looking dogs that were racing around a wide dirt track. Maggie bought a cheese sandwich and ate it as people holding winning tickets elbowed past her to a row of cashier windows. Then she wandered around in search of a restroom and found herself in front of a long, skirted table covered with glossy brochures.

"Do you want to adopt one of the dogs?" asked a large woman who straddled a stool that was pushed back from the table to accommodate her paunch. "This is our annual adopt-a-thon."

"No, no, I can't," said Maggie. "But why are they for sale?"

"They're not for sale," said the woman. "They're free to a good home if you pay the veterinary charges and adoption fee and make a donation to the rescue center."

Maggie picked up one of the brochures. Inside it were pictures of big-eyed dogs with bony faces and names like Little Bo's Majestic Queen. Apparently the dogs, which had been bred for speed, were not young enough or hungry enough for victory, and their owners didn't want them anymore. "I couldn't give it a good home," she said, putting the brochure back on the table.

The woman handed her a thick stack of photographs. "The dogs are in cages now. I'm pretty sure you could give it a better home than that."

"At least they're safe," said Maggie.

"Actually, they're not. The ones that aren't adopted will be euthanized."

Maggie riffled through the stack of photos she was holding. A dog's name was written in black marker across the bottom of each one. "Dancing Dinero," Maggie read from the top card. "That's kind of a fancy name. What would you call him for short?"

"What about Dino? Dino is cute. But feel free to look through the entire stack. You might find a dog you like better."

"I don't really like dogs," said Maggie.

"That's like saying you don't like babies," said the woman, but all Maggie could think of was Tomás. She pictured him trotting along the sidewalk behind her or scratching at the screen door, hoping to be let inside the house.

"We take credit cards," said the woman. "And debit cards and, of course, cash."

Maggie had a pocket full of rainy-day money, but taking the animal was out of the question. "I don't live in Phoenix," she said. "I don't even have a place to stay."

"Then you can really empathize with these dogs," said the woman. "Imagine that you not only didn't have a place to stay, but that someone was waiting to haul you off and jab you with a lethal dose of pentobarbital if you couldn't find someone to take you in."

Maggie was silent. The woman beamed out her disapproval from across the table, while Dino stared mournfully up at her from the photograph.

"I'll tell you what. If you adopt one of the dogs, I'll tell you where you can stay for free. You'll make back the adoption fee in just a night or two."

When Maggie still didn't say anything, the woman said, "So Dino is the one you like?"

"Isn't it more important that the dog like me?" asked Maggie. "It wouldn't seem right to send him home with someone he isn't comfortable with."

"Not that you're headed home," said the woman. She rang a little bell that sat on the table in front of her and added, "The dogs are all very friendly. If they weren't friendly, they wouldn't be candidates for adoption."

"What happens to the unfriendly dogs?" asked Maggie.

"Most of the dogs are friendly," said the woman. "Really, almost all. But where is Peggy?" She rang the bell again, and this time a person with an oily ponytail and frizzy bangs entered the room holding a nylon leash. "It's been wonderful chatting with you," said the large woman. "Now, if you'd like to meet Dino, I can have Peggy introduce you."

Maggie followed Peggy through a door into a room lined with tiered rows of steel cages. As soon as the women entered, the dogs in the cages started to bark and pace back and forth in the tiny space allotted to them. Maggie was immediately reminded of the prison. "Oh my goodness!" she exclaimed. Suddenly it didn't seem right to leave Dino in a cage when she could so easily do for him what she might never be able to do for Tomás or George. She mentally added the vet bill to the adoption fee to the donation and came up with sixty-five dollars. Dino was a mere sixty-five dollars from being free—she couldn't turn her back on him now!

"Don't look straight at him," instructed Peggy, handing her a bone-shaped biscuit. "He will interpret that as a threat."

Maggie turned sideways and stretched out the hand that held the treat. "Hello, Dino," she said, but just as Peggy was trying to coax the dog out of his cage, a logical corollary occurred to her: the same could be said of all the dogs incarcerated there. Sixty-five dollars would free each and every one of them, and there was nothing, really, to distinguish Dino from the rest of them except that his card had been on the top of the stack. What if some of the other dogs were more deserving? She should probably choose the one that was poking its nose out between the bars of the cage rather than slinking into a corner the way Dino was doing. Or the one that was happily wagging its tail. But then she stopped herself. She had already exhausted the subject of merit and rights in thinking about Tomás. A creature shouldn't have to earn its freedom, so being more or less deserving didn't come into it. Besides, what if Dino's card had been on top for a reason? But still she stood paralyzed by the grooming table, and only when Peggy called out, "Here he is!" did Maggie close her mind to further thought.

"Crouch down like this," said Peggy, dropping to a squatting position. "And hold out your hand for him to sniff."

The large woman trundled into the room with some paperwork for Maggie to sign. "The Catholic Charities is in an old church," she said. "I've written down the address right here on your adoption agreement. If they don't have room for you tonight, at least you can get on their list for tomorrow. And here is a starter kit with some dog food, a complimentary water bowl, and, of course, a leash."

Maggie squeezed the dog's things into her luggage and put the adoption papers into her pocket with the map. "I never thought of myself as a dog owner before," she said.

"Guardian," said the woman. "Owner isn't a word we like to use."

# 9.2 MAGGIE

Dino lumbered along at Maggie's side as she walked north and then west into the setting sun. Whenever she passed a couple walking hand in hand, she wished Lyle were there to see the palm trees and the pretty red-tiled roofs and the line of muscled mountains that turned from pink to purple in the fading light. Now that the sun wasn't beating down from above, the source of heat seemed to be the sidewalk beneath her feet, and she wondered again if the earth was the living thing and if all of its creatures were merely parts of a larger organism. Every now and then Dino sat down, so Maggie would stop to catch her breath and consult the map before encouraging him forward with gentle tugs of the leash.

It was nearly dark when she found herself in front of an old stone church. The spires and arches and leaded windows set Maggie's heart to soaring until she remembered something her mother had said about how steeples were meant to strike fear into the hearts of wandering marauders by resembling giant swords. Even churches are weapons, she thought. When a security fixture mounted on an adjacent building came on, throwing daggers of light between the etched black branches of the trees that grew in the space between the buildings, she made her way up the pitted stone steps and tugged at the heavy door, but it was locked. "It will take more than that to foil our plan," she said to Dino, who looked as if all of his plans had been foiled long ago.

She felt her way along a narrow path that led through a tangled garden, past a statue of Saint Francis and a dry fountain where concrete birds had come to drink, and then through a weedy plaza where the path abruptly ended. Maggie found herself facing a crumbling wall topped with a spiky iron fence. Just when she was about to retrace her steps, she noticed a small sign that was only visible because the security light was shining directly on it. The sign said DELIVERIES AROUND BACK, and an arrow pointed to a gap in the wall she hadn't noticed in the darkness. Maggie scrambled through the gap and found herself in a dank courtyard where a series of concrete steps led down to a grimy basement door.

Before trying the door handle, Maggie whispered, "If God wants me to find Sandra Day O'Connor, the door will open." Dino took a step forward at the sound of her voice, but he jumped back again when the door sprang open. "If God wants me to free Tomás and George, there will be a place for us to sleep," Maggie said to Dino as they slipped inside.

The church basement was windowless and dark, but as her eyes adjusted, Maggie could make out an opening, and through the opening, a narrow stairway led up to a landing where a small window allowed some of the security light to filter through. Just off the landing was the sacristy, complete with a tiny bathroom and running water, and through the sacristy, the sanctuary and long, narrow nave of the church. Maggie's footsteps rang out on the stones of the center aisle, and her heart nearly stopped when a cat jumped from a pew and hissed at her. Dino's ears pricked for an instant and then flopped back against his head. Maggie searched in vain for signs of the Catholic Charities, but except for the cat, the church appeared to be abandoned.

"This can't be right," she said to Dino. "Unless we're in the wrong place, or unless the Catholic Charities has moved."

Maggie's feet hurt. It had been nearly twenty-four hours since she had left home, and her heart sank at the idea of having to find another place to sleep. She sat on one of the pews and said a little prayer. Just as she said, "Amen," it occurred to her that she was in the right place after all. Ever since getting off the bus, her moves had been anything but random: the protesters had frightened her into crossing the street; the tour guide had called, "This way, this way," as if he had been waiting for her; the ticket-taker had opened the turnstile without asking for her ticket; the adoption lady had directed her to the church; the security light had come on just in time to illuminate the delivery sign; the sign had pointed the way to the door—a door that had opened almost by itself! Now her presence in the church seemed inevitable rather than inadvertent. She clasped her hands in front of her and whispered, "Thank you for watching over me, Lord. If you tell me what to do, I promise to do it as best I can."

It was the first time in her life Maggie had made a promise to God and the first time she had felt him so near. As she waited, a little awed by the solemnity of the occasion, the tiredness lifted from her mind and body. She felt happy and hopeful and filled with certainty that she was exactly where she was supposed to be and doing exactly what she was supposed to do. "I won't rest until I free Tomás and George," she whispered. Then she found some cushions and lap blankets in the choir stalls, poured some of the kibbles onto the stone floor, and filled the complimentary adopt-a-thon dish with water from the sacristy bathroom before settling herself and Dino for the night.

The next day, Maggie took Dino with her and sought out the attorney, who assured her he had once been an actor and knew exactly how to play these things. "Ha, ha!" he chortled when Maggie failed to respond. "It's just a little joke—never mind. But it's true that actors make great lawyers. Frankly, it's the secret of my success. Sometimes I feel sorry for my opponents, but not too sorry, of course—that was another little joke."

Maggie had expected someone young and vigorous, but the man's hair was white and he leaned heavily on a gnarled stick. "Experience," he said. "That's the thing you're paying me for."

"I'm not actually paying you," said Maggie. "I'm working for you and devoting half of my paycheck to Tomás's fees. That was the deal."

"Ah, yes," said the attorney. "That's something anyway."

"You told me that the arresting officer made a string of false arrests."

"Now I remember!" said the attorney. "Now I know exactly who you are. I don't mind saying that I'm very glad to see you. I've been without an assistant for weeks."

He took a stack of files from his desk and handed them to her one by one. "This man is serving twenty-five years for breaking into a church kitchen that had once given him food," he said. "And this one stole some videotapes for his nieces and nephews, and this one helped two girls shoplift a set of sheets, and, well, the point is, they were all handled by the same dirty prosecutor. One of the defendants was just granted a new trial, so now is the time to strike! Unfortunately, none of them can pay. It would help your man if we pursued all of the cases together and tried to establish a pattern, but I have to take three paying clients for each person I represent for free. So if you could contribute anything in the way of fees for the others ... "

"I have a little cash," said Maggie, and without thinking it through, she opened her backpack and handed over the entire packet of rainy-day money she was saving for her ticket home.

"Hmmm," said the attorney as he counted out the bills. "It's not much, but I guess it's a start. Yes, we'll establish a pattern of prosecutorial misconduct and see how it goes."

The attorney showed her to a desk that was overflowing with

loose papers and articles of clothing and unopened mail. "Why don't you start here," he said. "I have to be in court, but if the phone rings, answer it and write a note on this pad. I'll be back around noon."

Maggie left Lyle and Will a message saying she had arrived safely. Then she set to work imposing order on the chaotic office. When the attorney returned, he gave her two files and asked her to decide which case he should take.

"Can't you take them both?" she asked.

"He who takes on too much accomplishes nothing."

"That's the way it is, isn't it?" said Maggie. "The minute you choose a person to help it means you're not helping someone else."

"Yes," said the attorney. "That's the way it is."

Maggie spent the morning reading through the files and couldn't see that one defendant had a better claim than the other. First she thought it was the soldier who had given so much for his country, and then she thought it was the father who had five children to support.

"Let me show you a useful trick," said the attorney. He took the files and hid them behind his back. "Which hand?" he asked.

After choosing, Maggie put the files in the proper stacks and didn't look at them. That way, she wouldn't know which person she had consigned to unrepresented limbo. "There are other attorneys who might help him, aren't there?" she asked.

"That's what we have to believe," said the attorney. "Otherwise we'd shoot ourselves."

"And of course he might be guilty."

"Most people are guilty of something. Reminding yourself of that is another useful trick."

Before Maggie left for the day, she asked the attorney if he knew Sandra Day O'Connor.

"Who doesn't?" he replied.

"I was thinking she could help us."

"Darn right she could."

Maggie pulled the map of Phoenix out of her pocket and asked, "Do you know where she lives?"

"Somewhere around here." The attorney poked a bent finger at the map. "One day I was walking along the sidewalk right about there"—he poked the map again—"and what do you know? There she was, surrounded by people who wanted her autograph! Of course, that was a few years back."

Maggie used a pencil to mark the places on the map. "I'll see you tomorrow," she said. "What time should I be here?"

"Eight-thirty sharp," said the attorney. "Do you have a place to stay?"

"I do for now," said Maggie.

"And if you see Justice O'Connor, make sure to give her my regards."

"I realize it's a long shot," said Maggie.

"Everything's a long shot," replied the attorney. "Unless you have money."

"I'm afraid I gave you what I had," said Maggie.

"In that case," said the attorney, "what we need is luck."

# 9.3 LYLE

Lyle was alone when the police stormed up to the door with determined looks on their faces. He recognized the shorter of the two men, and it was obvious the man recognized him too, for his face flushed in embarrassment when he saw Lyle. "I'm sorry, Mr. Rayburn, but we need to speak to your wife."

"It's Lyle, Ben. It's Lyle from church."

"I know it's Lyle," said Ben. "But this is official business. The sheriff doesn't like us to use first names when we're on duty."

"Mrs. Rayburn isn't here," said Lyle stiffly. He didn't say, She got out in the nick of time, but that's what he was thinking when the taller of the two officers said, "You don't mind if we take a look around, do you?" He took a step closer as he said it, which had the effect of pushing Lyle into the glassed-in alcove where he and Maggie and Will hung their jackets and stored their muddy boots. When the man took another step toward him, Lyle didn't say yes or no; he merely shifted to one side as the two men barged past him and stood with their hands on their hips surveying the living room. Maggie's bill-paying desk was pushed against the far wall, and the man who wasn't Ben said, "You take the desk, Ben. I'll look in the back."

Lyle was vaguely aware that some defensive action was required of him, but he stood with his fists in his pockets and his tongue stuck to the roof of his mouth as Ben pawed through the neat stacks of bills and receipts. It finally occurred to him to call Jimmy Sweets for advice. When Jimmy didn't pick up, he called Lily De Luca and said, "Lily, it's Lyle. The police are here, and my house is being searched."

"Do they have a warrant?" asked Lily.

"Do you have a warrant?" asked Lyle, but Ben appeared not to have heard him. "Do you have a warrant?" he asked again.

"It's best not to make trouble," said Ben.

"Are you under arrest?" asked Lily.

"Am I under arrest?" asked Lyle.

Ben muttered something about stolen documents just as the

larger officer came back from the kitchen and reprimanded Ben for chatting.

Lyle remembered something Maggie had said in relation to the prisoners, and it frightened him a little that he was considering using words that usually pertained to brawny felons. "You're violating my constitutional rights," he said.

Once the words were out of his mouth, the fear started to change into something else. He was almost shouting when he said, "Get out of my house, Ben. You and your friend need to get the hell out of my house."

"Or what?" said the big man from the mouth of the hallway. "Or you'll call the police?"

Ben said, "Come on, Reilly. We can get the warrant and come back later."

"And let us know if you hear from your wife," said Reilly. "You need to tell us right away. Obstructing an investigation is something we can arrest you for."

"What investigation?" asked Lyle. "What investigation are you talking about?"

"You know we can't tell you that," said Ben as he hurried out the door.

Lyle rubbed his hand across his eyes as the sleek cruiser backed into the road and sped down the hill and around the curve toward town. Across the street, the hayfield was dotted with big round bales, left there after the summer cutting. If he didn't hurry, he'd be late for work, but he stood a little longer contemplating the familiar scene, which had always seemed friendly to him but now seemed indifferent and bleak. Lyle wished he had a dog so the two of them could sit on the stoop together watching the cars go by, or he could pat its head and say, Now what the hey was that all about? and not be talking to himself. As he stood gazing into the distance, a car came into sight. Instead of passing, it turned in at the drive. Darned if it wasn't Lily, stopping by on her way to work to find out what was going on.

"What do you think it was about?" she asked. "You don't have some secret life I don't know about, do you?" She gave him a smoky look before laughing at how unlikely that was.

"What if I do?" asked Lyle. "Am I as predictable as all that?" He was thinking of the time he had followed Lily home, but then he dropped the pretense and said, "It's Maggie they're after. I know you've heard the rumors ... "

"People always gossip when someone doesn't toe the line," said Lily. "That's something I know about firsthand."

"Well, some of the rumors are true! She's the one the *Sentinel* was referring to in that series on innocent prisoners! The reporter didn't use her name, but everyone knows it was her."

"Hmm," said Lily. "Don't tell me where she is, then. It's better if I don't know."

"I don't know where she is," said Lyle, but he said it a little lamely.

"That's good," said Lily. "That's exactly what you need to tell people. And next time you talk to her, tell her not to come home until you're sure the coast is clear."

It had been three weeks since the Glory Dayz celebration, three weeks since the official end of summer and the day Maggie had said, "I'm leaving tomorrow. I'm only taking the rainy-day savings. I'll send money when I can."

Lyle had been shocked by the announcement. But now he could see how everything that had come before had been leading up to it.

"It's now or never," Maggie had told him. "I started something, and I have to see it through."

They had been standing in the kitchen discussing the baseball game: Will's home run, a brilliant play at third, the heartbreaking loss—at least he had been discussing it—when Maggie pointed to a list of instructions she had taped to the refrigerator. Her eyes were bright in the darkness, reflecting the moonlight that came in at the window, but also, Lyle decided now, a burning inner conviction.

"Will told me you were serious, but I didn't think you were," Lyle had said. Now he wished he had asked more questions, but it hadn't occurred to him, and he still wasn't sure what those questions should have been.

Maggie had said, "Sleep well, honeybun. See you tomorrow." But when he awoke the next morning, the bed beside him was empty and she was already gone.

## 9.4 PASTOR PRICE

What would Maggie Rayburn do?"

Beads of sweat were dripping into Pastor Price's eyes, but he was on fire with the Holy Spirit. The arc lights had been installed when the television show was only a faint glimmering in his consciousness, and now he congratulated himself on his foresight. Here he was, on the last Sunday after Pentecost, preaching the word to the faithful, seen and unseen, his message blasting out across the radio waves, across the visible spectrum, beaming down from satellites and blazing along broadband and fiber-optic cables—who knew how far the signal spread? He could feel the spirit lighting up within him. He felt it burning down from above until he wanted to cry out with the beauty and torment of it. Tears were streaming from his eyes as he spoke the words of the Old Testament: *Woe to the shepherds who destroy and scatter the sheep of my pasture!*

He was filled with pain and love as he preached, but also with a righteous anger when he thought of Fitch's innocence series and how, instead of condemning Maggie for stealing prisoner records, some people were turning her into a hero. Didn't she realize she could go to jail? And then the question burst out of him again: "What would Maggie Rayburn do?"

He let the words echo according to the calculations of the acoustic engineers who had mixed resonant surfaces with sound-absorbing wood. A chord from the magnificent organ quivered and died. Then silence and only the hushed rustle of clothing as a thousand parishioners caught their collective breath to hear the answer to the very question they had been asking each other and themselves.

"I've heard some of you say it. I've heard that question fall from the trembling lips of the elderly as I held their fragile hands. I've heard it from the rosebud lips of little children and from the lip-sticked mouths of the mothers who only want the best for them. I've heard it from parents and teachers who have held Maggie up as an example of righteousness, an example of someone who put the needs of others before her own needs, someone who gave up everything to do what she thought was right."

Now the pastor adopted a conversational tone. "It sounds good, doesn't it? Self-sacrifice. Duty before pleasure, others before self. Following the still, small voice instead of the crass and shouting crowd.

"Don't get me wrong—I believe in those things. But whose version of the story are we listening to?"

Now he let his tone become honeyed and intimate, as if he

were gossiping to a circle of friends. "Haven't you ever been in a situation where one friend tells you something her spouse or another friend did to her, and you come away hopping mad that such a kind and beautiful person could be treated so unfairly? You're ready to shun the lout who did this to your friend. You're ready never to talk to him or her again. And your righteous anger lasts ... oh, maybe it lasts all the way until you hear the other person's side of the story, at which time you are equally outraged and convinced.

"Well, whose story are you listening to now? To Maggie's story or the Lord's?"

The pastor waited—one beat, two beats, three.

"Those of you who aren't from our community might well wonder who I'm talking about." Here, Pastor Price gave a nod to each corner of the church, where the television cameras were barely visible poking out through the acoustic slats, and then to the adjustable boom that was being operated from a control room on the balcony. He raised his eyes to the heavens—there was a camera there too—and said, "But Maggie's story isn't so special. We all know people who are put on a pedestal, people who are revered because they were blessed with wealth or athletic ability or good looks or charisma. We all know people like that, people who are considered good and righteous only because of superficial things and without regard to the truth of their characters.

"So what would Maggie Rayburn do?

"Apparently she'd leave her husband and her son. Apparently she'd leave her job without giving her employer so much as a chance to replace her. Apparently she'd take from her workplace things that were not hers to take."

The pastor's voice lacked emphasis. He let the facts speak for themselves.

"And the truth is that Maggie Rayburn took it upon herself to tell the judges and the prosecutors they were wrong. And to the juries made up of people just like you, she said, 'You don't know your business.' Why, I bet she'd walk right up to the president if she got a chance and say the same thing. And I don't mean the president of the Ladies' Auxiliary. I don't mean the president of the PTA."

Pastor Price let this sink in, and then his voice boomed out again. "I am referring to the President of the United States! I have no doubt she'd say the same thing to all of us who are sitting right here today. She'd say we don't know our own business. But Maggie Rayburn does. There's a word for this, and the word is 'hubris.'"

Price knew the word was foreign to many listening ears, but he didn't define it. He wanted people to ask each other about it at the coffee hour. He wanted them to look it up in their dictionaries and on the Internet. He wanted the conversation to reverberate long after the ringing of the end-of-service bell. And then, if Maggie dared to say anything about any of the other secrets she had stolen, people would remember the word and say to themselves, Hubris! This is exactly what the good pastor was talking about.

"So if you hear any of our lovely elderly people or any of the scions of our town or any of our beautiful little children ask each other, What would Maggie Rayburn do? you are not to sit silently by. You are not to let the question go unanswered, for silence in this case is the worst kind of lie. You are to tell them, Maggie Rayburn would spit in your eye. Maggie Rayburn would open the doors of the prisons and loose the murderers and rapists upon your sons and daughters. Let's just hope there aren't any terrorists locked up in there, for no doubt Maggie Rayburn would let them out too.

"You tell them that not because I told you to. You tell them that because it is the truth."

324

The sweat was pouring down inside the pastor's cassock. It was dripping from his neck and burning the skin behind his ears. His hair, which he had grown a little longer on the advice of his stylist and over his wife's objections, was slick against his collar. He gloried in the animal strength of his body, flesh and blood lit by the spirit, and he thrilled with the truth of how God and man had come together in Jesus Christ. When the choir started up, it was as if the holy waters had broken and an ocean of sound engulfed the room. The new blue satin choir robes shimmered like quicksilver, and when the arc lights went out, their metallic piping caught the light from a thousand candles that had been lit for the Church of the New Incarnation's television premier.

## 9.5 TULA

The studio audience was holding its breath while the girlfriend, who had clearly been coached to draw out the delivery of her lines, turned her poker face to the camera before opening her lips to declare, "Yes, Gary, you are the father!"

"Didn't I say?" Tula sighed. She had known it all along.

After Maggie left, Tula went to the house most Sundays to keep Will company, and now they were sitting on the couch watching TV. "Didn't I say it when she first came on?"

"You were right." Will was staring at the screen, but he didn't seem to be paying attention either to it or to Tula.

The announcer blared, "Next up on our program: an obese

teenager confronts the mother she believes is sabotaging her weight loss attempts in order to keep her daughter for herself."

"It's cold in here," said Tula.

"You can borrow one of my mother's sweaters if you want. I think she keeps them in the chest."

Without Maggie, the house seemed dirty and defeated. The kitchen counter was littered with empty soda cans and fast-food wrappers, and someone had left a pile of laundry on the floor near the washing machine as if it would magically wash itself. Tula's instinct was to gather everything up and either put it in the trash or wash it, but she stopped herself and made her way down the narrow hallway toward the bedrooms.

Only in Will's room was everything tidy and clean. A few of his Transformers robots remained on the bureau top, but they were lined up against the mirror instead of positioned for an attack. It seemed that things were missing from the walls too, even though she couldn't remember how the room had looked before. The closet was similarly spartan: shirts arranged by color; baseball uniform neatly folded; mitt freshly oiled, a new ball in its jaws.

Lyle's room was as chaotic as Will's was neat. Clothing had been flung here and there, and most of the bed coverings were on the floor. The blinds at the windows were cocked, and dead flies littered the windowsills. The drawers of a small chest were open to varying degrees, and a tipped-over chair hadn't been righted. Tula opened the drawers of the larger chest one by one, starting at the top: socks and underwear, nightgowns, T-shirts, shorts. The bottom drawer stuck on its tracks, so she had to kneel to open it. But when she reached beneath a blue cardigan, her hand hit a stack of magazines. She pulled one out at random and opened it, but instead of finding an article revealing the identity of the sexiest man alive, she found a government document with Top Secret written in red letters across the top. Folded inside it was a letter from Dolly Jackson introducing herself and asking Maggie if she had ever come across a report linking munitions to birth defects. Stapled to the letter was a photograph of a baby with a huge purple tumor growing from its mouth.

Tula sat on the floor and took out the magazines one by one. Then she looked through the house until she found a large cardboard box. As she packed the documents into it, she was thinking how the secret cache explained the recent changes in Maggie. She was also thinking how it would serve Mrs. Winslow right if she finished what Maggie had started and exposed whatever the great men of Red Bud were trying to keep quiet. It would serve Sammi Green right too—not that Sammi had ever done anything bad to Tula. In fact, it would teach a lesson to the entire town. You couldn't clean house without getting your hands dirty. You couldn't make an omelet without breaking some eggs. Purity, she thought, as she carried the box out to her mother's car. What did purity even mean?

Tula was trying to decide whether or not to show Will what she had found, but when she returned to the living room, Will didn't seem to notice that she had been gone for nearly an hour. He was still slumped on the corduroy couch, his eyes glassy and his ears red with cold. "Hey," said Tula, peering from Will to the television screen. "Isn't that the pastor from your church?"

Will didn't say anything, and it took a moment before it dawned on Tula that the pastor was talking about Maggie. "Hey," she said again. "Isn't he talking about your mom?"

Instead of answering her, Will got up and turned the television off. "Where would you go if you could go anywhere?" he asked her.

"Somewhere warm," said Tula. "Somewhere with turquoise water and white sand."

"I'd go to the Middle East," said Will. "To Afghanistan or Iraq."

"No you wouldn't," said Tula.

"Yes," said Will. "I would."

After that, Will grew more distant. He started to miss school.

Every so often Tula went by his house to look for him, but most of the time he wasn't there. Why had he mentioned Afghanistan and Iraq? But there was only one reason to mention them, or only one she could think of.

Tula, too, was restless. One evening she stood outside and watched a star shoot across the November sky, thinking, Where there's a will, there's a way. But the familiar phrase failed to comfort her, and the future, which she had always thought of as nestled in a sunny valley at the end of a pretty country road, no longer seemed so easily reached. The weather had turned cold, but when she thought about going back inside, her thin shoes felt heavy on her feet, as if the dense clay soil of the yard were pulling at her, and beneath the clay, the earth's magnetic core.

## 9.6 LYLE

Without Maggie around to tame it, the house started to make demands on Lyle. Great flakes of paint curled off the metal fretwork that held up the sagging roof of the porch, and a gutter rattled loosely in its bracket whenever the wind blew. A window cracked, seemingly without reason. The bathrooms sprouted mold. Even as they disintegrated, the objects around him seemed to have more life in them than they'd had before, if only because a thing first had to have life to lose it. The connection between the broken boards of the porch and the trees they had once been announced itself every time he mounted the front steps, and when he looked closely, he could see that the rusted screws that had held the boards in place for so many decades were slowly loosening their hold, as if the job was finished or they had somewhere else to be. Everything had a place in a grand scheme that was slowly making itself visible to Lyle, and the grand scheme was death and decay. The jagged piece of gutter, the rutted driveway, the rotting leaves, the screen door that had started to sag and whine. "Even the house misses your mother," he said.

"It's always been like that," said Will, but Lyle didn't think it had. Bills were piling up on the desk, and after brooding about it for a few days, he discussed the idea of paying them with Will.

"Go ahead and do it, Dad," said Will.

"But your mother was always the one ... "

"Well she's not here now, is she?" Will's usually placid face bloomed white in the darkened kitchen, where both lightbulbs had blown at once.

It wasn't like Will to lose his temper. "I think Will's drinking beer," Lyle said to Jimmy Sweets when they met at the Merry Maid one evening after work.

"Jeezus, the kid's seventeen," said Jimmy. "It's not as if he's motherless. And he still has you, doesn't he? He still has that hot little number he's dating. What more does a growing boy need? Three squares and a little cha cha cha."

"Don't be crude, Jimmy," said Lily, but everyone in the bar was laughing at the way Lyle's ears were turning red.

"Jeezus, Rayburn," said Jimmy. "You're as sensitive as a girl."

After that, all anyone had to say was "cha cha cha" and Lyle would slap a fiver on the bar and storm out the door.

"What's eating him?" Jimmy would say loudly enough for Lyle to hear.

Sometimes Lily ran after him and they would sit in the front seat of Lyle's truck and talk for a while before Lily got out and Lyle went home. It occurred to Lyle that he was being tested and he was failing the test. It was clear he had relied too much on Maggie, that she had sapped his strength in some way and it was up to him to get it back, but that seemed beyond him.

"I know what it's like," said Lily one evening when Maggie had been gone for almost three months. "Two years ago, my husband left me."

"Maggie didn't leave me," insisted Lyle, but he wondered if she had. And not only had she gone, but she had left behind a great suitcase full of responsibilities. For the first time, a little tendril of blame wrapped around his heart. "Do you think it's safe for her to come back?" he asked Lily. "I never heard from the police again, but I don't know what that means."

"No news is usually good news. If they wanted to go after her, they probably would have done it by now."

"Probably," said Lyle.

"But I guess you can't ask without opening it all up again," said Lily.

"No," said Lyle. "I guess I can't."

Lyle thought about how he had followed Lily home and how she had said, "You might as well come in," and how for a split second he had thought she was saying it to him. Now her eyes were filled with soft question marks, and he figured he had come to one of those moments where he got to decide something important about the future. He tried to look down the various roads that pinwheeled away from the truck where he and Lily were sitting, but all he could think about was how MacBride had said he wasn't a visionary. He guessed MacBride had been right about that, for try as he might, he couldn't see down any of the roads or even through the door Lily seemed to be holding open for him.

"MacBride told me I wasn't a visionary," he said, explaining his hesitation.

"Who the heck is?" asked Lily. "'Visionary' is just a word they slap on people who turn out to be right about something. For instance, if you come home with me now, I'm a visionary, and if you don't, well then, I'm not."

Lyle wondered if there was a way to go through a door and simultaneously not go through it, just so he'd know what he was getting into. "I guess I could come for a little while," he said.

"Aw heck, Lyle," said Lily. "Nobody's forcing you. Maybe you and I are better off as friends."

When Lily got out of the truck and started down Main Street, Lyle's first instinct was to run after her. But his second instinct was to stay put. The two impulses held a battle in his imagination, and by the time he decided he should follow her after all, it seemed too late to do it gracefully, not that he'd ever been particularly graceful. Then he had to argue with himself about whether there was such a thing as too late in this case and if it was just habit that kept him from acting decisively. It was too late, anyway, to be decisive. That much he knew. And being indecisive was probably insulting to any woman, Lily included, which meant he was probably better off waiting for the future to come to him rather than rushing wildly off to meet it.

Of all the things Lyle had learned to do over the course of his life, the thing he did best was to blend in. So he sat in the truck as the lights in the shop windows went out one by one and the citizens of Red Bud hurried past him as if he wasn't there until the only beacon for the weary left in Red Bud was the blinking neon Beer and Cheer sign in the window of the Merry Maid.

After that, he did what was expected of him the best he knew how to do it, and when people asked him how he was doing, he mostly said, "I can't complain."

Early one morning two weeks before Christmas, Ben and Reilly returned with a warrant to search the house. When Lyle protested, Reilly pushed in through the glassed-in alcove as if Lyle were just another jacket hanging on the row of hooks. Lyle watched silently as the two men turned everything upside down before leaving empty-handed.

Ben said, "Be seein' you, Lyle," as if the visit had been a social call, but Reilly stormed out without a word, rattling the windows and slapping the screen door against the side of the house.

"Hey," Lyle called out. "Are you happy now?"

Reilly didn't turn back, but Lyle heard him mutter, "What about the phone records? Do you reckon we could get a warrant for those?"

It was almost eight-thirty when they left and Lyle was already late for work. Still, he waited for an hour in the Redi Mart parking lot, dialing the attorney's office every few minutes until Maggie picked up the phone.

"The good news is that the police came back with the warrant, but they didn't find anything," he told her. "The bad news is that we can't use the house phone anymore. If you can get to the office early on Mondays, I'll try to call you then."

"How's Will?" was the first thing Maggie always asked when Lyle called. Then Lyle would tell her the local gossip and Maggie would tell him about her work. "That series of articles about innocent prisoners has sparked new interest in Tomás's case," she said now. "Did they ever figure out I'm the one who took his records?"

"Nothing official," said Lyle, which was true as far as it went. He didn't say anything about what everyone suspected.

"And how are you doing, honeybun?" was the last thing Maggie always asked before hanging up. Lyle would reply, "I can't complain," the way he always replied when anyone asked him how he was. If he had had a life philosophy, it would have involved not complaining and blending in.

## 9.7 DOLLY

Dolly had always thought that something astonishing was going to happen to her, something to erase the ordinariness of her life— something, rather, that was the reason for the ordinariness, so that when the time came, she would be free to devote her whole attention to whatever it was. Instead of sitting back and waiting for the thing to happen, she believed in helping the gods or fate or whatever forces were in control of her destiny, so just before Danny came home, she had fixed up the apartment. After that, every time she walked in the door, it was as if she had spent a weekend away and come home unsuspecting, the way it happened on *Extreme Makeover: Home Edition*. And when she looked up one day and saw that the clinic waiting area had undergone a similar transformation, she was as surprised as anyone, even though she herself had done the painting and even though she had scoured the classified ads for secondhand furniture and taken on some hours at the hospital to pay the cost.

For the walls, she had chosen a color called Quiet Moments 1563. Against it, even the folding metal chairs looked inviting. She had hung sheer panels at the windows and put a rustic table and mismatched armchairs in the center of the room. "Shabby chic," she said when the doctor cocked his eyebrows at her. But she was proud of her work.

"Decorating on a budget takes far more skill than your high-dollar projects," one of her regular patients told her. Another said Dolly definitely had an eye. Someday she'd do the geraniums and the parking lot, but someday had always included Danny, and Dolly didn't know what she was supposed to think about someday now that Danny had gone off with the members of his old unit.

"How's that soldier of yours doing?" asked the doctor one afternoon when Dolly went in to give him his mail.

When Dolly blinked at him in astonishment, he said, "I keep my ears open. I know a thing or two about what's going on."

"He's in New Jersey," said Dolly. "He and some friends are starting something there."

The doctor no longer seemed to be listening, but then he said, "I thought you'd be interested to hear that I've gotten involved in a study run by some people at the university. Don't you go telling anyone about it yet—no sense drawing fire before we're ready—but I thought you'd want to know." He smiled kindly, which made Dolly want to weep. It made her want to throw her arms around his stooped shoulders and confide all of her worries in him. She wanted to say that she hadn't told Danny about the tadpole because things were better with him gone, but she didn't want to burden the doctor with her own troubles when he had troubles of his own. Instead, she wiped her hand across her eyes and said, "This was a good day!"

And it had been a good day, because all of the appointments had gone smoothly, and because no one had thrown a fit or yelled at her, and because that day all of the husbands and boyfriends had spoken softly to the women and held their hands.

Why wasn't Danny there to hold Dolly's hand? Because Danny was better off with his comrades. He was better off making critical information available to the public than sitting around in the fixed-up apartment with nothing important to do. And, frankly, she was better off too. It was a relief that he was no longer jumping at noises or straightening the silverware or smoothing the coverlet on the bed or roughing it up again to test how much disorder he could stand. The problem was that now she was doing it. Now she was lining up the pencils on the desk and making sure the folding chairs were evenly spaced against the wall and organizing the magazines into separate piles: *Better Homes and Gardens* next to *Family Circle, Oprah* and *People* next to *Shape, Road & Track* off in a corner by itself.

The week before, a handsome but careless driver had dented Dolly's fender and sent her a check for the damage along with a bouquet of flowers. Then, when she called to thank him, he had asked her on a proper date of the kind Danny seemed to have forgotten about. Now she wondered if the tapestry of her life was the same as Danny's tapestry or if it was just hanging next to it. "Rain check?" the careless driver had asked, and Dolly hadn't answered yes or no. Whenever she was in a quandary, she liked to open the Bible and point to a passage at random. The last time she tried it, she had pointed to a depressing verse about the land of gloom and chaos. Now she thought of seeking guidance again, but instead of getting the Bible out of her desk drawer, she closed her eyes and picked up a magazine from the table in front of her—who was more likely to give her good advice, Job or Oprah? When she opened her eyes, she was looking at a headline that said: IS YOUR HANDBAG KILLING YOU?

She tried the November issue: COULD A MAN DRIVE YOU CRAZY? seemed pertinent. October: DO WHAT YOU LOVE! Then she opened *Road & Track: My attitude changed within about five minutes behind the wheel of the Azera.* From *People* magazine: *After 23 days behind bars, the heiress took back her freedom in a Petro Zillia blazer and jeans from her very own denim line.* From a book someone had left on the table: *So it goes.*

Out in the driveway, a car door slammed. It was a late patient, rushing to make the five o'clock closing. Dolly could see her hurrying through the mud with her scarf flapping in the wind and her arms around an unwieldy cardboard box. She hoped there wasn't a stillborn baby in the box because so far, it had been an almost perfect day. "Do we have time for one more?" she asked the doctor.

"If you're quick about it. It's nearly five, and I have dinner plans."

The young woman who entered the waiting room stood in the doorway, her scarf pulled up to her chin and her hood pulled down over her ears. She was shuffling her feet in a way that Dolly knew from long experience irritated the doctor. Before he could bark out that he was a busy man, Dolly said, "Please tell the doctor what you've come to see him about."

The woman glanced nervously from the doctor to Dolly and back again. It was only when she set the box down on the rustic table and took off her jacket and unwound her scarf that Dolly recognized Tula. "Tula!" she cried. "I haven't seen you in months! Are you all right? Are you here to see the doctor? I hope something isn't wrong!"

"No," said Tula. "I'm here to see you. There's something in this box that I think you'll want to see."

## 9.8 MAGGIE

Just before Christmas, a FOR SALE sign went up in front of the church, and soon afterward, Maggie returned to find a group of real estate agents inspecting the garden. She lingered on the sidewalk and tried to figure out what they were talking about, but she only caught snatches of their conversation: "nonessential properties," "abuse scandal," "not remotely worth what they're asking."

On Saturdays, Maggie took Dino for long walks through the city, always keeping her eyes open for Sandra Day O'Connor. Many of the citizens of Phoenix looked at her suspiciously when she asked about the former justice, and others merely shook their heads. "What business do you have with her?" asked a crossing guard in a disapproving tone of voice.

"You've chosen a funny way to go about finding someone," said a woman with two small children in tow. "I'm sure Justice O'Connor wouldn't take kindly to stalkers."

"I can hardly stalk someone I've never seen!" exclaimed Maggie.

One time, she tried to explain about the depleted uranium to a nice gentleman who was walking a retriever. He listened politely while the two dogs sniffed each other, and when she had finished, he said, "You shouldn't speak so loudly. The shadow government might be listening."

After that she stopped asking questions, only walked silently around the neighborhoods she had circled on her map with Dino trailing behind her, his long toes tapping on the pavement. And she did see the justice—at least she almost did. Once or twice a day she would spy a face with powdery skin and a halo of soft gray hair, or a small, gracious figure dressed in a smart suit. She would spy the figure from the back, from the side, just going around a corner or through a door. On those occasions, Maggie would call out, "Justice O'Connor!" and rush after her, causing bystanders to stare at her briefly before going about their business as if they had seen it all before—a woman in faded jeans accompanied by a droop-eared dog, searching for something she couldn't find. On nice days Dino would linger in a patch of sun and look solemnly after her before starting forward again, one paw in front of the other, until one day he stopped in front of a gourmet deli and refused to budge.

"Justice O'Connor? She was in here just last week," said the proprietor. "She bought a loaf of seven-grain bread and some of those Greek olives."

Maggie couldn't believe her luck—it was almost as if she had turned a corner to find herself face-to-face with the former justice herself. But past experience had made her cautious. She didn't want to say the wrong thing and see the jovial face before her cloud with misgivings. "How often does she come in?" she asked.

"Now and then," said the proprietor. "When she's in town."

"But she's in town now, isn't she?"

"She was last week, but she goes to Washington, DC, a lot. Her clerk said they were headed back there. She didn't say when they were going, and of course I didn't pry."

"Her clerk?" Maggie had assumed she would find the former justice alone, with no one else to interfere. She had envisioned a

338

kind woman in a long black robe sweeping toward her along the sidewalk or, in an alternate scenario, sitting on a portable dais and answering questions for people who stood in line before her, as if searching for the justice was not only acceptable, but common-place. She saw herself explaining about the top-secret documents and the Iraqi babies and then about Tomás and George and feeling her burden lift as the ex-justice absorbed the facts in preparation for making a pronouncement about what to do. "Do you happen to know where she lives?" she asked.

Before the proprietor could answer, a customer came into the shop and mistook Maggie for an employee. "Excuse me, excuse me," she said, tapping Maggie on the shoulder. "I need a little help."

Maggie had the sensation that the roles had somehow been reversed—that the customer was looking for her the way she was looking for Sandra Day O'Connor and that she would be expected to offer thoughtful suggestions on the basis of a disjointed set of facts.

"I can't seem to find that nice olive oil with the white truffle essence," said the customer.

"If only my problem were that simple," said Maggie when the customer had paid for her purchases and left. "If only I just needed a little olive oil."

"Try me," said the proprietor.

Maggie nearly burst into tears. She knew she would have to tell her story carefully so the proprietor wouldn't scoff at her or clam up altogether, but even though she took a deep breath and gathered her thoughts before starting, the story came tumbling out of her: the missiles that spewed radiation into the air, the munitions plant that polluted the creek, the policies aimed at providing ever more bodies for ever more prison cells, Tomás and George and all the wrongfully incarcerated. "I don't know what to do, and I thought Justice O'Connor could advise me."

"You got Tomás's file to an appellate attorney, didn't you? And someone wrote an article publicizing his case, and the attorney is making progress on the appeal, isn't he?" The proprietor was looking at her with admiration, as if she had done something out of the ordinary.

"Yes," said Maggie. "But even so, nothing's changed."

"Well, unless you plan to go to law school, there's not much else you can do. Most people wouldn't have bothered at all."

"How could I not have bothered? Once I realized all the terrible things that were happening, that's all I could think about. It seemed selfish to be concerned with myself or even with Lyle and Will when innocent people were in cages. So I started to look for evidence, thinking that was the way to convince other people of the truth. But I didn't convince them. They pointed to rules and procedures and only became more firmly entrenched in their positions. Which made me wonder—what if the important thing isn't reason or evidence at all? What if it's more to do with imagination? If you can imagine what it's like for someone else, you still might lock that person up—you might even kill him—but you'd comprehend the tragedy of what you were doing, wouldn't you?"

"Hmm," said the proprietor. "You might be overthinking it ... but at least you're overthinking it at the best little deli in Scottsdale! You might as well take advantage of it. You might as well sit right here at the counter and have a cold drink and my signature eggplant and feta sandwich."

The proprietor busied himself behind the counter before turning and presenting her with two thick slabs of bread pinned together with a toothpick and garnished with parsley and a radish.

If he had understood anything of what she was saying, he gave no sign of it. "Now," he said, "I want to hear more about Lyle and Will."

Maggie's heart leapt like it had finally been returned to water after lying helplessly on the bank. She had purposely put her family out of her mind, but now she poured out the story of her life in Red Bud. She told of dinners at the Main Street Diner and how the three of them had squeezed together in the front seat of the truck before she had quit her job at the munitions plant. She told how Lyle had loved turkey and cheese or ham and mayo in his lunch until she had stopped buying turkey because the birds were raised in such tight quarters that part of their beaks and toes had to be removed to prevent them from injuring each other and ham because of how the sows were confined to cramped gestation crates until they were too old to be useful, at which time they were killed. She was surprised to find herself voicing not only what she loved about Lyle, but also the things that irritated her. She described how Lyle would shake his head over a dilemma before declaring, "Who am I to say! There are experts for that sort of thing." She recalled how she was always sticking up for Lyle, but when was the last time Lyle had stuck up for her?

"It sounds like you had a lot of responsibility on your shoulders. It sounds like Lyle took advantage of you. No wonder you ran away."

"I didn't run away!" she exclaimed. "And Lyle didn't take advantage of me at all!" She tore a crust off her sandwich and tossed it to Dino, who was waiting for her by the door. It was disconcerting to be misunderstood. But how did a person tell his or her story exactly the way it was?

"When the responsibilities of your family became overwhelming, you traded them in for responsibilities of a different kind."

"That's not the way it was at all."

Right from the start, Maggie had assumed Lyle needed her more than she had needed him. Even worse, she had let other people think it. Whenever Misty or True said, "I hope Lyle knows how lucky he is," Maggie had never corrected them or said that she was lucky too. And if Lyle gave Will what she thought was bad advice, she would interrupt and contradict him, right in front of Will. Now she wondered if the proprietor was a little bit right about running away, and if what she was running away from had mostly been her fault.

# 9.9  LYLE

Every evening, the first thing Lyle would see when he walked into the house was the pile of bills on Maggie's desk. He tried putting a kitchen towel over it, but that only made the pile seem to be taunting him. The Saturday after the phone service was terminated, Lyle got up early and cleared a space on the desk. After setting the checkbook and a blue felt-tip pen in the space, he poured a cup of coffee and sat in Maggie's chair with his knees bumping up against the underside of the pencil drawer. He hadn't worked at a desk in over twenty years, and his eyes automatically flew to the door and then to the window. A flock of crows settled on the lawn, their wings black and gleaming. Maggie's bicycle, which he guessed now belonged to Will, rusted against the side of the shed, and the mud-spattered truck angled into its parking spot, indicating that Will had been the last to drive it. Lyle hadn't heard him come in—where was Will going so late at night? He wished he could discuss it with Maggie, but he didn't want to worry her. He wished he could discuss it with Jimmy Sweets without Jimmy always taking Will's side and acting as if Lyle didn't know his own son. When the crows flapped off, Lyle tore his eyes away from the window, half expecting Miss Proctor to slap her ruler against the side of the desk and say, Next time, Lyle, I'm slapping it against your head!

Each time Lyle wrote out a check, he sealed it in an envelope and fixed one of the self-sticking Liberty Bell stamps into the top right-hand corner. Then he printed his return address on the lines provided and dropped the envelope into a pile at his feet and carefully subtracted the amount from the balance column in the check register, just as Maggie had always done. "Look at this, Will," he said when Will came into the room rubbing his eyes. He tapped the checkbook with the pen.

"Good job, Dad."

Will's big hand rested for a moment on Lyle's shoulder, filling Lyle with something deep and joyful.

Besides bills, the pile contained credit card applications and mortgage refinance invitations and packets of coupons for things Lyle didn't use. At the bottom of the pile were two letters on official school stationery—one inviting Will and his family to a meeting at the college counseling office, and the second saying that Will had missed two counseling sessions and also failed to turn in his scholarship application forms. A week later, a third letter arrived suggesting Will consider a trade school course if he didn't plan to go to college. It included a final counseling date, this one printed in bold red type.

"What do you want to do?" asked Lyle.

Will seemed surprised that the counselor had taken the trouble to write so many letters. "I guess they believed their own story," he said.

Will spent the weekend picking the letters up and putting them down again. "About becoming a doctor," he said when they were clearing away the Sunday supper things.

"Yes?" said Lyle when his son didn't continue.

"I mean, how do people know who they really are?"

The question unnerved Lyle, who had started to wonder the same thing. "Why don't you call Mom in the morning?" he suggested. "She gets in early on Mondays. She's sure to have some good ideas."

"Mom's a perfect example of what I mean," said Will. "We went for years thinking she was one thing, and then, all of a sudden, she was something else."

"People have sides to them," said Lyle. "Your mother was just discovering a different side. Kind of like you discovering you want to be a doctor."

"But I don't want to be a doctor," said Will quietly. "I don't want to now, and I never did."

"But I thought ... " Lyle sat down at the table, stunned and silent. "Let's call your mother," he said. "I expect she'll have some good advice for you."

"What would Maggie Rayburn do—isn't that how it goes? The thing is, I don't want to know what Mom would do. It's what Will Rayburn would do that counts, so don't you go telling her anything about it."

Lyle understood that in some way the conversation was about him, for all around him, people were changing while he sat stuck to his chair. He alone had no facets or hidden agendas. He suspected that when the doctors eventually cut him open, what they'd find would be a brown zip jacket and a red felt cap.

After that, he spent ten minutes a day at the desk and watched the dwindling pile of bills with a deep sense of satisfaction. Less satisfying was the fact that the total in the right-hand column of the check register was going down. "I guess I won't be fixing that muffler," he said to Will, who was sitting on the couch staring out the window at the crows.

"Did you ever notice that when one flies off, they all fly off?" asked Will.

"That seems to be in the nature of crows," said Lyle.

"Yeah," said Will. "Sometimes I think I must be part crow."

One day a representative of the bank that held the mortgage on their house called to say the automatic payment had failed to go through for the second month in a row.

"My wife handles the mortgage payments," said Lyle.

"In that case, perhaps you could put her on the phone."

When Lyle couldn't, the bank representative informed him that payment in full would be expected within a week. Then he told Lyle the amount of money owed, including interest and late fees. Lyle wrote the number down on a notepad and said he would send a check, but when he used his calculator to subtract the amount the bank wanted from the balance in the checkbook, the display blinked out -623.58.

Negative numbers had always seemed highly theoretical and dangerous to Lyle. They reminded him of words like "antimatter" and "implosion" because they didn't correspond to real things, but to the opposites of real things. He tried to laugh it off—first to himself, and then to Will. "What's the opposite of a couch?" he asked.

"There's no such thing," said Will.

"That's my point," said Lyle, walking over to show Will the bank balance. "That's exactly what I'm getting at."

"What about your paycheck, Dad? And didn't Mom send you part of hers?"

"Oh gosh, of course," said Lyle, breathing a sigh of relief. He adjusted the numbers in the check register and experienced a warm rush of competence. But there was also a car insurance bill hiding in the pile along with an unpaid speeding ticket and a charge for filling the propane tank, leaving the bank balance still veering toward negative territory even without the mortgage payments. "I guess I don't absolutely have to pay the phone bill," he said. "I guess I don't absolutely have to fix the truck."

"Nah," said Will. "We can live without a telephone, and if the truck makes a little noise, so what?"

"Turn off the lights," Lyle said to Will when he went off to bed. As he said it, he remembered all of the things Maggie had been reminding him about in the weeks before she left. Had she been planning on going to Phoenix all along? "And we don't need the heat on high either," he added. "Let's use extra blankets instead." But Will just sank farther into the couch cushions and didn't answer. He didn't even turn his head.

## 9.10 WILL

The day after Will visited the recruiting station, he called his mother and told her he was following his dream just the way she was following hers.

"Will!" cried Maggie. "I'm coming home on the next bus."

"I won't be here," said Will, misrepresenting his departure date. Then he relented and said, "I'm proud of you, Mom. At least you're doing something you believe in. We can compare notes on our adventures someday. In the meantime, I'll be sure to write."

That evening he and Tula sat in their usual spot under the apple trees and had their first beer together. A few snowflakes sifted through the lacy branches as they laughed about how beer was a gateway drug and also about how straitlaced they'd always been.

"Every class has rebels and good kids," said Tula. "I guess we're somewhere in between."

"We don't fit in at all," said Will. It was something he kept realizing and then forgetting again. He thought being straitlaced was generally a good thing, but he also didn't want to be a stick in the mud. "Of course, I'll have to follow the rules in the army, but I won't follow them blindly. I mean, I'm going to think for myself." The beer had loosened the gear that usually got in the way of speaking his mind, and he added, "Moderation—that's the key, isn't it?"

The beer also made him feel good. Tula said it made her feel good too. Good and also a little reckless, a little like having a second beer. "Was there a reason we said we were only going to have one?" she asked. "It seems kind of arbitrary, but if there was a reason for it..."

"It was kind of an assumption—I don't really know."

"I can see how you might say you're not going to have any. That would be a line worth drawing, but I can't really see the difference between one and two, can you?"

"Two never killed anybody."

"That's what I think. I think two would be perfectly okay."

"It's probably not even a good idea to stop at one," said Will. "If a thing's worth doing, it's worth doing well."

But there had only been two beers in the Rayburns' refrigerator, and it wasn't easy to figure out how to get more. "Everyone in town knows us," said Will. "If we want to buy beer, we have to drive to Glorietta, which means we have to get the truck from my dad, who is probably at the Merry Maid . . ."

"Drinking beer," Tula finished for him.

"Exactly right," said Will.

The sky had been leaden and threatening all day, and now it started to snow for real, which only seemed to confirm that the world around them was changing and they would have to change too—either with it or in opposition. Either one would be good. They debated whether conformity was preferable to rebellion, and for once, they both agreed. It was exhilarating to run along the icy road in the knowledge that they had been marginalized by society and that, being excluded, they might not be bound by its laws at all. They whooped and hollered as they plunged down the hill past the athletic fields and through a dark stand of cottonwood trees to where a footpath ran beside the frozen slick of Ash Creek. They stopped for a long kiss, and Will located, deep within his alienation, a sense of belonging and completion.

The streets were unplowed and the snow was piling up, concealing the familiar. Then Tula tugged at him with her mittened hand and they were running again, past the turnoff to the Ash Creek settlement where Tula lived and past the municipal recreation center before heading up the slope to the Super Saver parking lot and down the street to where Lyle's truck was parked next to an empty lot where the foundation for a new office complex had just been poured.

"Go inside and ask him for the keys," said Will. "Tell him the truck is in the way of the snowplow and that you'll move it for him."

"I can't say that," said Tula. "It's a lie!"

"You'd be protecting him," said Will. "If he doesn't know our plan, he can't be held accountable for what we do. He can't be pressured into revealing it to anyone."

"Pressured by whom?" asked Tula.

"Whoever's out to get us," said Will, winking like a conspirator.

Tula blinked at him, her eyelashes heavy with snowflakes, and just when he was going to grab her again, right there on Main Street where anyone could see them, she pushed him away and sashayed into the bar, leaving him to stamp his feet on the icy pavement, trying to stay warm. After what seemed like a long time, Tula emerged, swinging her hips like a cheerleader and dangling the keys triumphantly above her head.

Will hadn't expected there would be side effects to drinking. He hadn't expected that he'd want to kiss Tula's neck and her belly button or that he wouldn't want to stop there. He hadn't expected that driving the truck would become increasingly hazardous or that it would get stuck in a snowdrift driving back from Glorietta or that he'd push Tula into the drift instead of getting it unstuck or that he'd dive in after her when someone in a passing car stuck his head out the window and shouted, "Get a room!"

"We've got the truck, don't we?" he said to Tula. "It's even better than a room."

"No, no, I can't," said Tula. She looked sorrowful and frail, shivering in her too-big parka. He wanted to protect her, so he put an arm around her shoulders, but instead of snuggling in close to him, she moved away. Tiny snowflakes were drifting down, and the light from a streetlamp made a halo around her head.

"Why not?" asked Will. Something had changed for him; or, rather, many things had changed. He was motherless. He had joined the army. He had a girlfriend. And pretty soon he'd be

349

quitting school. He was giving up a lot, so it seemed right that Tula give up something too. Not that she'd really be giving something up—they'd both be gaining. He said the word "sacrifice," but it wasn't exactly what he meant. Apparently it was the wrong word to use because suddenly, Tula no longer seemed frail. Will suspected she was even angry, but the alcohol was affecting his perceptions and he couldn't be sure.

"Give up. Abandon. Kill," said Tula. "What kind of sacrifice are we talking about?"

Will was confused as to whether having sex or not having it entailed sacrifice and whether sacrifice was a good thing or a bad one, but before he could ask, Tula stepped beyond the circle of lamplight and faded away behind a veil of snowflakes, leaving him to ponder the effects of the beer, which no longer made him feel happy and light-headed, but leaden and angry and thick. He ran partway down the road in the direction she had gone, skidding and panicked and shouting for her to come back. Now and then a car pushed past him, its taillights smearing in the snowy dark. Then there was only silence and a small but growing blister of loneliness and desperation. He was walking back to the truck when an SUV stopped and the driver helped him push the truck out of the snow.

"Christ almighty, son," said the driver. "You're already at the Loop Road. Your girlfriend probably just walked on home. You must have really pissed her off."

Will drove around the loop, slowly at first as he looked for Tula, but then more recklessly when he realized she had probably taken a shortcut across the fields to her house, which was no more than a mile away as the crow flies. He turned the wheel this way and that just to make skid marks in the pristine whiteness. He opened the window and shouted out into the swirling blizzard, "I think

I know a little bit about sacrifice, Tula Santos! I joined the army after all!"

The snow absorbed the sound while Will absorbed the strange quiet of the town where he had lived his whole life. As he drove, he gazed at it in wonder, as if he had already left it or returned after an absence of many years. He was as good as gone, and he thrilled to imagine the adventures he would have while the citizens of Red Bud plodded around the same old track. He slammed on the brakes, turning into the skid before speeding up again and letting the thrill overtake him until he was riding the razor's edge of chaos and control. He marveled at how the plumes of exhaust coming from a car that appeared in front of him turned red in the glow of the car's taillights, at how the shapes of things seemed sharper and more brittle in the frozen air. He marveled at how things were already changing and would never be the same again. And he marveled at how slowly and inevitably the collision happened when the driver of the car he was following suddenly hit the brakes.

# 10.0 VISIONS
# AND GOALS

*Danny's girlfriend sent us proof the government not only knew the munitions were toxic, but was taking active steps to cover it up. She sent photographs of damaged babies. She sent some doctored scientific reports.*

—Joe Kelly

*We got more submissions from soldiers than we knew what to do with. And then it wasn't just soldiers, it was government contractors and whistleblowers. Concerned citizens, that's who it was.*

—Penn Sinclair

*They sent evidence about the war, but also about cancer clusters, toxic waste dumps, government surveillance programs, journalists detained at airports, corporate malfeasance, manipulation of financial markets, politicians bought and paid for. It blew our fucking minds.*

—Joe Kelly

*SWAT teams breaking up college poker games, moms who lost their kids because of false arrests, first graders handcuffed for talking in class, babies shot in no-knock raids, property seizures without due process, militarization of the police. I would have posted everything on the site, but the captain said we had to remember what the mission was, and the mission was to tell the truth about the war.*

—Le Roy Jones

*They got their share of hate mail too.*

—E'Laine Washington

# 10.1 LE ROY JONES

Le Roy was alone in the warehouse when a visitor knocked at the door saying he was a reporter and asking to be let in.

"How did you find us?" asked Le Roy.

"A woman named Dolly Jackson sent me here."

"Hunh," said Le Roy. "Danny's girlfriend sent you? How do you know her?"

"A while back I wrote a series of articles on innocent prisoners. One of my sources told me that Dolly was on to an even bigger story, and Dolly told me about you."

"Hunh," Le Roy said again.

Three months before, Le Roy would have let anyone in. One day a serviceman who had been summoned to the building across the street installed a new Kenmore refrigerator before Danny returned and pointed out the mistake. Another time, Le Roy enjoyed takeout from a local Chinese restaurant that wasn't meant for them. After that, Danny helped Le Roy develop a method for sensing when something was about to go off track, and a surefire indicator was that the doorbell would ring when everyone but Le Roy was out of the warehouse.

"Don't answer the doorbell," Danny had reminded him just that morning. "If no one else is here, you should just let it ring."

But the reporter didn't ring the bell. He clomped up onto the front porch and rapped on the windowpane.

"The door's not locked," shouted Le Roy when he heard the rapping. He only heard it because he didn't have his headphones in his ears. He didn't have them in because the captain and Kelly had gone off somewhere and Danny had gone somewhere too, which meant he could turn the music up as loud as he wanted as long as the upstairs neighbors didn't complain. Headphones were a good invention, but they weren't as good as no headphones, which allowed the surfaces of the building to rattle and become part of the music, which Le Roy thought was not only the way the musicians intended it, but what the music itself wanted.

"Listen to this," he said to the reporter, who just happened to be carrying a video camera and some recording equipment. "Does this sound better to you or this?" He played two versions of the same song, one recorded in a high-tech studio and one out on a busy street.

"No contest," said the reporter in a smooth voice.

"Yeah," said Le Roy. "Fuck that other shit." He put the live recording on again and amped it up until the windows rattled and the computer speakers buzzed a little. "Even better, am I right?"

"So right," said the reporter.

"More real," said Le Roy.

"Exactly what I was going to say."

"I'm thinking of recording this and then playing the recording so it picks up other sounds and then recording that and playing—you know, keep doing that until I reach a point where it no longer sounds better—if I ever reach that point. That's what I want to find out."

"I've got a digital recorder," said the man. "Why don't we try it now?"

After a while the man reached over to turn down the volume and said that his name was Martin Fitch and that he was investigating how a particular top-secret document had found its way to wartruth.com. "The document is called *Countering Misconceptions,* and it showed up on your website a couple weeks back."

"Sure," said Le Roy. "I can help you with that." Then he opened the email log he had created to track all of the submissions they had received in the weeks since the site went live. "This column shows who sent it, and this shows what, if anything, we did in terms of authentication. And this is the date when I put it up on the site." He spent a minute scrolling through the log. "Oh, yeah," he said. "That's the one we got in the mail from Dolly Jackson. You know Dolly, right?"

"I do," said Martin. "She's the one who sent me here."

After giving Martin the information he wanted, Le Roy told him a little about how the website had started and how the captain felt responsible for Pig Eye and the others even though it wasn't his fault.

"Whose fault was it?" asked Martin.

"That's something I think about too," said Le Roy. "What if the world is just a giant computer simulation? What if the grand master isn't God, but a computer geek at his keyboard who just wanted to find out what would happen if we took out Saddam? Maybe he also wants to see what happens if we bomb Iran or North Korea or let the polluters run amok. Or what if he makes half the people warlike or hyper-religious or a combination of the two and the other half, you know, all goody-goody and passive. Or if he gives all of the money to a handful of people and everybody else has shit."

"Hunh," said Martin. "Cool."

Just then E'Laine and the single mother came in with bags of groceries. Le Roy had forgotten E'Laine had come to visit for a few days. He was glad to see her, but the gladness was more like satisfaction, the kind a person felt when problems were solved and blanks filled in. Like if he had been wondering where E'Laine was, now he'd know. "There's E'Laine!" he said, marking the instant a tiny gap closed up inside him.

"We're cooking for the guys tonight," said E'Laine after shaking hands with Martin. "You're welcome to stay for dinner if you like."

"Thanks. I'd like to meet everyone involved with this project. I'm hoping they can help me with my article, and in return, I can help them publicize the site. The more publicity, the more traffic, and the more traffic, the more donations—that sort of thing."

"Sure," said E'Laine. "I'll set another place."

Le Roy swiveled his chair to see E'Laine. He thought about how his chair could be turning on its axle, or it could be that with a mere push of his foot, he'd sent the entire universe spinning around his chair. "Oh," he said. "Oh, yeah."

Martin said he had an errand to run, so Le Roy got back to work. He put on his headphones. He turned up the volume to the point where the room went away and it was just him and the screen and the liquid slip of the keys under his fingers. He liked to tap in time to the music, which made it seem like he was the one playing the keyboard, and if the train just happened to come through as it did now, all the better for the bass. He entered another line of code and felt like a master of the universe, even if his universe was still small. Once he got tired of the website, he'd try something bigger. He wasn't joking about simulations, which were a combination of games and real life and were starting to get some press.

He kept his eyes on the computer screen, but the sides of his face could feel E'Laine walking toward the door with Martin.

Probably she was only seeing him out, but maybe she was going with him. E'Laine had a mind of her own. He knew he could tap and tap and he couldn't keep her from going with the reporter if that's what she wanted to do. The tiny gap threatened to open up again. Then she was waving—he couldn't tell if it was to catch his attention or to say good-bye to the reporter. He felt a slight unraveling in his chest as if he wanted to tell her something, but then he typed another line of code and E'Laine was gone. Martin Fitch was gone. Everything was gone but the screen in front of him until Danny came back with some books under his arm and a few minutes after that the captain and Kelly returned with the supplies. Danny made sure everything was in order—the tape on the tape shelf and the coffee on the coffee shelf—while Kelly answered the phone when it rang, and the thing that had clicked out of place when E'Laine went out the door with Martin clicked back in until Kelly started shouting at the captain about something and Le Roy tuned him out.

In his simulation, Le Roy would make a world where everything was in its place, at least at the beginning—at least at what he thought of as ground zero or the big bang. He could set the parameters so that if Kelly or Danny went out the door, they were guaranteed to come back in again. That way, the people in the simulation who depended on Kelly and Danny would feel secure the way he felt now that his friends were back and the supplies were put away. But then he thought, What would that prove? The point of a simulation wasn't to keep things static. The point was to shake things up. He'd like to see what happened if an alien race attacked those people who were feeling all safe—ha! Or if the icebergs melted all at once or if computerized robots started to make decisions for themselves. Like if the rich people somehow got the poor people to vote against their own interests and if the poor people ever figured it out. Or what if they were in a simulation now and just didn't know it—a simulation within a simulation, he thought. Now that would be a project worth working on. Now that would be fucking cool.

## 10.2 PENN SINCLAIR

After Fitch's article was published in the *New York Times*, leaked documents started to pour in to the site's secure drop box from anonymous sources.

"Shee-it," said Kelly. "Who's sending us all this stuff?"

"Martin says we don't want to know their names," Penn told him. "It's better for everybody that way."

Le Roy increased site security and developed a network of volunteers to help with encryption and document authentication. Some of the documents needed to be redacted, so they developed another network for that.

"We all know Dolly's name," said Danny. "Does that put her in some kind of danger?"

"She's not the insider who stole the document," said Penn. "Outsiders are safe."

"What about us?" asked Danny.

"We're journalists," said Kelly. "Journalists are protected by the First Amendment."

"But probably not leakers," said Penn. "Fitch says that the prevailing view is that they aren't protected, even though some scholars disagree. Everything in this arena is changing pretty fast, and the law is far from settled. But the bottom line is that the less we know about the people sending us this stuff the better."

The site's email box was even busier than the drop box. One soldier wrote anonymously of participating in the Haditha massacre, where twenty-four unarmed Iraqis were shot at close range. Others wrote about being advised to carry drop weapons in case they killed the wrong person. Soldiers wrote about indiscriminately rounding up all able-bodied men and sending them to Abu Ghraib for processing, and interrogators at Abu Ghraib wrote about being overwhelmed and undertrained. There was footage of an Apache helicopter firing on men armed with what turned out to be cameras and more footage where a wedding party was the target of attack. In the forum section of the site, the soldiers asked each other how you could tell the right person from the wrong one, and the answer was you couldn't.

They wrote about bellying up mountains through storms of artillery fire and about taking out snipers and disarming bombs and providing clean water and helping the local businesses that sprang up in areas that had been rife with sectarian violence, and then they wrote about how the sectarian violence crept back in as soon as the soldiers left.

Political operatives wrote about burying information in the run-up to the war and about inserting sentences into official speeches. A Vietnam vet sent a documentary of the Winter Soldier Investigation, which was intended to show that war crimes in Vietnam were a direct result of official policy, and another one told about how he'd been present at the Gulf of Tonkin—no torpedoes had been fired at U.S. warships that day, which meant a deadly and divisive conflict was started on a lie.

There were stories about how one third of veterans from the First Gulf War suffered from Gulf War Syndrome and how they were still fighting for treatment seventeen years later and how much of the debate centered on what to call the mysterious constellation of symptoms that was now starting to affect a new generation of returning soldiers and how what you called it had implications for how seriously it was taken. There were stories about how exposure to Vietnam-era Agent Orange was only getting official attention now that it was too late to help the men and women who had suffered from multiple myeloma or soft-tissue sarcoma or cancers of the lungs or larynx or trachea and finally died. There were stories of benefits delayed or denied, of soldiers who fought for their country overseas and then had to fight the bureaucracy at home.

There were statistics too: 148 combat casualties in the First Gulf War; 145 noncombat deaths. And explanations of the statistics: official figures for soldier deaths only counted those who died on the ground, not the ones who died on the C-130 taking them to the hospital or the ones who died after they landed in Germany or the ones who died at Walter Reed Medical Center or the ones who died a few years later from wounds or illnesses contracted during the war or the ones who waited eight or ten or fifteen years to die of worsening symptoms that were variously attributed to vaccinations, oil well fires, pesticide use, bacteria in the soil, anti–nerve agent pills, solvents, metal-laden dust, depleted uranium weapons, and infectious disease. Of 694,000 soldiers who served in Desert Storm, 115,000 would soon be dead. Of a group of eight friends, only two remained.

A soldier wrote to say, "Why are you doing this? People don't want to know all the risks because then no one would do anything."

But Kelly kept passing the stories on to Le Roy and Le Roy kept blasting them up on the site and Martin Fitch kept advising them on which documents to release to the public and E'Laine came more and more often to do odd jobs and the single mother was there almost every evening with a hot, home-cooked meal. Now and then one of the men would say, "Man, this thing is really taking off," but mostly they concentrated on the daily tasks, with Penn feeling good that the other men needed him less and less, because wasn't the whole point to set them up on their own? When he couldn't sleep, he tramped through the neighborhood on patrol. Once, he scared off someone who was trying to jimmy a lock on a building down the street. Another time, he chased two men from the shadows, gaining on them as they cut through an empty lot and circled back toward the river. He was running easily, his shadow catching up with him when he passed a streetlight before disappearing in the dark. The closer he got, the more infuriated their heavy, labored breathing made him. "You shouldn't go on a mission you're not ready for," he shouted.

When the slower of the two men tripped, Penn made the decision to keep after the faster one, sensing weakness there too, and panic. With panic, he knew from experience, came mistakes. The man took to the street where the running was easier, which gave Penn a further advantage because the path was predictable and because he could save a few feet on the curve. When his quarry ducked left, headed across a parking lot and toward a forested hillside that dropped toward the river, Penn knew he had won— because of a chain-link fence that was hidden in the tangle, which meant the man would have to retrace his steps back up between the parked cars to the road, and because he was faltering while Penn stayed strong. Penn hung back. It was better to tackle a spent man than one with some kick left in him. As predicted, the man cut up the embankment toward the highway. Penn turned on one last burst of speed, and in another minute he had the target on the ground.

"Okay, mister, okay."

When he saw it was only a teenaged kid, the anger drained out of him and he said with more violence in his voice than he felt, "This is my neighborhood. You mess with it, you mess with me."

"Okay," the kid said again.

His hat had fallen off. Penn picked it up and held it out in a gesture of conciliation. "Where do you live?" he asked.

The boy waved vaguely at the surrounding streets of ramshackle houses.

"Give me the exact address," said Penn.

The boy gave it to him.

"I'll tell you what. You bring your friend here tomorrow night at eleven and I won't tell the police about you. I need recruits for my patrol."

"What patrol?" asked the kid.

"You'll find out tomorrow. You'll start off as grunts, but you can work your way up."


In February, Colonel Falwell contacted Penn to say he was using his time stateside to check on his wounded troops. "The families said some of them are with you."

"Yes sir," said Penn. "Some of them are."

"I'd like to touch base with them. Do they want to come down here to Washington?"

"We were there in the fall," said Penn. "It didn't go so well, but I'll ask them."

"And if that's not possible, you might make the trip yourself. You live in Connecticut if I remember correctly."

Instinct told Penn to let the misinformation stand, so he said, "Yes sir, I do."

On the day of the meeting, Penn set off when it was still dark. It was peaceful in the car. He hadn't been alone for weeks, and he liked listening to the whoosh of tires on the damp road and watching the light come up and the scenery change. He liked seeing the small businesses pop up as he approached a town and the neat suburban lawns unspool into farmland as he left it. He liked pulling into a service station and smelling the mix of gasoline and coffee and saying, "Morning" to the station attendants in their neat gray uniforms with their first names stitched in red script on white canvas patches and knowing just that about them, nothing else. He wondered what Falwell would say to him, if he knew about the protest or the website. But something about the closed capsule of the car protected him from the birds of worry, so he fiddled with the radio as he drove and mostly he thought of nothing, just let impressions flow over him: a hill with fruit trees, an abandoned baseball field, a middle-aged woman on a bicycle, a man in a cap and faded jeans who had been pulled over by the police.

But now and then one of the worries would peck through and he would think about Louise and all of the people he had let down and about how, if things kept going the way they had been, they were likely to cover their expenses with donations alone, without tapping into any more of the seed money from Penn's trust fund. And just that week, Kelly had said he had thought of a way for the site to turn a profit.

"I've applied for nonprofit status," Penn had told him.

"Yeah, sure," said Kelly. "But what if I could find some advertisers in addition to the donors?"

Penn had been noncommittal, but now the word "profit" rattled around in his head like unexploded rounds. He should be happy the men were pulling in different directions because that meant he had accomplished what he had set out to do, so why was he so bothered by it? He supposed that alongside his desire to help them was an equally strong desire to prove himself as a leader, and what kind of a leader was he if his men weren't following enthusiastically along behind?

Just after the turnoff to Annapolis and Fort Meade, the highway cut through a thick stand of trees. He tried to imagine that he was lost in a primeval forest, that all anybody needed to live was a simple cabin with a rough pine floor and a plot of land with a river running through it and a few tools and some farm animals and of course a rugged inner core, but with cars and semis whizzing by, it was hard to hold on to the vision.

Anyway, he thought as he pulled off at a rest stop for another cup of coffee and a piss, there was no denying the fact that Kelly was developing a knack for business and that Le Roy was a whiz with computers and that Danny could go for an entire day without hitting the deck when the train went through. In that regard, the website was a complete success. It was Penn himself who lacked a real direction, and in the back of his mind he was hoping his meeting with Falwell would help him with that.

## 10.3 GORDON FALWELL

Falwell shuffled through the stack of reports on his desk—the one that said ten of eighteen benchmarks had been met in Iraq and the one that said eleven of the benchmarks hadn't been met and that only three had been completed. He found the report he was working on, and then he picked up a pen and changed "modest" to "significant." He changed "trained" to "empowered," and in front of "leadership" he wrote "committed and determined." Fuck the benchmarks. Was there a benchmark for understanding the enemy? Was there one for unit readiness and self-sacrifice and morale? Was there one for showing that Americans wouldn't put up with crazy fucking shit? "Unmistakable signs of progress," he wrote. "High levels of local cooperation and trust." The counterinsurgency was working. They were definitely winning hearts and minds.

Falwell was in Washington to provide input for an operational assessment and, if all went well, to be recommended for a promotion and to see someone about a persistent pain in his gut and a worrisome rattling in his chest. To top it off, now one of his after action reports was being called into question on the Internet. Miller, his old NCO, had brought it to his attention, and if certain other people saw it, it could torpedo his career. He could only surmise he had Captain Sinclair to thank for drawing attention to the inconsistencies. Sinclair was the one who had first written up the IED incident, and he was the one with the guilty conscience. Any report depended on the person writing it, as well as on the freshness of the memories and on biases and agendas the writer might not even know he held. A reasonable man could argue that Sinclair's version of events was less accurate than the more measured official version, but the colonel didn't want to have to make that case. Things were muddied enough without going down some he-said-she-said rabbit hole. Falwell wasn't angry so much as irritated. Mightily irritated. And, to be honest, his feelings were a little hurt. When he'd altered the report, he'd been looking out for Sinclair's interests as much as for his own.

Once, back when he himself had been a captain, he'd led a tank company in the wrong direction. Visibility had been next to impossible due to hundreds of burning oil fields. He'd had to make a split-second decision, and he had called it wrong. The lessons learned were many: to listen to his subordinates, to take a moment even when all hell was breaking loose, to realize that mistakes came with the territory in any pressured situation. Most important of all, he had learned that the reaction of a superior could foster learning and renew confidence, which is exactly what his commanding officer had done when he had called Falwell into his office and said, "You'll get 'em next time." That was what had been done for him and what he had tried to do in saving Sinclair from the consequences of his overly emotional report.

The very next day, Falwell's tank company had led the charge into occupied territory, and he had earned a Bronze Star for decisive leadership and superlative courage in the face of enemy fire. "Superlative" was a good word, one he liked to use whenever he could.

## 10.4 PENN SINCLAIR

What the fuck? asked the expression on Falwell's face when he opened the door of his Arlington hotel room. Falwell was up for full-bird colonel, and he was quick to make sure Penn knew it. "What the fuck?" he asked when the formalities were over and they were sitting down.

"I'm sorry, sir, but I'm not sure what you mean," said Penn, who had decided to listen and say as little as possible until he found out why he was there.

"You told me you deleted your statement."

"What statement?"

"Now someone has posted it on a website right next to my official AAR, and I'm guessing it was you."

"What if it was?" asked Penn, worried that the colonel knew more about the website than he was letting on.

"What the fuck for?"

"I'm just telling the truth," said Penn, grateful now for the fist that gripped his insides because it kept him from letting his guard down. And grateful for the guilt that was his constant companion because it kept him from backing off his commitment to his men. "I'm hoping it will even save some lives."

"Truth," said the colonel. "How exactly will your version of the truth save lives?"

*"Only by acknowledging a mistake can we learn from it,"* said Penn.

"Who said that?" asked Falwell.

"You did, sir. You said I could quote you."

Falwell picked up a sheaf of papers and put them down again. "Do you see this report?" he asked. "Sectarian violence is down; local law enforcement is up; a constitutional review committee has been formed. Ten of eighteen benchmarks met or exceeded."

Penn looked out the window to where a glossy bird sat on a railing and pecked at the glass.

"Damn bird is trying to get in," said the colonel.

"Why in God's name would it want to get in?" asked Penn. "We can't even understand ourselves, so how can we expect to understand birds?"

"I think we can understand birds," said Falwell. "At least a little

369

bit. Otherwise why would we care about them? Why would we create bird sanctuaries and set out birdseed in the winter? Why would we give a crap about the spotted owl?"

"We're so good at understanding that we barge right on in without realizing that we don't have a clue what we're hoping to accomplish. Nobody had a handle on the big picture, but they were too stubborn to admit it."

"But that's changing. That's what the surge was all about."

"Oh, *now* we understand. We didn't then, but now we do. There's nothing different about this time. That's the real lesson learned."

"Who really knows anything?" asked the colonel. "You do your best with what you have."

"And our best wasn't anywhere near good enough. The war has harmed countless soldiers and families, and it's made the world more dangerous."

"The world has always been dangerous," said the colonel. "We in America have an illusion of safety, but it's only an illusion. The war might have opened a few eyes—it might have opened your eyes—but it didn't change anything fundamental about the world. You want to see a dangerous world, just dismantle the American army and bring all of our soldiers home."

Penn remembered what he had learned from the man in the library, and he couldn't disagree. "Man is warlike," he said, but the heat had gone out of his anger. All he felt now was tired.

"What would our place in a peaceful world be, Sinclair? Do you think a peaceful world would be one where everyone agreed and justice magically prevailed? No, it would just be one where people didn't give a shit. No one standing up for anything. Everybody neutered and complacent." He laughed without smiling. "In a peaceful world, my daughters would be in charge of things, and much as I love my daughters, that isn't something I'd like to see."

Penn thought about what the world would be like if Louise and her friends were calling the shots. Everything would be attractive and well planned, with peonies and parsley garnishes and sparkling beverages served in champagne flutes.

"Everything becalmed and stagnant—is that the kind of world you want?"

"No sir."

"If there's nothing worth fighting for, there's nothing worth living for either."

"Yes sir," said Penn.

*"Far better it is to dare mighty things, to win glorious triumphs, even though checkered by failure than to rank with those poor spirits who neither enjoy much nor suffer much, because they live in the gray twilight that knows not victory nor defeat."*

"Theodore Roosevelt," said Penn.

"My point is that you take your best shot. That's all any person can do."

It was something Penn had said himself, most recently to Danny. He had not only said it, he had believed it. Now a tiny particle of hope started expanding in his breast. Maybe people could know, or if they couldn't, maybe partial knowledge was good enough.

"What do you want to do with your life, Sinclair? What are your plans?"

It was the question Penn had been asking himself. "I want to see my men back on their feet. I think that's happening—at least I'm hopeful. And after that, I haven't decided."

"I called you down here for two reasons," said Falwell.

"Sir?" The bird was back. Penn wondered if it had choices or only instinct and if he was more, or less, like the bird.

371

"One was to ask you if you are the one who posted the two versions of the IED incident on the Internet. And if you did, to ask you to take them down." Falwell drummed his fingers on a pile of papers, and when Penn didn't reply, he said, "And the other is to ask if you are interested in this." He took a sheaf of papers from the pile and passed it to Penn. The top page showed a group of soldiers standing at a safe distance while a robot dismantled an IED. "When I saw it, I thought of you."

Penn had wondered if the colonel knew who was behind the website, but as he paged through the document, he concluded he didn't. The knot in his chest dissolved as he listened to a rambling story about burning oil fields and a botched tank attack, where the moral seemed to be about second chances and where the punch line seemed to be "the smog of war."

"I see something in you," said the colonel. "And what I see is me."

"Yes sir," said Penn.

The bird was back, fooled by the expanse of glass and probably by the reflections in it of the view from the hotel window: the blue sky and the puffy clouds and a chevron of geese silhouetted against a disc-like sun. Penn decided it wanted in after all, but only because it thought that in was out.

"That was a defining moment for me," said the colonel. "Things could have gone one way and they could have gone another. The thing is, my commanding officer had my back. The thing is, I learned from my mistakes."

"But what if the war itself was the mistake?" asked Penn. "That's what I'm trying to figure out."

"I have to admit I think about that too, but the bottom line is, deciding that is not our job. Our job is to get the supplies from point A to point B. Our job is to find and defuse the IEDs." He reached out to tap the papers Penn was holding. "Our job is to run patrols and build infrastructure like water treatment plants and even schools. I'm here for another couple of months, but then I'm headed back. I can take you with me if you want."

"Let me think about it, sir," said Penn.

"It's another chance," said the colonel. "It's another chance to get it right."


## 10.5 JOE KELLY


Meaning had always eluded Kelly until he started fighting for his country, and then it suddenly seemed embedded in the smallest of events. He would be eating breakfast or loading a truck or cleaning his weapon or buckling into his body armor when a blast of meaning would nearly knock him over: One for all and all for one! You're with us or you're with the terrorists! Live free or die! Now he thought, People have a right to know. It felt good to see the big picture. It was gratifying to know the big picture had a place in it for him. Maybe he was a business-man after all. Maybe he'd buy himself a suit. Ha! Every now and then he got up to stretch and tried to see what Danny was doing because when Danny went down the rabbit hole with his epic poem, it was hard to get him out. But it seemed like that morning everyone was busy with work-related tasks. Everyone except the captain, who had driven down to DC to visit with the colonel.

Kelly worked through the emails, feeling a zap of pleasure whenever he handled one particularly efficiently. If he came upon something unusual, he would say, "Hey, Le Roy, I need your wizard skills," and now and then Le Roy would lean over Kelly's screen and say, "Ya got anything new for me to post?"

Kelly almost always did. In the past two weeks alone he had gotten photographs of flag-draped coffins and a story about how preelection fear-mongering had incited someone in Ohio to spray a chemical irritant into a room full of Muslim children and statistics showing that one third of female troops would be raped by fellow service members and that some of the victims would subsequently die under suspicious circumstances of non-combat-related injuries. He'd gotten reports that post-9/11 security measures had led to spying on American citizens and that a facility was being built in the Utah desert large enough to store data at the rate of an entire Library of Congress every minute and that twelve billion dollars in shrink-wrapped hundred-dollar bills had been sent to Iraq only to—go figure—be squandered or lost. And just that morning he'd received a story about a unit that was ordered to kill all military-age Iraqi males, after which four low-ranking soldiers were arrested and caged for twenty-three hours a day in seven-by-seven cells while sworn testimony was shredded to ensure they took the fall for their commanding officers.

At first, they were stories and reports sent to him by soldiers, but then it wasn't just soldiers posting on the site. There was Mark O'Hara of Tampa, whose war involved being sentenced to twenty-five years in prison for possessing a bottle of Vicodin for which he had a valid prescription, but because the prosecutor charged him with trafficking rather than possession, no prescription defense was allowed. And there was Genarlow Wilson, who was seventeen when he had consensual oral sex with his fifteen-year-old girlfriend, an act that earned him ten years in prison. Vaginal penetration would have been okay. Girls who were arrested for dropping chewing gum on the sidewalk—black girls, that is. The white girls could put their gum anywhere they wanted, but they couldn't jaywalk near the University of Texas without carrying an ID card. Then they risked being slapped in handcuffs and hauled off to jail.

There were Jennifer Boatright and Ron Henderson, who, under civil property forfeiture laws, were stripped of the cash with which they had planned to buy a used car when a police officer pulled them over, found the money, and threatened charges of child endangerment and money laundering if they tried to get it back. The usual constitutional protections didn't apply because it wasn't Boatright and Henderson who were the named defendants in the case, it was the $6,037, which went straight into the coffers of the police department that had seized it, where it joined the money that was supposed to pay for James Morrow's dental work.

There was Irma Alred, who got thirty years, and Theresa Brown, who got life, both for drug charges where no drugs had been found and the only evidence was the word of people who were given immunity in return for their testimony. There were the seventeen Uighurs who escaped Chinese persecution only to wind up in Guantanamo Bay and remain there because no nation wanted to upset the Chinese government by granting them asylum. There was Otto Zehm, developmentally disabled and wrongly suspected of robbing an ATM, who was batoned seven times from behind, Tasered, hog-tied, and fitted with a non-rebreather mask that was not attached to an oxygen tank. There was twelve-year-old DeAunta Farrow, who was playing with a toy gun when he died.

"I thought we weren't going to post that stuff," said the captain when he came back from DC. "I thought we were going to focus on information pertaining to the war."

"There's more than one war going on," said Kelly.

"But they're not our war," said the captain.

"That's 'cuz you're rich and white," said Kelly.

"Well, we can't post everything we get. That stuff just takes away from our mission. Tell Le Roy to take it down."

Ever since the *Times* article, the captain had been going on about tough choices, but it seemed to Kelly that "choice" was the captain's way of saying, This is how it's gonna be.

"And what's our mission?" asked Kelly. And then he said, "Captain, sir."

"Helping other soldiers, you know that."

"What if there's other people I want to help? People who didn't get to choose the war they're fighting. Believe it or not, I even want to help myself." Kelly was eager to explore the site's commercial potential, but he had been waiting for the right time to press the issue. "I'm thinking the human-interest stories might attract advertising, so if we concentrate on those . . . "

"Commercial potential is something I think about too," said the captain. "The practical answer is that it's pretty darn hard to make money on news. And the philosophical one is that I don't think we should be making money on the war."

"So everyone can make money on the war but us?" asked Kelly.

It was cold in the warehouse. Danny talked about installing storm windows, but they were expensive, so Kelly had been sitting with a blanket around his shoulders. Now he took it off and paced to the refrigerator, but it was empty. "Shee-it. We couldn't afford new windows, and now we can't afford beer?"

"The thing about making money off the war is, then there's no incentive for peace," said the captain.

"Is it wrong for farmers to make money off of hungry people or doctors off of sick people?" asked Kelly. "Or should everybody just focus on selling people shit they don't need?"

"Martin agrees with me that the documents are the important thing," replied the captain.

"Martin isn't my boss, and neither, frankly, are you."

Martin was working on a new series of articles, which would be published in the *Guardian*, and would only communicate with them via secure back channels or on the burner phones he sent them. "That's where our focus should be," said Penn. "The documents are the thing people can't get anywhere else."

Instead of arguing further, Kelly went on a beer run, and an hour later Danny said he wouldn't mind a little food. "Burgers or pizza?" he asked.

"I'd go for some Chinese food," said Kelly. He didn't really care what they ate, but there was a pretty girl at the Chinese restaurant, and if they wanted Chinese, he'd go for it himself so he could see her shock of black hair bob around her ears as she shook her wok back and forth and dipped rice out of a big metal vat.

The beer worked on all of them differently. Danny would get hungry, Le Roy would get even quieter than usual and eventually fall asleep, and the captain would start dwelling on everything he was doing or had ever done wrong. Kelly thought he was immune to beer. He wished he had some of those pills Harraday used to give him. If he had those pills, he'd go back and get to know the Chinese girl better. He'd like to see the shock of hair without the pointed cap the owner of the restaurant made her wear. It had been a long time since he'd really had some fun, but then he realized he was having fun now. Mostly he was having fun, even if it was of a tamer variety than he was used to.

# 10.6 JOE KELLY

Kelly was thinking about the Chinese girl, who had turned out to be engaged, when he opened an email that had no subject line and no signature, just a compressed file containing a clip of videotape and a message that said, "I want to make sure I have the right recipient. Tell me what this means to you, and if I'm satisfied with your answer, I'll send you the rest."

The video clip showed Kelly and Pig Eye up on the Toyota. It showed them raising their fists in the air. It showed Pig Eye stepping up on the truck and standing beside and slightly behind Kelly. "Stand right up next to me, motherfucker!" Kelly hissed at the screen, but even though he watched the video several times, Pig Eye never did.

Kelly played the clip a total of five times before it vanished. "Hey, Le Roy," he called out. "Is it possible for emails to self-destruct?"

"Yeah, man. I think I heard of that," replied Le Roy.

But what did the video mean to him, and what was he supposed to say to the person who had sent it?

He could answer with his name and rank, but the sender hadn't given a name, which made Kelly apprehensive about giving his. He finally wrote, "I'm the guy with his fist in the air. Who the fuck are you?" As an afterthought, he asked the date of the event. He figured that was something only someone who had been there would know.

The next bit of film didn't come until almost a week later.

Although Kelly had been expecting it, he jumped in his chair when he saw it in his in-box. The new clip was date- and time-stamped. It showed a television crew milling around while a convoy was preparing for departure. Thirty seconds into the tape, Colonel Falwell drove by and waved. Someone called out from off screen, "Colonel, is it true that Al Anbar Province is lost?"

The colonel gestured for the driver to stop the vehicle. "The situation there is certainly deteriorating," he said. "But lost? Not by a long shot."

"Should we go there then, or accompany this unit to Tikrit?"

"That unit isn't going to Tikrit," said Falwell. "But keep that to yourselves for now. They'll get the news soon enough. Now I've got a chopper to catch."

This clip didn't self-destruct, and Kelly watched it again and again, letting his head of steam build until he couldn't contain it any longer. When the captain came back with Subway sandwiches for everybody, he called out, "Hey, Captain! Get a load of this!" The captain didn't immediately answer him, so Kelly walked around the table and grabbed him by the collar of his jacket and hauled him over to his computer terminal and pushed him down into his chair.

"Did you know?" he shouted. "Did you know that we were never going north, that we weren't waiting for orders, that even the film crew knew the supplies were going west—that everybody knew it except for you?"

"I knew it was a possibility," said Penn. "Falwell told me I should sit tight until I heard from him. The new orders finally came through about three hours after you left that morning."

Kelly played the tape for the captain, and then he played it again, and again after that.

"Who sent it?" asked the captain.

"The television crew, obviously."

"Why is it obvious? Did they say so?"

"Because they were a film crew. Because it's a piece of fucking film. They must have seen our website. They must have seen your email exposing the cover-up of the IED incident and noticed that the dates didn't match up, and now I'm seeing that the colonel knew the supplies weren't going north before he even left for HQ."

"He didn't tell me," said Penn. "He acknowledges that right in the film. Maybe he wanted to be absolutely sure first. Hell, that wouldn't be the first time he held information until he couldn't hold it any longer—like the way he sat on the stop-loss orders."

Then Kelly told Penn about the vanishing email that showed him up on the Toyota with Pig Eye.

"The film crew didn't send it," said the captain. "Think about it. The first clip showing you and Pig Eye was the teaser. That was just to get your attention. The second clip was what whoever sent it really wanted you to see. But it wasn't sent for the website. It won't mean anything to anybody but us—who else is going to spend the time to work out where the convoy was going and when the orders changed and who knew about it and exactly when they knew it? And why would the film crew send you something that can only have one effect?"

"What effect is that?"

"Exactly the effect it's having. It's causing us to turn against each other. What if it was Falwell who sent it? What if it was from someone who wants this site to disappear? Whoever it is sent it to sow the seeds of discord. If they know you, they know exactly what buttons to push—hell, it was right there on the first film clip they sent you. You don't need to be a genius to figure out it's pretty easy to tick you off. Did you ever think of that?"

Kelly hadn't thought of it, and he didn't want to think of it now.

"Or maybe it came from someone who is trying to find out who we are, which you very obligingly told them."

Kelly wanted to let the steam rise up in him. He wanted to take something gigantic and make it broken and small. But then he found himself remembering how Pig Eye had stepped up onto the hood of the truck beside and a little behind him and how he had liked it that way. If Pig Eye had stood right next to him, he would have stepped forward a little, just enough to preserve the front-and-center position he had thought of as his due.

"If the supply convoy was going west, what about the road-clearing crews?" asked Danny. "Were those moved, and if so, when?"

"I was curious about that too," said Penn.

It was Kelly who said what they all were thinking: "That would have made the northern route even more dangerous than usual. It would have raised our chances of being hit."

## 10.7 PENN SINCLAIR

Penn was at his desk, but his mind was elsewhere. Falwell hadn't changed the date on the AAR just to give Penn a second chance. He was covering up his own mistake too. He hadn't passed on critical information, information that would have caused Penn to make a different call about the convoy and the school. But whenever he started to get angry at Falwell, he remembered that Falwell had told him to hold the convoy, and the bottom line was, he hadn't.

When the phone rang, he rushed to answer it, hoping, suddenly, it was Louise. He hadn't talked to her in weeks, but now he realized he was missing something and maybe it was her. Halfway to the phone, he stopped. Why would Louise be calling him out of the blue? It was his responsibility to call her first, and he would. He'd call her that evening, after she got home from work. Meanwhile, what if it was Falwell on the phone? Let Kelly answer it. Ever since the meeting in DC, Falwell had been silent, and even though no news was better than bad news, something told Penn the silence wasn't entirely good. Almost two months had passed since then—more than enough time for Falwell to have investigated the website and discovered Penn's involvement in it. More than enough time for him or one of his subordinates to come up with a plan for shutting the website down. Miller, thought Penn. I'll bet Miller's the one who sent the tape.

"Danny," called Kelly, rapping on the windowpane. "Dolly's on the phone."

A late-season storm had blown in overnight, and they had awoken to find the ground covered with snow. "What happened to spring?" Danny had asked before going with his notebook to sit on the stoop with his head resting on his hands and his elbows on his knees and tiny flakes turning his hair white. He'd been sitting in the snow working on what he was now calling his rap epic, but he was no longer there. An hour earlier he had stuck his head in through the door to ask, "Anyone have a synonym for 'help'? I have 'help' in there now, but it's missing the connotations I want. I want it to say 'solidify the position of.' I want it to hint at 'aggrandize' and 'enrich.' I want there to be an undercurrent of corruption, where one person helps another only because he thinks it's going to pay off for him personally. I want the emphasis to be on the subject, not the object of the verb. Altruism laced with greed—that's what I want. Nothing to do with helplessness.

Maybe there isn't a word for it after all. Or maybe there is, but it's in a language I don't speak."

"Where's Danny?" Kelly asked, and then he told Dolly that Danny would have to call her back.

The snow was coming harder now, slanting down and swirling where the wind eddied around the building. Penn and Kelly put on parkas and gloves and headed out the door, one going left and the other right, their movements perfectly in sync as they canvassed the neighborhood, up one street and down the next, meeting in front of the railroad crossing and then continuing together past the squat building where the single mother lived with her three kids before turning back across the tracks, which is when Penn noticed footsteps going toward Bridge Street and the river. The footsteps were just faint impressions, mostly filled with new snow, as if a ghost had passed through, only touching down lightly now and then.

"Over there," Penn said. Kelly followed Penn's gaze to where the prints left the road and plunged down the steep embankment to the railroad bed. The two men started down after them, stumbling at first and then getting their footing and doing what they had been taught to do—no words necessary, only gestures and bodies and eyes. Penn's adrenaline was pumping now. Inside the parka, his core was heating up. And then they were at the trestle bridge and the river, with the straight shot of the tracks over the gray-black water and, on the other side, Pennsylvania. He caught Kelly's eye. Cross?

Kelly nodded: cross. He held up his watch for Penn to see. It was ten minutes after the hour. "When does the train come through?" he asked.

Penn shrugged. He didn't know the schedule. Danny was the only one who paid attention to that.

Kelly nodded again, and they started across, sprinting now, legs working in a steady rhythm, eyes sharp and wide-angled, ears straining and sifting through the muffled sounds and slotting them into categories: interesting but irrelevant, pay closer attention, ignore. Penn paused to take in the ribbon of black water, made gray by the cross-hatching of snow, but Kelly didn't break his stride. And then they were on the other side, with better options for avoiding a train should one come through.

"Hey, Captain," said Kelly, motioning to the disturbed snow of an equipment yard where a row of open sheds housed lumber and lengths of PVC pipe and sheets of corrugated roofing. "He could be in there."

Penn nodded and circled left while Kelly circled right, each man ducking into the first shed he came to before shaking his head and moving down the row, sliding in and out with his back to the wall and now and then checking the other man's position and scanning left and right, alert not only for signs of Danny, but also for signs of anyone else who might be hiding there with less-than-benign intent. Their paths met at the far end of the yard, and they circled back toward the tracks, this time drifting silently between the buildings, quick and catlike in the snow. But Danny wasn't there.

The tracks curved behind the last of the commercial buildings before one set veered west toward the rail yards and one cut south along the river. Kelly pointed to some footprints going south. Above them, the clouds were low and shredded. On one side of the spur, a marsh. On the other, the steely expanse of the river, with the far bank only a faint pencil sketch of rocks and trees against the snow. They found Danny sitting on an embankment one hundred yards farther down the tracks, his eyes closed and his hands folded on his lap.

"Hey, man, what're you doing?" asked Kelly.

"Come on," said Penn. "You're coming back with us."

It took a long time for the words to sink in and for Danny to nod in their direction. But then Danny heaved himself upright and stood tall and straight, hands extended as if he were welcoming them to his white and blanketed kingdom.

"Dolly called," said Kelly. "She wants you to call her back."

Now it was the three of them moving abreast—Penn on the right and Kelly on the left, with Danny between them, eyes sharp, ready to dive onto the snowy verge if and when a train came, half-jogging so as to limit their exposure on the tracks.

"When does the next train come through?" asked Kelly as they passed the place where the spur joined the main line.

"East or westbound?" asked Danny.

"Either one will kill us."

"Two or three minutes," said Danny, "but the snow will make it late if it hasn't been canceled."

They walked a little farther in silence. Then Penn said, "We'll wait for it here. We can cross the bridge once it passes."

Danny stopped and turned, and the men on either side of him stopped and turned too. They stood side by side but not quite touching and waited, gazing out over the frozen river as if they were protecting it, listening to the silence and blinking their eyes against the snow, which was coming at them horizontally now, propelled by a stiff wind shooting off the water. They sensed it before they saw the light, a humming vibration that felt and sounded like a giant was running his violin bow across the tracks, with the faintest of bass notes resonating up from the earth's core. Then a bright smudge in the surrounding whiteness, a whitish-yellow halo, small and indistinct, but steadily growing in size. Penn couldn't tell how close it was. Everything was muffled. There was no depth to anything, no clear waves of sound. Just the three of them, arms linked now, surrounded by the pelting snow.

"Come on," said Kelly. "Let's get off the tracks." But Danny's feet were planted, and when Penn pulled on his arm, he encountered an equal and opposite resistance.

"We don't go until Danny gives the signal," said Penn. He held his right hand up, gloved fingers spread. "Count it out, Danny," he said. "Count it right on out."

But Danny was silent, immovable.

"I'm not going until you do," said Penn, and Kelly nodded in agreement. "All for one and one for all, man."

"One for all and all for one," echoed Penn.

The train was closer now, the smudge of light dead center in the white-on-white hollow of the tracks, the engine the barest silver with a streak of red. It was the whistle that seemed to have force and mass, though, and Penn had a vision of being destroyed by a thick and lethal blade of sound.

Danny opened his mouth, but it took another second for any words to come out. "Five," said Danny. Then "Four," then "Three."

With each number, Penn closed a finger against his palm. First the thumb and then the pinkie and then the ring finger, until he was making the peace sign—or perhaps it was the V for "victory." But even when the middle finger protruded alone—even when Kelly said, "Fuck you, Danny" and Danny finally said, "One," Penn wasn't sure if he would give the signal. And he wasn't sure if Danny would jump even if he gave it.

The tracks were screaming beneath their feet now, the train a silver tear in the softness. Stretching left to right was the water, and across the river, spread out for miles in every direction, substandard housing and urban decay laced with pockets of modest but vital renewal. None of it was visible in the snow, but Penn saw it because he knew it was there.

There was a long pause. Danny's mouth opened wider, but

whatever he said was devoured by the cacophony of the train, and then they were tumbling down the bank, laughing with relief and shouting, "Oo-rah" and scooping up handfuls of snow and throwing it at each other and Penn feeling considerably more alive than he had when he had rolled out of bed that morning.

It suddenly seemed so simple. He'd make sure the men were all right, and then he'd take Falwell up on his offer. He would marry Louise and they would buy a house somewhere, with mourning doves roosting in the hemlocks and swallows flitting between a little meadow and a pond. In the summer he would stand on the porch, looking on as Joseph and Jules tumbled down a new-mown hill. In the winter he would festoon the house with colored lights and the kids would ride down the hill on toboggans and then Louise would make hot cocoa while he lit a fire. Every year he would hold a picnic with races and games just the way his father had done. It could happen eventually, even if it didn't happen right away. He'd call Louise. He'd ask her to marry him as soon as his next tour was over, or maybe he'd marry her before he went.

## 10.8 JOE KELLY

Spring came, and with it came new disagreements. Now that they had their heads above water money-wise, the captain kept talking about "visions" and "goals."

"Advertising dollars," said Kelly, sounding like a broken record even to himself. "Donations are fine, but if we went after advertising dollars, I could definitely get me a car."

"It's not about money," said the captain, and Danny said, "Do you realize that if we actually stop the war, all of this goes away?"

"Fat chance of that," said Kelly. The week before, sixty-five people had died when two suicide bombers attacked a crowded Baghdad market, and just that morning, someone had forwarded him a link to a site that made a case for perpetual war. Not that perpetual war was good, but that it was inevitable.

One day in early May, Kelly received another email, and instead of sparking an argument, this one made the room go quiet. Someone wanted to buy the site.

Kelly was the one to break the silence. "If we sell, we'll have money for pretty much anything we want to do. We can have our cake and eat it too."

The captain asked what would happen to the stories people had trusted them with. "And the documents you can't find anywhere else—what will happen to those?"

"I assume the new owners will carry on with it," said Kelly.

"Assume," said the captain. "Ass. U. Me."

"Will they have the necessary programming skills?" asked Le Roy.

"I assume they'll keep some of us on," said the captain. "And our volunteers—they'll certainly need those."

"Assume," said Kelly. "Ass. U. Me."

"Doesn't it worry anyone that the site isn't worth a fraction of what they're offering?" asked Danny.

"You know what it's worth?" asked Kelly. "Exactly what someone is willing to pay."

Every day they were popping open the beer a little earlier, but when the purchase offer came in, Kelly made a case that noon was not too early. "Noon's normal," he said, and the captain laughed and replied, "I've been wondering what normal is. Now I finally know."

"I just don't know why they're offering so much for it," said Danny. "I can't make the numbers add up."

"Money's money," said Kelly. He was picturing himself in a convertible like the one in the coming-home parade. This time, though, he'd be driving, with a pretty girl beside him in the passenger seat.

"True enough," said Danny. "True enough."

"That's two hundred fifty thousand each," said Le Roy.

"Three hundred thirty three," said the captain. "I don't need the money. Which isn't the reason I think we shouldn't sell."

"Whatever's fair," said Danny. A few minutes later, though, he was back to worrying. "The numbers don't add up," he said. "Even if there was some way to get advertisers, it would take them years to earn that money back."

"Unless that's not the point," said Penn. "Unless they only want to shut us down."

Outside the warehouse window, two teenagers threw a rock at a stray dog. The dog yelped and ran off just as the third beer was sliding down, causing something to catch in Kelly's throat so that some of it came up again.

"Jeezus, Kelly, be careful of the keyboard," said Le Roy.

When the captain went outside to talk to the teenagers and recruit them for his patrol, Kelly stumbled after him and sat on the stoop thinking of the day he had lurked on a street corner while Joe Senior was stopped and searched, eyes down, arms out, compliant and sacrificial. The sight had filled Kelly with a bottomless swamp of bitterness and sorrow. When he had a son of his own, he wouldn't send him off to school telling him to keep his head down or to smile and make new friends. He'd send him with the name of a lawyer in his pocket and a checklist of do's and don'ts:

do be polite, don't make furtive movements, do ask if you are free to leave, don't tell the cop to fuck himself. But you can think it, son, he'd say. So far they haven't made thinking illegal, and you can think any damn thing you want.

The dog was back, eyeing him warily from across the street. Then it tucked its tail between brindle haunches and slunk into the bamboo that ran along the railroad tracks. "Hey, dog," called Kelly, but by then, the dog was gone.

"Any luck?" he asked when the teenagers got into their car and drove off.

"They'll come," said the captain. "If they don't, I'll track their asses down."

The magnolias were in bloom, and up the street, the single mother was digging in her garden. Kelly thought about the convertible he was going to buy. He told himself he hadn't made the world the way it was and he wasn't responsible for human nature, not even his own. If they sold the site, he could do anything he wanted, but what did he want to do? He seemed to have a head for business—he could make something of that. He could find a nice girl and get married. He'd figure it out once he had the money, but they should definitely sell the site. He'd call Hernandez and get him to come to New Jersey to help with whatever they did next, or maybe he'd go to Texas and Hernandez could give him advice about settling down. He dialed the number, but Hernandez's voice was guarded. "What?" he asked. "What do you want?"

Kelly tried to explain it, but the spoken words didn't sound the way they had in his head. It sounded like he wanted something from Hernandez, when what he wanted was only to reestablish their old connection. "Remember how you got the Humvee out of the ditch?" he asked. "Remember how Harraday smoked those guys down by the canal just before the helo got there?"

"Hey, man. I'm trying to forget."

"I was thinking you could come out and help us with the site," said Kelly. "If we don't sell it, that is, or if we start a new one. Either way, we could work something out. I can send you a ticket, just so you can see the place. And I might buy a convertible—I haven't decided yet. If I do, you can help me pick it out."

"I'll think about it," said Hernandez. "But I've got a kid, you know? He's already three years old. And I've got Maya, and a little house—maybe you should get a woman too. It's not perfect, you know what I mean? But it's sure as hell not bad."

"Yeah, that's something I've thought about. I've thought about that a lot."

But Kelly needed a woman who could stand up to him, which basically meant he needed a man.

"There are men in the army," said Hernandez.

"Ha!" said Kelly. "No way I'm going back there. Besides, I'm pretty good at what I'm doing now."

"Me too," said Hernandez. "Not great or anything, but definitely pretty good."

## 10.9 LE ROY JONES

An inspector from the building department knocked on the door one evening when Le Roy and the other men were eating fried chicken out of a paper bucket. "I heard you guys were living here," he said. "This area is zoned commercial. No COs for permanent occupation."

"Hey, man, nothing's permanent," said Danny, and Kelly said, "Hell, we've lived in bigger shitholes 'n this."

"We just work long hours," said the captain.

"I heard you're here day and night."

"This is a start-up, so we kind of are."

"I'm afraid you're gonna have to find another place to live. I'll give you a week or so, but I can't let it slide much longer than that."

"Fuck that shit," said Le Roy.

"Christ," said Danny when the housing official was gone. "It's like they don't want us to succeed."

"We've already succeeded," said Kelly. "We should definitely sell."

"I'm telling you. They'll buy it and they'll shut it down," said the captain.

"Why would they spend a million dollars on a website just to shut it down?" asked Kelly. And then everyone was quiet except the captain, who said they all knew why. Everyone but Le Roy knew why. "Why?" he asked, which started up another argument, with the captain going on about "visions and goals" and Kelly banging his fist on the desk and Danny pacing up and down saying, "Let's all calm down here. I'm sure we can work this thing out."

Le Roy couldn't fully comprehend the source of the disagreement, but he suspected it was located in the place E'Laine kept harping on when she talked about the things they used to do together or about how Le Roy's body had been taken over by someone else's soul. So when Kelly said, "What do you think, Le Roy? Weigh in here," Le Roy could only try to guess what Kelly wanted him to say. It was like hacking a password, but with no end run where you used machine language to reset the basic user information. "What if I make a memorial to the guys in the company?" he asked. "Or what if we make a second site?"

"We can't do that 'til after we sell," said Kelly. "We don't want to divert traffic and scare the buyers off." Kelly did the thing where he slammed the refrigerator door and chugged a beer and threw the can so hard it hit the wall behind the trash can.

Le Roy thought it might be time to bring out his new idea. "I'm thinking about a simulation," he said. Just the thought of it was calming. Just the thought of all that new-idea blankness turning into lines of code. He started to describe how in the simulation, the parameters could be set so that most of the people would be totally screwed, and then they would band together to take their country back. Wasn't that what the captain meant when he said "visions and goals"? It had occurred to him that they were in a simulation now. The odds of it were good. It was generally accepted that intelligent beings would eventually create realistic computer simulations, which meant that someday the simulated worlds would far outnumber the real worlds, which meant a person would have a better chance of being in a virtual world than in a real one. Maybe someday had already come. "In the simulation—" he started to say, but Kelly interrupted him.

"We're not talking about any simulation here, Le Roy. We're talking about real life."

"But what if we're already in a simulation? What if we only think it's real? In that case ... "

"Besides, there's plenty for you to work on finding people to help authenticate that new batch of documents. Whether we sell or not, we've got to keep going full strength for now."

Then the conversation died down, and after a while, everyone went back to work.

"Hey," said Kelly later in the day. "I got a funny call from Martin."

Le Roy had forgotten about Martin Fitch, but now he said, "What's up with Martin?"

"He's getting some heat about the sources for his new *Guardian* series, and he wants to make sure our security is up to snuff."

"Blast it on over here," said Le Roy. "Let me take a look."

"What do you think he means when he says 'heat'?" asked Kelly.

"I guess we can't expect to post some of this stuff without ruffling some feathers," said the captain.

"But Dolly's okay?" asked Danny.

"Yeah," said Penn. "Dolly's just fine."

"All the more reason to sell," said Kelly. "Get out from under while we can."

Here it came, Kelly yelling and throwing another beer can at the wall and the captain telling everyone to calm down and Danny taking his notebook out onto the porch and staring off up the tracks to where they disappeared behind a patch of urban bamboo and Le Roy snapping his noise-canceling headphones into place and trying to induce the sensation he got when someone was passing through his peripheral vision, when he could feel them sliding along toward being forgotten.

The issue of the sale didn't go away, and a week later Danny suggested they vote on it. "A yes vote means we sell," he said.

Kelly voted yes, Danny voted no, and the captain abstained. "The website belongs to you," he said. "Besides, I redeploy in another couple weeks."

"That leaves it up to you, Le Roy," said Danny. "You get to decide this thing yourself."

"That makes zero sense," said Kelly. "That makes less than zero sense."

Le Roy looked from Kelly to the captain and tried to figure out which of them had the more compelling expectation, but just then a glitch on the screen caught his eye and he was narrowing the cone of his vision and feeling the music of the ether coming up through the pads of his fingers and letting his mind resonate with the vastness of the universe, of all the worlds within the universe, of all the worlds within the worlds.

# 11.0 HOME

*The judge denied the warrant for the telephone records—partly because of incompetence and partly because of that brouhaha in Congress over domestic spying.*

—Deputy Ben Kincaid

*Our break came when some highly sensitive documents showed up on a website and two local business leaders lodged a formal complaint. Now we were getting somewhere. Now we only had to connect the dots.*

—Sheriff Hank Conway

*Alpha particles are not harmful until they are aerosolized and inhaled or ingested, but what about the gamma rays, x-rays, and neutron particles emitted by unexploded ordnance? All three have much longer penetration ranges than alpha radiation. Neutrons are especially harmful to living tissues, but you can't measure them. When they decay, they leave no trace.*

—Professor Stanley Wilkes, Oklahoma State University

*Hell, the guys at the plant were sitting right on top of that stuff, and so were the military drivers and pilots in Iraq.*

—Munitions Worker, name withheld

*My nurse is the one who convinced me to get involved. Soldiers are risking their lives every day. They have a right to know where the danger is coming from.*

—Levi Thomas, M.D.

*Everyone assumed Lyle and I were having an affair. That's how it is in Red Bud. People get wrapped up in the minor scandals and they miss the bigger ones.*

—Lily De Luca

## 11.1 WILL

In the days between joining the army and shipping out, Will was treated like a hero by everyone he knew. It reminded him of the brief period when he had wanted to be a doctor. Whenever he went into the Main Street Diner, Lucas Enright called out, "Coffee's on the house!" The mayor sent him a bottle of champagne despite the fact that Will was underage. He and Tula drank it while watching *The Bourne Identity,* after which they went for a walk and talked about what the movie meant.

"My favorite part was the beginning, when Matt Damon said, *I can tell you the license plate numbers of all six cars outside. I can tell you that our waitress is left-handed and the guy sitting up at the counter weighs two hundred fifteen pounds and knows how to handle himself. . . . Now why would I know that? How can I know that and not know who I am?*"

"How sad," said Tula.

"Sad? I think it's incredibly cool. He's kind of like Spider-Man. And anyway, who really knows who they are?"

"I do," said Tula. "At least I used to know."

"Everybody has sides to him, sides that are brought out by particular circumstances. So there's no telling who you might be under different conditions."

"I think that underneath, everybody has a solid, unchanging core."

Sometimes Will took Tula with him to the diner, but more and more often he went alone. The diner had always seemed special to Will. "Let's go out to eat!" his father would announce every now and then, and his mother would flutter back and forth between delight and consternation. "Oh dear, give me a minute to fix my hair," she would twitter. "Is this the right shade of lipstick for my dress?"

While they were waiting for her to get ready, Lyle would say to Will, "You can see why I married your mother—she was the town beauty, and she still is."

In the truck, Maggie would shrink up against Lyle in the front seat and put her hand on his shoulder as if she needed protecting, even though everyone knew she could handle most things just fine. Then they would park at the Super Saver and walk up Main Street to make the evening last longer. When they reached the diner, they would sink into the red leatherette seats of a booth and Lyle and Will would open their menus and Lyle would ask, "What do you say, Will? What looks good today?" All of it made Will feel older than he was, as if the occasion was both a festive celebration and a solemn lesson in how to be a man.

Some Saturdays, Lyle took Will to the diner for pancakes while they let Maggie sleep in. Saturday mornings were different from the evenings in that except for the waitresses, it was all men, which gave the narrow room a clubby feel. The men dragged out their breakfasts, tapping pipe tobacco onto their plates and talking about politics and the state of the world as they chewed, as if this were the spot where grave decisions about economics and foreign policy were made. Inevitably, one of the men would say, "Damn it!" or "Damn it all to hell!" which only made the subject seem more urgent, affecting not only the future of the planet, but the mysterious fate that lay in store for Will. He never spoke much at those breakfasts, but his protruding ears took in everything that was said, and his mind sifted through the various tidbits of conversation for clues about what that fate might be.

The worst thing about quitting school was that now he only saw Tula when she wasn't busy with other things. Ten days before his departure, she called to say she had a surprise for him—she would pick him up at his house at seven o'clock on Saturday evening. "Be there or be square," she said. All week long, Tula acted mysterious, and if Will pestered her with questions, she said her lips were sealed.

When Saturday came, Will put on the navy shirt with the pearl buttons and sat at the kitchen counter while Lyle ate some miniature sausages straight from the tin and washed them down with a can of beer. "Are you sure you don't want any?" he asked.

"Thanks anyway," said Will. He suspected Tula was planning a special dinner, and he didn't want to spoil his appetite. At 7:15, Will walked down the driveway to peer up the empty road, and at 7:25, he walked all the way to where the hill dipped and flattened out. When he got back, Lyle was sprawled on the couch, listening to a journalist explain that there were five Iraqs, not one, to a host who kept interrupting. The empty sausage tin was sitting on the countertop along with dishes from that morning and also from the night before.

At 7:45 he called Tula's house, but no one answered. By the time she finally arrived it was almost eight and both of them were flustered, dissolving the air of mystery that had built up over the previous week. "Where were you?" Will asked, but they both knew it wasn't a question so much as a complaint.

"My mother had to work late at the Winslows' house and I couldn't get the car," said Tula. "But it will be worth the wait. I promise."

"I hope we're going to eat," said Will. "I could eat a horse."

"Oh," said Tula. "I forgot about that."

"Who forgets about eating?" Even though Will had stopped getting taller, he was still filling out, and food was never very far from his mind.

"Men!" said Tula the way she often said it, but neither one of them was in the mood to laugh. Then she repeated, "It will be worth it. You'll see."

They drove for a little in silence. Sleet had fallen earlier in the day, and the moon was throwing its cold light over the frozen fields, washing them in silver. Instead of heading into town, Tula steered toward the highway and turned into the parking lot of the town's only motel, which catered mostly to long-distance truckers. Will wasn't sure what to say until Tula took a room key from her pocket and dangled it before his eyes. "I helped my mother today so she could get to the Winslows' early so she could get back with the car—not that that worked out exactly the way I planned it. Anyway, while I was at it, I took a key to one of the empty rooms."

Her tone had become teasing, and as soon as Will took in what she was saying, his hunger vanished, replaced with a burning sensation deep down in his belly. He drank in Tula's perfume, and the sight of her standing on the frozen pavement under the star-strewn sky filled him with wonder.

Tula's fingers fumbled with the key, but she wouldn't let him take it from her. "I can get it," she said. By the time the door sprang open to reveal the disarray of an unmade bed and the greasy remains of a half-eaten take-out dinner, the burning inside Will caused him to interpret Tula's gasp of dismay as a cry of passion. He scooped her up and tossed her onto the bed, choking a little on his own suppressed cry.

But Tula jumped right up again and said, "Why isn't the room made up? The rooms are always made up as soon as the guest leaves."

"He could have left too late."

"What if he hasn't left yet? He could be back at any minute!" Her eyes darted from the tangled coverlet to the door. "I wanted it to be so romantic, but look at it. It's a mess."

Will was willing to take the risk that a stranger would walk in on them, but Tula wasn't, so he spent a few minutes trying to convince her that the room had been abandoned. "If someone was staying here, he would have left his personal belongings lying around, and there aren't any. You said you and your mother left the motel early. If the guest left late, you wouldn't have been there to clean the room."

Tula's expression said he was missing something obvious, but he didn't know what it might be. She rushed around the room opening and closing dresser drawers and poking her head into the closet before scooping the dirty linen off the bed and into a pile on the floor. After replacing the coverlet, she took a towel and wiped at the surfaces in the bathroom before getting on her knees to swab behind the toilet. "Leave it, Tula. It doesn't matter to me what the bathroom looks like. It doesn't matter to me at all."

"Of course it matters!" Tula's eyes were glassy, and she was clutching at the porcelain fixture and gesticulating with the towel and nearly choking, all at once. Then her eyes caught and focused and she threw down the towel and jumped to her feet. With a great anguished howl, she pushed past Will, shouting, "What was I thinking? I should have known it would be like this!"

Will could only stand in a stupor and stare after her as she ran out of the room and across the parking lot to where she had nestled the car in behind a supply shed. He heard the car door slam and the engine sputter to life, and then the tires skidded on the icy asphalt and the car roared off, leaving him to walk the two miles back to town.

The diner was about to close, but when Lucas Enright saw Will at the door, he ushered him inside and set a steaming plate of spaghetti on the table along with a tall glass of Dr Pepper with crushed ice. "We're always open for you," he said.

"Good," said Will. "Because I'm so hungry I could eat a horse."

The girl who had laughed at him in the women's shop was sitting in a booth with her friends. When she saw Will, she came over and sat down across from him. "Remember me?" she said.

"Of course I do."

"My name is Dylan. I know yours is Will."

Everything about the girl was casual and put him at ease, so before he knew what he was doing, Will found himself pouring out the story of what had happened at the motel.

"I'll give you a ride home," said Dylan. "But you don't mind if we stop by my place first, do you?"

Will said he didn't mind.

"Tula likes things to be tidy and clean, but I'm afraid I like things a little on the dirty side. That won't bother you, will it?"

Will felt his mouth drop open, but he managed to say, "No, that won't bother me one little bit."

Will made a point of stopping by the diner every day after that, partly because he was killing time until the day of his departure and partly because he wanted to experience the hush when he entered, but mostly because he wanted witnesses to the fact that his life was finally unzipping and letting its possibilities out. One of the men always said, "Hey, there's Will," and Will had the strange sense that it was thirty years down the road and he was watching his own son swing through the door on his way to wherever life would take him. It reminded him of a movie he'd seen where a visitor to the past stepped off the walkway and killed a butterfly, which altered the entire course of evolution until he journeyed back through time again so he could make sure to stay on the walkway and change everything back.

Sometimes one of the patrons would call out, "Let's ask Will." Then Will had to be careful not to disappoint them, careful not to answer what he was thinking, which was that he did better with multiple choice questions, questions where he could apply answer elimination techniques before making an educated guess. So mostly he replied, "That's a good question. What do you folks think?"

"Funny you should ask," his interlocutor might say, and then the conversation would start back up again, for they all had opinions on just about everything. Even the quiet ones had opinions, and this was the place they dared to share them. Even the ones who were older than Lyle and Will put together had opinions, even the ones who were older than the folded sandstone hills.

## 11.2 PASTOR PRICE

God hadn't talked to Pastor Price in a long time. When he mentioned it to Tiffany, she tousled his hair and said, "Maybe that's because you're the one doing all of the talking."

"Only on Sundays," replied the pastor. "Most days, all I do is listen. Just this morning, I learned more than I wanted to know about sub-prime mortgages from Jack Baker and counseled a family whose son was killed in Iraq. And when have I ever said no to one of Mrs. Farnsworth's tales of woe?" He tried to sound good-natured about it, but his wife's words stayed with him and he vowed to redouble his efforts in the listening department. Lately, things had been moving very fast for the pastor, which was precisely Tiffany's point.

The April meeting of the pastoral council gave Price a chance to test whether he was listening or not. As he stood underneath a banner that proclaimed Grow Toward Tomorrow and greeted the council members as they arrived, it dawned on him that tomorrow was already here. The ambitious goals of the steering committee had been met or exceeded, and it wasn't lost on him that the Red Bud elite who were filing into the meeting hall were there because of him. He was the prime mover when it came to the Church of the New Incarnation's astonishing growth and success.

Congratulations on the pastor's recent performances eddied around more general talk of the television show—of whether or not it would bring the people of the parish together or drive them apart, of whether someone should tell the choir director not to preen so blatantly in front of the cameras, of whether the money it brought in should be used for local issues or national ones, and whether the parish should take a stand in the upcoming mayoral primary or stay out of that sort of thing.

Buddy Hutchinson arrived and said, "Did you see that editorial about term limits?"

"I did," said the pastor.

"It's got some people talking about throwing their hats into the ring."

"A man would have to be a damn fool to run against you," said the pastor. "Anyway, talk is cheap. Sometimes it's better to bide your time." No one could say he wasn't listening!

But there was one issue that wasn't being talked about. It wasn't being talked about because most of the council members didn't know about it even though it was probably the most pressing issue of all. A few days before, Winslow had called to say that the top-secret document calling for a cover-up regarding toxic munitions had surfaced on an anti-war website. That would have been bad enough, but then Lex Lexington had reported the same sort of thing—his missing draft legislation had shown up on a website called wartruth.com.

"What do prisons have to do with war?" the pastor had asked.

"Apparently there's a war on poor people," said Lexington. "Hell, how would I know what a bunch of crazy people are thinking?"

"The prison provides labor to the plant," said Winslow when they conferenced him in. "It's perfectly legal, though."

"Well, it sure doesn't look good if we're backing legislation that would incentivize incarceration," said Lex. "It doesn't look good if the munitions are harming soldiers and you're covering it up."

"Optics," said Winslow. "I have to admit the optics are bad."

That had been the day before. Now Price kept one eye on the clock. He liked to start his meetings promptly at seven, but Winslow and Lexington were late to arrive. When they did, they huddled in a darkened corner of the room, talking in whispers and trying to catch the pastor's eye. It irritated him that they weren't able to conceal their distress. Even when he signaled "later" to them and made calming motions the way he did when Tiffany was driving too fast, they scowled and twitched and grumbled to each other behind a leafless ficus tree. He had only persuaded them to keep quiet at the general meeting by saying it was better to figure things out privately, after everyone else had gone, but when he made his eyes bug out and drew his forefinger sharply across his neck, they merely scowled at him and made spastic movements with their hands.

Between his vow to listen more and his awareness that the sooner the meeting was over, the sooner he could address Winslow and Lexington's concerns, the pastor was unusually quiet at the general meeting, unusually agreeable, unusually willing to delegate to his advisors. "Good stuff," he said as the group broke up and reached for their coats.

The three men made a show of leaving the parish hall along with the others. They waved good-bye in the parking lot and got into their cars, where they fumbled with their keys and checked their cell phones as the parking lot emptied. While the pastor was engaged in this charade, his phone rang. It was Lex. "You're not actually leaving, are you?"

"Of course not," said Price. "We're just waiting for the others to go. Wasn't that the plan? I thought that was clear."

"That's what I thought, but then I worried I'd misunderstood."

"I think we're all on the same page," said the pastor. "Let's wait five more minutes before we go back in."

The parking lot was dotted with beautiful hand-forged lamps designed to resemble palm fronds, but now the pastor regretted them. For one thing, they looked out of place in the wheat field where the church was set, and for another, he longed for real darkness, for a time when people could disappear into the night and when a man's business was his own and couldn't be blasted out over the Internet for all the world to see. But then he realized that he was nostalgic for an era of hardship and privation, one without satellite television or even indoor plumbing. He thought of all the people who needed him—people in the here and now, lost people, people with struggles and torments. People like Winslow and Lexington. People like Senator Ewing, who had called that very afternoon to express concern about the missing documents because his signature was on one of them and it would upset his constituents if they saw it. People, frankly, like the president. The president needed him too, or at least he needed people like him, but since there were very few people really like him, the president needed him, Houston Price, to be just where he was and doing just what he was doing, right there in the here and now.

Price had seen the president once, at a meeting of religious leaders. It was disgraceful how those Code Pink people had crashed the gates and shouted things. And the Bare Witness people, without a stitch of clothing on. Right in the middle of the incident with the Secret Service, the president had caught Price's eye, and a look had passed between them. "I need ya," said the look, and Houston Price had promised then and there to do whatever he could to capture hearts and minds right there in Red Bud, right there where the president needed him most.

When the three men were back inside the building, they gathered in a windowless coatroom so the light wouldn't attract the attention of anyone passing by—not that the church was on the way to anywhere. It was surrounded by fields owned by the large industrial farm run by Tiffany's father and the nearest dwelling was a mile away. "So what do we do?" asked Winslow. "I'll not only be in trouble because those emails attribute some very forward-thinking ideas to me, but I'll also be in trouble because the document went missing over a year ago and I didn't report it."

"And I run a high-security prison," said Lex. "How secure does it look now?"

409

"Losing sensitive documents is pretty darn bad in and of itself," agreed Winslow, "but making the information they contain public is even worse."

Lexington said "losing" was the wrong word to use. "They were stolen, and it was Maggie Rayburn who stole them, one hundred percent. The mystery is how they got up on that blasted website. I'd ask the little bitch myself, but no one has heard from her in months."

Winslow glared at the pastor. "I thought you said the story about innocent prisoners would create a distraction. You said it would scare that Rayburn woman off if people knew she had pilfered records from the prison."

The pastor's wheels were turning—there was always a solution, even if it took some time to find it. "I think you should both report all of the thefts to law enforcement," he said slowly. "Even if it makes you look bad, you want to go on record that you weren't the ones who leaked them to the press."

"I don't mind getting the law going on it," said Lex. "But meanwhile, we've got to shut that website down."

"How in tarnation are we going to do that?" asked Winslow. "We don't even know who runs it."

"Can your army contacts help somehow?" asked Price. "There has to be a way to track that sort of thing."

"We don't have to know who it is," said Winslow. "We just have to reach them through the site. Doesn't it have a contact page?"

Lex paced to the end of the coatroom, where a schedule of filming dates was posted next to the altar-flower sign-up sheet. "We've got all that TV money, don't we?" he said. "Why can't we just up and buy the blasted thing?"

"All church money is reserved for God's work," said the pastor, and then he quickly added, "Don't get me wrong."

"If this doesn't qualify as God's work, then what the hell does?" bellowed Lex.

"Don't forget that you're only here because of us," said Winslow. "You might be the face, but we're the heart of this operation. We're the reason this church exists."

"August just wants you to remember who provided the seed money for this thing," said Lex. "We're the major stakeholders— along with a few others, of course—and now we're looking for a return on our investment."

"We'll buy it," said Winslow. "We'll buy the sucker and then we'll shut it down. I'll make some discreet inquiries about the website through military channels—just in case. Meanwhile, let's talk to Sheriff Conway. I'm sure multiple laws have been broken. There's no doubt in my mind about that."

"This isn't a democracy, Houston," added Lex. "It's not as if we have to take a vote."

Deep in Pastor Price's brain, there was a whole secret sector reserved for undemocratic principles. It was like looking at pornography—even if you knew everybody did it, it wasn't seemly to admit it. Then 9/11 happened, and people started making up new phrases that stripped old concepts of their negative connotations. The pastor found himself nodding or murmuring, "Just so" when some public figure or other used the term "enhanced interrogation" in the place of "torture" or equated freedom with domestic spying or morality with war. But much as he wanted to see God's Kingdom taking root right there in Red Bud, some of the measures people were talking about didn't sit well with him, and he didn't like being pressured to throw the resources of his church behind private agendas. Now more than ever, the pastor needed guidance from God, but even when he closed his eyes and said a little prayer, the part of his brain he counted on to light up with inspiration stayed dark and stupefied.

"Can I have a couple of days to think about it?" he asked.

"Two days," said Winslow. "We meet back here in two days to make a plan, and the sooner we execute it, the better. It would be a lot easier to do this with your help, Houston, but we're prepared to do it without you."

That evening, God finally broke His silence. The pastor was watching the news and trying to figure out how he was going to sneak a million dollars past the church finance committee while Tiffany paraded around in her apron and lace panties as she put the finishing touches on a new recipe. On the screen, a panel of experts was opining on the war and whether or not it was right to show photographs of coffins to the American people. A high-level memo on torture had been leaked, and new information about the man who had written it was coming out. Price had skipped both breakfast and lunch and he was only half paying attention because his stomach was growling and his head felt a little feverish and light.

"Guess what's for dinner," Tiffany called out.

It was Italian night, and she wanted him to guess from the smells emanating from the kitchen what she was making. It obviously contained tomatoes and basil and garlic. And the lid was rattling on the big pot, so he guessed she was boiling water for spaghetti or the colorful rotini she liked. "Rotini with marinara sauce," he called out, and the thought of the tough little spirals becoming pale and flaccid in the seething water made him dizzy and a little desperate, as if a similar fate lay in store for him.

Just then, the television showed a general—or perhaps it was a retired general. He'd missed that part when he was talking to Tiffany. Whoever it was, he was saying, *And when I stand up before*

*Christ, I want there to be blood on my knees and my elbows. I want to be covered with mud. And I want to be standing there with a ragged breastplate of righteousness. And a spear in my hand. And I want to say, "Look at me, Jesus. I've been in the battle. I've been fighting for you."*

Startled, the pastor turned up the volume. He wished he had one of those newfangled systems that allowed a viewer to replay the segment. Would a general really say those things? And then he knew it hadn't been the general talking at all. It had been God talking to him through the general. And now God was talking through a woman donating a sack of clothing to the local homeless shelter (*Clean house and do good at the same time!*) and through a life insurance team with its performance trophy (*Join the winning team!*) and through a man showing off his compact car (*So roomy, you could hide a million dollars in the trunk!*). It seemed God's message was that he could avoid being a loser by joining the winning side, and he could avoid unnecessary questions by routing the money for the website through a charity such as Tiffany's Mothers of Mercy group. He'd have to figure out how to tell Tiffany so she wouldn't become suspicious, but it was a good solution to the problem. Thank you, Lord, he thought just as Tiffany called him in to eat.

"Just in time," said the pastor. "I was feeling a bit woozy just now."

"You're half starved, not to mention overworked. A little food is bound to make you right as rain."

Tiffany had made a vegetarian dish, and the pastor ate it with relish.

"No meat?" he asked.

"No," she said. "I've been rethinking my policy on that."

Two weeks later, a small cadre of council members met and made an anonymous offer to buy the website.

413

# 11.3 TULA

At the spring assembly, Mrs. Winslow stood backstage holding a clipboard and checking names off of a list as the girls arrived. "It's hard to believe you're almost a senior," she said to Tula. "Do you have exciting plans for the summer?"

"I'll probably get a job," said Tula without conviction. "And I'll work at the clinic, but of course that doesn't pay."

Tula had worked as hard as anyone on Sammi's great men of Red Bud project, but where she once had felt like a central spoke in the functioning of the assembly, she now felt herself spinning helplessly at its rim.

"I guess you'll start looking at colleges too," said Mrs. Winslow, as if she didn't know that without a scholarship, Tula had no way to pay for books, much less living expenses and tuition. "You need to get in line," she added with an uncharacteristic wink. "The procession is about to begin."

The music started up, and the girls moved forward using a mincing step that made their gowns appear to be gliding of their own accord. After the procession, Mrs. Winslow stood at the podium and gave a speech about unity and transitions. "This is a happy occasion. A time to be happy about the office you receive and also about the office your friends receive. You are all sisters and you are all equal. Success for one is the same as success for all."

"*That's* not true," Tula whispered to the girl standing next to her. The speech had tapped an evolving vein of cynicism, and even though it shamed her to acknowledge it, she persisted. "Who believes that? Only people who are rich and successful, that's who."

"Shush," said the girl, adjusting her bouquet of sunflowers, which was identical to the bouquet carried by all of the rising seniors. When it was time to light the candles, the girl rushed energetically forward, as if to make up for Tula's rudeness.

Tula performed her small role in the festivities with a sinking heart. She had imagined the graduating girls dressed in long white dresses and the younger girls arrayed around them in a rainbow of colors as they walked in formation around the room before singing the song they had practiced and learning the results of the vote that would determine which of her classmates would step into prominent positions for their last year as Rainbow Girls. She hadn't dared to imagine herself as the new Worthy Advisor, but she saw herself in the lesser role of jewel officer, standing at the Worthy Advisor's side and filled with gracious benevolence for the girls who hadn't been elected to any position whatsoever. Most of all, she had imagined that white would have a new meaning not only for her, but for the entire assembly. That dream had shriveled and died, but as the lower positions were announced and hers wasn't among the names called, she started to wonder if she might be elected Worthy Advisor after all. She had worked diligently. Everyone liked her. And hadn't Mrs. Winslow just winked at her? Mrs. Winslow never winked! Tula quickly calculated that if Sammi and another popular girl split the vote, she had an outside chance at winning. She hardly dared to think of it, but it wasn't inconceivable that the cards would fall in her favor after all.

One by one, the newly elected girls floated across the room to stand on the dais with the outgoing officers until there was only one more result left to announce. Tula's hopes rose and sank with every beat of her heart. Sammi was popular, but she had become increasingly bossy over the last few months, so perhaps the girls had tired of her. In fact, it was highly likely. But when the drum-roll sounded and the new Worthy Advisor was finally announced, Tula was shocked but not really surprised to hear Sammi's name instead of her own. The meeting hall erupted into whistles and applause. Tula clapped her hands automatically, but when she looked around the room that had held such promise for her, tears welled in her eyes. Each time they threatened to fall, she reminded herself that the eighth bow station with purity as its central tenet still existed, if only in her heart. And purity included feeling happy for Sammi. Mrs. Winslow was right about that. It also included making something of herself no matter how insurmountable the obstacles in her path.

But there was another voice inside her head, and the more she tried to ignore it, the louder and more insistent it became. What if she had been wrong about purity, wrong about what white signified—wrong about everything! The incident at the motel had worried Tula. It seemed an indication that her instincts were wildly off-kilter. Why had she thought the motel was a good place to take Will? Why had she insisted on cleaning behind the toilet? And why hadn't she realized that no amount of scrubbing could ever change the motel's drab colors and flimsy wallboard into something more permanent and respectable? She still thought that the Rainbow banner should be re-envisioned, but now she wondered if the added stripe should be black, with all that blackness signified. In any case, the idea of purity suddenly seemed childish and naïve. Were the women who came to the clinic impure? And who had first thought to apply the concept of purity to women so that they could forever after be held to an impossible standard and found wanting?

Tula had resolved to do better by Will, and just before he left for the army, she had tried again to arrange a special evening. Mr. and Mrs. Winslow had gone out of town for a few days, and Tula had volunteered to keep an eye on their house. She invited Will to go there with her, and after making sure the plants were watered and everything was in order, she gave him a tour of the upstairs, ending with the master bedroom.

The room was dominated by an enormous bed that was draped in flounced bed coverings and piled with satin pillows. At the windows, silk curtains fell in shimmering puddles to the floor, and an entire wall was hung with paintings of beautiful women cuddling lapdogs or brushing their hair. The setting was the opposite of the motel room in every regard, and Tula's heart was thumping erratically as she drew Will across the threshold and sat down on the edge of the bed.

Instead of sitting beside her, Will wanted to peer into the closets and turn on the water in the roomy shower. "Get a load of this!" he exclaimed. "Who ever thought of making the water come out from the sides!"

The bathroom was scrupulously clean. No suspicious yellow scum or lint or curls of pubic hair marred its gleaming surfaces. Instead, there were stacks of fluffy towels and dishes of fragrant, unused soap. Only belatedly did Tula realize that it was clean because her own mother had worked herself to the bone to keep it that way. Will insisted on peering into every cupboard and sniffing every vial of perfume before he sat down beside Tula and told her he respected her too much to force her into anything. "I understand about purity now," he said. "It took me a while, and even if I don't completely understand it, I know that whatever's important to you should be just as important to me."

Tula wasn't sure how it all happened, but before she knew it, she and Will were eating ice cream at the Main Street Arcade and promising to wait for each other, and then they were kissing each other good-bye. Tears were oozing from her eyes as she said, "I'll think about you, Will. I'll think about you every day."

"I'll think about you too, Tula."

"Do you have the picture I gave you?"

"I'll keep it in a special pocket. Right next to my lucky crystal and my knife."

"I have your picture too. It's sitting right beside my bed, so it's the first thing I see every morning and the last thing I see at night."

And then she was waving from her doorstep and Will was gone and the waters of her life closed over him. Some days, if she didn't count the persistent ache in her heart, it was almost as if he had never been part of it at all.

After the ceremony, the new officers stood in a long line to receive the good wishes of the assembly. Mrs. Winslow breezed around the room, her head held high, curls bouncing stiffly on her head. "You still have a whole year to figure things out," she said when she saw Tula standing in a corner by herself. At first, Tula thought she was talking about Will, but of course she wasn't.

"Yes ma'am," said Tula.

"A lot can happen in a year! Just keep in mind that Mr. Winslow is always looking for good secretarial help at the plant. He might even have a summer position so you can start to learn the ropes. And of course I need household help every now and then."

"Yes ma'am," said Tula again. It was as if she had already given up on college, already begun scrubbing bathrooms alongside her mother, already started fading into the grimy shadows of the motel or flushing little pieces of herself down the sparkling toilets of the rich people's homes.

# 11.4 LYLE

By the time Will left for the army, Maggie had been gone more than six months. For weeks afterward, Lyle passed shadowlike through the concrete expanse of the munitions factory, avoiding people who approached to congratulate him, as if he were the heroic one. If Jimmy raised his hand from across the parking lot, Lyle pretended not to see him. Then, at the end of April, he took two days off to visit Will before he shipped out overseas. The day he returned, MacBride called him into his office and said, "I know things have been difficult for you, Lyle, but we have standards to uphold."

"Yes sir," said Lyle, snapping his shoulders back and speaking crisply. He had spent the last two days watching Will and his fellow soldiers stand at attention and salute, and some of their spit and polish had rubbed off on him.

"It's not that I don't know things have been a little rough," said MacBride.

"Yes sir," replied Lyle.

"The thing is, I need people who can give me one hundred percent."

MacBride went on about inputs and outputs and effort and reward while Lyle studied the worn face in front of him, with its squinting eyes and wrinkled skin and specks of ingrained dirt, and wondered if MacBride was happy or at least content.

"I hope you'll see this as an opportunity," said MacBride. Then he said he'd be happy to write a recommendation for Lyle and that his final paycheck would be sent to his home. Lyle scanned the cluttered cubicle for clues to his future, but the dusty workplace safety manual and the chipped metal task lamp and the grimy work orders tacked to the bulletin board next to the photograph of MacBride's son and grandson holding fishing poles seemed like artifacts from an exhibit about the distant past.

"I have a son," he said. He almost told MacBride that he had missed work because he had been seeing his son off to war, but the rule was that absences were to be cleared in advance, and he hadn't done that.

"Family," said MacBride. "That's what it's all about."

Most of Lyle's acquaintances couldn't remember whether he attended the high school graduation or not. Afterward they said, "Didn't see you up at school," despite the fact that Lyle had been sitting in the R section, right where he was supposed to sit. Will wasn't there to walk across the stage, but there was a flag with a wooden stick strapped to the empty chair between Rafe Rodriguez and Stucky Place. August Winslow had been asked to give the graduation speech, and the principal beamed out at the audience as he introduced him.

"Our speaker was recently honored as one of Red Bud's great men, so we are lucky to have him with us today," he said.

Winslow looked like a politician with his dark suit and silver hair. "I'm probably not the greatest of the great, but the others were unavailable," he said, which made the audience laugh since everybody knew that all of the other men on Sammi Green's list were long since deceased.

Winslow spoke about individual strands in the strong rope of the American economy. He said that local businesses like the one he worked for were always happy to welcome new graduates, but that some of the young people before him would spread their wings and fly before coming home again and others would soar farther afield, using what they had learned right there at Red Bud High to help make distant communities stronger. He said "freedom" and "heartland" and "sea to shining sea." He made special mention of two boys who were joining the armed services immediately after graduation, and then he saluted the flag on Will's chair and everybody clapped.

Lyle wiped the tears from his eyes and hurried out before the ceremony was over. He sat for a long time on the stairs that led down to the locker room, his knees as bony and angular as the metal treads, his khaki shirt blending in against the cinderblock wall, and his inner chambers as empty and echoing as the stairwell. He was proud of Will for going off to make something of himself, and he wondered if it was too late to spread his own wings. There had to be a job for him in Phoenix. He and Maggie could get a fresh start there. Now and then a group of students burst through a fire door from the hallway, their high spirits propelling them up a flight or down and out into the sunshine, and only by flattening himself against the wall did Lyle manage to avoid being kicked by a polished battalion of special-occasion shoes. When August Winslow rushed past followed by the mayor, Lyle craned his neck to watch them through the balusters.

"Goddamn it, Buddy," Winslow hissed. "Keep those kids out of the creek! I don't care what you tell them. No, don't say it's toxic! Chrissakes, isn't that the whole point? Make up something about venomous snakes—it doesn't matter what. Just get it done."

Whether it was Winslow's words or Will's absence or the fact that he hadn't eaten yet that day, Lyle experienced the kind of phantasm people who died and came back to life claimed to have had of the light-filled paradise that was waiting for them on the other side. What Lyle saw wasn't paradise, though, but a parallel world of privileged information and secret contacts and clandestine assignations. It was as if he had broken through the walls of his existence to find that what he had thought were hard limits and bolted doors were only flimsy illusions woven from the thread of his expectations and lack of confidence in himself. Now he saw that anyone who wanted to could tap on the barrier and break right through. He felt powerful and alienated, as if there was an important reason for his suffering and he was about to find out what it was. His own passivity made sense now too. It was what the people in charge wanted from people like him, and he had been only too willing to comply.

It was the sensation of finally seeing beyond the curtain that caused Lyle to drive carefully home, staying well within the speed limit even on the New Road Extension, where he had always revved the engine and banked the curve. It was what caused him to search through Maggie's things for some hint of what the police had been looking for or for some clue as to what she had meant about the Iraqi babies. But he found nothing, only a couple of sweaters and a few magazines with their pages missing.

The next afternoon, a representative from the bank that held the mortgage arrived to change the locks and post a sign in the front yard. "What are you doing?" asked Lyle, but the man merely handed him a business card and a pamphlet and asked him if he had somewhere he could stay.

"Why do I need a place to stay?" asked Lyle.

"Read the pamphlet," said the man. "If the pamphlet doesn't explain everything to your satisfaction, you can call the number on the back."

# 11.5 MAGGIE

Lyle's calls became less and less frequent. Neither of them said so outright, but with Will gone, there was little for them to talk about. "If I can't come home," Maggie had said the last time they spoke, "maybe you should come to Phoenix."

"That's an idea," Lyle had replied. And then he had asked, "Are you making progress on the case?"

"We should hear something any day now." Since Maggie had been working for the attorney, two of his clients had been granted new trials, so the office was busier than ever. "Everyone wants representation," she said to Lyle. "But hardly anyone can pay."

"Maybe if you prove Tomás is innocent, they'll forgive you for taking his prison records and you can come home," said Lyle.

"So they figured it out?" said Maggie.

"I expect they did," said Lyle.

Maggie didn't say that Tomás's records weren't all she had taken, and she wondered if each stolen document would count as a separate strike when they added up the charges against her.

When several Mondays went by and Maggie didn't hear from Lyle, she dialed her home number only to find that it was out of service. A lump of panic rose in her throat, and whenever she swallowed, the lump reasserted itself and made her gag. She called True, who promised to get a message to Lyle. Then she called Misty, who told Maggie the police were still sniffing around. "We would have heard if they'd found something new, but you probably should lie low for a while longer just in case."

That night Maggie tossed fitfully and awoke when it was still dark to find Dino whining and licking her face. "Okay, boy, okay," she said, but it took her a minute or two to remember where she was. When she took him out for his morning walk, she thought she saw Tomás dressed as a soldier. Good for you, Tomás, she thought. As she followed him up a side street and into an alley, she noticed he had put on weight and seemed taller than she remembered, but just when she got within shouting distance, he was swallowed up by the crowd. A few minutes later she saw him coming out of a coffee shop with a group of friends, and then she saw him selling magazines from a darling little cart. "Tomás!" she called out.

"Hello!" the magazine vendor called back, and it was obvious even before she crossed the street that it wasn't the little prisoner after all.

"Even if that's not Tomás," she told Dino, "it's someone he might easily have been. And it's someone who isn't in prison, thank the lord for that." Her voice scratched in her throat when she spoke, and the unfamiliar sound of it made her think that she was only one coin toss away from being someone she might have been too.

In the confusion she had gotten her turned around, and when she started up again, Dino planted his feet until she agreed to go in the opposite direction. "Okay, boy, okay," she said again, because just then she spotted a woman who looked like Sandra Day O'Connor. She hurried to catch up with her.

"What are you following me for?" asked the woman in a gruff voice.

By the time Maggie found her way back to the church, her head was spinning and her forehead was hot. She set out food and some fresh water for Dino and only saved herself from collapsing by grabbing on to the communion railing. Kneeling and letting bits of colored light from the stained glass spatter her face as the sun made its way up the firmament, she prayed. She prayed for Lyle and Will, of course. She prayed that someday Tomás and George would walk the verdant paths of freedom and warm themselves before a fire in a sitting room with rough pine floors and a worn corduroy couch that bore a striking resemblance to her own sitting room floor and her own sagging couch. But now she also prayed that the men could bear their incarceration bravely, that they wouldn't break on the wheel of American justice the way so many others had broken. She now knew that true Justice had been set far out of reach on some celestial shelf—more, she thought now, to taunt people than to teach them anything useful.

But she also knew that there were small pockets of justice locked deep inside each person's heart, so she prayed for the judges and the jurors—not only the ones who had convicted and sentenced Tomás and George, but for all judges and all jurors everywhere—good people, she knew, but people who had limited access to Truth, which reposed on the high shelf alongside Justice, people who pondered the facts as presented to them and who struggled with growling stomachs to put the pieces together the way, as a girl, she had put together the jigsaws in the forty-watt light of the lamp that sat on the game table in the lakeside cabin where the Rainbow Girls had gone together to spend the month of July and strive to understand Fidelity or Nature or Immortality or whichever of the bow stations was paramount that year.

There were always pieces missing. There were always girls who thought it funny to conceal a piece of the puzzle up their sleeves so that they could return to the table in the bright light of a July morning, crawl about on all fours, and emerge from underneath the table with a triumphant, "Ah-ha! I found it!" and so be the one to complete the picture while the other girls, who had searched high and low and underneath the table and couches only the evening before, looked on with mounting suspicions about where the piece had been all night. In later years, so many pieces were truly missing, vacuumed up by the August cleaning crew or taken home and forgotten by someone who wanted the last quiet laugh, that it took the fun out of doing the puzzles and eventually they were all forgotten or thrown away.

And, finally, she prayed for herself, but it had become a vague prayer. She didn't know what to pray for. She prayed to be true to her promise. She prayed for strength. She prayed for hope. Sometimes she prayed for tolerance unless she prayed for intolerance, for she thought it was probably a sin to be tolerant of injustice and evil—if evil existed and wasn't just a name people plastered on things they didn't understand or agree with. As she prayed, it occurred to her that prayer was the only thing worth doing, the only truly good thing, because all actions had unintended consequences and because people who acted were always in the gravest danger of being wrong.

But so, of course, were people who prayed. Perhaps it was wrong to pray for particular people or results. Perhaps the only thing she could do was to recite the words in the dusty prayer books that were tucked into the backs of the wooden pews. "Our Father," she whispered into the cavernous emptiness of the old church. "Lord Jesus, son of God." Or maybe the only good and true expression was a wordless cry to the heavens, a guttural sound of anguish, or a transcendental and meaningless "Om."

What was it she had meant to do? She had started off with such purpose, but then gone off track somehow. Tomás was only slightly better off than he had been before, since even if he was

426

approved for a new trial, the process could take years and he could be reconvicted, which was sure to break what was left of his spirit. And she had forgotten all about the toxic munitions—or if she hadn't really forgotten, she hadn't done anything with the information that God had trusted her to act on. The answer lay in her soul—she was sure of it, but when she tried to concentrate on the holy places of her innermost being, all was airy and dark, like the empty high-ceilinged church that had lost both its priest and its congregation. Her body ached. Her stomach heaved. Her head and brain were on fire.

A bird flapped loose from the rafters and swooped through the nave. It was Justice, she thought, or Truth. Her mind had wandered from the prayer she had wanted to make, and if the prayer couldn't even be formulated, how could it be sent? Was a vague feeling of supplication enough, or did she have to find the right words in order to make a connection across the universe to wherever the first principle was hiding? Could she use her own words, or did she have to chant official hymns and formulations? She didn't know, but just in case, she concentrated on the word "good" and all it contained within it and all it entailed. After trying in vain to keep the letters glued together, she let them go, and she saw that God was inside the letters and that he was talking to her, but he was speaking in August Winslow's voice.

—Don't you understand anything? Not that I owe you of all people an explanation. And not that you could understand it even if I did!

Winslow was right. What did she know about the history of the world or the intricacies of the law or the demands of politics or the competing needs of populations? It had been arrogance to think that she could change anything or that any change she might make would be for the better. How could she chart a just and true course when she could not know anything for certain? Causation, correlation, coincidence—how could she, Maggie Rayburn, hope to untangle any of the threads?

—You live in the greatest country on earth, said the voice.

And then it was Sandra Day O'Connor who was before her, dressed in a black robe and sitting in a patch of stained light on her portable dais, smiling benignly, flanked by her smartly dressed clerk and the proprietor of the deli and holding something behind her back and asking Maggie to pick a hand. The trip to Phoenix hadn't been for nothing after all, and Maggie strained to hear the words that the former justice had come to tell her.

"You came," Maggie said tentatively. "You came to see me after all." Her words echoed strangely in the ancient acoustics of the church. Outside the high, translucent windows, the light was fading. Somewhere in the distance, a siren blared, and somewhere close by, the dog stirred. She must have fallen asleep, for everything outside of her and everything within went silent, vacuous, and dark.

All through the night or a succession of nights, the voice called out to her, and whether it was God or August Winslow or the former justice trying to make contact, she clearly heard the word "Om."

—Om, said the voice, unless it was saying "home."

She fell back into a deep sleep, and when she finally awoke, clearheaded and hungry, Dino was gone. Even though she searched every corner of the church and then circled the block calling his name, she couldn't find him. The one good thing she had accomplished had come to nothing after all. Everything was a circle, she could see that, and it both made sense and didn't make sense that at the end of her journey she would find herself exactly where she had begun.

# 11.6 DOLLY

Lord have mercy," said Dolly. "This is a mighty fine young man." She hefted the baby against her shoulder before swaddling him more securely and passing him to the mother, who was smiling tiredly from the bed. "Are you ready for your husband to come back in?" The mother nodded and said she was. Dolly straightened the bedcovers before opening the door to where the woman's family was waiting in the reception area, with its pretty sheer curtains and comfortably upholstered chairs. "You can come in now," she said.

It was almost 5:30, but Tula, who was working nearly full time during the summer, had stayed late to help out. She was sitting at the desk, the stethoscope Dolly had given her as a present peeking from the pocket of her smock. When everything was clean and orderly, Dolly turned to Tula. "Even if things don't work out for Danny and me, I'm saying a prayer for you and Will."

"So am I," said Tula. "But something tells me Will and I will be just fine."

"You will be," said Dolly. "You absolutely will." She was remembering the Fourth of July picnic where she had met Danny and how she had known instantly that he was the one.

"We argue a lot, but maybe that's a good thing," said Tula.

"I wish Danny would argue," said Dolly. "He used to go for days without saying a word, although now when I call him, I can hardly shut him up."

"That's a good sign," said Tula. "Talking's always the first step in the healing process."

They talked for a little while about how some women could just feel things and how Dolly and Tula were like that themselves. Tula said she could sense a world of possibilities hovering and ready to descend: college, children, a little house of her own—hers and Will's—all of it waiting for her, all of it one tick in time's cycle closer to coming true. "I not only get feelings," said Tula, "but I see honest to goodness signs. Just yesterday I was walking through the apple orchard where Will and I used to meet, and I saw him—he was sitting under a tree, plain as day. There wasn't anybody there of course, but I saw him. It was his way of telling me he's coming back."

Dolly had been getting conflicting signs for weeks. Only that morning, a crow had landed on the new hand railing at the front steps just before the doctor had diagnosed inoperable tumors in a twenty-five-year-old woman. The doctor sent her home with assurances that he would make some phone calls to other specialists. That had seemed like a good sign, but as soon as the woman was gone, he turned to Dolly and said, "I know what you're thinking. I know you're thinking, What's the point?"

Dolly had been thinking, Hang in there, girlfriend! She had been thinking, You got to hold on to hope! Even though she knew the doctor was talking to himself, she turned to him and answered anyway. "The point is to let her know we're doing everything we can. The point is to give a miracle time to happen."

"Miracles," said the doctor. "Now there's an idea. When's the last time you saw one of those?"

"Every blessed day," said Dolly. Quiet Moments 1563 was one of them, as was her pretty apartment, as was any boy who held his

430

pregnant girlfriend's hand. The biggest miracle of all was sleeping in a basket near the reception desk because Dolly's mother had been unable to babysit that afternoon. Every now and then Dolly or Tula would peek into the basket and catch her breath. "He's perfect," Tula would say. Or Dolly would say it, and Tula would reply, "He absolutely is."

New tumors had appeared on the woman's body and throat virtually overnight. She would die within weeks if not days, yet she was making lists of baby names for a baby that would never be born. "What do you think of Verna?" she had asked Dolly while her husband pulled the car around.

"Verna is nice," Dolly had replied.

"If it's a girl, of course. Just Verne if it's a boy."

The thought of little Verne or Verna just about broke Dolly's heart, but she reminded herself that most of the babies were born healthy—that's what she needed to focus on. But then she remembered the grapefruit baby and the baby with the whitish glaze, and while she believed in focusing on the positive, it didn't seem right to forget them. But they weren't forgotten. There was the website, and recently the doctor had been asked to speak on television, which was a major miracle all by itself.

"You sure you don't want to introduce him to Danny?" asked Tula.

"I'm thinking about it. I just want to give it a little more time."

"He's gonna need his daddy," said Tula.

"I know," said Dolly. "I know you're right."

"Do you ever think about what his life was like? When he was in the army, I mean."

"I try not to think about it. I try to focus on the positive."

"I do," said Tula. "I've been reading about the war and trying to imagine what it's like for Will. It makes me feel closer to him, and not just emotionally. Sometimes I even think I'm there."

"Where?" asked Dolly. She was half listening to Tula and half listening to the music that was softly emanating from some recently installed ceiling speakers. *I Feel Like Traveling On* was one of her favorites, and now she tried to decide if the song was telling her to go to Danny or if it held a darker message. She used to be so sure about things!

Outside the window, the men Dolly had hired to spread the gravel were arguing over who would shovel and who would drive to the stone yard for another load. Their negativity carried in through the open window, and Dolly was relieved when the larger, gentler of the two men picked up a shovel and the lean one strode over to where the truck was parked in a patch of shade. The gentle man reminded her of her father—was it better to fight or to give in peacefully to the inevitable?

The men were only halfway finished, but already the driveway looked fresh and welcoming, and Dolly could easily envision how lovely everything would be once she had filled the new planters with geraniums and ornamental sweet potato vines.

"Speaking of sweet potatoes," said Dolly, holding the baby up to her face and breathing in his milky fragrance. "You're just about sweet enough to eat."

"Did you pick a name yet?" asked Tula. "You can't keep calling him Tadpole."

"I'm thinking Danny Junior fits him. He's the spitting image of his dad."

As she said it, the baby blinked its long eyelashes and gaped at them with the wisdom of the ages shining from his eyes. Miracles were everywhere—to see them, you only had to look.

# 11.7 LYLE

Lyle tried calling Maggie at work, but it was the attorney who answered the phone and said he hadn't heard from her in over a week. "May I inquire who's calling?" he asked.

"No, no," said Lyle. "I'll call back."

"I'm sure it's nothing to worry about," said Lily. "You can try her again tomorrow."

Some nights Lyle slept on Lily's couch, but most nights he slept in the truck. He had a few leads on jobs, but if those didn't work out, he'd go to Phoenix. There's nothing stopping me now, he thought. Nothing he could put his finger on anyway.

He'd had an interview at McKnight's earlier in the week. The manager had said he'd get back to him in a day or two, but it was already Friday and he had heard nothing. He knew by now to talk in terms of the interviewer's interests, but it was hard to know what those might be for the pencil-necked man with the rash of acne who had beckoned him in from the waiting room. Lyle had mentioned cars, the war, and the Texas–OU rivalry in quick succession, and then he decided to turn the tables and ask the manager right out.

"What are your interests?" asked Lyle, and when the manager just stared at him, he added, "What is it you want most in the entire world?"

"I'd kind of like a cheeseburger," said the manager. "Can you get me one of those?"

"You need to be thinking bigger," said Lyle. "You need to be thinking of your career, which is something I can help you with."

"O-kay," said the man, smiling for the first time.

The interview had lasted only ten or fifteen minutes, but it got Lyle thinking about the munitions plant and how when it came to bosses, you couldn't do much better than MacBride.

"I know the manager," said Lily as she headed off to work. "I can put in a good word for you, but you still oughtta go on over there today and see what's what."

"Good idea," said Lyle. "I guess I will."

It was almost noon when Lyle got in the truck and started it up, but instead of driving toward the chicken farm, he found himself in the part of town where Tula lived. The houses on Ash Creek Circle had once been identical, but over the years their owners had made additions and improvements. The Santos house was one of the few without a second story or a sunroom added on. A dilapidated swing set squatted in the dusty yard, and the spokes of an ancient wash rack clattered in the wind. Over the past weeks Lyle had driven by several times, but except for once when a load of washing was hanging out, he never saw any signs of either Tula or her mother. He wanted to know if Tula had heard from Will, but he hadn't seen her since the day of the high school graduation.

Now he got out of the car and knocked on the front door; he didn't expect anyone to answer it and no one did. His reflection in the glass panel startled him because it looked like someone else's face, and he couldn't help thinking about killers lurking in the dark and waiting to attack him.

After checking behind the house, Lyle returned to the truck and drove along the creek before circling back toward town. He had just turned onto the Main Road when the sheriff's pickup pulled him over and Hank Conway got out and swaggered over. "What did I do?" asked Lyle. "Is my taillight out again? And I've been meaning to get that muffler fixed."

"No, no, nothing like that," said the sheriff. "I'm just wondering where you're headed, is all."

Lyle knew he didn't have to say anything. He knew a man's thoughts were his own and nobody had a right to force them out of him. He knew it wasn't legal to pull people over and interrogate them without just cause, so he didn't say anything, only waited for the sheriff to continue.

"I want to show you something," said the sheriff. "Something you might appreciate. Something that might make you sleep a little better at night."

Lyle unbuckled his seat belt, got out of the truck, and walked with the sheriff around the back of the glossy pickup. The sheriff ran his hand along the truck's flank where COUNTY SHERIFF was painted in gold letters outlined in black. He pointed to a gun rack bolted to the reinforced frame of the truck, drawing Lyle's attention to two hunting rifles and two military-style weapons, and then he waved at a pile of SWAT team vests that were stashed in the cargo bay and also at a locked box that contained, he said, a thousand rounds of ammunition. "We've got the exact same gear as Will's got in Iraq," said the sheriff. "Only some of it's a different color. And when the current conflict ends, where do you think all that surplus military equipment is gonna go?"

"Where?" asked Lyle.

"Cities and towns just like Red Bud, that's where. It's amazing what you can get if you agree to certain priorities."

"What priorities?" asked Lyle.

"Drugs, terrorists, illegals, that sort of thing. Those are Uncle Sam's priorities, and there are a lot of financial incentives for communities like Red Bud to make them ours as well."

Lyle didn't know what the sheriff was getting at, so he asked, "What are you getting at, Sheriff? Do you think I'm into drugs?"

"Heck no, Lyle." The sheriff gave a snort and squinted up at the sun before fixing his sights back on Lyle, who asked, "Are there terrorists in Red Bud?"

"I'm just thinking you'd like to know that for a tiny little town, we're pretty well equipped for keeping the peace 'n' all. You might like to know that we're dedicated to keeping our citizens safe and that it's better for a person who's done something wrong to turn his or herself in."

"How does a person know if he's done something wrong?" asked Lyle. His heart sank with misgivings. He wondered if it was legal to sleep in his truck or if he was breaking the law on the nights he didn't stay at Lily's.

"Jeezus, Lyle. What kind of a question is that?"

As the sheriff drove away, Lyle tried to think of what else he might have done wrong. If it didn't have to do with the truck, then perhaps it had to do with the house, but the house no longer belonged to him. His bank account was overdrawn—that was sure to get him crosswise with the law. It was possible it had to do with the munitions plant, even though he didn't work there anymore. And then it dawned on him—the sheriff wasn't interested in him at all.

## 11.8 MAGGIE

The first driver took Maggie as far as Flagstaff. "In case you're interested, it's a straight shot to the Grand Canyon," he said. "You may as well see it, now that you're here."

Why not? thought Maggie. She had always wanted to see the Grand Canyon, and there was no telling when she'd get another chance.

When the second driver let her out at a visitor's center, it was as if she'd been dropped onto another planet, or as if she were seeing her own planet for the first time. It was as if all the churches of the world had exploded or turned inside out or been transformed in some way so that all that was sparkling and glorious now lay before her. Every stained-glass color, every vertiginous drop, every astonishing element of the universe was spread out like an all-you-can-eat buffet of miracles. Even surrounded by a crowd of sightseers, she felt alone with the majesty. Even hemmed in by the safety barricade, she felt as if she could fall at any moment, as if she was falling, as if she had fallen and then her wings had caught and held the way the wings of the birds that drifted in slow circles over the chasm had caught and held and lifted. Her breath came in short gasps. Her heart expanded in her chest. Her eyes bulged and didn't blink. How she had come to be there seemed both strange and inevitable. None of it made sense to her, but perhaps that was not a useful way to think about things. Perhaps senselessness was the entire point.

Maggie made her way to the big wooden map that showed her location in the string of parks that stretched north almost to Utah and west nearly to Las Vegas. Only slowly did she realize that the spot where she stood was a speck in the vastness, that there were other observation points, just as stunning and true. There were boat rides and dangerous rapids and treacherous paths and hot air balloons and helicopters and so many points from which to view the canyon that no one lifetime could absorb or comprehend them. And the canyon was only one part of the world, just the way the world was only part of the universe, and the universe . . . It was too much to contemplate all at once, so she shut the thinking part of her mind and opened up the part that allowed creation to fan out before her without asking her to ponder what it meant.

A man leading a scrawny donkey by a rope approached to ask if she wanted her picture taken with it. He showed her a Polaroid camera that hung from his neck by a greasy strap. "Only ten dollars," he said. All around them tourists were pretending to ignore the man as they surreptitiously snapped pictures of the donkey with their phones. The photographer's hands were grimy and his gaucho hat shaded his face so that Maggie couldn't see his eyes. "Nobody wants Polaroids these days," he said, his lips curling over broken teeth in a smile that couldn't quite mask his desperation.

"Well, I want one. I don't even have a cell phone," Maggie told him.

"Why not?" asked the photographer.

"Money, for one thing," said Maggie. "But I'd love to buy a photograph from you." She searched her purse and found the envelope the attorney had given her on her last day of work. "I wish you weren't going," he had told her. "You're the best office manager I've ever had."

"My family needs me," Maggie had said.

She handed the donkey's owner a ten-dollar bill, and a few minutes later he handed back a smeared Polaroid. "A souvenir of your trip," he said. "Something for your memory book."

"Yes," said Maggie. "Thank you very much."

In the photograph, the canyon was a featureless gulf behind her, but despite the runny colors and the sad expression on the donkey's face, it made her smile. The image only hinted at the grandeur that surrounded her, but it was enough to prove to Lyle, and more importantly to herself, I was here.

## 11.9 LYLE

After his encounter with the sheriff, Lyle drove to the Redi Mart and called Phoenix again. This time he told the attorney who he was.

"I think she might be headed home," said the attorney. "Hasn't she called you?"

"It's a long story, but she can't," said Lyle.

"Well, when you see her, tell her I have some good news to report."

Lyle wished he and Maggie had made one of those plans everyone talked about after 9/11—a plan of where and when to meet in case of a national emergency. Then he and Maggie would know where to go now, not because they were facing a national emergency, but because they were facing a personal one.

What did a person do in the absence of such a plan? He wished he had ESP. He wished he or Maggie were clairvoyant, the way True Cunningham claimed to be. Then the one who wasn't clairvoyant could just choose a time and place to meet and think about it really hard, and the one who was clairvoyant could pick up the signals merely by concentrating—problem solved.

But that was wishful thinking. Wishful thinking was why Maggie had started down this path, and he guessed he wasn't the only one who had been unable to see where it would lead. Lyle sat in the truck while the sun reached its zenith and started its slow descent over the boxy Multiplex. Finally, he jiggered the key in the ignition and drove down the street to the diner, where he ordered a cup of coffee and tried to piece together a plan of action. The clock above the counter ticked past four o'clock and then past five. All around him noisy families were gathering to celebrate the weekend by ordering from the giant plastic menus that had always fascinated Will and that Lyle still saw as evidence that the world was big and filled with opportunity. When the waitress began to frown and snap her gum, Lyle realized that instead of pondering the problem, he was only staring blankly at the Formica counter-top and waiting for inspiration to strike.

He had to think, but he didn't know what to think about. It wasn't until he had paid the bill and stepped out into the soft June breeze that it occurred to him that instead of bemoaning the way things were, there were two questions he should be asking himself. The first was, How would Maggie solve the where-and-when-to-meet problem? As if that was not difficult enough, he would also have to ask if Maggie even knew about the problem.

Since there was no way to answer the second question, he could only assume she knew and work on an answer to the first. He should have made sure she wouldn't come home unexpectedly by telling her the police investigation wasn't over instead of trying to protect her by holding information back.

Then he remembered what Jimmy had said about goal-setting, about tactics and execution. The goal was to meet up with Maggie. As for tactics, he had to put himself in her shoes. What would she be thinking? Even more critical to the solution was, What would she be thinking he was thinking? Was there something so obvious that it would not only be obvious to her, but it would also be obvious to her that it was obvious to him? And it struck him with the eureka force of discovery that there was an obvious time to meet! It was noon. They had met in the lunchroom after the twelve o'clock bell for the four years they had worked together at the munitions plant, and he knew with absolute certainty that noon would be obvious to Maggie just as it had been obvious to him. Just in case he was clairvoyant after all, or Maggie was, he closed his eyes and sent a message to her, wherever she might be: Noon, Maggie. We'll meet at noon.

But now the matter of where to meet arose. The first place he thought of was the munitions plant lunchroom, but that wasn't realistic. Maggie no longer had an employee badge; nor, for that matter, did he. But again, as if the coffee shop had been inhibiting his problem-solving skills and the fresh air was the thing needed to jump-start mental activity, the answer came unbidden. The bus station! A transportation hub was the obvious place, but on what day and in which city? The last time they had played the travel game, he had wanted to go to Tahiti. How realistic was that?

Lyle hurried along the sidewalk to where the truck was angled in between two sleek late-model cars. The fender Will had dented in the snowstorm was starting to rust. A crack spidered across the windshield, and the defective muffler was hanging nearly to the ground. But it still started right up every time he turned the key, and he didn't reckon a man could ask much more of his truck than that.

Just as he was backing out of his parking space, he saw True Cunningham walking along the sidewalk, surrounded by a group of friends. "True," he called out. "Hey, True!"

"Why, Lyle, I haven't seen you in I don't know how long! Maggie called me a few days ago, but when I looked for you at the plant, they told me you were no longer working there."

Lyle motioned her over to the open window, hoping the others wouldn't follow her. "I want to get a message to Maggie," he said. "I know you have experience with, well, with sending messages via—"

"ESP," True finished for him in an exhibition of the very skill he was looking for.

"Exactly. I was hoping you could help me with that."

"Sure I can, honey. Now what kind of a message are you hoping to send?"

True's friends were standing on the sidewalk, craning their necks to hear what she and Lyle were talking about. Even if he took True someplace private and swore her to secrecy, it was only a matter of time before she broke down and gossiped about his business. And if, for some reason, she tried to keep his secret, the police might get it out of her, or it might be picked up by the hidden surveillance cameras everyone was installing, not to mention the fact that cell phones could surreptitiously be switched to record. Lyle put the truck in gear and tried to look as if he were late for something. "Never mind, True. I'll call you later to explain."

When he turned onto Park Drive, he had to stop while a group of boys crossed the road, loaded down with gear and headed toward the town baseball field for an evening practice. Lyle had never been on a baseball team, never had a bunch of buddies he could rely on. It was just as well, he thought now. It might have made him soft, and first and foremost, a man ought to rely on himself.

He nestled the truck in behind a grove of cottonwood trees and spent the night alternately dozing and sending Maggie messages via ESP. Don't come home, he thought, but he didn't know if he could send the messages or if she could receive them. The sweat pooled in his armpits and on his brow. It had upset him to see the firepower in the sheriff's truck, and now a horrible dread came over him. What if the bus station had come to mind because Maggie was sending a message to him? Where would she go if she could go anywhere? Suddenly he knew, and it wasn't New York City or the Grand Canyon or Niagara Falls. It was Red Bud, Oklahoma. Don't come home, he thought again as he drifted on the edge of sleep. And don't go to the bus station. Whatever you do, Maggie, don't go there!

# 12.0 TACTICS & EXECUTION

*Lyle said he'd call me later, but he never did. I sent a telepathic message to Maggie anyway. I knew what he wanted to tell her. He wanted to tell her to come home, so that's the message I sent.*
—True Cunningham

*We figured if she didn't come to him, he'd go to her.*
—Sheriff Hank Conway

*Were we cooperating with law enforcement? Absolutely. But buying the site was our insurance policy*
—Lex Lexington

*I told them they should consider moving their headquarters overseas, but they just laughed at me. They said, "Hell, we're just some guys trying to make sense out of the war."*
—Anonymous

*Just before he left, the captain asked if I thought we were in over our heads. He said that if the buyers seemed at all competent, maybe we should sell.*
—Le Roy Jones

*The captain and I were kind of opposites. He was changing his mind about selling just as I was changing mine.*
—Joe Kelly

*Being told not to write the article about Maggie lit a fire under that Fitch boy. After that, he started poking his nose into everything. Wait a sec—what did you say your name was? You're him, aren't you? You're that reporter fellow, Martin Fitch.*
—August Winslow

## 12.1 PENN SINCLAIR

Penn spent his last day in New York City shopping for an engagement ring. He hadn't known it would be so complicated: How much did he want to spend? Which cut of stone did he find appealing? Should the band be platinum or gold, and if it was to be gold, what about alloy and purity?

At each store he went to, a sales associate laid a velvet tray on the countertop and set out a selection of rings for Penn to admire. He had always been sure of himself, but now he couldn't seem to make up his mind on anything. "Perhaps you should bring your fiancée in with you," suggested an unsmiling salesman. "The ladies tend to have definite ideas about these things."

"She's not my fiancée yet," said Penn.

"I see," said the salesman, arching an eyebrow as if what he saw was not entirely pleasing. "I assume you've discussed marriage with her, though. These days couples usually discuss the ring."

They talked about marriage endlessly, but it was always in the context of another bridegroom and another bride, and now Penn couldn't remember anything Louise had told him. He wondered if he was supposed to feel happy as he shopped, or at least as if he was trading his money for a chance at happiness. He supposed he wasn't unhappy, even if he was a little irritated when the saleswoman at Tiffany's ignored him to wait on a woman who clutched an expensive purse and disapproved of invisible flaws in an array of pearl necklaces.

"Pearls are a natural product," said the saleswoman. "Natural products have flaws, which is one of the reasons we value them."

"But why so pink?" asked the customer. "These aren't for my daughter, after all. They are for me."

"What about this double strand?" asked the saleswoman. "They're really lustrous. Or, have you considered yellow—or even black?"

"Heavens, no," said the woman. "Those are far too modern for my taste."

When it was his turn, Penn found out that there was color to diamonds as well.

"Color is just one of the four Cs," said the saleswoman. "Cut, clarity, color, and carat. Your job is to balance these attributes without straining your budget. Even an imperfect diamond can appear quite brilliant to the naked eye."

"Only quite brilliant?" asked Penn.

"Quite, quite brilliant," said the saleswoman.

Perhaps he should come back with Louise even if it ruined the surprise. Or he could buy a cheap glass ring for the proposal with the idea that they could replace it with the real thing down the road. He tried to imagine the scene: the little blue box, Louise's trembling fingers, the inevitable awkward seconds between the moment Louise first saw the substitute ring and the moment she realized it was only temporary. Much as she might be a costume jewelry convert, he didn't think she would settle when it came to an engagement ring, and he didn't want his first words after "Darling, will you marry me?" to be a long-winded explanation for why the ring he was putting on her finger was only standing in for the one they would choose together. And when would they choose it? He couldn't expect Louise to wear the temporary ring for the long months he was overseas.

Penn walked down Madison Avenue, pausing now and then to gape into the shop windows and trying not to feel defeated. It was a warm summer Friday and clutches of excited shoppers gave the city a festive air, but he couldn't help feeling critical of their high spirits. By the time he reached Forty-second Street, the crowds had thickened and changed. Now it was men and women in suits who crowded the sidewalks talking into their cell phones or rushing to catch an early train to the suburbs or the beach. Instead of turning west toward Louise's apartment, where he planned to shower and change his clothes, something made him jump into a gap in the revolving door of the library just as a woman with children was coming out. "Hi, kids," he said, but the girl ignored him and the boy peered at him suspiciously from behind his mother's leg.

He made his way up the escalator to the room where his eyes had been opened, fully expecting to encounter the homeless man sprawled on the floor where he had first seen him, but of course he wasn't there. "I'm looking for a man who used to come in here to read books on war," he said to a librarian sitting at the information desk. "Have you seen him lately?"

"I'm new here, but I can ask my colleague."

Penn waited while the man went off and came back again with an older woman. "You must mean the professor," she said. "He hasn't been here in several months, but there's a soup kitchen two blocks away. I know he used to eat there."

Penn hurried along the sidewalk to where a group of haphaz-ardly dressed people were clustered near a recessed entryway. It was 4:40, and a sign taped to the inside of a window said the door wouldn't open until five o'clock. He was supposed to meet Louise for an early dinner before heading to the airport to catch a flight to DC, where he would board a military transport plane. He hadn't yet told her he was going back to Iraq, and he had counted on the ring to soften the blow. But now he concluded it might be better to put off the proposal to a day when he had more time and less on his mind. That morning he had gotten up early with the pleasant sense that the day stretched endlessly before him, but now he felt rushed and indecisive. It would be folly to propose in such a harried state of mind—that and the news of his departure would ruin the atmosphere for a romantic celebration. In any case, he didn't have a ring. He leaned against the side of the building and ran his fingers against the grimy stone cladding. He still had to shower and change his clothes and head uptown to the restaurant, so if he waited until five for the soup kitchen to open, he risked being late for Louise.

He paced the length of the block and back again. Just when he had decided he was compounding his folly by waiting when he didn't even know what he was hoping to discover, an old man came around the corner tapping a gnarled stick in front of him. It took Penn almost a minute to recognize the professor. Something fundamental about him had changed, and when he banged his stick on the ground, it was without his previous air of conviction. Penn introduced himself and explained what he had been doing in the months since they had met, but the man showed no sign of recognition.

"We talked about war," said Penn. "You told me that man is warlike, but that he doesn't like to think of himself that way."

"I say that to everybody," said the professor, stopping to cough into a grimy handkerchief. "Everybody who will listen, that is."

"I gave you half a bagel."

"Ah," said the professor. "Half a bagel."

"We talked about philosophy," said Penn.

"Philosophy!" wheezed the professor. He squinted at Penn and leaned forward, balancing on unsteady feet with the help of the flimsy stick. "It seems to me that there is only one worthwhile philosophical question, and it isn't whether or not ... " He started wheezing again. His eyes were red and runny, and his skin seemed to erupt in new boils while Penn watched.

"It isn't whether or not man is warlike. Of course he is. It isn't whether or not the system works to sustain itself. Of course it does. So the question is not whether it is even possible to be outside the system or whether man is doomed to be a cog in a killing machine, it ... " He coughed and scrutinized his handkerchief and seemed befuddled by what he saw.

"What is the question, then? What were you going to say?"

"It is whether it is possible to be both moral and ... " Here, he was taken by a paroxysm of painful coughing, accompanied by what seemed to be a memory lapse. "Where was I? Where was I?" he asked. The professor poked his stick in Penn's direction, hitting him on the kneecap, but his grip was so feeble that it bobbled and dropped from his hand.

Penn stooped to pick it up, trying to conceal his agitation. "You were saying there is only one worthwhile philosophical question."

"Thank you, young man. Yes, exactly. I believe there is."

"What one is that?" Penn felt increasingly desperate, and while it occurred to him that he was listening to an old man's ramblings, he was certain the professor possessed the kernel of truth he was looking for.

Now it was the old man's turn to say, "What? What one is what?"

"The question!" cried Penn, but the professor's response was interrupted when a volunteer in a red apron came with a ring of keys to open the door for the long line of people that had formed on the sidewalk.

"What's for dinner?" shouted the professor.

"Come in and you'll find out," said the volunteer.

"I'm hoping it's not meat loaf," said a scrawny woman who was standing near them.

At the sound of the keys, another horde of people had materialized, and now they were jostling for position in the line. The professor used his stick to clear a space for himself as the volunteer called out, "One at a time, please! There's plenty for everybody!"

"But it's not yet five!" cried Penn. His wristwatch, which had been given to him by his father when he went off to college, was finely calibrated and had neither lost nor gained a minute in the nine years he had owned it.

"One at a time," the volunteer called again. Cooking smells wafted out the door to mingle with the exhaust from a passing bus and the stink of rotting garbage that curled up from the curb.

"What's the one philosophical question?" Penn was shouting now, but the old man had scuttled up to the door and was vanishing through it. "Can you at least tell me that?"

The volunteer smiled benignly at Penn. "It's hard to think about philosophy when you're hungry," she said. "Come back after dinner. Maybe you'll get your answer then."

Penn slung his duffel over his shoulder and wandered through a nearby park where an art class was experimenting with line and form. "Solids and voids," said a bearded man when Penn stopped to peer over his shoulder at the abstractions on his canvas. The face of Penn's watch showed 6:04. It was too late to shower, too late to change his clothes, too late to be on time for Louise. He walked another block west and turned north on the Avenue of the Americas. It was seventeen blocks to the restaurant overlooking Central Park. He imagined hailing a cab and getting locked in rush-hour traffic or jogging up the avenue on foot, becoming sweatier with each block while Louise tapped her long fingers on the tablecloth and ordered a bottle of imported water and then a selection of appetizers when he still didn't appear. He saw her choosing an expensive wine and sending it back when it wasn't quite what she expected.

Suddenly it seemed easier to go back to the war than to face Louise without a ring, without a life plan, without a polished sense of who he was or how he was going to answer life's big questions. With only a vague sense of what those questions were. All around him, people were making small protests against fate: the taxicab drivers fighting over a customer, the fat woman enjoying a candy bar, the thin woman shaking a tambourine and belting out a gospel song. Even the proprietor of a nearby newsstand waved cheerfully at the headlines: MARKETS SLAMMED BY BIG OIL, RUSSIA WIDENS ATTACKS ON GEORGIA, CRISIS DEEPENS AS BIG BANKS FAIL, OKLAHOMA WOMAN SOUGHT IN LEAKED DOC PROBE. He followed a carefree young woman who tossed her hair and crossed against the light. Then Times Square exploded in front of him, and he felt a wave of happiness wash over him, or if it wasn't happiness, it was at least a sense that cross-purposes and conflicting messages and questions with no clear answers weren't necessarily bad and might even be evidence of progress. He told himself that he had done a little good in the warehouse. He and the men had started something, and whether or not they finished it wasn't up to him. He'd call Louise. Or he'd leave a message with the maître d' of the restaurant. He'd send her flowers. Meanwhile, he had a plane to catch.

On the plane, Sinclair went over his orders again. He was being assigned to an engineer battalion that had undergone intensive stateside training with a new generation of robotic devices that were now being deployed overseas. The first wave of combat robots had been plagued with technical issues and precipitously pulled from the theater after reports of malfunction and friendly fire. But improvements had been made and hopes were high that the new devices would save soldiers' lives. He re-read the spec sheets: the Groundhog was equipped with an M249 light machine gun that could shoot a thousand rounds per minute with 100 percent accuracy; the Parakeet could fly thirty miles per hour and hover in place as long as its power source lasted, which depended on factors like wind resistance and operator skill. If only they'd had a robot scouting the supply route that terrible day. But now he was being given a chance to save future soldiers even if there was nothing he could do about the past.

He put his head against the seat back and closed his eyes, happier than he'd been in a long time. He wondered what the new troops would be like. He wondered if there would be a businessman like Kelly or a computer whiz like Le Roy or an escape artist like Pig Eye—Edwards, he corrected himself. Paul Edwards was his name. Or a poet like Danny or a captain like himself, given leadership before he was completely ready for it. He knew that in some respects the men and women were all unique—of course they were—but in other respects, they were all the same.

## 12.2 MAGGIE

It was early morning when the last truck driver let Maggie out at the Red Bud exit. Now and then a car sped off the highway heading toward town, but she didn't try to flag it down. What if it was someone she knew? She wouldn't know how to answer the inevitable questions and she didn't want to lie, so she walked with her head down, eyes glued to the dirt. Every time she caught a glimpse of her shadow stretching behind her, she thought it might be Dino, but of course it wasn't. She tried to decide whom she had let down more—God, because she hadn't kept her promise to him, or Tomás and George, because nothing she had done for them had made a tangible difference. She remembered how she had declared so confidently to anyone who would listen, "Saving someone else's son is the only way to save my own." But she hadn't saved someone else's son. So far, she hadn't saved anybody. All she'd done was to raise the hopes of people who couldn't stand too much more disappointment, which didn't seem particularly kind under the circumstances. When she turned onto Old Oak Road, her heart started knocking like the engine of the truck on a cold day. Lyle! she thought. Will! And then she knew who it was she had let down most of all.

The driveway was hidden by a bend in the road. First the hay-field came into sight, nailed in place by the big old oak, and then the mailbox, which hung open as if panting in the June heat. It was all uphill from there—up the last stretch of road, up the driveway, up the cracked front walk with its embellishments of dandelions and tufted grass, up the steps and across the worn porch with its broken boards and rusted nails. The door was locked—why had Lyle taken to locking it? Maggie didn't have a key, so she jimmied a loose window and climbed through it into the dining alcove, where she had hoped to find Lyle and Will drinking their Saturday morning coffee in companionable silence. But Will had joined the army, and the alcove was empty even of Lyle.

She saw by the battery-powered kitchen clock that it was

already ten o'clock. Of course Lyle would be up and about by now. She washed her face and fixed a tall glass of water, which she sipped as she tidied first the kitchen and then the living room. She had always been too busy to clean properly. She had always been rushing from one thing to another: taking a hurried shower before her family was awake, eating breakfast as she slapped together the sandwiches for lunch, reminding Will about his homework and hustling everybody out the door. And then the busy day at work before coming home to dinner, household chores, and bed. Now she could take her time. Will's room was spotless, so she started in on Lyle's room, folding the scattered clothing and making up his bed with fresh sheets. Her bed—rather, hers and Lyle's. It felt good to concentrate on each task, on each object, on each slow tick of the clock that was marking the seconds until Lyle would come home to find her waiting for him with dinner bubbling on the stove. She unpacked her duffel, putting the dirty clothes in the laundry basket with the sheets, the worn-out shoes on the rack in the closet, the sweaters in the sweater drawer—no, sweaters in the closet. She was pushing the sweater drawer shut when she realized it should be full of the evidence she had carefully hidden inside magazine covers all those months ago, but the evidence was gone. Lyle! What had Lyle done?

Maggie rushed back to Will's room, only now noticing that nothing of Will remained in it. The emptiness frightened her. Her heart rattled in her rib cage like a broken clapper. The house seemed to be telling her something, so she stood very quietly, listening to the stillness and smelling the musty, closed-up smell. It wasn't a home any longer, it was only a house.

She crept back along the hallway to the living room. The curtains hung heavily on their rings. Years ago, she had stitched them herself from fabric she had saved up for months to buy. Now she noticed that the hem was coming out and pinprick holes in the floral weave allowed tiny galaxies of light to come through. The once-bright cushions on the corduroy couch were used-up squares of dingy fabric. Dishes with the crusted remains of a meal had been kicked underneath the couch. The desk was piled with unopened mail, and propped up against the desk lamp was a letter from the attorney that started off "Good news!" It went on to say that the appellate court had agreed to a new trial for Tomás, and could she send another installment on the fee? She sat down at the desk to write out a check, but when she flipped through the check register, she saw that Lyle's paycheck deposits had stopped over a month before.

The desk held other answers: a sternly worded letter from the bank that held their mortgage, a notice of termination from the munitions plant, documentation that Will had passed his army intake physical, had achieved a high score on his vocational aptitude test, was being deployed to Iraq. Maggie gazed out the window, but the oak tree and the rolling landscape were the only things in their proper places. Will had gone off to fight a war she had forgotten all about. How could she have forgotten the very thing that had started her on her current journey? Had she lost her way or found it? Or was life a series of mostly blind turnings guided by instinct and luck? And her husband of almost twenty years, where the heck was he?

She thought of the where-would-you-go game they had played when Will was little. But how was the game relevant? Surely Lyle hadn't gone to California or Tahiti. And then she wondered if there was something else about the game she should be remembering. The last time the three of them had played it together, Will had only shrugged and said, "I'm too old for that." But Maggie had played along. It had been before she had found the top-secret document on Winslow's desk, before they had stopped driving Will to school together, before everything about her life had changed. Before she herself had changed it. She had said, "I'd hop a bus and go clear across the country to New York."

"A bus," Will had scoffed. "If you could afford to go any-where,

couldn't you afford to take a plane?"

"I want to look out the window and see the sights," Maggie had said, but without Will's participation, the air had gone out of the game. They had driven the rest of the way to school in silence, but as soon as Will got out, Lyle had patted her shoulder in a consoling way. "I'm with you on seeing the sights, but it might be hard to take a bus to Tahiti. That's the place I really want to go."

Maggie had gotten her bus trip after all. She had seen Phoenix and the Grand Canyon, and it was deeply unfair that Lyle hadn't been with her. But she didn't think Lyle would go off without her now no matter what had happened. Still, the idea of the bus station stuck in her head. It was a hub of transportation. It was the place, on the day she had departed for Phoenix, she had left the bicycle with a note attached to it that said, Please Return to Lyle Rayburn Who Lives on Old Oak Road. Now, she hoped someone had returned the bicycle and she would find it in the shed.

The clock in the kitchen said it was 11:40. Something told her she should hurry. Hurry for what? she asked herself, but there was no answer to the question, just an inner ticking and the image of the squat brick building on Hill Street with the bench outside for waiting and the silent morphing of the liquid crystal numbers on the kitchen clock and the familiar weight of the threadbare backpack as she slung it once again over her shoulders and left the house.

## 12.3 JOE KELLY

Kelly took his coffee outside to watch the street come to life: the white panel laundry truck starting on its rounds, the road crew putting new sewers in the street, the single mother walking her children to the corner and waiting with them for the bus, the muscled brothers who owned the car parts shop rolling up the metal awning and smoking a cigarette, passing it back and forth and calling out to Kelly, "This way only one of us will get cancer." On the surface, everything was the same as usual, but something tickled Kelly's attention. For one thing, he wasn't used to the starched and buttoned cuffs that were poking out from the sleeves of his new jacket, and for another, the captain was gone. For the first time in his life, Kelly felt like the master of his own fate, but he also felt a little disconnected and alone.

He walked across the tracks toward the school bus stop where the oldest child was telling the younger ones horror stories of what awaited them in third grade. "What are you going to school on Saturday for?" he asked.

"Make-up days," said the oldest. "Because of all the snow."

"Da-amn," said Kelly. "Well, come and see me when you're out."

"You boys are on your own this evening," said the single mother. "I started that new job, but I'll see you tomorrow for sure."

"Things are looking up," said Kelly.

"Yes, I think they are."

The bus rolled to a stop. Shiny faces peered down at Kelly through the glass. The driver said, "Hurry up, kids." The single mother blew three kisses, and together she and Kelly watched the bus chug up the street toward the intersection.

When it was out of sight, she said, "Me oh my, you look good in a suit! What's the special occasion?"

"Big meeting today," said Kelly. He would have liked to linger in the cool morning air and enjoy the sense of change and possibility, but he had work to do. The buyers and their lawyers were coming at noon to deliver a draft of the sales contract and to answer any questions the men or the attorney they had hired might have. When Kelly had asked to make it a condition of the sale that the site wouldn't be shut down and that the new owners would keep Le Roy and Danny on if they wanted to stay, the representative for the buyers had said, "No problem, man. Why would my clients pay a million dollars for something only to turn around and shut it down? They believe in this mission is why, and they have the money to do it right. They're hoping you'll all stick around for a while."

The sewer crew started up their jackhammer, splintering the morning quiet as Kelly walked back down the street. Above him, the clouds exploded with brightness and the air was sharp with the smell of new-mown grass. With the captain gone, there was no one to question his decisions, but no one to help him make them either. It was both liberating and disconcerting.

He drained the last of his coffee and headed back inside. Le Roy had gone on his morning run, but Danny was standing in the middle of the room adding his voice to the din from the jackhammer:

*The rich get richer and the poor stay poor*
*While we're knock knock knockin' on the devil's door.*
*The Defense Department isn't keeping score,*
*And the generals talk about esprit de corps*
*As they sign you up for another tour*
*So the rich can get richer while the poor stay poor.*

Sinclair's absence made the decision to sell the website easier, but now Kelly wondered if it was the right thing to do. He was beginning to feel at home in the warehouse. They had applied for an occupancy waiver, and the sense of being somewhat settled astonished him. Besides, now that the captain was no longer around as a force of opposition, Kelly had started to see the mission of the website from the captain's point of view. He had started to wonder if making a profit off the sale was ethical and if he should divide the site into two separate entities—one for the everyday horror stories and one for hard-core revelations like those contained in the classified documents they had already published and the ones Le Roy said they were getting from a new source at the NSA.

He wished he had someone he could discuss it with, but Danny had started talking about going back to Oklahoma and it wasn't the sort of question Le Roy cared about. If Danny left, he would be shorthanded if he wanted to turn the website into something bigger and more significant than it was now. Unless he decided to sell and get out from under the shadow of the war once and for all, the way Hernandez had done.

Closing the door on the street sounds, he poured himself another cup of coffee and sifted through the morning's email correspondence. One of the volunteers wrote to suggest moving the site overseas, and the captain to say they were in over their heads—as if they couldn't handle things without him! But he couldn't worry about that now. The buyers would be there in just under four hours, and he still had to print out the spreadsheets and figure out his strategy regarding the sale. Then he had to loop Le Roy and Danny in on whatever the strategy was and remind them to let him do the talking. He guessed they could play a waiting game. He guessed they could listen and give the purchasers just enough information to buy themselves a little time.

The question of what Kelly wanted for the website was complicated by the question of what he wanted for himself, but that was becoming clearer. The idea that he was positioned to do something truly good took hold of him the way the starched collar and cuffs took hold. "Unsettling"—that was the word for it. Equally unsettling was a new and insistent desire to talk things over with Joe Senior, who was his father after all. He'd missed Christmas and Easter, but he'd go home for a weekend soon—the Fourth of July was approaching—he'd go home for that. Not that Hoboken was home. Of course it wasn't. While he was there, he'd call up that Rita woman and get to know her better. An election was coming up in a few months—hell, maybe he'd even vote.

## 12.4 LE ROY JONES

While Kelly got ready for the meeting with the buyers, Le Roy generated a string of random numbers for use as an encryption key in preparation for receiving some explosive documents from his contact at the NSA. It was also a good idea to encrypt any encryption key and store it in a safe place. Le Roy believed in Kerckhoff 's principle, which said that an encryption system would remain secure if the key was secure. Even if everything else about the system was known to the enemy, the key was, well, the key. That made where to store the key the most important decision he had to make. While he was thinking about it, he sent an email to E'Laine:

> I just did 5 miles in less than thirty minutes and I hardly broke a sweat.

With the captain gone and E'Laine back in Detroit, the warehouse seemed empty, like there was a blank place in Le Roy's peripheral vision despite the fact that the row of sturdy, mismatched desks and the metal lockers and the cots and the kitchenette were still in their usual places—everything solid and just as it should be. As soon as he got back to work, the hole in the universe closed up until the next time he happened to raise his head, always scuttling just ahead of his line of sight. It was almost noon when he saw it—a shadow moving on the porch, an incomplete silhouette creeping and crouching silently, smoke-colored and indistinct. He sat cemented to his chair, afraid in a way he hadn't been afraid since that day in Iraq, trying to figure out what it was. Just then his email pinged with a reply from E'Laine, and he turned his attention back to the screen.

> Good going, track star.

Le Roy went back to figuring out where to store the encryption key and decided he could send it to E'Laine.

I'm putting something in your drop box. Keep it in a safe place until I ask for it.

You can count on me.

I know I can.

Now that that was solved, Le Roy could get back to work on his simulation. He felt good about the arrangement, but he knew that encryption programs and even keys weren't the most important link in any security chain. People were.

# 12.5 DANNY JOINER

When the stapler misfired for the third time, Danny threw it across the room. "Who bought this piece of shit?" he wanted to know, but Kelly was printing out documents and Le Roy was deep inside his simulation. They had their headphones on, happy in their separate bubbles of isolation.

As Danny watched them, his irritation was replaced by an unfamiliar sense of belonging, and when he walked over to retrieve the stapler, he put a hand on Le Roy's shoulder and left it there for a moment before getting back to work on his epic. He had changed the beginning several times, trying to get it right. A possible title was "The Mars Hoax," which referred to both the Roman god of war and to a widely believed but erroneous report about the planet that was based on a misread email. "Are Ares and Mars the same?" he had asked the captain a week or so before he left. "Or are there subtle differences between them that will color the meaning of whichever one I use?" The captain had studied classics as well as philosophy and seemed to have been placed right there across the room from Danny in order to answer his questions about the two ancient gods of war.

"They're different," said the captain. "Ares was destructive and destabilizing, whereas Mars saw war as a pathway to peace."

"Awesome!" crowed Danny. "Just what I was looking for!"

Sometimes he wanted to zero in and sometimes he wanted to telescope out, and the word "Mars" allowed him to do both. It was a vast red planet with impact craters and frozen polar caps, but it was only visible from earth as a pinprick of light. Not only was the entire solar system swept up in those four little letters, but also the color red, which was the color of anger, the color of passion, the color of blood and lust and love. The word was tailor-made for his purposes, and finding out about the opposing war connotations had given him a sense of order and control he had never experienced before. He thought how time was like a funnel for events, where everything in the past made the present seem ordained: the World Trade Towers had led to the war, which had led Danny to his unit and the IED and the warehouse and the epic, and finally to just the word he wanted—"Mars." It might be an illusion, but it all felt inevitable and fated. And then he wondered if inevitability was the same as determinism, which didn't allow for choice. Choice seemed just as real as inevitability did, but they couldn't both be true.

"Do you believe in free will?" he asked, but no one heard him, and even if they had, free will wasn't something Kelly or Le Roy thought about. The three of them were as close as human beings could be, but the truth was, the only thing they had in common was the war.

The epic had to work on several levels at once, with particular words, like "Mars" and "red," acting as bridges between worlds that existed simultaneously, that could be sensed but not inhabited by a single person all at once. How did a linear and specific string of words portray both vastness and minuteness, simplicity and complexity, possibility and finality, choice and inevitability, self and other? How did he indicate that horror and beauty coexisted—in the same moment, in the same heart?

The Mars thread was finally working, and he had devised a system of footnotes to indicate that not only were there layers to the epic, but there were layers upon layers. He just needed to find a synonym for "help"—or did he?

*War, war, what's it for*
*Help the rich and draft the poor.*

Whether he needed it or not, the perfect word was out there, and he was going to find it. It was in the air. Could be it was already in his head—he could feel it hovering, somewhere between his ear and his eye. He knew it was there, but he couldn't quite catch it, and now for some reason Le Roy was trying to get Kelly's attention by making faces and jumping up and down. Kelly was standing in a corner with his headphones on and his back to Le Roy, working on what he was going to say at the meeting. Kelly didn't want to be distracted, and Danny didn't want to be distracted either. He wanted to hold on to the sense that things were falling into place. He arranged the pens and pencils on his desk and squared the edges of his manuscript. Then he set the blue mechanical pencil he had been using down in the very center of the top page. Vertical or horizontal? He left it where it was. What was it? What was going on? Why was Le Roy opening and closing his mouth like a fish? Was it because the website was about to be sold and he didn't do well with change? Why did he look like he was going to fly out of his chair and grab Joe Kelly by the neck?

"Chill, man," said Kelly, heading to the printer. "The buyers will be here in ten. We need to be collecting our thoughts and I need to copy these spreadsheets, so don't bug me now. I'll talk to you later, K?"

But Le Roy wasn't making any noise. His neck bulged above his collar and he seemed to be choking. Danny thought he was having a heart attack or some sort of seizure. Then he thought that a train must be coming through, but if the clock was right, it wasn't due for another five and a half minutes—and anyway, Le Roy wasn't bothered by the train.

Then he heard breaking glass and boots on the porch, and when he turned, kind of in slow motion, he saw men swarming into the room and weapons being drawn and sited. Black bulletproof vests, legs squared and braced, helmeted heads held low like battering rams, barrels burnished and menacing.

"Everybody on the floor! Everybody on the fucking floor!"

Mars had been the perfect choice. When the captain had told him that Mars was complex and peace loving, whereas Ares was pure aggression, Danny knew it was just the sort of gossamer filament that would float over his epic, that would weave through it, inform it, give it shadow and lightness and depth. A crimson thread running right through the black-and-white words and tying them together.

Kelly had taken off his headphones and Le Roy had shut his mouth and dropped to the floor, but Danny looked instinctively for the captain before he remembered that the captain had gone back to Iraq. It was just the three of them now, unless he counted E'Laine, who had come to visit them a few times—but she wasn't there now so he guessed he shouldn't count her. He wished Le Roy would pay more attention to her, but E'Laine thought she was making progress in that regard, and who was he to disillusion her? He didn't know if things would work out with Dolly—she deserved better, but he was beginning to think they had a fighting chance.

"You, you! Face down! I'm giving you ten seconds! Nine seconds! Eight!"

The meeting with the buyer was coming up. He'd changed his mind and now he thought they should sell. They'd have money. They could do anything they wanted—or almost anything. Anything but go back in time to what Danny thought of as before. The three of them—five if you counted E'Laine and Dolly—could get a fresh start somewhere else or stay where they were and start a new venture, or Danny could finish college, which was an old dream of his, one he had lost hold of but might be able to reel back in once the sale of the website went through. The captain had bought the building and put it in their names, so they could stay there by the railroad tracks as long as they wanted or they could sell the building and move on—alone or separately. Everything was up to them. "The sky's the limit," Sinclair had said.

## 12.6 LYLE

Lyle's hands gripped the steering wheel as he sped through town. The clock on the dashboard ticked like a quiet bomb. His nerves tingled, and something flared in his guts as if he were the one with the threadbare tires and an internal combustion engine fueled by petrochemicals and a series of tiny explosions. He powered around the corner and past the muffler shop, gathering speed down the hill and past the bus station before skidding into the parking enclosure and wheeling around a row of cars so the truck was facing out again before ramming the gearshift into park. But he didn't kill the engine. Instead, he let the car idle, and while the truck chugged unevenly and the minute hand on the dashboard notched forward, Lyle felt the thing inside him continue to get bigger, as if a fuse had been lighted, as if a combustible pocket of gas had started to expand.

He was sure Maggie was coming. He blasted out another mental warning, but he guessed that all those days of wishing Maggie home had set things in motion, and it was too late to stop the dominoes from falling. He sensed the police presence. They could be hiding inside the cramped waiting room with its wooden benches and ticket window or in the alley behind the boxy brick station house. The sun was ricocheting off the cars lined up along the chain-link fence, and even the unwaxed surfaces of Lyle's truck emitted a dull, unnatural sheen.

By the clock on the dashboard, it was two minutes before noon when Lyle saw Maggie coasting around the corner onto Hill Street and pausing at the top of the hill. His heart almost broke. No, Maggie, no! He had expected her to come by bus, and he had planned to drive by and scoop her out of the disembarking crowd of passengers even though that would only initiate a high-speed chase if the station was as filled with police officers as he thought it was. He imagined them arrayed in their surplus military gear, crouched behind the plate-glass window or creeping along the sides of the building, waiting for the bus to arrive. But she wasn't on a bus, and that gave him an advantage.

He willed her to turn around, but she pushed off with her feet, and then she just kept coming, the angle of the hill and gravity causing the wheels of the bike to spin faster and faster until he thought for sure that she would crash. He couldn't give anything away just in case the police were surveilling the parking lot from the south-facing windows of the station. He couldn't show he had seen her by any movement of his body, so he just observed the scene woodenly, as if he were watching a news clip of a disaster that had already occurred.

And then the pocket of gas caught fire, and Lyle was filled with a great and liberating inspiration. As he revved the engine of the truck and aimed it at the sidewalk outside the bus station, he thought of the man pushing the Plunge-O-Sphere to the edge of Niagara Falls and getting in. He pictured the improbable orb spinning along in the current and then barreling over the edge as he aimed for the empty bench on the sidewalk, for the weedy shade tree, for the plate-glass window behind which he was sure the men in their bulletproof vests were waiting for Maggie and the bus.

But now a woman was easing her bulk onto the bench, looking expectantly down the road in the direction the bus would come from and shifting from side to side to settle her skirt around her knees. Lyle couldn't sound the horn or he would alert the police too early, before Maggie had a chance to see him. Before she had a chance to see that something was wrong. And before she could turn into the side street just uphill from the station house and pedal out of sight. Woman-in-a-skirt or no woman-in-a-skirt, there was no stopping what he had started. It was as if Lyle was running on gasoline or the truck was running on rage when he hunched into the wheel and shouted out the open window, "Get the hell out of my way!" At the last second, the woman saw him coming and jumped clear, and at 11:59 by the clock on the dash, Lyle rammed the truck right through the rickety bench, right through the skinny tree and into the metal awning supports, where it came to a stop only inches from the glass.

Out of the corner of his eye, Lyle saw Maggie's bicycle veer into the side street. The bicycle skidded and she almost fell, but then it was safely around the corner and Maggie was gone and the police were streaming out of the bus station, swarming like hornets, aiming their guns and shouting at Lyle to put his hands in the air. Lyle had to laugh to see the look on Ben's face when he said, "What the fuck, Lyle." He had to laugh when the sheriff said, "Lyle Rayburn, you're under arrest." He had to laugh to see the disappointment on the SWAT team's faces as they realized they weren't going to get a chance to fire their military-style weapons after all. And he had to laugh because it had never occurred to him that anger could feel so good.

## 12.7 MAGGIE

Maggie was glad to see the bicycle leaning against the shed. She had left her empty duffel in the house, but she kept her backpack with her as she mounted the bike and started pedaling. The crunch of the gravel beneath the tires brought to mind the free, almost floating feeling of heading off to Phoenix all those months ago. This was entirely different. With every revolution, the front tire rubbed against the fender, which was rusted and bent, and the brakes squealed whenever she slowed down. Even the wind generated by the bicycle was dusty and seemed to suck at her rather than blow. But the tires were new, and they bounced obligingly over any potholes or stones they encountered.

When she turned onto Main Street, she kept her head down in case there was traffic, but even though it was nearly lunchtime, everything was quiet. It was as if the town had shrunk in her absence, or she had somehow grown. She passed the town's lone office building, although now, from the looks of things, they were getting another, and the Main Street Diner had a freshly painted sign indicating it was now called the Main Street Café. She peered at the window as she went by, but the glass storefront only reflected her image back at her, and if any of the customers were watching her from the leatherette booths, she couldn't see them. She thought of eating dinner there with Lyle and Will and wondered if she was having a memory of the past or a happy premonition of the future.

An oil truck whizzed past, frightening her because she hadn't seen it coming. It was as if the film of her life had been spliced, leaving out the vehicle's approach and also its departure, for just as suddenly, it was gone. Even the air seemed jumpy, as if it were attached to her nerves and images were painted on it in thin colors rather than seen through it, or as if the town she had lived in for her entire life was only a mirage or an elaborately constructed set that could be changed at the whim of an unseen director, someone she envisioned smoking and laughing at her from a canvas chair with his name stenciled on the back or flirting with a winsome assistant rather than caring about what was taking place on stage.

She recognized the feeling as a combination of apprehension and loneliness, and then she realized that the apprehension was turning into full-blown fear. Where was Lyle? She passed the

472

turnoff to the Church of the New Incarnation and thought of going there to seek refuge in its sparkling vastness. She missed having the shell of a church around her, and if she went there, she could ask the pastor for advice. She could ask God to forgive her for reneging on her promise. But all she could think about now was finding Lyle.

The bell on the Catholic church was chiming the hour when she turned the corner by the muffler shop. A group of men were sitting outside smoking cigarettes and drinking Dr Pepper. She wondered briefly what their lives were like, whether the good in them outweighed the bad. Now she could see the bus station far ahead. It was little more than a storefront with a park bench outside for waiting. An old metal awning and a thin tree provided a stripe of shade, and just beyond was a chain-link enclosure for long-term parking. She thought she recognized Lyle's truck at the end of a short row of parked cars, but the glare of the noonday sun made it difficult to tell. She paused for a moment at the top of the hill before pedaling forward again.

The truck's window was open, and as she got closer, she could see that the driver of the truck was wearing aviator glasses and a blue shirt and a baseball cap that she imagined—no, she knew!— was made of crushed red felt with the letters OU stenciled on the front. Lyle! He was looking in her direction. He was looking and she knew in her heart he had recognized her. But even when she took one hand off the handlebars and held it up in joyful greeting, causing the bicycle to teeter dangerously beneath her, Lyle didn't wave back. Worse than that, he turned away. Of course he was angry with her. Anyone would be.

Anyone, she thought, except for Lyle. Lyle didn't get angry.

Maggie pressed her sneakered foot on the brake just as the truck lurched through a gap in the chain-link fence, wheels spinning.

It careened sideways into the road and gained momentum before slamming up on the curb, across the sidewalk and into the bench and the spindly metal stanchions. He had seen her! He was warning her away! A side street was coming up. As Maggie skidded into it, the bicycle's tires shimmied and slipped in the gravel. She almost lost her balance, but then the tires bit, and by some saving miracle, she didn't fall.

## 12.8 DANNY JOINER

—The what? I can't hear you, soldier. You'd better speak up.
   —The dust. Just there . . . in the distance . . . eleven o'clock . . .
   —What dust?
   —About three or four klicks up the road.
Danny could see Kelly crouching now, lowering himself on strong arms. And Le Roy, who only that morning had laughed for the first time since anyone could remember, was flattened in a patch of striped light from the barred window, muttering, "Fuck this shit," over and over to himself. He looked from the shiny barrels of the guns to the FBI logos to the laced and polished boots and tried to decide if he was experiencing a flashback or a dream or just a particularly vivid scene for the epic. It seemed very real, but all of the scenes had seemed real before he turned them into words and wrote them down.

*By the waters of Babylon...*

—Get going. You should have left when it was dark.

—Just let Pig Eye stay. He was supposed to go home last week.

—We were all supposed to go home.

—But Pig Eye.

He got slowly out of his chair, adjusting the blue mechanical pencil so it was horizontal now rather than vertical, the plastic barrel of the body arranged so that it lay just underneath the last words he had written—words that might make a fitting last line, which would make his epic shorter than he had imagined it, but lots of things were either longer or shorter than he had thought they would be—the war, for instance, and innocence and life. He felt sharp and clearheaded, if somewhat unhinged, and then not unhinged, but brittle and coldly righteous. Strong. A bell was ringing. It was the bell at the railroad crossing. He felt a bullet of comprehension click into its chamber. That's all it was—the train! But a train didn't explain the guns and the boots and the voices that were finished shouting at Le Roy and had started shouting at him. One of the agents took a step forward, and through the thick plastic visor, Danny saw Harraday's eyes staring at him, the hollow eyes of a natural killer.

"What do you think you're doing?"

"I'm writing a rap epic."

*By the waters of Babylon,*
*A soldier makes a lucky shot . . .*

—Tell them who you are.

—I am an American soldier.

—Tell it to *them,* and say it like you mean it!

He turned to face the door. The perfect word was out there. It was somewhere between his ear and his eye. He could feel the guns aiming at it, and then it shifted ever so slightly until it was dead center, right in the middle of his forehead. Help, he thought.

Le Roy had his eyes closed. Kelly was moving his mouth, but no sound was coming out. Or, if sound was coming out, he couldn't hear it. Maybe he was deaf. He didn't think he was deaf, but he couldn't absolutely rule it out. Where was the captain? The captain should be there to tell them what to do. Or his recruiting officer or the doctor or the sergeant who had always smoked him in basic training but who had taught him everything he needed to know. He straightened his shoulders.

*By the waters of Babylon,*

He stood with his head up and his feet squared.

*We sat down and wept.*

—Tell them who you are!

"I am an American soldier! I am disciplined, physically and mentally tough!"

"On the ground, now!"

The captain had gone back to Iraq—he remembered that now. But Dolly was coming. Last time they had talked, she had said she would. "Not right away," she had told him. "Ask me in a couple weeks." He would call her and ask her to marry him again, just to make sure. He'd plan something special for a celebration. No sparklers. No alcohol. No tablecloth with stars and stripes. "I will never accept defeat!" he shouted, this time a little louder, just in case. Then he looked into the middle distance and thought of Pig Eye and also of Joe Kelly the day the two soldiers had stood together like brothers on the Toyota—and then he rammed his right fist into the air.

It was as if he had punched through a sound barrier, for as he did it, Kelly shouted, "Hit the deck, Danny! Hit the deck!" and the bell stopped ringing and the train blasted through right on schedule or even a little early for once, rattling the glass in the barred windows. But then Kelly was drowned out by a deafening crash, as if the train had jumped its tracks. Danny saw stars, and among the stars, a planet—Mars! At first it was the barest pinprick of light, and then it became big, blood-red, and molten before it exploded the way Pig Eye had exploded, into a thousand new pinpricks as everything disintegrated and settled into a kind of shrouded, starstruck peace.

## 12.9 MAGGIE

The side street intersected with an alley that ran behind the bus station, and as she tore past it, Maggie could see three squad cars and the sheriff's big pickup parked there, gleaming in the sun. She gripped the handlebars as tightly as she could. Sweat pooled in her armpits and dripped from her brow. Were the police after her? Had they found the stolen documents? Was she a fugitive from the law?

She sent a prayer into the ether and hoped Lyle would hear it. And then she thought about the army and the war and how she had taken her eye off the ball, but was the ball the depleted uranium munitions, or was it Tommy and George, or was it her poor, neglected family? Please, God, she thought, take care of Will!

She was pedaling as hard as she could, keeping her head down and taking back roads to a track she knew of that followed Ash Creek from the park with the baseball field where the summer league games were played all the way to the Church of the New Incarnation, where the narrow trickle of the creek widened out into a glassy man-made reflecting pool before meandering through the fields and eventually into a concrete culvert that funneled it beneath the highway. When the undulating form of the church came into view, Maggie was already tiring. How would she make it the hundred miles to Oklahoma City? How would she make it to wherever she was going with only a rusty bicycle and scarcely a dollar to her name? Almost of its own accord, the bicycle turned up the long driveway toward the twin domes of the church, the domes that made the church look like a female torso toppled over on its back.

As Maggie entered the vestibule, she could hear music emanating from the nave: the big pipe organ accompanied by what sounded like the full choir. It was Saturday. It must be a special holy day, but she couldn't think of which one it might be. Just as she was tiptoeing forward to peek through the double doors, the pastor's wife burst through them and almost knocked into her. "Maggie!" she cried. "Whatever are you doing here?"

Maggie was taken aback by the perfectly waved hair and the made-up face and the tightly wrapped summer dress and the air of voluptuous good will. When Tiffany put out her arms, Maggie allowed herself to fall into the softness and burst into tears. "I'm tired," she said. "I'm just a little tired is all."

"Of course you are," said Tiffany. "Let me get you a glass of water and a bite to eat."

It turned out that the producers had wanted to film some background segments for the television show, so for the previous week, a camera crew had been shadowing the pastor and his wife. Today was the day to shoot the choir and the interior of the church. "The show's going national," said Tiffany. "They even want to do a segment on me."

She led Maggie to where a tray of fruit and sandwiches had been set out for the camera crew. She poured two glasses of water and took Maggie to an inner room where they wouldn't be disturbed. "I heard you talking to Houston the day you and your husband came to him for advice," she said. "I heard you talking about the prisoners, and I haven't been able to forget what you said. As you know, I lead a group called Mothers of Mercy, and you inspired me to take on something more significant than providing school supplies for the prison and sewing quilts for wounded soldiers."

The backpack was still cutting into Maggie's shoulders, and now she took it off, reminded of the day she had met the representative from PATH. A lot had happened since then, but what had she accomplished?

As if she were reading her mind, Tiffany said, "Long story short, the MoMs group has recently received some money, but we don't have a mission—not a real one, anyway. If I'm going to be on television, it would be nice to have something important to talk about."

Maggie recognized the tone, the set of the jaw, the refusal to be dissuaded. Don't do it, she wanted to say. She wanted to warn Tiffany about all she stood to lose, but the sensation that she was looking at a younger, better version of herself destroyed her ability to speak.

"I'm thinking ... well, I'm actually thinking two things," said Tiffany. "The first is that there is some money—quite a lot of it, actually—in the MoMs account. And the second thing is that you might have a few ideas about how that money can best be spent."

"You have to focus in," said Maggie. "It's easy to get distracted if you take on too much at once."

Maggie wanted to ask how a person chose just one thing in a world where so much needed doing. She wanted to warn Tiffany that progress on any one of the items was impossibly slow. She wanted to say that there were sacrifices involved. Instead, she said, "Tomás is getting a new trial, so it would be wonderful if you could send something for his legal fees. And I've completely neglected George . . . " She held out the backpack with the same mixture of reluctance and relief with which the PATH woman had passed her the quilted bag with the name George appliquéd on the side, and the woman in front of her took it with the same eager confidence Maggie had once had. It was as if Maggie were both staying and leaving, both giving the prisoners up and holding them close. When the pastor's wife transferred the files from the backpack to a locked drawer of her desk, Maggie noticed that there were no other papers in the drawer. The surface of the desk was clean too, arrayed only with a set of matching implements, no doubt purchased from the office supply depot in town but never used.

Tiffany went to the donation closet and filled a small duffel with clothing. "What size are your feet?" she asked. She repacked the backpack with food and money and gave Maggie the telephone number of someone she knew in San Francisco. "I'll be sure to give the same telephone number to Lyle," she added. "And don't you worry, I'll check on him as soon as I'm finished here."

"And Will," said Maggie. "Can you find out where Will's unit is stationed and give him the number too?"

"Of course I can. Don't you worry about a thing. And don't forget to call me now and then to let me know how you are."

Tiffany gave Maggie her cheerleader smile and accompanied her to where the bicycle was tipped over beside the reflecting pool. "This is just between us," she said. "Not that the pastor wouldn't fully support everything we're doing, but he has a lot on his mind right now. What he doesn't know won't hurt him."

"I'm not sure that's true," said Maggie with some of her old fire. "But of course, my lips are sealed."

"If he has a problem with it, I'll just tell him it's my one crazy thing." When Tiffany laughed, Maggie felt a burst of joy, and better than joy, she felt hope—for herself, for the prisoners, and for the world. Where would she go if she could go anywhere? She'd stay right there in Red Bud, of course, but life was a narrowing down as much as an opening out, and for now Red Bud was the one place on earth she couldn't be.

She wheeled the bicycle to the top of a low rise and looked around her at the green fields of wheat waving gracefully in the breeze. Please take care of Will, she thought again, but this time it wasn't so much a prayer to God as to the other people out there, people who might lend a hand to a stranger in time of need.

In the distance, a straight ribbon of highway stretched all the way to California. On either side of it, a flock of oil derricks bowed and preyed on the rich Carboniferous sludge deposited millions of years before, when Oklahoma was a steamy and suppurating swamp. Behind her, the double-domed Church of the New Incarnation had doubled again—it was sprawled on its back giving comfort to the sky and it was also flipped upside down, drowning in the reflecting pool. As she surveyed the familiar landscape, she wondered again if she had done any good at all, and if she had, had she done right? When she had started down this path all those months ago, she had assumed that things would be clearer than they were and that she would be able to look back on her choices and accomplishments with certainty and satisfaction. Partial knowledge, she thought. It was all anybody had. Overhead, a plane tipped its wings at her, filled with people who had other problems and other destinies awaiting them. As she watched it disappear into the distance, a hawk plummeted from the heavens and rocketed up again with a field mouse in its talons. She was sorry for the little creature, but there was nothing she could do for it. Even she knew that saving too many mice would doom the hawk. The world was paradoxical, and if there was a solution to the paradox, it wasn't for her to know.

# 13.0 BABYLON

*People have been at war for all but twenty-nine years of history. What makes anyone think we're going to stop now?*
— The Professor

*I learned that there's a heck of a lot of mom power out there, and if you just figure out how to harness it, there's no telling what you can do.*
— Tiffany Price

*Of course it wasn't just the moms, it was the money. Winslow and Lexington were all up in arms about it, but when we didn't need it for the website, Tiffany refused to give it back.*
— Pastor Houston Price

*Those guys were getting in pretty deep, so we helped them mirror their site on other servers. They needed to protect themselves.*
— Anonymous

*Once a simulation gets started, it can pretty much run itself.*
— Le Roy Jones

*We found him sitting on the sidewalk outside, and when we brought him into the building, he walked straight up to his old cage and got right in.*
— Director of Greyhound Adoptions

*I hope they don't find her. I like to think of her out there somewhere, making the world a better place.*
— True Cunningham

# 13.1 WILL

The morning was still and hot, giving the desert a timeless, lacquered look. Will took out the controller and attached the joystick before lifting the Parakeet he called Polly out of its case. It weighed six ounces and only resembled a bird in the rounded fatness of its body and the beaklike sensors attached to its head. Instead of wings, it had four rigid appendages topped with rotors for vertical lift and a stabilizing rotor in the middle of its back. The payload port on its belly was fitted with a camera that relayed signals to the computer pack that Nate carried over his shoulder.

"I kinda wish I'd been issued one of those Groundhogs," said Nate, nodding to where third team was climbing into the Humvee that would follow behind a robot that resembled a mini tank. "Those things are awesome."

"I don't know," said Will. "I think the Parakeet is cool."

"It doesn't have a gun," countered Nate. "That's a major negative right there."

"But the Groundhog can't fly. Anyway, UAVs are where it's at if we want good jobs when we get home."

Will's platoon had been training an incoming unit to take its place—first the training exercises of two days before and now the mission to find a downed helicopter—and then he'd be leaving

Polly with Nate and going home. Not that going home was without its complications.

Nate hoisted the computer pack and strapped it on while Will flipped a switch to activate the camera, which he could toggle between wide-angle and high-resolution zoom. When Nate said he was ready, Will tossed the Parakeet into the air as Nate manipulated the joystick and nudged the throttle with his thumb. The bird took off and the two men watched until it was only a tiny, glittering speck.

"Let's roll," said Will, climbing into a Humvee with the rest of his team.

He patted his thigh pocket. Through the heavy canvas fabric he could feel the flat photographs he carried with him along with a small jumble of other things. He had given the magnifying glass and Transformers robots to some local children, but he still had the razor blade in its paper wrapping. He still had the twist of sturdy wire, the extra paracord, and a tiny pair of pliers he had won off another soldier in a poker game.

"The girlfriends?" asked Nate.

Will smiled and said, "Yeah, man. They're my COG." But now that he was going home, his center of gravity didn't feel quite so centered. For one thing, his parents had moved to California, and for another, he was feeling a little guilty about leading both Dylan and Tula on.

"I can't believe you have two," said Nate. "Anyone with two should be required to share."

"Very funny," said Will. "But I'll let you look at the pictures later if you're good."

As they drove, Nate told a story about a soldier whose girlfriend had dumped him and asked him to send her picture back. "He didn't want her to know how badly his feelings were hurt, so he

486

collected all the pictures of women he could get his hands on from his friends—pictures of their girlfriends, of their wives and aunts and sisters—over fifty in all—and he sent them to his ex with a note that said, 'I can't remember which one you are, so please take your picture out and send the rest back.'"

"Ha, ha," said Will. And then he said, "You can see the pictures, but you can't have them."

"My girlfriend didn't dump me," said Nate.

"That's because you don't have one."

"Technicality," said Nate. "Anyway, I've got Polly now."

Will focused his binoculars. "The wind's coming up," he said. "That's one of the things you've got to be careful about." As soon as he said it, the Parakeet was dive-bombed by a giant hawk. They watched helplessly for a few seconds, and then the hawk flew off. "Hawks are another thing," said Will.

"That was a close call," said Nate. He allowed the Parakeet to fly ahead while Will scanned the sky with his field glasses and took readings on the wind. Their search sector extended west to a series of low hills, and beyond the hills to a road. Early that morning a helicopter had gone down, and the mission was to find it. What looked like a stretch of flat terrain could be seen on the portable monitor to be riddled with rocks and fissures, making the going too tough for the Groundhog, which would drive around and enter the search area from the north. Twenty minutes in, the screen showed a one-lane track winding between some boulders, so they steered along that until Nate zoomed in on what appeared to be a vehicle that had fallen into a shallow fissure.

"Is it one of ours?" asked the leader of the new team, whose name was Robbins.

"I'm guessing it is," replied Will. "Hey, Nate. Get Polly to circle back around so we can take a better look."

Nate manipulated the controller, and ten seconds later the screen was filled with a close-up of the vehicle, which seemed to be abandoned. Except for a helmet lying on the ground and a second set of tire tracks, there was no evidence of the people who must have left it there.

"What do you think it means?" asked Nate.

"I'm guessing it was part of the training exercise," said Robbins.

Will hadn't thought of this. "Yeah," he said, "maybe it was."

Together the team came up with reasons why the vehicle might be abandoned: (a) it was part of the training exercise; (b) it had broken down in the last few hours and been temporarily abandoned; (c) it was bait for unsuspecting soldiers who would approach to find it booby-trapped; and (d) it was bait and being covered by hostile snipers who were hidden somewhere nearby. Will remembered the answer elimination techniques. He remembered that sometimes there was only one correct answer and sometimes there was more than one. He remembered there was always one answer that seemed right but wasn't, and that was the one they called the sucker choice.

"If it's D," said Nate, "Polly should be able to see the snipers."

"Keep circling," said Will. "She should be able to see the bomb too, if there is one."

Nate worked the directional button and adjusted the resolution of the output. "If there's a bomb, it's hidden pretty well."

"Could someone be hunkered down in that gully? Or hiding in those hills?"

"The hills are covered with boulders—someone could be hiding anywhere. But I guess we can confirm or eliminate answer A by radioing back to base," said Robbins.

The radio operator spoke into his handset, but the line was filled with static and he couldn't get through.

"We're missing something," said Will, aware of an unfamiliar shimmy in his belly. "It's the helmet that bothers me. What's that helmet doing there?"

"I'm thinking it was part of the training exercise," said Robbins. "That's the only way the helmet makes sense."

"Try the radio again."

Will followed Nate out of the vehicle for a better look. The sky was the color of metal. For some reason, he could feel ghosts all around him, and he wondered if they were real ghosts or only figments of his imagination. It was probably just the wind, which was blowing in gusts and eddies. He took the controller from Nate and brought Polly in low, but a crosscurrent pushed her off course. "The wind is Polly's biggest thing," he said. He struggled with the controls and was relieved when he got a visual—a bright spot against the ragged aluminum sky. "Okay, I see her now," he said, but the wind was scuffing up dust, making visibility difficult, and he immediately lost sight of her again. "Hey, Nate," he called out, "do you have a visual on Polly?"

The two men scanned the sky. Then they bent their heads over the computer screen to see what Polly was seeing, which would give them a clue to where she was. The feedback video bucked and whirled as Polly hit a trough and then settled as the stabilizing rotor took hold.

"Freeze that!" said Will when the output showed something moving in the distance, but the camera had already lost whatever it was.

"I sure wish we had one of those Groundhogs," said Nate.

"Shit! Switch back to the wide-angle view."

"No, wait," said Nate. "Look at this."

Now they could see the ravine on the screen, and the helmet, and the vehicle.

"Check the coordinates," said Will, and Nate said, "It's about half a klick north of our current position."

Will tried to circle the Parakeet back over the ravine, but the wind was blowing in circles and swirls of dust obscured the view. A minute passed and then another. "Nothing," said Will. "I don't see a fucking thing."

"Should we go and check out the vehicle ourselves?" asked Nate.

There were only two possible answers to the question. After the *Turn of the Screw* quiz, Mr. Quick had said the best answer was both, but that clearly wasn't an option here. "I don't know," he said. "I wish the radio was working."

"What if there are men inside?"

"We didn't see signs of any men, and the helmet is too far from the truck to have fallen. It seems like it was planted as part of the exercise. Hey, Robbins. Can you try the radio again?"

"Get Polly to go back around," said Robbins.

Will nodded, but Polly was nonresponsive.

"Maybe the hawk got her," said Nate.

Inside the Humvee, the radio crackled to life. Will couldn't make out the words, but he heard Robbins say, "Roger that," before calling out, "The vehicle was part of the exercise. They want us to bring it in."

While the driver navigated between the boulders in the direction of the abandoned vehicle, Will marked the coordinates of Polly's homing device. "She's up there," he said, pointing to the line of hills. "We can go after Polly while you all deal with the Humvee."

"We'd better check with base," said Robbins.

The signal was better now that they were higher, and a second later the captain's voice came through, relaying instructions from the busy operations center: "Third squad found the helo, but do not leave that bird in the field. I repeat: do not abort."

The homing device indicated that Polly was approximately one klick away from the stranded vehicle, which Will figured would take them just under the second ridge, about halfway to the road. "You heard the man," he said to Nate, who cracked a grin and laughed a little, as if he had thought of something funny. Then Robbins said, "Go get that bird," which was when Will realized he would miss Polly and the desert and the team.

The two men adjusted their goggles and patted their weapons. They made their way along a gully before climbing to the top of the first hill. The desert stretched around them, hazy and brown and kind of corrugated where the wind had made patterns in the dirt. Below them, Robbins and the others were attaching a tow bar to the stranded vehicle. Will pointed down the backside of the hill. "She's somewhere down there," he said.

The wind was howling now, the air gauzy with particulates— unless it was the ghosts Will was still imagining. "Do you believe in ghosts?" he asked.

"Hell, no," said Nate, but he didn't sound too sure.

Will could imagine the ghosts wailing and screeching and saying their prayers. He could imagine them telling their stories—as a warning, as a history lesson, as a way not to be for- gotten, as a final comment on life and futility and all there was to be won and lost. He too would have stories to tell when he got back home. If he found the words for them and if they were worth telling. If people cared enough to listen. That morning, he had added a small notepad to his pocket just in case. Just in case he needed to write something down. Something final, he thought now, because it was his last mission before going home and because the shimmy was back and because he suddenly had a bad feeling about things. But then he countered the negativity by saying "Spider-Man" quietly, to himself, and the bad feeling peeled away, leaving his nerves steady and his senses stripped and sharp.

He tapped his pocket to make sure his knife was there, along with the two girlfriends. He thought about how he loved them both and how things that seemed crazy at home made perfect sense in Iraq—and vice versa. Anyway, he'd figure it out. He tried the launcher again, but Polly wasn't responding. The wind was almost shrieking now, filled with fine dust and occasional larger particles, and even though it was hot, a deep chill ran from his stomach to his toes. "Something bad happened here," he said. "I can feel it."

"This is a war zone," said Nate. "What did you expect?"

When the wind died down, it was hot under the heavy gear, and the rocky terrain made the going difficult, but still they put one foot in front of the other, three feet per step, 1,312 steps per klick. In the distance, Will thought he saw a cloud of thicker dust rising skyward, as if a vehicle was coming toward them, but then the wind picked up again and there was dust everywhere, and anyway, whatever he thought he'd seen was obscured by the brown crust on his goggles and also by the brow of the second hill.

"Nah," said Nate when he mentioned it. "How would a vehicle get up here over all these rocks?"

"What is it, then?"

"Hell, I'm saying it's third squad. The sergeant said they found the helo."

Will worked the controller, hoping he could get the bird to launch itself if it was grounded, but Polly wasn't moving. "I won der what the deal with Polly is."

"I hope she's okay," said Nate.

The cloud of dust was bigger now. There was something there, and it was getting closer. "Yeah, it's got to be third squad," said

Nate. He raised his field glasses to his eyes. "I guess they're coming to help us out." And then he said, "Holy shit," and then he started to run, which was difficult on the rocky terrain. And then, for some reason, he stopped running and fell face down in the dirt, and Will's first thought was, It's a sniper after all.

"Hey, man, you okay?" He dropped down beside Nate before looking up to see what Nate had seen. He focused and refocused—far out and then closer in—registering that Nate wasn't breathing and that he had a hole in his face and that he wasn't as heavy as Will had expected him to be, but otherwise not seeing anything he hadn't seen before, only hearing a low, motorized hum and thinking it was Nate, whirring back to life. Or maybe it was Polly, finally responding to the controller and lifting off. Where was Polly when he needed her? Where was his extra set of eyes and ears? And then he did see what Nate had seen: the swivel gun mount of a Groundhog coming up and over the second ridge.

Will said his cue word and felt the power surge through him— inward from his hands and upward from his feet—accompanied by a blast of heat in his groin. He experienced the resonating moment and visualized success. His adrenaline kicked in, right on cue, making time slow down, which gave him a split second to decide whether to run or take cover behind a nearby pile of rocks. His legs were ready, muscles tensed. He took a lead and tried to pretend he was stealing home. He could make it. He knew he could make it in any test between him and the player with the ball. Unless it was only luck that counted. Unless everything was due to chance. He wondered if the other soldiers were right when they said that it had all been set in motion long ago. In that case, it didn't matter what he did.

Out of the corner of his eye, the rock pile dissolved into light and shadow, solid and void, suggesting a depression in the earth or a recess or cave. He adjusted his hold on Nate and pressed his lead foot into the ground. He visualized his parents cheering from the stands. He heard the coach shouting at him to run like the devil was after him, and he thought it probably was. He remembered the drill sergeant who had smoked him in basic, and he remembered that can't was not an option. He hoped Tula was right that a person could change things. "Spider-Man," he said on the chance that he could defy whatever destiny was hurtling toward him. Maybe he couldn't, but maybe he could.

# Acknowledgments

Beyond the world of this novel is another world of people who helped bring it to life—writers and thinkers who opened my eyes or caused me to question, soldiers who shared their experiences, experts who took care of the details of publication, and editors and early readers who understood what I was trying to do—or didn't, which was helpful too. My heartfelt thanks to you all, particularly to Reagan Arthur and David McCormick, who were there from the beginning; and to Ursula Doyle, Terry Adams, Heather Fain, Matt Carlini, Betsy Uhrig, Shannon Langone, Carrie Neill, Susan Hobson, Bridget McCarthy, Emma Borges-Scott, Ayad Akhtar, Kevin Shushtari, Jami Attenberg, Melissa Sterry, Syndi Allgood, Graham Pulliam, and others who prefer to remain unnamed.

Special thanks go to Bruce Smart for the title; to Kapo Ng and Nico Taylor for the covers; to Kevin and Stephanie for the faith; to Nick for the insights on ethics, eternal return, and *amor fati;* and to Olivia for her sharp eye and even sharper opinions, as well as for sending me this, from Camus:

*Maman must have felt free then and ready to live it all again. Nobody, nobody had the right to cry over her. And I felt ready to live it all again too. As if that blind rage had washed me clean, rid me of hope; for the first time, in that night alive with signs and stars, I opened myself to the gentle indifference of the world. Finding it so much like myself—so like a brother really—I felt that I had been happy and that I was happy again.*

FLEET

To buy any of our books and to find out
more about Fleet, our authors and titles, as well
as events and book clubs, visit our website

**www.littlebrown.co.uk**

and follow us on Twitter

**@FleetReads**
**@LittleBrownUK**

To order any Fleet titles p & p free in the UK,
please contact our mail order supplier on:

**+ 44 (0)1832 737525**

Customers not based in the UK should contact
the same number for appropriate postage
and packing costs.